Dear Linda,

Happy Birthday!

Tricia

12/31/88

Also By Kate Braverman
Fiction:
LITHIUM FOR MEDEA

Poetry:
MILK RUN
LULLABY FOR SINNERS
HURRICANE WARNINGS

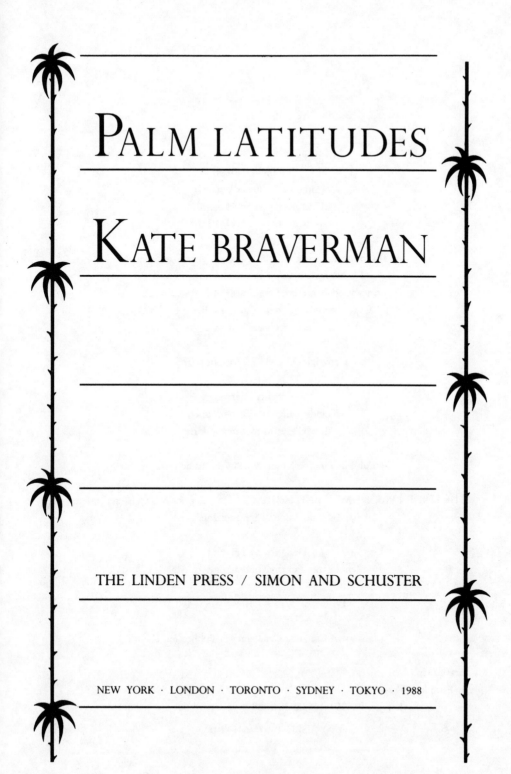

Palm Latitudes

Kate Braverman

THE LINDEN PRESS / SIMON AND SCHUSTER

NEW YORK · LONDON · TORONTO · SYDNEY · TOKYO · 1988

The Linden Press
Simon & Schuster Building
1230 Avenue of the Americas
New York, New York 10020

Published by the Simon & Schuster Trade Division

THE LINDEN PRESS/SIMON AND SCHUSTER and colophon are registered trademarks
of Simon & Schuster Inc.

Designed by Liney Li
Manufactured in the United States of America

1   3   5   7   9   10   8   6   4   2

Library of Congress Cataloging-in-Publication Data

Braverman, Kate.
   Palm latitudes.
      I. Title. PS3552.R3555P35 1988   813'.54   88-3018
               ISBN: 0-671-64542-0

PART ONE

I n this City of the Angels, you can trust nothing, not even the dense and erratic air. There is La Migra, la policía. Fire in the hills. Ash that falls from the skies. In this City of the Angels, en Nuestra Señora la Reina de los Angeles, it is best to be silent, invisible. You who are brown in this white realm, be as your stained courtyard walls, hidden, camouflaged. Become part of the grain of the landscape. Vanish into the indigenous. Be as the seared grass and cast no shadow. You who have no visa, no passport, no identification.

La Puta de la Luna is a flagrant exception. She leans against the enormous stalk of a palm tree planted beside a bus bench near an intersection, in daylight, exposed, without fear. She searches for American businessmen exiting the emptying downtown spires with their twin arrogances of dimension and light.

Here, at this particular intersection chosen by happenstance, she arrived as a shell might be tossed upon sand after a storm. Here, at this juncture where the city flattens out, allowing wooden frame houses, stucco apartment buildings, weeds and wildflowers to spill across the low hills, she is oblivious to danger. In this area that exists tentatively, by the indifference of the city, she paces and hunts. When the Queen of Angels wishes to expand herself, when the bloated diseased woman craves new edifices and glass spires, she will erase these hills of their temporary clutter. She will consume them without thought or argument. She will eradicate them as if they had never been.

It is always this way, La Puta de la Luna thinks. The pattern of this city is familiar, the scent and rhythm and texture. It is a design she has memorized. It is repeated everywhere. Sunsets through half-drawn drapes, sending a coral flush across alleys of bougainvillea and dust and dogs. The earth shivers as if with fever. Palm fronds merge with shadow, inventing night bodies with deceptively expressive faces. Later, these fronds will nod and sway, as if in perfect agreement. They are conspirators.

La Puta de la Luna knows they are plotting against the sun. One dusk they will find the place where the sun comes to sleep. Branches and leaves will lock in an intricate embrace. Vines will bind the captured sun to the dirt. A monumental yellow mountain will form. Then the blind trees will rise from their subterfuge of ruin and silence and reign. Such a birth is possible.

It is late afternoon. Soon the city will wear its night face, erased of myth and purpose. Night will strip it as if by scalpel. The central city will stand without pretense, deserted as if by a collective perception of contagion. Citadels will be revealed as they truly are, brick, dirt and mud dug from the earth and returned to rot under stars and banks of gray tin-scented clouds. In the cold dusk, the air will rattle with wind in branches and fronds, a form of music, subtle, vaguely metallic, like the sound of syncopated amulets. Dogs will run in packs again. And night will fall with the weight and power to dull a world.

La Puta de la Luna prefers to experience the night as it actually is, raw, hungry and lawless. She will feel the press of deep gulfs above, in the hollows and paths where planets come to feed in a sky littered and beyond reconstruction. Then the center of the city will be barren as a meteor, its excessive profusion of light will mean nothing, its spires and towers less significant than the craters pitting a dead orb in space. La Puta de la Luna never forgets that this city, like all others, is an hallucination.

It is a warm afternoon. She takes in the street with one glance. The Café Jalisco, with its large advertisement of naked women dancing within, is not yet lit by bands of red and yellow neon. There are no naked women in the Café Jalisco. And the working men and transients who drink beer at the scarred wooden bar cannot afford her. She turns her back and studies the acre of city park with its permanently grayish lake of ducks and water weeds and young boys in boats. It is like a wall behind her. And the perimeter is in order.

La Puta de la Luna is unhurried, absolutely alert, as any animal freshly risen, tasting the first implications of dusk. There will be prey. The night will be as all others, treacherous, studded with disguised traps and graves. She will survive it. There will be gold and the danger of barter with strangers, foreigners with metallic mouths of invisible eaten coins and greed, with mouths that are miniature replicas of the city, voids, empty, less than mud or clay, which are fundamental.

These are the white corridors. Here the albino vultures rush west through smoke, brown haze, coughing trucks, as if the area near the sea were a form of absolution. La Puta de la Luna knows the details comprising their lives, their pathetic contrivances, their attempts to render the night tolerable and erased of danger. It is said that the sea air is purer. She wonders why such a concern would be significant to men who have no lungs.

There are occasional moments when these men feel black wings beating within. He wonders what this means, this wavering, this sense of openings, inexplicable channels in that which was solid. His head will flood with alien images. A sky crowded with clouds of unknown intentions. Crescents and orbs of red moon. A sudden vision of a hotel with mahogany corridors and white windows facing a lagoon placid and green as jade which the sea has polished and engraved. A natural artifact. A man enters an apartment building he has never before seen where a young woman waits. New breasts. She is spreading her legs. There are acres of her. He could not reach the borders. His lips will twist on polished grooves. He will take the air as if to speak. But there is only one word. And the word is no.

Of course, the Spanish-speaking men are no better. She has brushed them away as she would insects, as she did the enormous black bugs born of heat and water she saw on the floors of the airport in Puerto Vallarta. They were a minor surprise, something to step over. The Mexicano gangsters boast of their sheer number of stolen cars and kilos of smuggled contraband as if quantity were itself quality.

The Mexicano hoodlums both offend and bore her. They are marginal thieves. They still smell of dirt roads, muddy, rain-ruined plazas in insignificant villages. They have never been to a tailor. They only dream, and their dreams are small.

Later, these Mexicanos will smell of jails and bus stations and tequila. They will smell of waiting and schemes that collapse, over and over, recurrent as waves in an ocean. They will marry women and beat them, father children and desert them. It is a pattern they will repeat past exhaustion. Their longing for a definable manhood will remain incipient, damaged, illusive and unprovable. Later still, their lies will multiply, becoming lavish, elaborate, more the product of alcohol and inadequacy than any recognizable reality. She is of another species entirely. She clarifies her position. And they disappear.

She has also driven off more serious men, encountered by rumor and accident. Such men have accountants and the suits of Anglo bankers, appropriately gray with perfect parallel lines ingrained within the fabric, as if they were garbed in a vision of highways, of precisely etched rows of asphalt asserting some final and meaningful destination. They have erased their accents. They flaunt the expensive American smell which is partly leather and leisure and a tangible future arriving in predictable installments, like a fully charted sun which brings gold on cue.

Of course they think they are Montezuma as he should have been, without neurotic paralysis, a warrior correctly deciphering the auguries and ordering the tiny squad of diseased white men driven back into the sea. Or brought into Tenochtitlán, where their hearts could be cut out slowly, at celebrations, through decades. Always, these men claim the uncorrupted blood of Mayan or Aztec royalty. Or they insist their grandfathers were born in Spain or France or Italy. She is mildly amused by how conventional and unimaginative their invented histories are. The possibilities of surprise are legion, but these men are oblivious to subtlety, to the rare and unexpected juxtaposition. They wear their aesthetics on the outside, as if a silk suit could alter the fibers of their flesh. She thinks they are ridiculous. Were they less ignorant, they would be pretentious.

La Puta de la Luna does not need them. They know nothing of the interior complexity, the intersections of chance and ambivalence. She has sat in their cars. She has stared at their suits with the gray lines within the gray fabric. Their lives are also parallel lines they must follow like terrible actors with only slight natural grace and an overwhelming compulsion to memorize. They leave no impression. She slides out of their cars, unsoiled.

They offer her protection, arrangements, guarantees, hotels with cocktail lounges decorated with chandeliers and fountains. They expect that this vision of fraudulent glamour will arouse her, as if she were a peasant newly arrived in a capital. Or perhaps less, an Indian eager to sell her hunting lands and the grounds where the bones of the fathers rest in sacred burial for strings of glass beads, trinkets, appliances, cheap furs. They know nothing of the chemistry of a city dying, surrendering to weeds and wildflowers, to eruptions of orchids and jungle vines. They do not recognize that one exists not by the blessing of the gods but by their indifference.

She explains nothing of her history. It is not for sale. She does not mention Mexico City, where she stayed at the Camino Real. A car waited to take her to the museum, to the Paseo de la Reforma for shopping, to the Catedral de la Virgen de Guadalupe. In Caracas, in Managua and Guadalajara, always, cars waited for her command. Often, she simply had the chauffeur drive while she embossed the landscape across the soft fabric of her eyes. In San Juan, she stayed for six weeks in a tenth-floor suite at the Hilton Hotel. She ordered bouquets of roses, a dozen each day. Her room became a garden. In Las Vegas, she stayed at Caesar's Palace and the Sands. She did not work in these hotels. She was a guest.

Boys with blond hair handed her bath towels, like blanched supplicants with terry-cloth offerings. They arranged her slatted lounge chair, finding the most beneficial angle for her flesh to meet the sun. They called her madam. When she raised one oiled arm, gin fizzes or piña coladas simply appeared. She merely signed the number of her hotel room to checks. Her sunglasses were manufactured in Paris. Her sandals were leather. She was never required to show her room key.

Always, there were swimming pools, she remembers this. The blue jewel, cruelly brilliant oasis of cool tiled pool. The sudden sapphires of water, as if a passing god had chanced to drop one of his precious stones, a lapis lazuli perhaps. Always, there were the palms with their shredded bark skirts like the grass skirts of certain island women. The palms, casting their meager suggestion of shadow onto lawns perpetually watered, a moist green, whatever the season. Always the sky was molten, livid, outraged by birds blazing between neon.

The elements became mutable and fluid. The air itself was a form of liquid. She drank it, intoxicated by the accumulation of accidents which made her what she was. She recognized that it was all random, a matter of sudden portals opening of their own accord. You enter a bus or a plane. You answer a doorbell, a letter, a telephone, and the course of your entire life is changed. And the cool tiled swimming pools. The air which was not quite air, which contained hidden gulfs and channels into which she could drift, could float. If one learned certain intricacies of navigation, the world could be an unceasing June on a planet of red wild sunsets and abnormal gravities. The fevered air flared, circular. And she had risen as a red cloud, gossamer, cleansed by disaster. Her bones were pure. And she was a summer madonna, nude and languid after mating. She was a flesh sculpture, the product of invention and inexplicable grace. There are certain forms of metamorphosis from which one never returns.

From one terraced hotel suite or another, in one early steaming afternoon or another, she watched young Spanish-speaking women plump as pomegranates calling their Manuels or Josés back to the casa, back to sweets or beatings. She looked down at their tenements and rows of identical projects as she perfumed her body, as she waited for trays of strawberries and brandy. The world below was a geography she had transcended. She had dared to wander from the compound. With one inspired juxtaposition, she had scaled the illusionary walls. They were made of clay. Her feet left imprints in their soft surfaces. They were symbols she had decoded. Such walls meant nothing.

Always, there were oceans to walk beside, the constant waves purifying her flesh, engraving their calligraphy across her skin. In Santa Clara and Mazatlán, in Puerto Vallarta, in the Caribbean and the Pacific, in the Gulf of Mexico, in the gulf of chance and destiny, she discovered a form of absolution. Fog crowded into the foam. Faces of saints washed lamplight amber at her feet. Waves were lime and irridescent where they broke, cracking like translucent insect wings. And the oceans were the soft red of wines. She could drink of such seas as if they were holy water.

Her hair was black, a mane held by tourmaline combs as she fell back, opening the place where the earth intersects, deathless, pure, a stasis of orchids and midnight. Her lips were a scented red. The air was salty, wind and quartz. And it was summer in Mexico City, Miami or Los Angeles.

No, she informs the men with the pose of American stockbrokers, with suits in three pieces, gray as the asphalt webbing the white world. You have nothing to offer me.

They do not understand or discourage easily. They take her to restaurants they consider elegant. She finds the food, the wine list and ambiance mediocre. They take her to nightclubs they perceive as lavish. She thinks the setting is garish and unremarkable. No, she tells these men in English and Spanish, she does not wish to dance. She has no desire to put white powder in her nose. And no, she has no interest in meeting men who might wish to marry her. She declines their offers with finality and grace.

She dismisses them, but carefully. She accepts their business cards and says only that she will telephone them, perhaps later. When they have left, she throws these papers away and washes her hands, removing the stain from her flesh.

Eventually, these men decide she is crazy. She does nothing to alter their perception. She has seen the core. It is liquid, in constant motion. There is the sudden severing of the ordinary, portals, doors leading into the camouflaged regions of the inviolate interior. This is the essential and irrefutable pattern. All else is delusion, contrivance, forms of fraud which are irrelevant. And La Puta de la Luna is impatient with words, whatever the language or accent.

On the streets bordering the city park with its miniature and somehow damaged and squalid lake, on the winding narrow avenues of wooden shacks and stucco or brick apartments with slats of poor gardens and overgrown sidewalks, here, where the city curves downward and the skyscrapers suddenly stop, it is said she hisses and scratches like a jaguar. They say she carries a cuchillo, her fingernails are claws. Perhaps she is a stranded bruja. Or a thing still part jungle with connections to ancient rituals best left undisturbed. She wears certain odd jewels which resemble amethysts and rubies. It is said they radiate heat and glow in the darkness. It is possible they are real. Or perhaps they are amulets or shards from some not yet comatose god.

The boy-men in the local gangs pass her in silence. They say, softly, when they are beyond the sphere of her hearing, that she is more trouble than she is worth. They dream of raping her beside the lake, or ripping her silk clothing from her flesh and taking her with force in the back seats of cars. They would like to grind her skin into concrete. They wonder whether she would break as simply as ordinary women, if she would bruise and bleed beneath their weight and the puncture of their fists. They do not speak of this. They simply spit Puta, puta into the gutter and feel uneasy in their laughter.

Of course, these boy-men with their identical headbands and jackets intuit that she is somehow inviolate. They recognize something insistently red and sharp about her. Ambiguities, alluring and metallic. They find themselves mute before her. They lack the necessary concepts with which to form a vocabulary that would describe her. They cannot equate her boldness and courage, her ease with the streets with their own. It is obvious that were she a man and were she insulted, someone would die. There would be the flash of a cuchillo then, and blood that spills slow and hot across pavement, remaining like a scar in the asphalt even after a season of rains. But she is a woman.

Her name is Francisca Ramos. To the men who pay to push themselves into her, into any area within her that will open, she says her name is María. Men can pay for her body, but not for her personal history, the images she wears hidden, like delicate stitchings across her inner eyes.

La Puta de la Luna wears a skirt the color of a red orchid. Her blouse is a burgundy; from certain angles of lamplight and shadow, it seems coral. She saw such magnificent explosions of orchids near Caracas, where the filtered green noon air was strung thick with the scent of rum. She remembers the mountains of rubber trees, mahogany and coffee trees, the palms, of course, the cactus and ferns and then the anomaly of conflagrations of orchids, magenta and reds that seemed lacquered, inflamed. They opened elaborate, deceptive, their embroidery and veins fragile and indelible. Their centers looked like insects. They were obviously alive, prepared to spring, to fly. If they wished, they could erase the stars. They had red mouths, vermilion tongues. They spoke in the language of thunder and waves and vines, of all that was intrinsic and elemental. They could sing. They dreamed only of themselves, dreams in which they saw themselves frozen, endlessly beautiful, beyond narcissism or corruption. They were their own definition.

The profusion of orchids. And the jungle rising into veils of clouds containing not simple rain but strange pollens, spices and particles that stirred and produced sounds which were a form of music. They entered first her flesh and then her blood, like an infection or a narcotic. And her breath turned red, not a burning but an awakening.

It seemed to begin in the port called La Guaira. They had docked in a dawn tangle of cruise ships, oil and war- and freight ships, boats of coconuts, plantains and mangoes. She stood on deck with Ramón, counting out loud the different flags as they leaped and danced in the green-scented wind. Banners of yellow, red and green, Italian and Mexican, British and Venezuelan, released to the air like streamers or kites. It seemed a kind of celebration, and Ramón had laughed with her.

The sound of his laughter was physical, warm and moist and familiar. Their bond was unassailable. For him, she was beyond naked. She was mud and stone. She could shake gourd rattles and pray herself hoarse, immaculate with immutable proofs like a village woman with visions. Or a woman whose family has inhabited the same valley for one hundred generations. They were birthed by volcanoes, mysterious ash, a rumble across jungle orchids. They were that which had existed before the creation of seasons or increments, hierarchies or sin. In the beginning, there was only a dance. Their dance.

Yes, Ramón Cárdenas, her third patrón. The importer of art objects and artifacts, with the American wife who looked prematurely aged. La Señora, with her face of angles and lines, with her flesh like the bed of a dried river, mud bleached and cracked, savaged by wind. La Señora, with her skin the color of nothing, nameless, dust, fields that are barren, mute with contagion. Ramón Cárdenas, the Colombiano who said, when they traveled together, that his mother had been Australian.

Ramón stood at her side on the deck of the cruise ship. Then he bought her blue leather sandals with high heels, a sun hat with silk flowers stitched across the brim, and sunglasses manufactured in Paris. In the boutique of the ship, he studied her as he might one of the vases or paintings he purchased and sold. Then he said she looked almost American.

"But my skin," she had protested gently. Francisca was uneasy with his playfulness. She could not yet determine when he was serious. Still, she was willing to be whatever pleased him. She was the leaf that accident had blown to his feet. "I am so dark."

"It's not the color of the skin," Ramón laughed, "but the sense of money."

Then he explained the textures that mattered. She memorized them, as if they were an alphabet. And they were silk, leather and linen, suede and sable, but never mink. No, mink was unthinkable. But those were merely of the exterior, less resonant than the intangible fabrics one wore on the inside. There were books, music, ideas. Ramón was telling her this as they walked from the boutique of the ship. There were scents and sounds that must be absorbed. She was to wear perfume, never cologne. Now Ramón was speaking about a certain quality of light. It must be soft, amber as the arcs of streetlamps in autumn in northern cities. Amber as the lights on boats, as flesh draped in the caress of the moon. Amber, never raw yellow, which was an offense to the sensibility.

Francisca listened to Ramón and returned his smile. She felt tentative. With Ramón, all things became exaggerated in clarity. Even before he first made love to her, he ordered her to master English, and, by his command, the language revealed itself to her. It opened simply, like an antique Spanish lace fan. The night itself became singular, startling. Night was a woman, impeccably dressed, draped in black silk, black sable. Night was an ebony beauty, with shoes and gloves designed in Italy. It was the spring of the prophecy, becoming specific, committed.

When Ramón watched her move across a room, she felt as if she were decorated with silver and turquoise. She was twenty-one. It occurred to her that she was still young. Make me your child bride, she thought. Pluck me like a glistening stone, a charm. I will demand nothing. I will be motionless as a mountain, calm as a peasant anchoring the horizon, that which has always been. I am your daughter, your sister, a deity of the moon and wild roses. I am a carved-in-clay statue of an Indian goddess of the harvest, pitted with incising and rubbed with cinnabar. Yes, cinnabar, the blood pigment. That was how they recognized each other.

Ramón brought her coffee with rum while they sat in the crowded harbor, stranded like a random collection of fish beached after a disaster. They were a museum of sea vessels, some wind-eaters, others diesel-powered, all stalled at the edge of judgment. When she told this to her patrón, Ramón, he did not smile. She watched his eyes tighten and she was afraid.

Her mother often said that she did not watch her mouth, that what her eyes saw tumbled from her lips like a waterfall, agitating the river. This was how chaos and floods were born. One should not permit a stream of syllables to erupt unrefined from the mouth. Such a string of oddities was dangerous and unattractive: it was like spitting stones or bullets or arrows. She harbored a defect within. She was incomplete.

Her family doubted she would ever find a husband. Even the village curandera, Josefina Jiménez, the woman who had birthed her, said she was too delicate. Her skin lacked insulation, the ability to bear sun and wind and the shifting of seasons without pain. The curandera noted that Francisca was subject to unnatural wounds and deviations. Such women belong to the air. They must drift like leaves or smoke. Such women bear an allegiance only to the currents, the tides and channels clouds carve in the air, in the chameleon regions ordinary women do not see.

Francisca Ramos spent the long afternoons of her youth dreaming and sleeping. The river was a soft green indistinct rustling. The curandera prescribed recipes of herbs, juices of healing plants, insect blood and rum, but Francisca could not be fattened. It was noted that she walked to the one village store not for sacks of beans or rice but only for magazines with pictures of cinema celebrities. She pasted photographs of women and men, faces of angles and huge eyes, on her bedroom walls where other young women hung images of saints. Francisca stared at these alien too-thin images, these absurd faces where even the men looked starved and overtly feminine, as if these distant aberrations had a tangible application to her life.

The curandera doubted Francisca could birth children, with her flat chest and angular hips. The moon burned her skin, and the stars were a form of torment. One could be abused by radiance. For some women, the planets could scar and the phases of the moon sting like a lash.

It was said that the war was edging toward the pueblo, slow, corrosive and inexorable. The power lines were felled. It was said the guerrilleros had bombed the power plant. Many marriageable men went to the capital searching for work with machines. Some entered the army of the government, which fed and clothed them. Other men crossed the border or journeyed into the mountains to join the forces of the insurrection. Francisca barely noticed their absence. The loss of electricity was unexpectedly soothing. She felt as if night were finally assuming its proper dimension again, uncorrupted by the follies of men.

Then one morning, without warning, she found her belongings packed. She was being sent to the capital, to her tía, Petra Mendoza. The once-weekly bus rattled into the plaza and stopped, still shuddering, like an exhausted beast. Francisca Ramos was fully aware of the fact that she was staring at her destiny. It had come as a tin shell. She would enter this vehicle, and the entire course of her life would be changed. She wanted to remember the village, the plaza, the palm trees near the church doors, the dog barking near the wheels of the bus. But the village was already losing its clarity and dimension, as if the outlines were being rubbed away and the colors somehow muted.

Josefina Jiménez was whispering into her ear, "Remember, God is a man and therefore harsh with his judgments. But Maria Magdalena was no less a saint then La Virgen de Guadalupe." But Francisca could not quite hear the curandera or understand why she was imparting this information to her. Francisca could only think of climbing the steps onto the bus, of sitting at a window and watching her village disappear with a finality that both exhilarated and terrified her. The bus rattled around one bend in the unpaved road, and the pueblo of her birth ceased to exist.

In the capital, she was assaulted by noise. Night was tortured by neon. Even the statues of saints embedded on the sides of the boulevards were forced into perpetual wakefulness, as if they were being punished. Francisca Ramos did not understand why such a desecration was permitted. She found herself weeping. This was not what she had expected. Early in the second week after her arrival, her tía Petra Mendoza found her work with a family in the suburbs.

Héctor González, her first patrón. She could could remember he traveled frequently, with his leather briefcase and matching suitcase, both of which bore his initials carved in gold. Francisca had no idea where he went or why. He smoked cigars and left their fat stumps on the edges of tables and shelves. When he was in the house, he shouted at La Señora, his wife. Occasionally, La Señora shouted back. Francisca could hear their arguments cutting like knives into the soft underbelly of the darkness. She found sleep was becoming difficult.

La Señora wore sunglasses when her husband blackened her eyes with his fists. An invisible tension filled their house, like a poisonous vine growing colossal and disguised beneath the polished mahogany floors and rooms of orange tiles. Perhaps the camouflaged plant with its tendrils of venom spread telepathically, nurtured by abuse and hate. She began to walk carefully, fearful, as if the poisons could reach out from the floors and sting her ankles. She would awaken, startled by the sound of glass shattering. In the morning she would sweep broken lamps and crystal ashtrays from the orange-tiled floors. She would bend down on her knees to remove individual glass splinters from the hand-woven rugs.

Francisca neither expected nor was given an explanation. Once, La Señora chanced to pass her as she swept glass shards from the floor. "You know men," La Señora said simply, with a shrug of her shoulders. "Los hombres son perros." And Francisca had nodded in agreement, although she did not know men and did not know that men were dogs.

When the patrón, Héctor González, was gone, La Señora spent entire days shopping in the city. She returned to the house at dusk, laden with boxes, bags of garments and objects she rarely wore or used. La Señora chatted on the telephone incessantly, like a kind of bird, frenzied, rushing from one mirrored seed tray to the next, careless, spilling debris as she fluttered past. La Señora made the air around her swirl in a strange and twisted dance. She moved in an accelerated sort of trance, oblivious, in a constant flurry of senseless activity.

Each afternoon, Francisca bathed their baby girl. The infant nestled in her arms like wood warmed by sun. Francisca held the girl baby until her arms were numb and the infant seemed to grow into her and they merged like the branches of a tree. Then Francisca polished silver platters. She was not unhappy.

She was careful with her mouth. It did not occur to her to ask La Señora why her husband blackened her eyes, why they broke lamps and vases, why they bruised the night with curses and fists. Occasionally, she wondered why La Señora did not wash her own daughter, why she did not brush the girl baby's silken black filaments of hair or kiss the tender belly of the infant until she laughed. She wondered why La Señora deprived herself of this pleasure, but she did not ask. Her job was washing and polishing, waxing and ironing and scrubbing. Her life was a dance. These were the elements of her choreography. And within these limited possibilities, Francisca discovered a certain grace, a fluidity and purpose which soothed her.

Francisca Ramos had been given a square room with one arched window. The door of her room opened onto the kitchen. She was given an electric clock that glowed orange in the night. She turned the clock to face the wall before she went to sleep. She could not bear the orange glare of it. For two years, this was the room where she would come to sleep after she had finished washing and drying the dinner plates, after she had placed the girl baby in her crib and sung and rocked the infant to sleep. The room she slept in, after La Señora dismissed her for the night.

When Francisca was dismissed early, when she was not too exhausted, she would sit on her narrow bed and write an occasional card to her sister, Delfina, who was only two years older and already five years married. And Francisca circled new births on her calendar, careful each niece and nephew would receive a card on the appropriate date.

On Sundays, when the patrón was with them, they rode in his black Cadillac to the cathedral in the capital. Francisca was given special shoes for this occasion, a dress and a mantilla. La Señora and the patrón sat in a reserved area in the front of the church. It was expected she would stand in the back of the church, as she had been instructed. Francisca Ramos positioned herself near the huge carved mahogany doors. As soon as La Señora and the patrón and their daughter were seated, Francisca left.

Francisca had nearly three hours of liberty. Often, she would rush to a stationery store on the boulevard where La Señora shopped. She had learned which boulevard contained the most exclusive stores by memorizing the labels on the innumerable boxes she helped La Señora carry from her car into the enormous gate-enclosed house.

Francisca walked up and down the aisles of the stationery store, selecting dazzling cards to mail to her family. The clerk wrapped them in paper for her and she hid them in her purse. For that instant, that unique vortex of a moment, standing in front of the clerk, she imagined she was someone else entirely. A woman who inhabited rooms dense with hand-embroidered cushions, perhaps. A woman who wore sixty rings on one hand, and painted a river of purple half moons across her eyelids like bridges. A woman who pushed the noon-heavy air with a silk fan smuggled by barge and horseback from a forbidden territory on the other side of the ocean. A woman who waited for others to climb marble stairs carrying trays of strong coffee and sliced melons. It would rain. She would lie on silk sheets beneath a quilt soft as the petals of flowers and read adventure stories. And always, she would clap her hands at store clerks and fill net bags with chocolates sculpted like ornaments.

Then she rushed back to the cathedral. She met the patrón and La Señora in the courtyard. She sat in the backseat of the car with the child. The patrón and his wife drove in silence, subdued not by their experience with God, she recognized, but rather from an irredeemable mutual boredom. They smoked cigarettes. She wondered, idly, whether they ever confessed their sins, how they cursed repeatedly with the name of God, how they ate meats in French sauces on Friday nights with regularity, how La Señora took the anticonception pills. Francisca had seen them hidden within her jewelry box. Did they confess they filled their house with the poison of hate? And she wondered whether such married loathings had a specific category in the catalogue of sins.

Francisca lost interest in the nature of their possible confessions. She was elated with her deception and how easy it was. La Señora and her husband noticed nothing. Francisca sat silently in the back seat of the black Cadillac. She was invisible to them. She could be air or smoke. She could be like a place not yet born. It occurred to her then that there were holes in the fabric, sudden portals where escape was possible. There were legions of women who simply disappeared. Cars were found at bus stations and airport terminals. Suitcases were often discovered, purses and identification. But not the women. These women had suddenly woken and jumped off the edge of the world as it was ordinarily known, vanished, armed only with the clothing on their backs.

And Francisca Ramos realized that there were variations and anomalies. Doors could open, gulfs and channels. Names could be shed. One could create an identity from dust and rubble. One could weave the outline of a fiction and breathe life into it. There were precedents.

Then she returned to her half-life, her partial existence, her masquerade where she pretended to know less than cactus or stone. She waxed and polished. She waited to be called or dismissed. She kissed the belly and the feet of the girl child and made her laugh. And Francisca realized that her life was a kind of permanent Tuesday, a day when nothing happened. She forgot her name, her age, her village of birth. She knew what a bridge or a field of sugarcane or maize knows, which is only sun and wind and the earth beneath its roots, the fixed water below its span. Somewhere on the periphery, bells repeated themselves like pebbles tossed into water. She dreamed she was sleeping. The ocean poured in. Time stalled and each day was like a harbor in August, horizon filled by one great lemon-colored sail.

By the second summer, when the fighting reached the streets of the capital, the patrón and his wife and daughter fled to Guadalajara. Francisca had accumulated dozens of cards embossed with flowers and candles and birds. She took them with her to her new job, the next family, her second patrón.

There was a new room near the kitchen. There was another child to wash. She accepted the limiting details of her present existence because she intuited there were eddies and streams beyond counting, rivers and oceans. Always, these surfaces could be drifted across, rafted, sailed. It was a planet of water. Someday, the liquid would reach for her. There would be a fluid calligraphy. A blue mouth would open, would call her by name.

Now the harbor wind was caressing her face. Ramón was taking her hand. He was guiding her down the ramp of the cruise ship. After the week at sea, the smell of the tropics was immediate and raw. Here the revelations will be green, she thought. The inhabitants will flaunt fibrous bodies and sit in pools of shade comparing green dreams. The alphabet would be one of green nuance, leaves and winds, unspoiled. And she told the patrón Ramón only that she was grateful for such a luxury of green.

The day erupted opulent, verdant, mysterious. She thought of emeralds, of splitting them apart with her teeth and bathing in their exquisite green liquids. At that precise instant, with the harbor of stalled ships at her back and the continent staring her in the face, she realized the entire world was simply a collection of jewels.

Surely, in another life, she had stood on a shaded terrace while a hawk fluttered vaguely west. Slow drugged clouds leaned against low ridges of muted hills. She sewed gems on the saddle of a lord's war horse. Ten thousand diamonds for stars, for emphasis. She lived within walls dark blue and cool with tiles. Hillsides were rounded like the resting arm of a carved-in-jade god. Flutes were played. Everything outside was lime.

Ramón had hired a car to drive them into Caracas. Such cars were simultaneously mundane and inviolate like a confessional or a shrine.

And she had learned to wait for a brown or black or white man to open the car door for her. She waited, as the wives of the patrones waited in bougainvillea- and cassia-covered patios, on brocade-draped beds or cane-trimmed terrace chairs, waiting for their coffee or iced rum drinks or their polished silver trays of tiny elaborate sea creatures and fruits arranged like geometric sculptures. And it occurred to her that waiting was a form of art. It required patience and precision, the body assuming a certain posture, a collection of deliberate angles, an arrangement of the limbs almost indistinct from indolence. It was similar to the foods and drinks Ramón ordered for her, oysters and pâtés and liquors which lingered on the tongue like burnt oranges. He called such substances an acquired taste. Francisca felt she could acquire these tastes and gestures without effort.

Then she leaned back into the leather seat of the car as it wound into air steaming with coconut oil, rum and the slow monkey rhythms of red-and-black mahogany trees. She realized the trees had also mastered the art of waiting. Perhaps this was the natural expression, to simply be as a rooted thing, to ask nothing more than what the air and clouds and stars in their profusion and monumental indifference decided to offer.

They stopped for lunch in a restaurant which had once been a monastery. It was nearly three hundred years old. Ramón held her hand as they walked down the original corridors which were hard, chipped and endlessly erotic, the color of bone and opening into sudden shrunken rooms still smelling of sin, young men beating their backs with metal belts in chalky cells, intuiting a blood connection which must be denied, banished, an obstacle in the path of absolution. She almost laughed.

She felt as if she were breathing secrets into her skin, in the special air of Spanish silks, antique brocades and cool polished tiles brought by ships across the ocean. When her leather-sandaled feet moved across their oddly cold surface, she felt as if she were walking across water. And she recognized that all rooms were actually gulfs, harbors, and lagoons. The perimeters were liquid, constantly shifting. We exist by the grace of invisible bridges that will open or collapse of their own accord, she thought. There is nothing more.

Then they were driving, passing cathedrals constructed with the specific species of gray stone required by the imported God. They glared through the green haze like aberrations, the monstrosities invented by acute personal disaster or fever. And she wondered how the Europeans could think their bizarre contrived angles and embellished eccentricities would ever settle without struggle into a jungle that was insatiable, in a land where orchids were an unceasing eruption and the vulture was considered a sacred bird.

Their car was twisting up cliffs of agave and banyan. Ramón was describing the legions of men who had gone mad with sun and the delirium to discover gold. They lost their identities in a chaos of green. She could imagine them, stumbling between vines in a region of green streams, green gullies, green clouds where compasses and maps and prayers were irrelevant.

Then the dirt was turning red and soft as if newly born. Blue tin and orange bricklike shacks appeared on the cliffs like terrible festering wounds, lesions, rotting, untreated. She had been startled by this sudden juxtaposition, this thin metal perching on the hillsides like a deformity.

"The pus of the poor," Ramón commented, lightly.

Ramón was telling her of the ignorant farmers who had abandoned the safety of the interior, of the perpetual cycles of red and green coffee beans, to nest on scalped hilltops punctuated by television antennas. The new gods spoke from electronic boxes. Everyone could own one. There were no more penances. And the colors streaming from the screens were more vivid and compelling than any painting of any caped saint, bluer than the robe of La Virgen de Guadalupe, whiter than the banks of clouds on which angels sat.

She saw the city through his eyes. It was an hallucination, impermanent. Each season, storms washed the hovels away. The people returned like blind cattle, sculpting the debris into new dwellings even before the ground beneath their feet had again hardened. They returned like a lingering fever, a form of malaria ringing the illusionary city.

Francisca held a cigarette. Ramón leaned into her, lit it. The knew what they were. Earth and fire. Words were redundant, a violation. They were the skin of the world itself, the skin which repeats itself in precise patterns on the hides of jaguars, on the enameled wings of butterflies. Between them, the current was lush, fluid, undamaged.

Their car sped past the poor who appeared everywhere like weeds after rain. The women were young, yet they were already bent by children, betrayal, abandonment and poverty. The failure of rituals and governments, chants and incantations, gods and vows was etched across their flesh. And the women stood heavily beneath the inadequate shade of palms, listless, like a species of imperfect plant. She thought of her family.

"Will you weep for the hungry and lame? The victims of ill planning, with their ruined teeth, coughs and congenital lack of imagination?" Ramón asked, watching her face. "Are they not wet enough with the spit of God?"

Ramón removed his eyes from her face. Clouds burst from the earth and rose to form a veil across the sun. She felt a sudden chill. The day stalled, stillborn. Then Ramón was pointing at the round tanks of oil reservoirs, the huge vats where the black blood of a gutted jungle sat.

"It is not the Communists or the Americans," he noted. With his hand, Ramón indicated the billboards which erased entire hillsides. They were advertising Japanese tape recorders and trucks. "Propaganda," Ramón said. "That is what is ruining this fucking world."

Francisca was considering the poor whom God spit upon, in monsoons and seasons of inescapable floods. But this did not apply to her. Ramón had given her a gold bracelet wide as a fat man's thumb. And a ruby ring bright as Mars that one night in August when it hangs low and close, almost touching the earth like a great rare moth. The red ring. When they traveled together, she wore it. She was wearing the ruby ring now. It was a fortunate season. She slept well.

They were passing spires of centuries-old cathedrals rising on an horizon green and strung with stone crucifixes and freeway overpasses. The streets were crowded with chickens, rusty wires and strips from abandoned, partially completed edifices. She recognized there was an equation in this, something definitive and resolvable. It was asserting itself at the periphery, just beyond her grasp. And the car was moving too fast. And the streets seemed filled with the spilled intestines of something rotting forgotten beneath a screen of bamboo and a relentless August sun in a region where time curved and bent and lost its sense of purpose and proportion.

These are my green lessons, she thought, my portals into revelation. But the car was speeding and she let her thoughts drift. And the city was everywhere not quite built. It was an experiment someone had begun without conviction and then impatiently and irrationally abandoned. A bored and restless god, perhaps, anxious to journey to another world.

Now she is sitting on a bus bench at the edge of a city park. It is a city like any other. La Puta de la Luna senses the palms at her back. They are the too-tall variety, common to this area, all stalk with heads shockingly small, pitiful, defective. For more than a century, they have pushed themselves up into the sun and in the end, frail and deformed, utterly debased, found nothing.

This late afternoon, Francisca is aware of a woman sitting, almost motionless, at the shore of the gray slate of lake in the center of the city park. The woman is watching her with an intensity Francisca finds disturbing. The woman is old as bone, as stone, as a muddy pueblo bordered by dull fields of sun-singed crops and no hills, only clouds of dust and an arbitrary relentless river cutting the horizon in half like a curse. This old woman has seen the river in seasons of abundance, when there were crops enough and babies with fat bellies. She has witnessed the aging of the river, its channel slender, an irridescent green, crusted with flies, typhus, water-borne plague. Francisca senses that this old woman has seen war, fires, early widowhood. The years when locusts come with a vengeance, as if deliberately summoned. An old woman who knows that the sun is clearly and cruelly gold as the eye of a brutal and decadent god, forever unappeased.

Between them, there is a recognition. They realize they have been bored and dissatisfied in this life and others. They know that the wind comes or does not. They know that he limps home, eventually, or does not. Always a palm rises and shines greened, glistening after rain. Always beggars squint into a malicious sun, in the archetypal plaza, where their wounds are nests for insects. A princess is lifted on a litter of jade inlaid with human finger bones. Between them, they understand this.

La Puta de la Luna banishes the old woman from her consciousness. She wills her skin to glow and it does, as if she had somehow mastered the art of transmuting simple materials like neon and a static dusk, here, at the edge of a city park with its standard-issue miniature lake surrounded by deformed palms, here, at this intersection of accident and happenstance where the contrived grandeur of the office buildings and the municipal halls suddenly stops. It is a lazy city, eating its way outward slowly, she realizes, like a beast fat enough to be selective. Yes, a creature utterly assured and absolutely corrupt.

This late afternoon, Francisca has painted her eyes with the blues from feathers of extinct birds. She saw such colors in the elaborate capes of Aztec lords rendered in paints in the museum in Mexico City. These colors seeped into her skin. That was the day before Ramón left her. Now she allows the tentative sea breeze to rustle her silk skirt. Her legs are crossed at the knee, slender, like a piece of carved mahogany. The bus bench softens, ambers, beckons. It cannot resist her. She stares into the passing traffic and thinks, I am your last oasis. I am the final answer, what you were born for.

A car slows, circles the block once and drives on. Perhaps the man is startled by her face. She is a corrupted madonna, not alabaster but wood, darker and more resonant. Her flesh is a layering of teaks, ebonies, spice, a dense jungle mist, steaming, symmetrical and insistent. She wills herself to be radiant with heat and she is, creating a sphere of red like a beacon, a promise of an intangible and intimate connection with earth and clay. She is that which has been sculpted and baked by an older and more forgiving sun.

She is content in her waiting. It is a form of art, like ballet or weaving or arranging flowers. Women wait on bougainvillea- and cassia-covered patios. Women wait on terraces of fuchsias and geraniums. In the waiting, she observes nuances, appearing instant upon instant and dissolving back upon themselves as the sun shifts, as a window shade is pulled open or shut, a door, a pair of sea-blue drapes perhaps.

Francisca lets the transitory details fill themselves in as they will, as they must, each unrepeatable and unique. In this waiting, civilizations rise and fall, alphabets, gods and rituals, science and magic. And individual moments have their unassailable geographies, their music and silence and integrity.

Behind her, like a painted backdrop, the acre of city park assumes the deeper green of late afternoon. The lake is an empty slate reflecting shadows and the palms standing in a tortured circle around the shallow and dirty water. The old woman sits like a sculpted stone at the water's edge. The old woman is watching her with a kind of longing. And beyond, the palms prepare their frail heads to bear another night when the moon will tell them nothing, the stars will remain silent and the sky will deny them even the solace of sleep.

In the muted and still unformed sea breeze, Francisca watches automobiles pass like strange unpatterned pythons. She knows such mutations cannot reproduce. They are both the beginning and the end of their line. They exist in a realm beyond awe and pity.

Buses are white and numerous, painted with borders of a serene yellow and orange. They are clean and predictable. In the windows of the buses, Francisca observes the faces of the women who work in the suffocating edifices which are the sole definition of the center of this city. Their eyes are confused and empty, like eyes of travelers in airport terminals in the middle of a night. Any terminal in any night where the plane is indefinitely delayed, where a loudspeaker advertises cities in a profusion of languages and all the syllables lack meaning. One sits in the interminable gray, unhurried and disoriented, while enormous clocks offer the precise instant in Jakarta, Rome, Nairobi, Caracas or Miami. One sits mute in an identical cubicle, waiting not for the flight that will never come but for a more profound announcement, something definitive, like the end of the world.

The women in the bus windows let their shoulders slump. Their arms are bare, thick, the skin slack. They are draped in beiges and grays, without variation. They will leave these buses and walk up low hills in the stained shoes they once wore to church on Sunday. They will enter wooden houses in which they are no longer certain they actually live. They will prepare frijoles and tamales, dust surfaces and objects without meaning. Even the rudimentary details have failed them. They will wait for children and husbands, never fully convinced these men will actually reappear. They will sit at formica dining-room tables and say nothing. The hiss of the city will fill their ears like seashells in which waves have belligerently engraved their stories. And the seashells will recite their histories indefinitely, even as the women sleep.

Francisca searches for one particular woman. She does not see her today, has not seen her in weeks, in fact. Always, their eyes would connect. And Francisca intuited a rage that startled her. That bus woman was a wound that walked. She was dangerous, her hate dense as smoke. And Francisca would call to her, would command her to step off the bus, to free herself from the configuration strangling her, to recognize there were no borders, no houses or men that could not be left, abandoned or run from. Names and identities can be shed, changed, invented.

Always, the women in the bus windows stare at her openly, too exhausted and shocked to be discreet. Protected by their clean white metal shells, they allow their brown eyes to widen. Francisca senses their contempt, their wordless wonder and repressed anger. Perhaps they once dreamed of wearing diaphanous veils, ivory combs and perfumes smuggled from distant ports on the other side of oceans. Perhaps they craved round and mirrored beds in rooms ambered by the light of candles and vases of dramatically fragrant flowers. They do not permit themselves to remember this, would form a circle around her and hurl stones, bricks, their stained imitation-leather pocketbooks, but their buses are moving again. The serene clean predictable buses that all wear as their tattoo the word LOS ANGELES.

Francisca Ramos consideres Nuestra Señora la Reina de los Angeles and smiles. The city bears an absurd name. But it is no worse than San Juan or Santa Clara or any pueblo or metropolis desecrating the name of a saint. Francisca has come to understand something about the hallucinatory scraps of adobe and metal that men designate as cities. They are simply a transitory imposition of syllables, a trick of the mouth and of cartographers which will be erased by an army or a decade of unprecedented storms. The fundamental process cannot be altered, is a shamelessly unremitting compulsion to turn what was sacred into rubble.

Suddenly, La Puta de la Luna longs to tell the bus women she cannot harm them. Always, their husbands return. She is like an island that men visit once and briefly. They snap photographs of her lush flamboya- and cassia-embossed hillsides, her gullies erupting with magenta orchids and enormous metallic insects which sail like kites and sing. They are dazed by the greenery. Night becomes verdant. The moon is swallowed. They have been given maps, but they lose all sense of direction. In truth, they are anxious to depart. There were storms and swamps, fever and dysentery. She is better in memory, once they are home again, under a safe and predictable sun. I am a kind of postcard, Francisca thinks, do not be afraid.

Of course she does not want their husbands, with their calloused hands and arms engraved with snakes and daggers in black inks, with their smell of sweat and discontent, with their trapped dark dying eyes. She wants no husband at all. And she is without desire for their stucco cottages, their lack of aesthetics, their bruises, their ignorance, their cycles of sleep and sporadic violence. She does not want their sons who will join gangs just as dogs that are wild find packs; these sons who will plunder, listlessly, retrograde as cannibals, killing their own.

And Francisca is aware of the aged woman at the shore of the lake behind her, staring, measuring, somehow evaluating her. Francisca knows without turning that the old woman is sitting motionless, is carving the air between them with her thoughts. Yes, the old woman knows the art of waiting. Were she to turn and glance at her, the old woman would appear radiant, hypnotic and beautiful. It occurs to her that this ancient woman understands what La Puta de la Luna does not want. Perhaps the old woman at the edge of the catatonic lake has been married, has been installed like an appliance, has been ordered when to speak and when to remain mute.

Francisca does not desire the married midnight, the frozen hour of impenetrable fear, the paralysis at windows with small iron-grated terraces above miniature suggestions of gardens, wondering whether he will return this night or ever. The terror of waiting for the police or the hospital to call. And the moments become suspended. Perhaps he has found a new woman or crossed some actual or symbolic border. Perhaps he has crashed the car, drunk. You bathe your rooms with lamplight, yellow and specific as beacons. You reach for your rosary, your tequila. You hear sirens and the barking dogs, always the savage eruptions of dogs. And suddenly you understand why howls rip their throats. It is the passing of some other they sense, some unnameable evil. You wear a frayed chenille bathrobe or a silk gown, bare feet or high-heeled sandals. You stare into the night which ignores you. And you realize that perfumes, priests, amulets and the recipes of curanderas, vows and curses and preparation and invention cannot save you.

And Francisca is suddenly aware that the aged woman at the shore of the shallow gray lake understands this. There is a fabric, an embroidery, a design they share, a sense of texture and fragrance, opulent gestures, the significance of amber and orchids, and the recognition that this cannot save you. The illusionary boundaries tear from their temporary moorings. Channels and currents and gulfs open at your feet, always.

As Francisca studies the boulevard, she decides that she does not dislike this City of the Angels, with its alleys of bougainvillea, with its insistent yellow and bright-orange canna studding narrow paths between bungalow-walled courts where only blood relatives dare walk. Now this collection of angels and asphalt, of stunted shrubbery and bamboo-fenced alleys dense with magenta crepe bougainvillea calls itself Los Angeles. She shrugs, feeling the wounded density of the city settling across her skin. It is a geography with themes that are recurrent like the bands of color in weavings. It is a specific design she had learned to navigate and survive.

There are no surprises in this particular fabric, with the packs of dogs and barefoot children with black hair and black almond eyes. She barely notices when they call her puta and toss bits of gravel near her. They are careful. No rock has ever grazed her flesh. She is an object of curiosity and fear. She is what glows in the night, the eye that does not sleep. She might be a sort of religious symbol. She leans against the wooden bus bench, reassured by the nearby garages and restaurants painted an aggressive yellow or red. The assertion of primary color is fundamental to the fibers of this weaving. It is lulling, like sleeping beside an ocean.

From her bus bench, she can see the orange-tiled roofs of Spanish-style houses planted in the sides of hills like a series of terra-cotta pots, almost ornamental. From a certain angle, this area could be Mexico City or Santa Clara, Caracas or San Juan. The pattern repeats itself like an insane weaver or a cancer, even in this southern city which seems only peripherally and accidentally American. This city which was once an outpost of Spain and once a region of Mexico. This city webbed with boulevards bearing the names of Spanish psychotics and saints. This incomplete city which seems to have no recognizable past, no ground that could be called unassailably sacred. This incomplete city that speaks of an impending terror.

It occurs to her that what she most appreciates about this City of the Angels is that which is missing, the voids, the unstitched borders, the empty corridors, the not yet deciphered. She is grateful for the absence of history and its physical manifestations, the granite cathedrals of the imported God, the wide tiled plazas and the assault of church bells, the church bells that scarred her later, in Mexico City, with Ramón.

It was a Sunday. Church bells were screeching everywhere, maniacally, like legions of lunatics or birds, millions of trapped and enraged jungle birds scratching at the air. Ramón was giving her twelve thousand American dollars. He was pressing an airplane ticket into her hands. But her fingers would not open. She held an invisible silk fan in her hands, pearls, a bouquet of orchids, white as a wedding gown. She was his concubine. They were of the same substance, indivisible. In time, he would shed his too-thin American wife, that woman of granite and angles. She was an aberration that did not belong, like cathedrals in the jungle. He would banish that bleached white bitch and marry her. There was no other possible resolution.

And she did not understand what Ramón was saying. The car was moving and she noticed only that her suitcases were packed, not his. Bells were ringing everywhere, birds were flying in sharp formations, frenzied, with no place to perch. The spires were poisoned with danger and clanging. The stones were a contagion. The sky crowded with low-flying demented flocks of shrieking birds, and something had gone wrong with her ears.

"What are these?" she asked in English. Ramón always insisted they speak in English. Even in her panic, she did not violate their ritual. "What are these?" she repeated. She was pointing at her suitcases.

"They are your bags, obviously. They are packed. We are driving to the airport. You are leaving," Ramón informed her. But she was deaf. She was reading his lips.

Yesterday, they had toured the museum. She had studied the feathered capes of Aztec lords, intricate and stunning with the green-and-purple plumage of long-extinct birds. She had seen the great round stones which measured time with an accuracy and precision mathematics could not begin to imagine. She understood the civilization on display before her. The Aztec Empire erected pyramids without the wheel. The implications of magic were irrefutable. She had experienced a grandeur and a majestic heat old and holy. And Ramón was a lord. He should wear the skin of jaguars and sandals of snakeskin.

They embraced in front of the Aztec clock and she was naked, air to air with everyone, dead and alive, real and imagined. They were beyond bodies. Time split, cross-sectioned. Borders were erased as simply as lines of chalk on a sidewalk during a storm.

This was the culture the Spaniards had destroyed. They had gutted the temples, burned holy books, artifacts, the magic and plumes. A band of exiled syphilitic renegades had pronounced this civilization as savage. And the priests had blessed them in this. Ramón wrapped her in his arms as she stood in the museum and wept.

Then the enormities were defined. There were steps down to the core of the earth. The path was captioned and mapped. She knew exactly who she was. Her fingers were flowers, flames. She owned the wind, the seasons, the paths of stars and the artifacts of all women and men. Now Ramón was speaking and she could not hear him.

"I have refined your sensibility, given you an outline of art and history, a vocabulary and reference points in two languages. The world is divided into women who ride buses and women who hail cabs. You know who you are. You will survive."

Then Ramón was giving her the box he had purchased for her in London and kept hidden in his office safe. He was handing her the marble box lined with black velvet. Within the box were the silver and gold bracelets which were also kept locked in his office. She was wearing the ruby ring. Ramón was placing small square pieces of paper in her uncomprehending hands and explaining the intricacies of bearer bonds. He was her patrón. She was being dismissed.

But she could understand nothing. The air had dissolved into a sharp and formless static. Deaf and mute, she kept pointing to the back seat, to her suitcases. They glared at her like a deformity, like a leper in the cobblestone-stained alleys of certain almost deserted ports, a leper begging without hands for dimes.

"They are Louis Vuitton," Ramón said. He seemed simultaneously sad and frantic, partly because of her, she realized, and partly because of the suitcases. "They are the only Louis Vuitton bags you will ever own. Try to hang on to them."

Hang on to them? She stared at him through her French sunglasses. Did he think she was mad, that she would lose her suitcases or simply throw them away? Did he think she did not yet understand how to travel, how to present a claim check, nod with one finger to summon a porter, a taxi, a concierge? Did she not often return from their trips alone, to prepare the house for La Señora, to be there as if she had not moved farther than the patio since La Señora left?

A dark-blue car stops. Francisca slides in. It is a short drive around the park with the grayish lake of water weeds and ducks, two blocks precisely. She glances at the ruined Los Angeles sky and realizes it is better this way, cloudless, bells silent, without the hypocrisy of rituals that have been too long obsolete. It is less offensive to forget entirely than to remember incorrectly, defectively. And Ramón was saying, You must go, this afternoon, now. I am falling in love with you. But, she was saying, but, she was saying, but, like a record struck, but what on earth do you mean?

Francisca leads the man up the stairs to her apartment. Across the narrow hallway, a Mexicano couple turn their radio louder and casually, with elaborate grace, close their door without once looking directly at her. The white man behind her has light hair turning gray at the edges like an unkept plot of land surrendering to dead weeds.

La Puta de la Luna eases herself out of her skirt. She lets the silk drift to the floor like petals from a flower. Then she erases the man with the weeds at his temple from her consciousness, thinks instead of her sister Delfina's last letter, now three months unanswered. She must respond immediately. Delfina said the government finally restored the power plant. For three days there were radios and phonographs, lights that blazed, fiestas and dancing. Then los guerrilleros bombed the power plant again. She must express her regrets.

There is a man above her, gray like a cloud or smoke. He has no weight. He is merely the illusion of space. And Delfina wrote, "You tell us nothing of your new patrón or the nature of his family." Delfina, whose firstborn son died of pneumonia the previous winter. And she must re-member to express her regret that the son of her father's cousin, Alberto Gómez, she can almost remember him, was killed fighting in the hills near the capital. Once she had been diligent with her communications. Once she had sent cards embossed with candles and birds and flowers. Now she can no longer bear addressing a card to the village of her birth. It seems an act of subterfuge, a form of impossibility, like communicating with the dead or attempting to telephone someone you have encountered only in dreams.

The American man is quick and clean, wanting almost nothing. Pale bastard, she thinks, afraid to drop your pants in dark alleys. Or to tear the sheet with your teeth when you come, like a woman giving birth, in pain and exhilaration. White erased thing, you cannot even imagine boarding a strange train that has no destination, a vehicle where they ask not for dollars but for your mouth.

Her contempt for the man passes. She is particularly grateful he does not speak. Americans crave the exotic, but they are streamlined like their highways, gray as the asphalt they invent to surround them. Their desires are predictable, run in cycles, like fashions. They do not know that the sea could wash them like paint.

She glances at the graying man, who is lighting a cigarette, already impatient, reclothing himself with rapidity, ashes fall upon the sleeve of his dark-blue jacket. He has the look of a man who realizes he has made not a terrible mistake, but rather an avoidable miscalculation. A man who drank an extra martini and missed an airplane, perhaps.

La Puta de la Luna is fastening her skin of burgundy. The man is hurrying and silent. She encourages him to remain mute. Yes, American men are clean and simple. The most offensive aspect of American men is their relentless desire to talk. They lack the facility for intuition, even in a primitive form. Such impulses have been removed from them. They do not understand it is all an ebb and flow, a shearing and an adornment, a ceaseless flowing where nothing is permanent. Their sky has been sealed, welded shut, tight as a coffin. The relation of stars to the side of a hill, the purpose of the winds and migrating birds, are phenomena they can no longer imagine.

Of course Americans are severed from their earth connections. The flesh exists only as a metaphor for them, a symbol. They have no sense of boundaries, as if the entire world were one concrete parking lot. They violate her integrity with their questions, their assumptions, their compulsion to identify. They want her history, bare and naked. They want not just her body, which is easy, but her secrets. When they speak to her, they sound as if they were all writing books or working for La Migra or planning to start a church.

Young men who cannot afford her describe their occupations and anxieties, as if she could provide them with answers, definitions, absolution. The young men who cannot afford her reveal hidden fears, admit that the towers and Municipal Court buildings sicken them. At night, alone, they write movie scripts no one wishes to purchase. They look at her as if she were a curandera, a gitana. It is as if they expect her to sing for them, to decipher lost tongues, dance with veils, read the tarot, decode their dreams and draw maps of their destiny. The flesh is not enough. It is abstractions, pyramids of words they crave.

After the perfunctory caress, passionless, with their hands like leafless whittled branches, they stare at her, longing for more. She stares back through eyes painted with the flawless blues of long-extinct birds. She can outwait them. Any woman could.

Women have waited millions of years, growing separate as another species, with visions and priorities no man-words, no man-measurements can comprehend. Women spark dark cracks in the wanton night. Women exist in isolated unfathomable perfection, creatures of nuance and implication. Women are like aberrant stars, suddenly changing orbits. Or an unconforming sea, resisting the obvious structures of piers and harbors, refusing to be merely blue or green, tame as a formula. It is women who shift the borders. The seasons run wild. Women flow and slide. Men are larger. Women eat the silence. Women survive.

The man with the graying hair and nicotine smell staining the skin of his fingers is quiet in the car. His silence comes not from respect, she realizes, but rather from an internal preoccupation. He switches on the car radio. It is the news in English. The terrible heat wave that set the mountains ablaze, poisoned the air and closed the downtown factories has abated. The night will be cooler. And they sit, unconnected, at a traffic light.

Francisca exits the car and walks slowly back to her bus bench. She glances at the park behind her. The aged woman is still sitting at the edge of the lake, staring into the shadow-dented water as if it were a page of a book that she could read. And it is possible this old woman has mastered the art of deciphering the fluid nuances of water and shadow, the intervals of silence and what they imply.

Tonight, the moon will be full. Francisca is suddenly aware that the ancient woman is also thinking about the moon and its impending fullness, how it has once again completed its journey into the round and temporary whole. Women turn on a lunar cycle. It is not mathematics or equations but the pull of the moon which makes them bleed. It is men who seek to chart space. Women already know that space is inhabited. Each month, women feel eggs and stars and infant unborn moons die and squeeze through their wounded wombs.

Francisca cannot erase the presence of the old woman on the shore of the lake. Somehow, this woman seems familiar. But no, she cannot possibly know this aged mestiza who is studying the surface of the lake as if decoding hieroglyphics. Francisca knows no one in this city. Yet there is a sense of recognition between them. She admires the old woman's patience, her graceful surrendering to mere waiting. This particular aged woman knows that the world is composed of rented rooms where women in faded half-slips sip sherry and pills. Their shoes strap at the ankle. They soak their feet in salted basins. Their painted toenails are chipped. The body is going to ruin like an insignificant and deserted port the jungle has begun to swallow.

In Madrid or Caracas or Los Angeles, it is the same indifferent neon, a radio, a phone call which does or does not come. There is a bouquet of carnations or roses two days past dead. You pretend that someone sent them, that you did not buy them yourself. This small subterfuge infuses the decaying petals with a dignity, a significance. Always, there are the trivial details, the tiny invented anchors designed to keep the waters from flooding in. A standard-issue bird in a cage or a standard-issue cat to be fed. The plants in terra-cotta pots to water. The button or hem to sew. The sun goes down and it is all less than you ever planned.

La Puta de la Luna stares into the passing traffic. She thinks of the card she must write to her sister. Delfina knows nothing of Ramón or the airplane which carried her, deaf and mute, from Mexico City to San Juan. Or how, after being mistress to a patrón, she could no longer keep her place, her pose of subservience, her falsely cemented lips. The rocks and pebbles had been spit from her mouth. Her fraudulence, her pose of ignorance, it was a thing she shed simply, naturally, as one tosses off an old coat.

And the first American family in Miami, with their sandy-haired blue-eyed boy-children, called her arrogant and sullen. She understood their English perfectly and more, what their words implied. They demanded the illusion of gulfs and uncrossable rivers. It was intrinsic to their functioning that she be perceived as different, as a thing with distinct and recognizable borders. She must be like a miniature country in the jungle mountains that one squadron of American airplanes could entirely destroy between breakfast and lunch. This is the design they understand, the configuration they insist be repeated in the exterior geography of nations and in the internal geography of people.

But she had sailed that particular gulf, had navigated and mastered that current. She could no longer merely pretend to be a lamp, a toaster, an oven waiting for their white mouths to order her off or on. It was the tone, Francisca now realizes, the same staccato precision that might be used to order the decimation of the farmlands of a small and insignificant nation. A region inhabited by women and men with brown or yellow-tinged skin.

She longs to explain to Delfina that she has learned certain intricacies of the body which are not a transgression but a blessing, a removal of self-imposed infirmities. Is it a sin for a woman who has been crippled to walk without a cane?

Once, she felt desire in the slow warming morning while Ramón slept and she waited for him to wake, in Caracas or Mexico City, in Puerto Vallarta or Managua, or in Santa Clara in the West Indian islands where the patrón and his wife had their second home. Santa Clara on the Caribbean, the youngest of God's oceans, the still green sea. There she waited for Ramón silent as clay, open to the bone, stripped as a bride at dawn on her wedding day, beyond breathless and becalmed.

She brushed her long black hair and thought, I was born to love you. It is my destiny, what I outwitted a starved and aborted girlhood for, entire sections of me intact, vast and unused like an uncharted continent or an absolute vow.

As she watched Ramón sleeping, she thought, I am every woman whose flower-print sheets you ever lay on. I am every woman wearing white silk slips and French perfume, bending above plants on terraces and balconies in whichever country or sunset. It was my lips that promised to love you forever, that moaned Siempre, por vida, oh baby. It is my face lingering unique and fragrant in your corridors, in the hollows anchoring your bones, in the blood canals where birds thought to be extinct call in your sleeping aviaries, eating the darkness with their mouths.

After Ramón she could no longer lie in a back room shared with a child, where a door might be opened without warning at any instant, a lamp switched on. She no longer slept easily, like an appliance turned off, like a candle blown out. Now she took sleeping tablets from the medicine cabinets and jewelry boxes of the patrón and La Señora. She drank their liquor.

Now she touched her body in the darkness and made herself shudder, sinning both in the act and in the remembering. And she had said to Ramón, Take me, my dreams of fish and rain forests, all that is lavish and green. I give you my skin to paint. Tattoo your name to my thigh. Christen me with your hands and tongue. Love me as if I were pulled from your loins, as if I had nested months in your belly, your chest, and exploded your groin with my birth.

Sometimes, in the night, in the room of a stranger, she would remember specific incidents with a clarity that amazed her. She sat with

Ramón on a restaurant terrace in Puerto Vallarta. They drank rum from the shells of coconuts. Men in red-and-white parachutes dropped from the undamaged fields of blue sky. The breeze took them like red-and-white petals. The waters were warm, calm, adorned with small black sharks. Ramón had glared at the American tourist at a nearby table and said, "If you look at my woman's leg again I will kill you." She remembered Ramón's words, parted her legs and with her fingers made herself feel thunder.

Now Francisca paces the pavement bordering the acre of city park, restless and agitated, surprised that the images still burn. And in the park the palms are beginning their hopeless surrender to the dusk, to the night that will be luminescent beyond expectation, brilliant and devious, more an equation than a lullaby and, as always, absolutely empty. This is a configuration which cannot be resolved.

La Puta de la Luna tosses her cigarette into the gutter. Perhaps she will answer Delfina's letter tomorrow. She will invent conventional lies. She will not attempt to describe what it is to be swallowed by a borderless other. It came to her with an urgency she could not deny or resist. And it was not an act of innocence.

On the other side of the illusionary waters she discovered she was subtly altered. She allowed herself to merge with a certain slice of city view, a particular collection of angles and shadows, spires and the green glaze settling across a terrace of philodendrons in terra-cotta pots. At such moments, her fingers stopped polishing the silver tray the family rarely used. She would abandon her assigned task and stand in a sunlit study instead.

Of course, the flesh had its own life, she recognized. The pulse was natural, was a river carving its own channel, employing temporary human vessels. And she realized that rooms and walls were transitory illusions, symbolic, meaningless without the consent of shared context. And she could no longer consent.

Her body seemed to shrink and swell. She stumbled into morning, blinded. It occurred to her that sometimes women turn to their secret, sexual side. Men were different. They were born with the sun on their bellies. They had absolute direction from inception. Women were daughters of the moon, with circular seasons, with one portion of themselves exposed and the other perpetually hidden and dark.

Then there was a second American family, a third and a fourth. And the next family called her lazy. La Señora suspected she was ill and suggested she consult a doctor.

Francisca remembers this and smiles. There is no doctor for her, no curandera, no prescription or herb potion, however exotic or difficult to gather and combine. There are no vaccinations for her disease, no Hail Marys, incantations or amulets, no composition of elements which fortune or imagination can invent. She has merged with the virus, the infection, the delirium that invaded her. They are one. She cannot be saved by candles lit in cathedrals or a visit to a sanitarium or a distant and indisputably hallowed shrine, not even a house where a saint was born and a certified miracle performed.

Once, in a pueblo near Miami, Francisca Ramos confessed her sins. The church was set behind a cactus-and-dust tourist courtyard where postcards and miniature plastic saints could be purchased. Blue-eyed replicas of the Madonna were also sold, large idols that plugged into walls like appliances and became electrified so that their blue eyes glowed. She could not bear to look upon them.

In the chapel, electric candles flickered and bled red across the carved breasts of martyred saints. She knelt on the holy stones and wept. I am through with this siege, this unhealing inflammation, the men and wind and hotels, she vowed. And she told the priest she would scrape the sin from her skin if it took a razor, if it took forever, if she had to learn again from the beginning. Even if the alphabet were granite blocks she must chip one inch at a time with her teeth and carry strapped to her back like a pack animal through eternity, itching in scrub brush and taunted by stars.

She placed a hundred-dollar bill in the collection box, and then a second. She lit candles for everyone whose name she could remember, sisters and brothers, nieces and nephews, the infant she had bathed in the capital, the girl-child of her first patrón who had fled to Guadalajara years ago. Then she sat for a long time in the courtyard of cactus and dust and orange trees. She felt the hot night rising, a stained red, calling her name, demanding her presence, insistent. She was necessary for this choreography, this conflagration, this disappearing sun. And three hours later she took a man for money.

Suddenly, Francisca remembers the curandera in the village of her birth, Josefina Jiménez, who had pulled her from her mother's womb. It was the morning when she was packed, without warning, and sent by bus to the house of her tía Petra Mendoza, in the capital where even the statues of the saints were lashed by neon and denied the possibility of sleep. She was watching the slow rattling and rusted bus approach, stumbling like a sick tin animal. She was standing in the plaza of her pueblo. She noticed chickens in the windows of the bus, held on the laps of old women. She was paralyzed by this moment, this portal, and the ancient vehicle summoned, as if magically, to transport her to her destiny. The curandera was whispering into her ear.

"You are an oddity here, an orchid among weeds," Josefina Jiménez said. The curandera was a religious woman. Her voice had a clarity, a direction. Her words were points, arrows, markers.

"Many and varied are the dominions," the curandera was whispering. "God is a man and therefore severe with his judgments. Remember this. Maria Magdalena was no less a saint than La Virgen de Guadalupe."

But Francisca Ramos could not comprehend the curandera then. Francisca was watching the bus, rusty, dented, bent by the weight of luggage and cartons strapped across its roof. She was staring at the face of her destiny. It had come at last, more or less on schedule, and it was indisputably three-dimensional. Then she climbed the thin metal stairs and entered the chamber of dream.

Yes, many and varied are the dominions, Francisca agrees with Josefina Jiménez across the illusion of time and borders that concurrently separate and bind them. Of course the curandera in the village of her birth knew the fundamentally fluid nature of distance, the sudden openings and transitory bridges. It was not a matter of prophecy or sorcery. There are only four elements, only fire and earth, air and water, and their infinite permutations, that is all.

In Puerto Vallarta with Ramón, the elements were revealed. They exposed themselves, raw and savage. It would be their last trip together before Mexico City. La Señora was with her family in Connecticut, a northern province of the United States where trees changed color with the seasons and their leaves were shed entirely in winter. In Connecticut there were stone haciendas and fields of snow, and the banyan, bougainvillea and even the palm were unknown.

Ramón had shown her photographs of La Señora's family home. It was winter there. The trees looked as if they had been burned, blackened, only their ruined spines remained. They might have been wire sculptures. The house was surrounded by a gray stone fence. And the house was enormous, with gray stones and angular embellishments, it might have been a cathedral. The photographs had made her nervous and oddly breathless. Nothing seemed to stir in them. She felt as if she were looking into an open coffin.

Before she left for Connecticut, La Señora had found fault with her. She said the coffee was too strong or too weak and dumped it down the sink. She sat on her patio waiting for Francisca to brew a second or third pot. La Señora watched her arrange lilies in a crystal vase. She turned to Ramón and said in English, "This girl is devoid of aesthetics."

It seemed La Señora was constantly staring at her. Her eyes were hard. La Señora studied her movements as if she were auditioning a dancer. La Señora was looking into her skin as if her flesh were glass, as if she thought she could discover bruises, the indentures of fingers.

"She is suspicious," Ramón said casually.

It was noon. They were sailing the warm harbor of Puerto Vallarta. The shore was a dense uninterrupted green, iridescent, the color of the wings of certain insects. A veil of green punctuated by waterfalls. On the sand, iguanas and boars stood, motionless as rock. The ocean was jade and tame. Young boys dove from low cliffs, swam to their boat for coins, opening sun-blackened hands that looked like fins. They drifted, drinking rum, eating cheese and melons. They found a green lagoon, transparent as unformed flesh, and swam to the smooth shore. Palm trees bent over them, draping them in bolts of angular shifting shade.

Yes, Francisca thought, as the sun blazed across their skin and the water spilled hot and tired near their feet, we will live beside a calm ocean. It will be cliffless, where no buoys float, no boats or drowned men. Dawn will be the color of chiffon scarves drifting from the suntanned necks of beautiful women. They would embrace at dusk, hour of the small blue openings, hour of enameled butterfly mouths. Hour of the flute and echoing bell, the air a recurrent phenomenon of cerulean. They would eat what the sea offered, the pale-green and Mars-red rocks that lay with round polished bellies up, moon grazed, sacred and healed in the tideline, set in the pattern of random revelation. They would fill straw baskets with these rocks and string them around their necks. They would feel the cool stones around their flesh as they slept. The sea would marry them.

Then, suddenly, the late afternoon turned strange, became raw with wind and a sense of disaster. Without warning, a veil had simply been stripped from the gauzy blue sky. An armada of gray clouds appeared, warrior clouds, prepared for battle. The sky was sealed as if by a lid of metal. The pale whitened sun disappeared. Perhaps it had been sucked dry by too many incautious lovers, she thought, startled and disturbed by this idea. She said nothing. The sky was invaded. There would be a war. They sailed back to their hotel, the water whipped by wind. The water felt hard, like stone. Dusk was a stasis of rocks and dried flowers. From their hotel terrace, the moon drifted through clouds and glared, a garish ebony. She was cold. A taste of onyx and crushed moths settled inside her mouth.

The hotel itself seemed to buckle beneath the thunder, the force of the wind, the torrential, angry rain. Waves of black insects crashed against the glass of their terrace windowpanes. Water above, rock in the sea. The elements were confused. It was a tear in the fabric, a wavering deep within the fibers, and she was afraid.

Francisca took a bath. Then she lay down on their bed. Ramón was smoking a cigarette, his hands were shaking. Yes, he was agitated. He had put the white powder into his nose again. Then he pulled the drapes shut. The black insects were erased, the dark-violet sky, the moon that burned behind the bruised clouds. Ramón sat down on the bed. She was naked. He was still wearing the blue jeans and yellow t-shirt he had worn on the boat. He smelled of rum and melons, salt water, tobacco and something metallic and faintly lemon scented.

The rain was louder, abusive, an eruption, beating against the sides of the hotel like an army of savages with sharpened sticks. Somewhere, a god had been defiled. His mouth of thunder and lightning and wind opened. The room shook. It occurred to her that the hotel might collapse. Then she could die as she longed to die, in his arms.

"It is the night I love," Ramón said, his voice odd. The sounds did not actually seem to be coming from his mouth. "The night unrolling like bolts of black antique Spanish lace."

He was staring at her, naked, in the center of their bed. "Do you know who I am?" Ramón asked. He laughed. "I am your caballero come at last. Your knight of prophecies and cataclysm."

She laughed. Then she realized that his face had become hard and distant, hooded and remote. His face had become a kind of stone. She remembered the photographs of the enormous house of gray stones belonging to his wife, the house in Connecticut. Instinctively, she reached for the sheet to cover herself.

"No," Ramón said with the voice that was not his. "Stay as you are."

Ramón took a small vial of the white powder from the pocket of his blue jeans. She had never seen him breathe the powder into his body before. Always, he did this in secret. They never spoke of it. Now his eyes widened and he trembled again. The thunder seemed poised directly above their room. The elements had deliberately chosen them. And even with the drapes shut, their room was lit by random bursts of lightning, intermittently an electric blue, eerie, cold. She shivered.

"And you are my whore, my longed for," Ramón whispered. "You are what waits with the red rose and lips scarred from thorns. The trophy after the bullfight."

Everything seemed to be happening in slow motion, at a distance, as an image shattered into fragments. Ramón was taking off his belt. It was a thin strip of brown leather. He had worn it on the sailboat, yes. "Look into my eyes," he commanded.

In the storm light, his eyes were blue, blue as the flames on kitchen stoves in cold rooms in rainy seasons in great houses with courtyards surrounded by gates when you are alone, when the patrón and his family are gone, when wind rips the patio walls, when palm fronds fall against the polished glass of the windowpanes. Blue as a stove's flame in a winter yawning skeletal, where darkness opens queer and incalculable. His eyes were the blue of betrayal and desertion, of oceans that cannot be crossed. And above them, the sky and sea were the identical electrified liquid, pouring into one another, disordered and enraged.

"Say this is not a game," Ramón demanded. "Say, This is a real part of me."

"This is not a game. This is a real part of me," Francisca said and laughed. She thought it was a game.

"Say it again. Say it like you meant it," Ramón instructed, the words strange in his mouth, as if he were talking from beneath water. "This is not a game. This is a real part of me."

Francisca repeated the sentence, word for word. Then he made her say it again. And then again. He commanded her to repeat the sentence thirty times. He counted. And the rain was falling in a steady pattern, monumental, furious. It was as if the world had turned upside down and the sea were pouring onto them. And the sea was stone. And Ramón's eyes had turned dark, the black of obsidian, cold and sharp. His eyes glowed, lit somehow from within. There was a disturbance in the elements. The ocean was inverted. And Ramón did not have eyes at all, but stars or volcanoes, embers that were charged, fused, a form of metal. And Francisca Ramos realized that he was no longer fully human.

He did not take her on their bed. He told her to lie down on the floor. The tile was surprisingly cold and hard. It might have been the surface of a remote star. She was lying on her side. Ramón instructed her to place one hand on his shoulder. He said, "Don't move your hand from my shoulder."

Ramón hit her thigh with his belt. He whipped the belt against the soft, sunburned flesh of her inner thigh. Then he lashed the leather against her skin, harder. There was thunder. The elements were convulsed, shuddering in spasms. The sea fell into their room. The ocean was composed of bruised clouds and black rocks, obsidians and ebony, chipped and pointed. And fat insects were crashing into the glass of the terrace windows.

"Don't move your hand from my shoulder," Ramón said. "I am going to hit you thirty times. You will count each one out loud."

"One," she began, and her flesh stung. And the sound of his leather strap against her bare skin was a kind of thunder. They were the center of the storm. It lived within them. It was possible they had created this physical manifestation, this derangement of water and rock by their thoughts alone. "Sixteen. Seventeen," she counted, and her voice was a gasp, a whisper, something startled and wounded. The words did not come from her lips or mouth but from a far more distant and hidden realm, like the place where winds and stars are born.

"Next time, you will say thank you each time I whip you. Next time, you will beg me to take off my belt," Ramón was saying, his voice soft. He carried her to the bed. He was rubbing cream on the red welts he had created across her flesh. Her skin was numb. She could no longer determine whether she was awake or asleep. It was difficult to breathe. The air was fluid. The thunder. The inverted ocean. She considered the possibility she was drowning. I could be as a shell in the waters, she thought. All beaches are the same. I could be refined by the incessant beating of waves. A shell that is found, is lost. I could be a daughter of the salt-webbed waters, blue into blue where there is liquid and rhythm only, a camouflaged and more final reality.

"I could fuck you like I would a man," Ramón said. He had been breathing in more of the white powder. He was smoking a cigarette with hands that trembled. He was above her. She lived on the floor of the sea. He moved in slow motion, a kind of hunter, searching the currents for her. He put out his cigarette. He unzipped his still damp and sand-stained pants.

"Hold your breath," Ramón said. "And open your mouth as wide as you can."

She was a sleeping sea creature. She lived within a shell on the soft floor of an ocean. Then he was pushing himself down into her throat. He was holding her head with his hands, pressing her head tight to his hips, and his fingers were a kind of vise around her skull. She gagged and could not move. Something rose from her throat, spilled from her mouth. It stuck in her hair, on her face. Ramón kissed her face, later. He ran his fingers through the fluid, the yellow of melons and rum. He painted her flesh with it. Then he streaked his own skin with it.

There was a mirror above the bed. Ramón told her to look into it, to watch them with her eyes wide open. She was kneeling. He was above her. She stared with wonder at her face. She did not recognize herself. She seemed otherworldly, like a saint or a film star. Then Ramón spit on her face. The air in the room sparkled, broke into patterns that shined and glistened, glazed as the bellies of abalone shells. The lightning had turned her face white as pearl, as alabaster, as a carved cameo. The thunder. The inverted ocean. The electric blue-and-white light.

This is how it happens, she realized. There is a door. It is opened by accident. You enter another region. And she heard the rain falling and the waves battering the shore below their hotel and the sky was liquid and the sea was rock. She considered the elegance of uninhibited water, its depth, its dolphins and black sharks, its sudden islands, shells and salt.

"Tell me your secret name," Ramón said. He lit a cigarette.

Because she did not know her secret name, she said nothing. In the silence between them, rocks were falling, rain, slabs of round onyx, glittering shreds of the garish moon, the blue thunder, blue lightning, blue sand and glass.

"Your secret name is slut," Ramón told her.

"Yes."

"Say it."

"I am a slut. I am a slut," Francisca Ramos said.

Then the rain began to soften. They left the hotel and walked along the edge of the deserted beach. The ocean washed across their feet. The rain was a drizzle, a warm mist and cleansing, a form of liquid blue flame. They were purified. The moon reappeared, removed her black veil and bathed the sand in white light. They walked barefoot across a tossed pebble beach and found a sudden driftwood-littered cove, a graveyard of branches wind-heaped in a random whitish anatomy of skullwoods, arrows and thighs. The sand where they slept was wet.

She woke with the sun on the lip of a lagoon webbed with red kelp. The day seemed sheared and unsolid. The sky was blue as a flame's belly. They draped their clothing across driftwood logs as the sky reddened. The glistening wet sand shifted, inflamed near their feet. Spent waves collapsed against the mute rock. The pivotal juncture of sea and land, sea and land at a moment of crisis and decision.

There were cliffs behind them where birds nested in rock tunnels which winds had cut. The ocean was quiet. A seal let the sun graze his belly. Three pelicans drilled north with rare purpose. The moon rose in the blue daylight above cliffs flushed pink on the naked rock where the vines and palms and banyans stopped. In the noon sun, her shadow was a long arrow across the hot sand. At the lip of the shore, she noticed the deeper dents of round glossy pebbles dislodged by the storm, tossed up on the sand while the sea dreamed and mermaids combed their red kelp hair with empty abalone shells.

The sun dried their clothing. They held hands as they walked slowly back to the hotel. She looked at Ramón and thought, Understand, I am more quiet than the young troubled cliffs, ambivalent and crumbling, strangling with their own abundance. I ask nothing.

At lunch, at a terrace restaurant, Ramón grew tense and agitated. He smoked an entire package of cigarettes. He took a pill from a bottle she had never seen before. He ordered a fourth Bloody Mary. He glanced at the beach, and his eyes seemed clouded and stained. She followed his glance and saw small waves the color of fine jade opening like fragile flowers on the sand, like the hands of infants, like antique lace fans. This was part of the calligraphy of the sea, she thought, stunned by the density of the ocean's alphabet, its motion, the infinity of slates it etched and erased, the creatures it invented for amusement, the lands it birthed and then flooded.

"Puerto Vallarta bores me," Ramón announced. He stubbed out a cigarette. His hands were shaking. He took another pill and finished his blood-red drink. The waves were strands of fine jade. Men fell from the sky in red-and-white parachutes that floated down to the sand like enormous flowers or a fantastic mutation inspired by clouds.

"In time, all oceans become identical," Ramón was saying, "their distinctions too vapid to recite." He glanced at the beach. "Still, the Pacific is one of the least attractive." She stared at him. "We will fly to Mexico City tonight."

Then he left her, alone, at the terrace table. She stared at the cloudless sky, recognizing with absolute clarity it would never be so seamless and vivid a blue, so of a piece with her flesh again. And the sky was blue as the flames on kitchen stoves in houses where she had lived in rainy seasons alone. And it occurred to her that somewhere a door had opened. Somewhere, it would close.

She lingered on the restaurant terrace until dusk, until the beach began to darken, until Jupiter appeared, pale, a matter of suggestion and the need to impose direction on the restless and uncontainable night. She memorized the thatched huts and the palms adorning the beach, the red-and-white parachutes drifting like flowers from the untainted blue acres of sky, the red and yellow sails of the boats sliding across the harbor. She sat on the terrace until abrupt stars, sharp as wind-ripped quartz, forced back the dark-blue folds of sky. By then, Ramón had packed their suitcases, and a car, as always, was waiting.

Now, in Los Angeles, the sky is slowly shattering, opening in gulfs and eddies, permitting the sun to begin its uneasy ordeal of setting. Francisca will tell Delfina she has won a lottery ticket or taken a job in an office. Any banality will suffice. Francisca Ramos actually longs to describe her apartment, this dwelling which belongs to her alone, where no rooms are shared, where doors do not open without warning, and she is not instructed, reprimanded or dismissed. Her own apartment, overlooking a miniature lake of young boys in brightly painted boats, ducks and water weeds. A lake with a soft shore where old men sit fishing and young men sometimes fight and die. She wishes to describe the lake, how it mirrors the sky, how it is sometimes greasy and stagnant, sometimes a flawless blue. The lake is encircled by palms that rise like many arms beckoning to the sky. Here, the palms are abnormally vertical, she will mention, as if they desire to make themselves more blatantly attractive to the wind.

Francisca smiles at herself, at the part of her that longs to boast of her triumphs and extravagance. She considers her many sets of matched pure cotton floral-print sheets. And the dozen thick bath towels she keeps in a special closet with sachets. Everything she touches is scented. Her soaps are sculpted in the form of tiny roses. Her bedside lamp is porcelain, and the bulb is amber, soft as petals of a flower or the skin of an infant.

No, she does not shop in the ugly center of the city, in El Centro, where the streets are crowded and the gutters and sidewalks erupt with debris. El Centro is for refugees. She takes a taxicab to Bullock's Wilshire. The man who guards the door nods his head, he knows her. Each Wednesday, she has her nails manicured in the salon there. She has her hair tinted or trimmed. Sometimes she eats lunch in the tearoom where women present fashion shows, passing between the tables, making their expensive skirts swirl.

She perceives herself as beyond brazen, as a creature lavish and eccentric. Of course La Puta de la Luna is a creature. She has learned to adapt to this city as the coyote who finds habitable hills just blocks above the boulevards. The coyote, who refuses conventional boundaries and definitions, who follows the San Gabriel Mountains through manicured back lawns, oblivious to fences and gashes of asphalt. She also stalks the periphery of disaster.

Within this region of her creation, she has not betrayed her sensibility. She does not polish floors or sleep in a small square room near a kitchen where a door could be opened without warning. She is convinced there is an integrity in this.

Francisca studies the street. On the other side of the intersection, the walls of a liquor store have been spray-painted with the emblems of local madmen and incarcerated heroes. This script is primitive but graceful and bold, unexpectedly geometric, like a kind of pyramid. The expression asserts itself, even in a degraded form. The impulse cannot be erased. She stares at the graffiti, noting that the signatures are perfectly arched like the arc of a matador's cape, powerful and fluid. This too is part of the fabric, an intrinsic element of the fibers and design.

Later, when it is darker, the liquor store will be iron-grated. In this city, darkness wears steel bars, windows are webbed and doors double-bolted. In this city, only monsters, and men who are marginally human, who forage for silver, watches and latches that can be broken dare to walk in the night streets. She is an exception. She trusts her intuition. She is rarely frightened.

She could write to Delfina of the fires which burned the hills of the city, indiscriminate, decadent, flames consuming the scrub brush almost delicately, in slow motion, with obvious pleasure. Then ash fell from the skies, brittle and ugly and gray as the last snowfall on a dying planet. The fires were brutal with intensity, the night sky was more red than black, but even that phenomenon has passed. Here the air is bad, Francisca could say, but Mexico City is worse.

Mexico City, where Ramón abandoned her, where the air was dense and chaotic. The infestation was deeper there, a litter composed not of simple paper and glass and smoke but the accumulation of centuries of ruin. The air was bone, ash, blood, parchment, cloth, feathers and gold. The smell of an eradicated civilization, the sense of intangible and uncountable loss rising, webbing the clouds, the bad air, savaged, irredeemable.

And the city had been called Tenochtitlán. Then the Conquistadores had gutted the pyramids, the temples, the plazas, the aqueducts of fresh water, the gardens, the magic, the flowers. The Spaniards and their priests burned books which were images inscribed on the skin of animals and bark. They erected churches where the pyramids had been. They buried, dismembered, scattered. And the wound of ash and dust was renamed Mexico City. And the air was bad, like a lingering curse.

Perhaps cures for madness had been burned, tonics for lameness, insomnia, tumors. Powders to reduce the grief of mourning and tragic love. They were ash. Entire alphabets were gone, with their unique possibilities and confluences, the hieroglyphics which were pathways, channels into enormities, unrepeatable arrangements. And the sense of a dying people rose into the bad air, forming music that could not be deciphered, wounds that would resist cure. She had not imagined such loss possible, not merely the external structures of a people but their internal fragile dimensions, the inspired connections they had invented which were gone, erased, extinct. It was in the museum in Mexico City that she wept.

Mexico City was hot. It was Sunday. A gouged-out white tequila-colored sun hung above them, obviously a portent. The ground beneath her became unsolid. She was stalked by cathedrals festering like abscesses on plazas where women from the provinces, draped in shawls, squatted beside tin beads they had arranged to form small pyramids. She remembers the geometric compositions of cheap candies, there on the edges of the plazas of the imported God where the impulse still stirred. The sidewalks swayed as if they were mere illusionary strips floating across invisible waters. And Ramón was the sun god and she loved him. Then the bells were screeching and she did not understand why only her suitcases were packed and what, exactly, Ramón was saying.

La Puta de la Luna turns from the street and studies the park where the old woman is still sitting along the shore of the lake, staring at her with intensity. Something is passing between them, a wordless current. Of course, this aged woman knows that the worst is possible, is recurrent, a theme almost predictable. Betrayal, lies, the inexplicable accidents, the chance occurrence that opens into a portal of personal cataclysm.

And the old woman who is reading the surface of the lake, the water and wind and shadow, knows what it is to polish and dust surfaces posthumously. Obviously, she has experienced nights when saints speak and when they are silent. Always, anchors are torn from moorings and you drift, sky inverted, a sheet of liquid, and the surface you slide across is black rock. The confusion of the elements. The confluence of chance and circumstances, relentless, inexplicable. Why this intersection, this bus bench, this city park with its standard-issue acre of grass, its standard-issue liquid fist of a lake, and not some interchangeable other?

A tarnished Volkswagen slows, stops, asks her how much, where? The car is dented, the victim of accidents which have twisted its yellow metal shell. La Puta de la Luna intuits that these collisions are self-induced. The man is young, uncertain, either frightened or angered by her price. She opens a mouth lacquered with the vermilions of certain sails in stalled southern ports, in calm harbors where noon elongates, edgeless, brilliant, and the wind is tame. And her mouth is a red portal. It has all the answers.

On this day, La Puta de la Luna has painted half moons above her eyes, vivid, iridescent, the blue of plumed capes once worn by Aztec lords. These eyes are fluid, gulfs and channels that say I am the opulence of love you crave.

The man nods his head and motions her into the car with a gesture of his fingers. It is almost obscene, how he points to her and the car seat with his thumb. His hands are calloused, blackened by a certain form of grease or oil that cannot be removed, has merged with his flesh, become part of the texture, the fibers and grain.

The man wears a tight white t-shirt which ends abruptly, as if severed, halfway across his hairless chest. His blue jeans are dirty, slung low, almost at his hips. His garments expose large sections of him. He is lean and strong, without excess, like certain birds which divest themselves of plumage before a storm. He can move like a cat, a dog, a panther. He is obviously dangerous, perhaps when drinking or provoked. But he is not intoxicated now. His car smells of gasoline. On the floor, there are empty beer cans, yellowed newspapers, pieces of stained and greasy cardboard boxes that might have once contained food.

He is a kind of animal, graceful, at ease with his flesh. A predator, perhaps a transient in this urban wound. He forages, buys food on street corners, sleeps in his car. She notes there are tools in the backseat of this dirty automobile. Perhaps he works during the day and then uses these tools to break the locks of houses at night.

"I don't like doing this," he says in a dialect of English she does not know. His words are as slow as the southern drawl, yet they are cold and angular. She thinks of granite churches in regions where there are stone haciendas and snow and in the winters trees shed their leaves and stand like wire sculptures. He is from a northern province, she decides, a state near the other ocean, the Atlantic. He parks his dented vehicle in front of her apartment building.

"I don't like paying for it," the young man says in his impossible dialect.

"Of course," she concurs absolutely and immediately, accepting, understanding. She opens her mind into its warehouse of immeasurable varieties of indifference.

His eyes are startling, a ruined blue, pools of glacial water clotted with red lines. A man who drinks excessively and cannot sleep. She can decipher his disease with a single glance. His hair is blond and long as a woman's. It is tied behind his head with a band in a style traditional to Indians. It is a fashion worn now only by American workingmen. Usually, such men cannot afford her.

He is standing in the doorway of her apartment, studying her rooms as if expecting the gangsters of his imagination or past experience to suddenly spring from the hallways, the closet, armed with pistols or machetes. Tense, taking in her apartment by inches, he notices the ferns in heavy woven baskets below the arched living-room window. He glances at the woolen hand-woven rug on the polished wooden floor near her bed. Each Wednesday, when she is having her nails manicured and her hair tinted and trimmed, a Mexicana scrubs her floors, cleans her windows, mops and polishes and dusts. She pays the woman thirty-five dollars for this.

The man assembles his money slowly, a stack of creased bills which seem exceptionally worn. The denomination of the money is small, fives and tens. They form a stained green plateau in her palm. He keeps one hand in his pocket. She assumes he has a knife.

For a moment, she senses a wavering in the fabric. Then she remembers that all workingmen are peons and identical. Brown-skinned farm workers in pueblos of coffee beans or maize or white men with blond hair and ruined blue eyes. Such men have calloused hands. Nationalities, languages, rituals and gods are irrelevant. Such men are defined by the abuse of the elements and the damage their labors leave engraved across their bodies, like fences. They are caged, limited.

La Puta de la Luna knows what the church knows. You must give them stained-glass cathedrals that imply God has prisms for eyes. You must provide parades and drums and confetti. Their lives consist of lethargy and a debilitating waiting, punctuated by the annual carnival, perhaps, with its standard-issue flame-eater and fortune-teller, the chained elephant with eyes wide and gray and catatonic. Each year, such men will stay at the carnival until the gates lock, trying to knock down glued bottles with a ball. They will beat a hammer against a metal disc that promises to set off bells until their hands bleed. They will spend their last coins attempting to win garish pink rabbits of synthetic material and poor design, objects offensive to the aesthetics. The man watches her place the money he has given her in a marble jewelry box purchased in London. He is still disturbed.

"But this is cheap for you," Francisca suggests, her voice soft, moist. Green gullies of moss, green mist, tame green. She moves slowly, carefully toward the bed. "A woman you would have to take to dinner, no? You would have to send flowers, meet the father, clean your car, no?" She pauses, but the man has no capacity for irony. "And even then, you could not be certain she would give in."

La Puta de la Luna sits down on the bed. She lets this information filter into the man. He is slow to relax. A man who has experienced terrible severings, promises broken, a horizon which is never solid. A man who must be convinced. "This way, you are certain," Francisca reminds him, gently. She smiles. "Imagine I am her."

"You must invent your own indifferences," Esmeralda told her later, when they parted. "The alphabets of indifference are a form of art."

Esmeralda, implanting suggestions, implications of how it was possible to dream with eyes open. There were trances that could be self-induced. The essential self drifts from the body like a flower embraced by a green sea breeze or a red-and-white parachute floating down from an undamaged ocean of sky. The body that remains on the bed is empty.

After the sixth American family fired her, almost immediately, as if they could detect her unsuitability with a single glance, she had stopped, on impulse, to have her fortune read. It was a dreary undifferentiated Saturday in a warm but not quite discernible season. The heat lacked character and direction. It was simply sun without nuance. It meant nothing.

Francisca Ramos considered the possibility she was dying. It seemed particularly unbearable to die in an alien and insignificant city where even the seasons were indistinct. Then she glanced across a boulevard no different from any other and saw the sign. El Futuro, Advice, Consejos, Tarot Cards, Problemas de Amor, Palm Reading. And because she did not believe that the future could be predicted or altered, she crossed the boulevard without effort. She would sit for a moment in a darkened room. It would be preferable to die in a chair within a house rather than on the street in raw daylight.

It was Miami, and the gitana proved to be Cubana. Francisca was surprised by the room where they sat, a spacious area, intimate, with filtered light. The lamp contained a soft amber bulb. The table was mahogany, finely crafted, an antique. Francisca had anticipated garish props, and there were none. The room asserted a subtle sense of aesthetics, a kind of caress.

Esmeralda, the Cubana gitana, wore a red silk scarf around her head and long dangling gold earrings. Francisca could measure their worth. Ramón had taught her that. And Esmeralda had the eyes and the hands of a curandera. She could heal if she chose. The gitana studied her openly, dispassionately, making private measurements and evaluations.

Francisca felt poised at the edge of an enormity she simultaneously longed for and feared, that which she sensed and concurrently banished from her consciousness. It was as if she had always suspected she had a terminal disease or an incurable disability and, suddenly, the reality of this intuition was being confirmed.

So this is how it happens, Francisca recognized. One turns a corner, crosses a boulevard that appears to be like any other, rings a doorbell, enters a room which is not a room but a hidden region, a physical manifestation of what is still unformed and inarticulate, and the course of your life is changed. It happens at intersections that masquerade as innocuous. It happens on meaningless afternoons in landscapes without resonance. The sudden widening gulfs, the openings into other worlds.

"You have a question about love?" Esmeralda asked in her dialect of Spanish which seemed warm and curved and spiced like certain islands.

"No," Francisca replied without hesitation.

"Marriage?"

"No," she said, laughing out loud.

It was in San Juan, after she had checked out of the Hilton Hotel, after she had taken an apartment in a poor barrio on the outskirts of the city, that she had learned about marriage.

It was even possible that in his own fashion, which was tentative and limited, Pedro Diego had attempted to please her. He delivered a speech. "You are clearly a woman of great elegance. A man without honor discarded you, perhaps? I am unworthy of you. But if you would marry me, perhaps I myself could become more."

She recognized that this man with skin darker than her own, had rehearsed this introductory dialogue for weeks. Perhaps he had even written it down, committing it to memory. In indolence and desperation she married him. Then she moved her few remaining belongings into his apartment. He lived in a cubicle similar to her own, several doors farther down the corridor in her apartment building. She was not without a certain curiosity about marriage. She also had less than five hundred American dollars by then. She had pawned the bracelets and the ruby ring. She had not yet sold her Louis Vuitton luggage.

Pedro Diego woke before dawn, took a bus into the city while she still slept and returned after dusk. She did not ask him what he did, nor did it occur to him to volunteer this information. Obviously, he was some sort of pack animal, a carrier of cartons or bricks perhaps. She was not interested in the specific details of his daily abuse, a configuration she suspected did not alter, was one simple and recurrent task only.

"Perhaps you would feel better if you took a shower," she suggested, softly, as he entered what had become their apartment. To please her, this wife, this discarded woman of elegance, he agreed. She offered him a martini. He studied the glass as if it were a rare poison, shook his head no, opened their small refrigerator and drank beer directly from the can. She averted her eyes.

Each apartment came equipped with a Formica table. Since he owned no linen, she covered the table with a beach towel. Anything was preferable to the naked glare of the plasticlike surface. The apartment contained no vases. She cut flowers and placed them in a water glass in the center of the table. Pedro Diego did not seem to notice the flowers or the paper she folded neatly to resemble cloth napkins. He simply ate.

The silence had a certain familiar quality to her. She thought of all the patrones and their Las Señoras, sitting on patios or at dining-room tables, mute, erasing each other's presence.

Francisca recognized that she was decoding an entire process, detail by detail. She was learning a certain alphabet, a geography, a language which would become a revelation. This compelled her to stay. There were artifacts everywhere. She was assembling a lost civilization. When she viewed it in its entirety, she would become someone else.

Pedro Diego was her stumbled-upon site, her buried city. She charted his movements as if she were carrying an invisible notebook. Connections appeared, paths, chambers and plazas. After Pedro Diego ate, mute, he rose from the table. He did not say thank you. He sat on the sofa and watched television. She realized she was supposed to wash the plates, sponge the table and prepare herself for bed. This is grotesque, she thought as she washed the dinner plates, but there were discoveries, remarkable, simply appearing, moment by moment. She washed the plates, wondering whether it was any different with the patrones and their wives.

The patrones did not watch television. Instead, they rose from their dinner, also wordlessly, and carried briefcases into their studies. They shut real or invisible doors. And, always, the woman disappeared.

Occasionally, Pedro Diego would verbalize an enthusiasm, an interest or an idea. Such expressions were, without exception, banal, a boxing match or a specific American film perhaps. She realized she was expected to encourage these enthusiasms, however trivial or brief. And it occurred to her that it was little different for the wife of a patrón. Had she not seen the strained smiles on the faces of Las Señoras when their husbands glanced up from newspapers or magazines to mention a distant event, a political configuration of one kind or other that did not affect them? Yes, the strained smiles of Las Señoras when the patrones spoke of a business triumph or a object he planned to purchase. Las Señoras hid their boredom, the rage of constant exclusion and the assumption of invisibility upon demand.

One dusk, Francisca put curls in her hair and rouged her cheeks. She drew light-blue circles above her eyes. When Pedro Diego entered what had become their apartment, she handed him a can of beer and smiled.

"You look like a puta," Pedro said, taking the beer from her hand. "Wash it off, please."

She removed her makeup. Was it any different for Las Señoras, shopping on an exclusive boulevard all day, returning in the late afternoon to bathe in oils, to dab their flesh with perfumes, to stand wearing a new dress perhaps? And the patrón did not notice them at all, walked past them as if they were merely an elaborate potted plant and immediately picked up his mail. On occasion, the patrón might notice the new dress and say to his wife, La Señora, that it was too low-cut or too tight, too light or too bright, and take it off, return it to the shop tomorrow. You look ridiculous, the patrón might say, carrying his briefcase into a study. And La Señora was listening to the door upstairs, the door that was closing.

Pedro Diego was a primitive, but still, by implication, an archetype. She began to understand certain subtleties. It was only the image that men loved, and their own sense of control. When she was dull, Pedro Diego felt whole. He ate illusions. He was malnourished. He would learn nothing.

So this is marriage, she thought, standing on her balcony at midday, suddenly aware that legions of women stood on similar balconies or terraces, all of them watching the fronds of the palms rocking back and forth like confined mental patients struggling for absolution with gestures mimed from a mute and disfigured god. And she realized that marriage demanded a certain posture. In the climate of deprivation, in the barrios of the poor, the women seemed listless, lazy and beaten. Las Señoras appeared lethargic, and indulgent. Now she recognized that neither description was accurate. Marriage simply drained that which was unique from a woman. They were neither apathetic nor indolent. They were gutted shells that walked in dusty alleys or on the boulevards of capitals. They were the half-dead. They cast no shadow.

Francisca swept the kitchen floor with its torn linoleum, with its edges ruined by water and rust, and realized that marriage was not very different from working for a patrón. You cooked and polished or instructed some other to cook and polish for you. In either event, there was the seamless, endless silence. Perhaps marriage was more difficult than working for a patrón. Additional tasks were required, the webbing was more intricate and dimensional with psychological exchanges, however shallow, sex and the pretense of a shared future.

The married night was made of stone. It slammed shut like a cell. It would be better to have a small back room near a kitchen than to violate one's sleep by the presence of an alien body. She would lie by Pedro's side as he slept, thinking her life had become an excessively severe punishment. She sensed that this man did not dream of her.

In the darkness, it occurred to her that the married night was no different for the patrones and their wives. They had nightmares on silk sheets in rooms of Spanish tile. But sleep did not come easily to Las Señoras, who also sensed that their husbands did not dream of them. Surely, they had once wanted more than their patios of imported garden furniture imported from across the ocean where they sipped black coffee and watched the flowers, the shadows, the silence as the patrón read the newspaper, oblivious to their existence. This manifestation asserted itself in mansions and in the cubicles of tenements. The difference was one of external textures. The difference was essentially negligible.

She took baths constantly, submerging herself in burning water as if it would purify her, as if the heat of it would awaken her flesh, this body which was becoming a shell, driftwood, numb. She brushed her hair until it had the shine of rare black pearls. She realized this was why Las Señoras spent their afternoons in bathtubs, rubbing themselves with oils, creams and lotions. It was not for their husbands. They engaged in this ritual, which would be unnoticed, to remind themselves they still existed, if only by implication, in a degraded form, if only to themselves.

This was the reason all Las Señoras posed on sofas at dusk with their cheeks rouged, prepared to flaunt their wit and intelligence, the books they had read. This was why they ate only melons until their necks and cheekbones were exposed like mountain ridges, until their bodies resembled sculpture. They wanted their husbands to love their skin, to open and close them like a fan, like a carved ivory or jade box he had always owned. They longed for their husbands to take pieces of them, like an armful of captured ravens or bolts of imported silk.

Of course Las Señoras knew it was useless, all of it, the baths, the satin, the perfumes, the starvation. She had misperceived their posture entirely. They were compelled not by indolence but by irony.

"You look pretty," Pedro Diego said as he entered the apartment, and, in the same breath, "What's for supper?"

He turned on the television, already either bored or assured of her. And in the tiled dining rooms, mahogany tables set with linen, crystal and silver, the patrón also asked what was for dinner. As La Señora opened her mouth to reply, to recite a rack of lamb with mint sauce, wild rice, endive salad and chocolate mousse perhaps, the patrón was dialing the telephone, was opening a newspaper, a letter.

"I want you to smile more," Pedro Diego informed her one morning.

She was startled. She realized she existed in a state of probation. More was required than she had dared imagine. It became difficult to speak. Words were sharp. They tore at her mouth.

"I am unhappy," she finally said. Somewhere, walls were collapsing in sheets of stained beige plaster. Then Pedro Diego left the apartment for the bus that would take him to his work in San Juan. She stared at the door that had closed. She thought she would never see him again. This thought both terrified and consoled her. And she remembered Las Señoras at dusk, pacing in their silk gowns, staring out of windows, drinking martinis with trembling hands.

The following morning, Pedro Diego told her he did not like her hair. She did not ask him why. She simply considered yanking it from her scalp, strand by strand. That evening he suggested that she should gain weight. She recognized a theme in this. Of course, every day would bring a new bruise, a fist punched not into the flesh but into a more tender and vulnerable region. Then she had nightmares. Her skin erupted with a red rash resembling welts. She lay in bed for days. She stopped bathing completely. Her bathrobe smelled of cigarettes and sweat and the undefinable odor of something metallic, of sparks, of a body transforming itself from within. There was a twisting, a carving deep within her flesh, in her cells.

"I thought you were more of a lady," Pedro Diego said one morning. He was looking down on her, on her seemingly motionless body, on the shell that did not even wash itself. His eyes seemed sad.

Francisca walked the half mile of barely differentiated apartments down to the ocean. Of course the sea was a woman, an emerald, with glittering sun-induced brooches, her enormities and magnitude. But she was also a moody bitch, given to savage seasons. I am her daughter, Francisca thought, I am no different. Did one love the ocean less because she had a pulse intrinsic to herself? Must she be only and always a monotone of blue, erased of urgency and passion? Did men not realize that if the sea were fully charted she would bore them?

Slowly, she began to define herself. No, she was not a lady. She planted geraniums in tin cans on their balcony, thrilled by the touch of the earth, her rich smell and generous body. She broke her fingernails. Images swirled outward from her wild interior, making havoc of her hair.

She felt herself growing beyond simplicities. She recognized that her

femininity was layered and complex, in flux, gusting with flame-blue and
flame-red sparks.

That night, Pedro Diego gave her a bouquet of daisies. Dyed pink,
they were garish and cheap. She put them into a water glass, listlessly. Was
this any different from La Señora, waiting for her husband to return from
a business trip to the capital and present to her a silk scarf in a shade she
found abhorrent, or a dress which did not fit, a pair of earrings that
duplicated ones she already possessed?

Time stopped as it does for a woman serving an indeterminate sentence, a woman in a prison. Francisca could not longer measure the
redundancy of her days. Marriage was a kind of prison. Women deliberately entered a gray cell, compelled by convention and delusion.

She paced their apartment, her borders marked by music floating
through the windows from a stranger's radio, from the clock on the
bedroom table, an increment of measurement that no longer applied to
her existance. She had been installed in place like the small refrigerator in
the kitchen, like the geraniums in their tin cans on the tiny implication of
a terrace.

There were moments when she wanted Pedro Diego to know her as
she was, beneath the controlled smile, the lips she had learned to twist
into an appropriate configuration like a lamp turned off and on. She
wanted him to know that she was a beast, a bad girl, angry, suspicious,
afraid of the darkness and her own anger. There is a mad dog inside me,
she longed to scream, and a child, relentlessly crying. There is a monster
with claws under the illusion of gloves you once called elegant. Are you
man enough for this?

"Don't you want to know who I really am?" Francisca asked finally,
idly, expecting nothing.

She realized that this was a similar exchange to one between a patrón
and La Señora, one La Señora or another, standing with a new hatbox on
one terrace of bougainvillea or one cassia-draped patio or another, asking
her husband if he wished to look at her most recent purchase. Surely La
Señora had come to expect nothing, to hear the rustle of a newspaper
turning, the scraping of leaves across patio brick, a car in the gated
distance, a bird. Certainly La Señora realized that their silence was without punctuation, was three-dimensional and solid, like an entity, like cer-

tain regions of forest so profuse with growth the sun is permanently screened.

"Don't you want to know who you are living with?" she repeated, her voice almost a shout. She remembered the wife of her first patrón, how she raised her voice to her husband, how he blackened her eye, broke vases and lamps. And beneath their house, thick vines with blossoms which were venomous grew monumental. She could feel them rustling beneath the polished floors of their house.

"I know who you are," Pedro Diego said. He was watching a boxing match on television. "I am going to tame you."

Francisca considered being tamed. She translated his words. He meant he wished her bleached, erased, rubbed smooth of visions and exhilarations. He recognized the caged thing within her and thought he could transform her. She did not bother to ask him how he proposed to perform this molecular surgery. He lacked skill and imagination. Such a procedure was beyond his limited capacity. There were not hatboxes or candles or bottles of perfume on all the shelves of all the stores in the hemisphere to fill the gulf between them.

Pedro Diego no longer existed as an actual entity. He was an outline of a form, a symbol. The concept of being tamed intrigued her. She woke in the middle of the night. She stood on the miniature terrace of their apartment building. She was certain she did not wish to be tamed, not by Pedro Diego, certainly, who no longer registered upon her consciousness, with his unspeakable dyed pink daisies, with his plastic dining table in his slum cubicle. It was rather that she did not wish to be tamed by any man.

This thought came to her with the clarity and power of a revelation. She looked down at the street of apartment buildings, each with minuscule orange terraces lined with geraniums in tin cans, and she felt she had discovered a sudden new room within herself. There were stairways and expanses of reddish-tinged wooden balconies overlooking bays cold and blue as a bruise. The linear assumptions were shattered.

Of course no man could tame her, not a patrón with leather luggage on which his initials were embossed in gold, or a man with calloused hands who had never ridden in a black Cadillac, who rode a bus to a job a mule could do. It is my imagination that created me, she recognized, each syllable and breath.

She stood all night on the square cell of an orange terrace. She considered the nudity of clouds, streams, the hills of this blue world, slow-growing and benign. And refinement, being stripped to essentials, as a cliff of bare rock.

She stood in the darkness defining herself. She was an exile without papers. She would always live on the edge. She would inhabit all the possible rooms, the shuttered windows, the fluttering polished-cotton drapes, the windows facing alleys where the sounds of wind and dogs mate and rise. Her allegiance was to the tides, to the moon, to the random lust born above bougainvillea and neon. She was that which serves fate, a vessel, a leaf, a sail, a thing oblivious to borders and ordinary increments. They meant no more to her than such configurations would mean to a cloud.

Francisca knows her secret name. Ramón was wrong. He sensed her difference, but his interpretation was banal. She is a mutation. She was born to the green felt and dice. Some women open their eyes on the ride. Some women glide through days as if they were made of glass. No surface can resist her. She must live behind the eight ball, in a darkness icy past blue, past grace, glazed, almost innocent.

Francisca Ramos watched morning slowly assert itself across the inert, static sky. She understood the thing called marriage in all of its permutations, its costume changes and accents. It was identical, in the village of her birth or in Caracas, in Madrid or Santa Clara or San Juan. The design had been revealed, the equation solved.

Between being the servant girl, living in a tenement cubicle, and being La Señora, pacing the orange-tiled corridors of a seaside villa, there is little difference. La Señora, with her hand heavy with jewels, trembling as she watched the servant girl, wondering why this creature without aesthetics had begun to glow, why the dull inhuman thing now had eyes sparkling like crystalline orbs, translucent as rare pearls. La Señora would feel the weight of the gold wedding band encircling her finger. The bishop had married them. Still, there were unofficial forms of abandonment, prolonged and inexplicable absences that made accepting dinner invitations difficult. And La Señora glances at the servant girl and decides she will say nothing.

In the morning, after Pedro Diego left their apartment, after he took his bus into the city, Francisca walked three blocks to the nearest telephone. She called a taxicab. In San Juan, she sold the luggage Ramón Cárdenas had given her and purchased an airplane ticket to Miami.

Now it is Los Angeles and above her the American workingman is deliberately abusive, trying to hurt her. He drives himself into her with precision, like a man with a hammer and a stake. If he could break her in half, he would. It is only the compulsion to wound that motivates him.

"You must invent your own indifferences," Esmeralda said when they parted. And the man above her is beginning to moan, finally, like a kicked dog.

In Miami, on an undifferentiated Saturday, she crossed a boulevard which was not a boulevard, was a channel, a portal. She rang a doorbell and the room was subdued, quiet, the light soft and filtered.

Esmeralda, the Cubana gitana, opened a wooden box and removed a tarot deck. The red-silk-scarfed gitana created an arrangement with the cards. Her movements were slow, as if the cards were flowers, perhaps, a special bouquet. There were tens, she remembers, scepters and cups. Lightning. The moon. A man who was a king. And in the future, young men on horseback carried orbs of yellow coins.

"The village of your birth is lost. It was incidental to you, a region you never fully inhabited. Return is impossible. Water, so much water." Esmeralda stared at the composition the cards formed. "You were damaged by a black-haired man of wealth and intelligence. He was cynical and, perhaps, unwell. Water and struggle. Storms. Perhaps he tried to drown you? You traveled with him. There were revelations. Antiquities. An abundance of color, brilliant, indelible. Your eyes were changed. Awakenings. A deciphering. You speak English? This is all accurate, yes?" Esmeralda asked.

Above her, the young white man with the long blond hair is still moaning. His eyes are open, a stunningly ravaged blue. He is a high tide only. He will subside and pass. She is a cliff of rock, the ridge where a continent starts.

In Miami, the cards formed a low pyramid across the wooden table. Faces were rising from the mahogany. She felt as if she were looking at photographs or into a mirror. She nodded, yes, and remembered Caracas.

The city, finally, after the brutal mountains where men had been lost in a delirium of greed which they justified as adventure. Green the vines, the fronds, the skies, iridescent and insane this green, dense this green, mysterious. And the jungle swallowed them. Vultures ate their eyes, which were green rocks.

After the mountains the city seemed a mirage, a place where the jungle was held back only by delusion, crude artifice and sheer will. It was temporary, an aberration, a juxtaposition imposing itself where it did not belong. A massive stone thinking it could float upon water. The plazas and offices were a deranged architecture. The ancient triangle resurrected and reinforced with steel. The design was recurrent and familiar. The outlines were viable. Only the substance was missing.

Ramón took her to a hotel, newly built and pointed as a pyramid. Room service brought her strawberries with cream in a silver bowl on a silver tray. Below, glass sides of triangular buildings reflected passing clouds and the flush of the sky. Everywhere, clothes were flapping, drying in the sun like rippling streamers, red and white confetti. Shirts and sheets, hanging from the terraces of shacks, apartments and condominiums. Everywhere, the drying of clothing in the air above them, in the wind, fluttering. It seemed a kind of celebration above them, across slow streets, crowded and dirty, the air thick and sweet and reeking of pastry. The red and white streamers in the air above them, above the Pepsi and mango stands framed by neon. And she was losing her sense of direction. A strange greenness was settling across her flesh, a mist, leaking into her. And in the dark heat, she watched the moon turn salty and green.

"Water. A density of color, green perhaps. The destruction was not irrevocable. Rather, your transformation is incomplete," the Cubana said. She poured them both a glass of rum. She said, "In the present, you are nameless, unformed. Still, you intuit your nature. You are an animal, innately cunning, potentially lethal."

Now, in her apartment overlooking the acre of city park with its lake like a liquid fist, the young white man is finished. He is languishing on the bed, lying on his side, racing-dog lean, watching her with ghastly blue eyes that are disturbed, alarming. He is saying something in his impossible angular, gray dialect. Can it be something about machines in office buildings, how he repairs them? "I pass you every day," the man says. "I had fantasies about you."

La Puta de la Luna is buttoning her blouse. She allows the man to notice she is glancing at her watch. He perceives this gesture, slowly sits up and slips his stained and incomplete t-shirt across his lean chest. He is lacing up his heavy workingman boots. She is thinking about Esmeralda, the Cubana *gitana*, who opened up a deck of cards like a bouquet of flowers. The heiroglyphics of her future revealed themselves with an indisputable clarity. In the future, there would be young men riding horses. They were not carrying swords, but coins.

"You are alone to the bone, alone past the bone to the place where the green heart sings of its opulence and misery," Esmeralda sighed.

The Cubana patted her hand. "There are answers you will never have. You have seen the world, yes? It is a standard-issue planet. One palm tree and plaza, one church and cop and whore on every corner. Still, there are possibilities, myriad, deceptive, limitless. Identities can be exchanged, discarded, invented."

The white workingman with his blond hair in a pony tail is clothed, his boots are laced, yet he lingers. He stands in front of her windows, stares down at the lake surrounded by palms where the old woman is still sitting at the shore and asks, "Got any beer?"

She shakes her head, no. She straps her red leather high heels around her ankles. This Wednesday she will also have a pedicure. It occurs to her that her triumphs are private and intangible. Of course it is the intricacy of the details which define us, the rituals we invent in secret, in the corners and edges where it is always dark and silent and our hearts beat like waves relentlessly breaking, eating at the shoreline where we stand, pushing the great nothing into temporary shape.

"A hundred bucks and you don't get a fucking beer?" The white man with the blue eyes that mirror his interior disease accuses. "You ain't worth it."

Francisca stands near the door. I'm a whore, not a bar, she thinks. Yes, it is strange, American men and their chatter. Surely these men know the unassailable connection of time and money. This is their motto, what they have etched across the surface of the earth. It is their only epithet. As she leans against the front door, she realizes that the pollution and ruin and misery are merely symptoms of a deeper rot. Americans have no sense of intuition, of when to stop, when to cease plundering, when they have dug enough wells, built enough power plants or dams, made sufficient profits. They outwit themselves, like the Conquistadores, so loaded with gold artifacts they fell into the lake surrounding the ruins of Tenochtitlán and drowned.

The blond-haired American man is staring at her. The air between them is tense and hostile. She remembers she is La Puta de la Luna, potentially lethal, a puma, a cobra. She lets this image saturate her flesh. A certain stance, an invisible armor. The man senses this. She watches him walk down the stairs and toward his car. "You think you're so fucking special? A hundred bucks," he accuses from the street. "You punch a clock, same as everybody else, bitch." She watches the dented vehicle drive from her street. Then she locks her door. Then she removes her clothing and bathes.

In Miami, in a room that was a confluence of rare elements, a fluid gulf, Esmeralda poured her a second glass of rum. "These symbols seem a bit primitive in the post-Freudian age," the Cubana noted. "We can decipher your situation without them, yes?"

Francisca agreed. She watched Esmeralda remove the cards from the table and replace them in her wooden box. Then they discussed the intricacies of the possibilities, the men on horseback, the coins, the nuances, the methods of navigating this unique geography. And Francisca remained in the house with the Cubana gitana until she understood the terrain fully, until it was a region she had charted and mapped.

She would leave Miami with a man named Jerry. He came from the South. For months, she thought all American men were named Jerry and came from a region they referred to only as the South. They shared a slow and not dissimilar rhythm. He took her to a hotel along the lip of the ocean, not to make love to her, but rather for her company, her aura, a silk cobra on his arm. In the hotel suite overlooking the ocean, there was a card game. There were many men in the room and several women. Even with the windows open, the room was dense with smoke. This particular Jerry was a poker player. He would win that night and the next, pulling money from the center of the table close to his chest while she stood near him, pressing her lavender silk dress against the edge of his chair. It was this sense of lavender silk he desired from her, nothing more.

"You are my Lady Luck," he told her, laughing, as they walked from the hotel into the steaming Miami night. His suit pockets bulged with money. They were walking along the ocean. The wind rustled her gown, and the dress was translucent, like wings. "Ever been to Vegas?" he asked, pausing to look into her eyes. It was an invitation. She accepted.

He took her to Las Vegas the next week. Their flight arrived late at night, but there was no darkness. The taxicab was carrying them through streets which were irradiated, domed, everywhere embossed by neon like a demonic sultan's drug-induced vision of an oasis. She recognized this as a form of insanity.

Jerry took her to a hotel called Caesar's Palace, a name chosen for its irony, perhaps. There were fountains, she remembers, but even the water did not seem real. Then they entered the hotel and she was blinded. It was like a cavern in which a madman had stored the jewels of an entire civilization, glued them to the walls, strung them in a web from the ceilings. The air was unnatural, smoke and a constant tinkling, metallic sound of coins and bells.

She stood near this Jerry while he played cards, in the casino or, more often, in hotel suites. He sat easily in his chair, one chair or another, stacks of black chips near his elbow. He built small black pyramids. Each black chip was worth five hundred dollars. When he won, when he pulled the black chips from the table to his chest, he would place handfuls of the discs in her evening bag. She learned to carry nothing in this purse, not even lipstick.

When Jerry slept, when he said he did not require her presence, she cashed the black chips and took a taxi to the airport. She rented a locker and stored the cash in a leather overnight bag she had purchased in the boutique of the hotel. She knew that the city was not real. No city was real, but this one most particularly, this outrage of neon, this demonic calligraphy imposed upon a sleeping desert, a region quiet as the moon. She knew that luck ran in unpredictable cycles, like seasons of good and bad weather. Luck was a matter of random confluences, similar to the love of women and men, an ebb and a flow, a trite recital of gray-worn tides that sway and die, come and go, mostly go.

This Jerry rarely wanted her in bed. He simply desired her to glisten near him, his private amulet, his personal piece of neon. He purchased black and red gowns heavy with sequins in the hotel boutiques, dresses with long skirts and low necklines. He bought her gold earrings so heavy they made her head ache. She purchased a bottle of aspirin.

In the long afternoons, when he lay in their suite and slept, she swam in the blue-tiled pool. She raised her arm and drinks simply appeared, gin fizzes and piña coladas with miniature parasols bobbing on their thick white surface. She watched the palms planted on the perpetually moist lawns, and the palms were unmoving as sculpture. It occurred to her they might not be trees at all but rather a simulation, a contrivance of synthetic fibers with fronds of a dyed green plastic. She resisted the impulse to touch them.

She was not surprised when this Jerry's luck began to change. It was the hotel, he said. They took a taxicab to another structure, a hotel called the Sands. There were fewer black chips now and less laughter. Now he sat upright in his chair, one chair or another, tense and drawn. Now he asked her to leave him alone at the table. He suggested she play the slot machines or watch a show. She stuck silver dollars into machines offering an alphabet of fruits, oranges and lemons and cherries and bells. She disliked the machine, pulling its metal handle, watching its limited arrangement of elements appear. There was no revelation in this.

Jerry handed the maître d' a fifty-dollar bill. She was given a booth near the stage where she sat alone, sipping mineral water and watching women draped only in strands of sequins and feathers parade like a flock of trained birds, wings clipped, escape impossible. She was close enough to see their eyes. They were vacant. She found the spectacle terrible, a debasement which seemed simultaneously lurid and pathetic, contrived and dull. She left shortly after the performance began.

In the morning, while they were eating the breakfast which room service had delivered, Jerry told her he was leaving. He did not look at her when he said this. She held a slice of toast in her hand. She put it down. The drapes in their room were pulled shut. Their hotel suite was a permanent shade of night.

Of course it can come at breakfast, she thought. The sudden severing of the ordinary, the unexpected cataclysm. It can come with daylight too. And she considered the sheer number of women who were, at that precise instant, sitting down to breakfast, watching their lives shatter above toast and jam. It happens on undifferentiated mornings, at tables in hotel suites, or in linen-draped breakfast nooks in apartments with city views. It happens on patios, with bougainvillea and cassia swaying, with the shadows of banyan or orange trees spilling across tile and brick. You are the servant girl or you are La Señora, married in a cathedral in a capital by a bishop.

She did not care that this particular Jerry was leaving. It was merely the event as a symbolic manifestation that intrigued her. One moment you are spreading raspberry jam across the surface of a slice of toast. He does not look at you, says only that he wants a divorce. He has found someone else, perhaps, is moving into an apartment with his receptionist. You are buttering toast, perhaps, and he says, We have nothing in common but the common and it is not enough. And you put the knife down. You put the toast down. Perhaps you are pregnant, wrapped in a bathrobe, and he says he can no longer bear the sight of you, you are a stain upon his aesthetics, a visual abuse. Or he says the farm of his youth is besieged by floods or locusts, his mother is sick, he has an obligation. He will not be gone long, a few months perhaps. Whatever he says is banal. The apartment he must take, the plane, the house where you live which he is going to sell. All that matters is the harsh glare of daylight, and that instant when your face splinters and cracks.

They rode in a taxicab to the airport together. He took an airplane to New York. She did not ask him why. Then she removed the leather overnight bag from the locker she had rented. There was a flight to Los Angeles in twenty minutes. She let that confluence of random chance, that particular implication of fate, determine her decision.

Yes, La Reina de los Angeles. She lived briefly near the ocean. It did not satisfy her. She has borne an excess of water. The sea with its relentless sense of demand, the salt that stings her wounds, invades even her dreams and forces her to remember Santa Clara, Puerto Vallarta and Ramón. Then she rode a taxicab inland, away from the constant pale-blue liquid abuse. There was a lake in a city park, a contained body of water, erased of danger. There was a sense of familiarity. The cab stopped. She rented an apartment, walked to an intersection at the border of the city park, which could have been any palm-draped acre in any tropical city, Caracas or Mexico City, Havana or Miami. The exterior names mean nothing. There is an inner structure, an insistence of the indigenous that resists boundaries and the contrivances of man.

She walked to the intersection bordering the city park. It was an intersection like any other. She draped herself in corals and reds. She leaned against the aged stalk of a palm tree and became La Puta de la Luna.

Now she glances out her window. The aged woman is rising from the shore of the lake. She is moving across the grass and settling herself beneath a tree. The old woman is carrying a serape, is draping it around her shoulders. Why does this ancient woman seem familiar? she wonders again. And it occurs to her that she would like to cross the park, walk across the small expanse of grass and talk to her. Then La Puta de la Luna walks down the stairs to the street.

Night drapes itself across her skin like another layer of silk. The rush of traffic has picked up a momentum. Vehicles hurl themselves forward as if of their own accord, blind, rattling, compelled. She has reached her corner, her particular manifestation of happenstance and accident. She is thinking about the old woman, draped in a blanket, lying beneath a palm tree near the lake, when a car honks.

The vehicle is old and battered, its original color muted into an indistinct gray. She notices that it has recently been cleaned. The man is still young, but slackening. His flesh implies a lack of purpose. His skin is dark. He is dressed simply, as if, like the automobile, exterior indications mean nothing to him. He might be a student. She tells him where to drive, where to park. She wonders whether he is drunk or drugged. He seems somehow unconnected, adrift.

He walks behind her on the stairs. He seems tremulous, climbing the steps in a seeming trance, as if he intuits he has reached the edge of an enormity. They enter her apartment. She has no sense of fear. There was a slight wavering in the fabric earlier, the long-blond-haired man smelled of danger. This man smells of nothing. He is speaking in Spanish. His accent is atrocious. He is the American-born son of Mexican parents, she decides, a Chicano. She strains to understand him and suggests, gently, that they speak in English. She walks toward the bed.

The man cannot seem to focus his eyes. She will help him. She switches on the cream-colored porcelain lamp. The light is a soft pool of amber, the essential color of what lives in the night. The eyes of predators, of rain scorched by lightning. Amber, the color of sleeping orchids, dreaming of their own beauty, locked in exquisite stasis where there are no mists or storms or seasons. Amber their petals, amber the air, amber the lamps in lighthouses and on the masts of ships.

The young Chicano does not seem to see her breasts. They are small but compelling, pushed up and contoured by lace. But he is staring not at her body but at her face, staring beyond it, into it, as if she were a blank space of a canvas.

"Yo quiero savez condiciones en su país," he says.

Conditions in my country, she thinks, letting her skirt slip to the floor. She is struggling with his Spanish. He seems to be saying, with inappropriately elaborate reverence, that he respects los guerrilleros in the mountains. He is lavish in his praise, in his estimation of their motivation and courage, as if they chose to enter the wind-whipped northern rocks by the strength of ideals rather than the pull of starvation and necessity.

La Puta de la Luna stretches her body, naked, across the bed. She notices that one of her fingernails is chipped. She will not wait until Wednesday, she decides. She will go to Bullock's Wilshire tomorrow. She will have a manicure and a pedicure. She will have lunch in the tearoom and watch the fashion show. They will be displaying winter clothing, of course. Black velvets and black satins, she imagines. She is interested in this. Then, in the afternoon, after she has eaten a salad, she will select an appropriate card to mail to her sister, Delfina. Then she realizes the room is dense with silence. This is unacceptable.

"Conditions in my country?" she repeats, filling the silence with syllables which say nothing.

She knows that this man wishes her to recite a list of atrocities committed by the government of her country, by the greed-poisoned psychotics who call themselves presidents and colonels. He wants her to tell him a story that includes a dead brother and a murdered child, perhaps. Her face is a canvas on which he desires her to recreate the village of her birth, to paint the surface a serene and unmolested green. She must include a plaza abundant with flowers, no doubt a gentle pink. The air should be filled with wild purple jungle birds which do not shriek but sing. There must be church bells, of course. A river laden with fish would be a nice touch. The banks should be dense with orchids and moss. And no mud, no dust, no storms. Obviously, he wishes her to create a postcard for him.

Then there must be the moment of drama. She walks to the well in a perfect lime-green dawn and, within the water, she finds a pile of severed limbs, ears and hands, floating across the flawless blue surface. Or perhaps they are not floating, they have sunk beneath the surface and appear in the pail she pulls up. Yes, that would suffice. Or perhaps she should provide more. How her family huddled in their shed and wept while the army of the government burned their crops, raped women, took everything, even the chickens. She could describe the troops that violated her body. Of course, it is not her flesh that excites him, but rather her connection to his imagined cataclysms. She is symbolic, like a bulto in a pueblo church, a saint of carved wood and paint.

Francisca senses he will give her more money if she produces the correct arrangement of words for him, if she will paint the images he seeks. A leg floating like a log in a stream. A stain of blood on the shed floor even a season of rains could not erase. She wonders whether this would be enough. Perhaps he requires more. Jeeps, soldiers with automatic weapons, tanks, mass graves and nerve gas. Radiation sickness, would that be enough?

La Puta de la Luna resists. She observes the identical forms of a captured soldier who will reveal only his identification number. She tells him, as she tells all men, that her name is María, her mother is aged and her children are sick. The Chicano is disappointed, like a peasant who has journeyed to a shrine, a house where a saint was born and the structure is closed that day, is being repaired, perhaps.

Of course she will not tell this man with his terrible Spanish anything more. He has paid for her flesh, not for her personal history, which is inviolate. She is not American. She has retained a sense of what is enough, of what is ripe, of when to pluck. Americans would let the fruit of the earth go rotten on the branch. Or they would eat in a frenzy until they became sick. Then they would lie in their vomit, praise and applaud it, announce it as a discovery, a miracle. Then they would package and sell it.

This Latino man takes a long time. It is not her mouth or her body he wants, though he uses them, as if to be polite. He finishes, dresses, walks behind her on the stairs and into the street. She remembers that his fingers trembled as he counted out her money, as he paid her with ten- and twenty-dollar bills. Everything about him is slow and tedious. Now he is still behind her, like a shadow, like the smoke from a powerful spell that only gradually dissipates.

"Che Guevara," he says again as they stand on the pavement in front of her apartment.

"No," she repeats. "I have never heard of that gentleman."

"It must be my accent," the man concludes. He stops, extracts a pen and a matchbook from his pocket. He writes the name down on the cover of the matchbook, carefully, in block letters, as if she were a child. She stares at the letters. No, she repeats. She has never heard of this Che

Guevara. The man seems stunned, lost. He has planned this pilgrimage to the house of a saint for months. A long journey in a rattling, rusted bus, the old women and men holding chickens on their laps. The landscape was sharp and tortuous. Then, as he walked slowly toward the shrine, the adobe house, a uniformed guard told him that it was closed.

She has rendered him silent. They drive the two blocks back to the park without exchanging a syllable, particularly not in Spanish. For this, Francisca is grateful. She thinks of the guerrilleros in the mountains near her village, of the bombed power plant, of the night which settled softly across her then, uncorrupted by neon and the inventions of men. She thinks of the Conquistadores drowning with their horses and gold in the ruins of Tenochtitlán. She remembers the museum in Mexico City where she spent her last day with Ramón.

It was in the museum she realized that the boundaries are illusionary. They have always been open to negotiation. She would like to tell this young man he should die for an unconventional cause. She longs to tell him that she will vote for the regime which offers to cover the airfields with acres of roses. She will campaign for the colonel who promises free dancing shoes and a piano in every house. But she watches her mouth. The shrine is closed for repairs. One cannot even touch the exterior walls. And she says nothing.

At her bus bench, she is restless. She paces the sidewalk now, her rhythm deepening with the first surge of authentic night. Tomorrow, after lunch in the tearoom, after the models in black velvet and black satin have passed, she will select a card for Delfina, a card embossed with soft pink and lilac flowers. She will simply say she is well, and enclose five or six crisp one-hundred-dollar bills. In the village of her birth, let them make an augury of it. Let them trace the green paper with their fingertips, memorizing the special scent and texture of dead American presidents. They will stare at the engraved faces of the dead American presidents as they would the faces of saints. In the pueblo of her birth, they will hear God speak. They will hear the syllables with absolute clarity. Translation will be unnecessary.

The Chicano with the battered automobile and the pathetic Spanish is gone. Perhaps he will actually journey south to her country and fight in the mountains. He could learn the language, make himself useful in some minor capacity and harden his still-young body. La Puta de la Luna smiles.

"You know men," La Señora, the wife of her first patron said. "Los hombres son perros." She was on her knees then, extracting shards of glass from hand-woven rugs.

Of course men are like dogs, with their intoxication of blood, their petty lusts and nonexistent attention spans. Men, with their collapsible lives, their insignificant artifacts, the trivial details they can pack into one single cardboard carton. A jacket, a photograph of a son not seen in a decade, a sweater a mother or a sister knitted, a guitar perhaps, and it is done. Then they drive into the pastel distance they perceive as perpetually open and beckoning like desperately lonely arms, like the limbs of love-starved women.

This man will go nowhere, she decides. His eyes lacked the capacity for passion, for the extravagant gesture, the instinct for urgency and sudden risk. There were buses he could have boarded, trains, planes. He knows the name of the intersection and has many times passed it. The shrine is closed for repairs. It lives only within him, like a dream, a sealed-shut impossibility. He has already surrendered. He is draped in an invisible white flag. It is the region of the half-dead he serves.

He will return to an apartment or a stucco bungalow. He will yell at his wife, enraged that his dinner is late, burned, somehow flawed and inade-quate. She will not ask him where he has been. He will accuse her of having not swept a floor or ironed a shirt. He will say her hair is too long or too short, the color of her robe too innocuous or too bright. She could be La Señora in a marble hallway. She is silent. Then the man will take an inordinately hot shower. He will spend half an hour soaping himself in clouds of steam until he has erased her, La Puta de la Luna, the locked shrine, from his pores. Then he will drink beer from a can and watch television.

Now the wind begins to stir. They call this a Santa Ana, this wind which comes from the desert beyond the city, unpredictable and fierce, scenting the irradiated night with sagebrush and sand. She takes pleasure in the way it howls through its broken Spanish mouth, shattering leaves, breaking the branches of trees, etching its insistent southern story in a braille of twisted fronds. She enjoys the stillness in the mornings after the winds have passed, after the winds have ripped the palms, made confetti of the pale listless fronds, dragged their anemic sun-drained fronds to the ground. Then the city has been purified. A sense of salt lingers. The calligraphy is obvious. At such moments she understands exactly what

God is saying. His voice rises with the clarity of church bells above the debris. And God is saying the party is over.

Francisca senses the traffic settling into its smooth night pattern. The chaotic rush westward has passed. The sky is a tarnished burgundy, a ruined wine.

From the Cáfe Jalisco half a block away, the neon lights have been turned on, the insistent red and yellow bands, beckoning, insatiable. Francisca hears the noise of Mexicana disco rattling into the night, all rhythm without substance, the pounding tinny and constant. There are no variations. The music hurls itself into the darkness as if to mutilate it.

La Puta de la Luna turns from the boulevard and studies the park. The old woman is wrapped in an ordinary serape. This old woman has mastered the art of waiting. It occurs to Francisca that this aged woman might be a curandera or a gitana. She senses a certain force, a subliminal power. She realizes the old woman is cold. Perhaps she should bring her a blanket, water, fruit. There is a wavering in the fabric. Then she is looking beyond the old woman and the park, to the hills turning reddish and steep as the mountains of Caracas, into this Los Angeles nightfall exotic with bird of paradise, wild iris and red geraniums.

Often, she would walk with Ramón in Santa Clara, on the island in the Caribbean where the patrón and his wife, La Señora (her name was Emily, Francisca suddenly remembers), had their second house. She had been with them for eight months, almost the length of time required to birth a child. But there would be no baby, of course. Ramón had procured the anticonception pills for her and she swallowed one each day, precisely as he instructed.

Francisca made La Señora's bed while La Señora sat and drank coffee in the patio garden with Ramón. The banyan above them was monumental, ancient. Cassia and bougainvillea covered the fences. There were a profusion of vines, trunks of coconut palms and mango trees embossed by moss and spikes of flowers resembling claws and wings. Ramón read the American newspaper and did not look at either of them, not at La Señora and not at her. Francisca refilled their porcelain coffee cups, careful not to brush against his body. She camouflaged the waves within her eyes, the incessant rhythm making them glitter and dance. She had jewels in her face. She hid this, forcing her eyes to be mud.

She still knew how to cease to exist then, how to be inanimate, a silver tray perhaps, polished and returned to an antique cabinet. A platter which sat silently, undemanding, simply waiting to be used. She memorized the configuration of stasis which was required, the posture of subservience and ignorance, the fraudulent trance. La Señora instructed her in the arrangement of flowers in the numerous cut-crystal vases which she never once chipped or broke. The linens she ironed and never once creased or stained. She was silent, her disguises immaculate, flawless. She dusted and polished, as if their objects were religious symbols and she a devout supplicant.

La Señora, with her frantic darting movements, her endless bowls of fruits and constant diets. One day she would eat only melons. The next, only berries. And her hands, startling with diamonds and the whiteness of flesh bred pale for millenniums. Francisca was breathless in her white presence. La Señora did not permit the sun to touch her skin, wore a hat and sunglasses, always. Her flesh seemed to be marble or porcelain, glistening.

Then she washed the dishes from their breakfast. She cleaned La Señora's bathroom, scrubbed the toilet and the bathtub with American soaps. She replaced the crystal containers of bath soaps which were sculpted in the form of flowers. And Francisca was careful that their fine scent did not drift upon her skin. She had no skin. She was a platter sitting silently, waiting to be used. Her name was peasant girl, servant, mop.

When La Señora was gone with her family in New York or Connecticut, or, once, simply visiting a friend on a boat in the harbor, Ramón would take her walking. Beneath lamplit arcs glowing in a sudden grove of mango trees and coconut palms in a miniature plaza with the sea beating near them, gauzy, pale and creamy green as jade the ocean buried and polished for centuries, Ramón kissed her eyelids, gently, as if enameling a leaf. His lips were brush strokes, a form of calligraphy, a part of a process too complicated and refined to refuse.

They began walking in the late afternoon. Wooden houses perched on the hillsides as if they were flowers which bloomed in annual cycles. Or perhaps they had just perched on the soft ridges of cliff like a certain species of sea bird. Goats pushed up puffs of coconut-palm hills. Flamboya erupted a liquid red, framing the port below them with flames. The edges became thermal. She could navigate by heat. The context expanded. There were no borders, no increments or divisions.

This time, La Señora would be gone for ten days. Ramón was unhurried. He told her the history of the island, how the British and the French had fought repeatedly here. When she asked why, Ramón laughed. "All wars are identical," he said, "fought from habit and boredom, from too much rum and sun."

Francisca imagined the British and the French punching their cannons into the lilac afternoons. They staked crosses into the soft earth, leaving cobblestone streets engraved with the names of their kings. Edward. Charles. James. George. Ramón was holding her hand. The air was opening, caressing, charged, charmed and electric. The air was fever-warm and rising in concentric waves. She recognized the alphabet of the elements, how they could transform themselves at will, from fire to earth, water to air. And the air swayed and burned.

In the marketplace, below an English stone church and the Black Cat Bar, cars were painted yellow, blue and red stripes, primary, crucial. The world stalled, a smeared oil palette. Barefoot black women wearing gingham print aprons and head scarves squatted beside pyramids of tiny silver fish in baskets. Breadfruits and plantains and mangoes were spread on burlap sacks. The sun was calm. There were no shadows.

She breathed green tides and ebbed and flowed as she walked. Wind encircled a church steeple, rustled cassia and banyan. It occurred to her that God was different here. God had spice in his blood. He floated without vengeance as a cloud, a mutation, splendid and unforeseen. The blood of this God was the orange of ginger, tiger's claws and orchids. This was the air of intoxication, of genius and dream. Here, in one inspired juxtaposition, God had formed the sea, the original drum, that it might beat a green rhythm upon the island, that it might rock it like a cradle, this infant, this favorite of his children.

They were walking down a path of smooth grasses to the beach. The jungle, the moss and vines, the cliffs of banyan and palm. The music, the constant rhythm of the ocean, the air which was flame.

They were sitting on a beach, the sand so white, so finely etched it seemed like a painted line. She realized that God had visions here. He sat on this precise beach and created music and detail. It was here that God first conceived of paradox and redemption. Here, in the green waters he had invented, God dived for black coral and sculpted the archetypal ear, that it might hear the recurrent drumming of the sea, the music of the wind, of the elements in constant transition. It was here, she decided, that God had discovered love.

Later, she surrendered to the night. She mated with the night and she was shameless. La Señora would be gone ten days. She wore La Senora's lavender silk dress with slits at the sides which exposed her legs to the thigh. She wore La Señora's high-heeled shoes, her gold bracelets, her diamond rings. And it occurred to her that bodies, like the elements, could be transformed, could rise from mud into water, an elegance of jewels and silk, a fluid elevation.

Ramón told her to bathe in La Señora's bathtub, to use her oils and her soaps which resembled perfect pink roses. Ramón sat smoking a cigarette, watching as she applied his wife's perfume to her neck, her wrist. When he pointed with his smoking cigarette to her breasts she did as he bid and placed the perfume where he indicated. His hand was a flame. This was a geography of conflagrations, the seamless red that speaks.

She realized at that moment that sin had a certain texture, shade and scent. Sin was not an abstraction. It was a form of art. It was a region, an entity, an island, a continent. It was ancient. This terrain was not amorphous. There were rules, lines of demarcation, gestures and nuances to master and absorb, seasons, cloud patterns, winds.

Flesh endures like rock, she thought then. In this realm, flesh was harder than stone, more resonant and absolute. Hands, tongues, the blue flowers that teeth leave engraved on the thigh. Only blood could be trusted. And the mystery was unraveling, simply, without effort, clarifying itself like an equation.

Then they were walking through the village that was Santa Clara. Night purpled, as if everywhere fushsias had simultaneously risen. Sunset in a debauchery of magenta. Night seemed lit by candles. Night had a mouth. She spoke in whispers and incantations, each syllable a secret illumination. Francisca had a sense of orchids, petals fragile as the skin of infants, a sense of alabaster, sculpted, ambered, a faint yellow like antique Spanish lace and something indescribable, deceptively delicate and verdant. She had the certainty that the sea was near and that finally it would birth her.

Beneath her leather high-heeled feet, the grass deepened, turned damp, dense with moss. Ramón's arm encircled her waist, embossing her, locking her within an invisible ring more binding than gold. She could define the separate components of night simply, like a page in a newspaper, like a script. And she thought then, I will never forget this texture, this particular shade of red, this sky of escaped fuchsias, this sky like a flock of dipped-in-burgundy jungle birds and this slow sea wind choreographing the fronds of the palms like a chorus of flamenco dancers.

Francisca Ramos turns to study the city park. She notes that the moon has assumed her night position, settled into the center of the sky like a great Spanish dancer in the middle of a stage. Tonight, the moon is perfectly round, absolutely full, polished, delicate as an amulet designed for a child.

The old woman is sitting beneath a palm, staring at the moon as if she were taking communion. Of course this old woman knows what the moon thinks, what she has learned and keeps hidden. The moon who masquerades as barren. The moon with her pretense of mute rock, her listless charade. It is an act of fraudulence. Beneath her illusion of craters and dust, there are oceans of orchids and roses.

She will cross the park and cover the old woman. The night air has the bite of wind to it, a studding of sharp brush and salt. The old woman has not moved in hours. She must be thirsty. Their eyes have connected. A recognition exists between them. This aged woman could open her mouth and it would be a portal, a revelation. Her feet touch the grass when a car honks, when a car on the boulevard honks and stops.

La Puta de la Luna slides into the car. Night rushes against her face and for an instant she feels as if she is reeling drunk at a cheap carnival, assaulted by color, eruptions of music, bells, tinny and metallic. The sound of coins. She leans back into the leather and the streams of neon and the man says, "You ride like a lady who has seen her share of Cadillacs."

La Puta de la Luna, who has learned to hear words without hearing them, who has mastered the art of seeming alive when she is not, finds herself unexpectedly laughing. She is experiencing a strange sense of intoxication. Somewhere, the persistent image of a hillside terraced and filled with orchids. Orchids and angels. Orquídeas y ángeles. And, no, they are names, she recognizes. Orquídea and Angelina. They are women, yes, and someone is calling them. The scent of leather in this new automobile. This sense of sudden drunkenness. The startling sound of her own laughter.

The man parks the car. He is obese, younger than he seems, perhaps even boyish. His features have been swallowed by flesh. Even his expensive clothing seems ill-fitting. He glances at her as if he has decoded the mystery of the whore song, which is precisely the same in all times, regions and histories.

It is oblivious to frontiers. It says my name is young. My name is use me. It says I am naked, a child in your arms, your sister, your slave. I am waiting on my knees. I am spreading my legs like compass points. There are acres of me. You cannot reach the borders. It says it is gold I crave, silk, jade and the danger of barter with strangers. It is the cool coins I must have, the metal discs etched with the faces of temporary gods that I long to press with my hands, to fill a tall vase with. And the sound of these coins is like an amber rain.

The man has opened the car door for her. She has been sitting, in a kind of stupor, feeling the pull of some other. It occurs to her that the fat man might be a policeman.

Every day women disappear. They enter a bus and chance upon la policía. They do not return for supper. They are placed in a cage near the illusionary border. They will not be permitted a telephone call. Later, they are taken into Mexico, a country which does not want them.

The fat man has the sense of a man who has seen certain explicable confluences, the tears in the fabric. You stand in an insignificant plaza in a meaningless village. A bus appears, rusted, crowded with old women holding chickens. You enter the vehicle, and the course of your life is changed. You cross a boulevard that seems like any other, ring a doorbell, enter a house where a woman wearing a red silk scarf creates a configuration of cards across the surface of a wooden table, and the course of your life is changed.

Always, there is the ground which is not solid. The enormity of water. We are ships. We drift where currents and seasons are unpredictable. Direction is an illusion. It is all happenstance, coincidence, the mysterious geometry of the transitory. And they are walking up the steps to her apartment.

No, she reassures herself, his clothing is hand-tailored, too fine for a policeman. And something within her shrugs. Would it matter if she were deported? All cities are similar, temporary configurations desecrating the name of one saint or another. She remembers she has lived in this La Reina de los Angeles for nearly a year and the police have never molested her. She is like the palms and the stucco-gated bungalows squatting on their square lawns, like the bougainvillea spilling across the alleys, like the wild red geraniums on the hillside. She is intrinsic to this landscape, and, by implication, invisible. She is like a lamppost, a dog, a rosebush. She is part of the fabric, the natural flow.

The fat man enters her apartment, surveys it quickly, expertly, and sits down in a chair. It is 10 P.M. precisely. Somewhere, she hears and counts the bells. She has lived in this apartment for nearly a year and yet she has never before heard the bells. She is struck by this oddity. Of course, the church has outposts everywhere. The bells reach into the darkness, subliminal. The bells too are fundamental to this design.

The fat man who is probably not a policeman takes out an expensive leather wallet. He removed three hundred-dollar bills. He places them on the table near the chair where he is sitting. "Pour your good scotch," he says, "then sit down and relax."

La Puta de la Luna takes a bottle of Chivas Regal from a shelf. It is still 10 P.M. She can hear the echo of the last church bell, floating through the night, leaving a small wake in its path like the tender liquid scars boats leave across water. The moment is frozen, seamless. It elongates, enormous. Suddenly, Francisca Ramos thinks of all the women lying in darkness, in Mexico City or Caracas or Los Angeles, considering their marriages, with the dresser mirror thus, and the fading roses or carnations in a blue vase thus. Through the half-drawn blinds, street sounds rise like a smoke that chokes.

Francisca pours two glasses of scotch. She hands one glass to the fat man and carries her glass to the window. Below, the lake seems comatose. The park is deserted except for the old woman, who now lies beneath a palm tree. The palms are insomniacs, she realizes, lashed by passing headlights and neon. And she wonders how many women are standing at their windows in their separate and identical darkness, in this seamless 10 P.M., standing on cell-like implications of terraces, or balconies above expanses of wrought-iron-gated courtyards and lawns, all the servant girls and Las Señoras, surveying the damage beneath this intense and disinterested moon. How many women in nightgowns or stained slips, glancing in mirrors, recognizing that their youth is barricaded on an impassable avenue in a city they can barely remember, in a city with an architecture that aggressively asserts a premise they cannot comprehend. Birds assault them from trees they do not recognize.

"You are pale," the man observes. "Sit down."

La Puta de la Luna sits down. She feels the sheer weight of the uncountable women who have learned by trial and fire their petty abilities and grotesque limitations. Acts without resonance. The dense silence. The illusions, the defending of nonexistent borders. All the women swinging with the arcs of style and fashion, knowing the leap the hanging man takes. It means nothing.

It is 10 P.M. It will always be 10 P.M. This is what the woman are thinking, in Caracas and Puerto Vallarta, in Miami and Los Angeles. The women have known nights when the saints called and nights when they were silent. And the nights the saints spoke with the mouth of a dog or with metal hooks. Always, the process remains hooded, inexplicable. All one ever learns is that it is finite, the music, the orchids, the moon, the monsters under the bed, love and the tumultuous follies it spawns.

She can still hear the last echo of the final bell. How is this possible? It is 10 P.M. It will always be 10 P.M. And the legions of women thinking, Mother, it is all so frail. Mother, I am terrified. 10 P.M. Hour of the ghost, the lost drunken husband, the ambulance siren. Hour of the bullet that ricochets. Hour of the rosary that lies.

The fat man sips his scotch. "I am interested in why you are pursuing your business in such a self-punitive manner," he says.

"It is a long story." La Puta de la Luna glances at the three hundred-dollar bills sitting in the center of the table. "And extremely complicated."

She is thinking of how many women are, at this precise instant, making a list of the chances they missed. They are painting their nails, studying the color beneath lamplight, half expecting him to telephone, to not telephone. How many women are watching this precise full moon, studying her from windows, balconies, terraces, realizing it has been six years since that last cruise to Jamaica.

It is 10 P.M. It will always be 10 P.M. They are wondering whether he will come back this night or tomorrow or ever. Perhaps he has found another woman, even the servant girl. They have the ring, the bishop blessed it. But there are unofficial forms of abandonment. Or perhaps he has simply forgotten. It is a century of sudden amnesia. We remember our addresses but not why we live there. Maybe he crossed a frontier, changed his name, was shot. Or he could appear at midnight, still angry, prepared to beat her. The heart cannot be calm. He might return with flowers, confess, weep at her feet, beg to fill her belly with a child he will not remain long enough to see born.

"You must hate this," the fat man says. He gestures toward the window.

This, she wonders, turning from the window with its view of the serene and empty park, the polluted lake bathed and luminescent with neon, reflecting headlights, the constant lash of light. And the barely alive palms who must continually bear witness. And the old woman, sleeping now, the woman she does not know who seems somehow familiar.

"This city?" she tries. The man nods, yes.

She is flooded with images. The walls and the floors buckle and sway. It is good that she is sitting. Once, outside Caracas, in a town collapsed back on itself, retrograde, with rib-thin streets of goats, dust and mud ruts, the village idiot played his guitar and hopped up and down in a torn raincoat while tourists snapped photographs.

In Saint Lucia, after the wharf and four blocks of cobblestone alleys, shacks perched at random in a forest of palms and banyan. Women sat with infants and piglets at their feet. Mangoes fell from trees. The air stank of rotting fruit and urine. Chickens and dogs cluttered the paths between shacks, and the paths led into nothing. The children limped, had injured eyes and obvious physical deformities. Ordinary symmetry dissolved.

"No, I do not hate this city." Francisca sips her scotch. The three hundred-dollar bills stare at her. "Mexico City and Miami and San Juan are worse. Particularly, San Juan on a Monday."

She remembers that day clearly. It is etched in acid across her nerves. A tattoo within her flesh. And it was a Monday in San Juan. It was when Ramón left her. It was when Ramón stared at her suitcases and told her to hang on to them, as if he thought she were demented, as if she were going to throw them away or tear them to shreds with her teeth. She sold them, of course, but that was later. That was after she deciphered the alphabet of marriage and before she met the Cubana gitana, Esmeralda, who showed her the future.

She had stepped off the plane from Mexico City. She was disoriented, jammed into early morning, the glare of the sun, the assault of the mon-strous urban again, the crowds and smog, the enormous banner on the wall of the airport saying BIENVENIDO A LOS ESTADOS UNIDOS.

She waited for her Louis Vuitton luggage. Near her, a blond woman stood holding a pocket mirror, meticulously tweezing hairs from her chin, oblivious, as if she were shrouded by invisible fronds. Or perhaps she thought everyone did this before breakfast. Francisca found standing difficult. She thought she might faint. She kept thinking, We are all dying, instant upon instant. We are all dying, like great cities, like Tenochtitlán. We are all miniature civilizations, constantly bombed, gutted, napalmed without warning. We are human beings and we are all ruins, our museums gone, our temples, our bridges, our gold and magic, our gods and rituals of solace, our broad avenues of statues and flowers. Gone, instant upon instant. We are like long-buried frescoes. In the moment of revelation, we are simultaneously eaten by sun. In the instant of our birth we are struck down.

"San Juan?" the fat man repeats.

It was 9 A.M., the air static, indefinably hopeless, corrupt, brutal and unmistakably American. She thought of Ramón asleep in Mexico City, sleeping badly, subliminally oppressed by the chaos of oceans, time zones and jungles separating them. Between them, an uncountable number of small men leaned out from shadows in alleys to carve obscene gestures in the air. And the air smelled of banyan and coconuts, ginger and urine, rum and sugar, silver fish the size of fingers rotting in baskets, diaphanous clouds bearing scars of the cathedral spires which had briefly trapped them. And the air was ash, bits of quartz, scorched parchments of the holy books, the erased possibilities, yes, this lingered above the gulfs and ports and floated across oceans. The elements were disrupted and stained.

She handed a porter her claim check. She hailed a cab and drove aimlessly through miles of orange terraced projects, apartment buildings planted in neat rows like a senseless crop in an insane farmer's field. A deranged botanist, making atrocities rise from the earth. The terraced projects, clothing drying everywhere, the clothing forming a web between terraces. And the plants pushing out of old oilcans on cell-like balconies. Disabled cars and occasional sad horses standing on patches of irregular lawn. The air steamed greasy. A vague breeze pushed the palms growing alongside wooden shacks, growing beside fruit stands, Shell stations and pizza parlors. The palms that shaded the police who stood guarding every corner.

"What happened in San Juan?" The fat man is staring at her.

"I grew up," Francisca Ramos replies. She refills his glass.

She had walked at random. On Calle San Francisco, under palm trees and a bronze statue of an American President named Theodore Roosevelt, a black woman wearing a red turban had pointed at her and screamed in English, "Get out of here. Puerto Rico belongs to us."

And Francisca wondered whether she looked American. She realized she did not have a passport. She felt odd on the street, exposed. She was too visible. The sun was pouring down on her, relentless, a liquid yellow poison. And because she did not know what to do, she told the man driving the taxicab to take her to the Hilton. Ramón had taught her that. If one was ever stranded, simply go to the Hilton.

Of course Ramón would come to San Juan. He would remember he had told her. He would come to the Hilton. He would find her. He would stop putting that white powder into his nose. His hands would cease trembling. Each morning, she stopped at the desk and asked for her messages. He would telephone. There would be a telegram. She purchased two new swimming suits, nightgowns, slippers, perfumes, an evening dress. She lay at the lip of the pool, drinking vodka on the rocks. She drank until the pain in the center of her head stopped. Sometimes this took an entire day.

Later, she sat alone in her suite. It occurred to her that flowers would improve her mood. She picked up the telephone and ordered a bouquet of roses. Then she ordered another. She filled her suite with roses until the air was so dense with their fragrance she could barely breathe. Now she ordered food from room service. She could no longer walk. The floors, the corridors, the carpeting and tiles, no, nothing seemed solid. The entire world was tilted, it buckled and swayed.

At the end of her fifth week, the hotel manager informed her that her bill was now close to seven thousand dollars. She accepted this information graciously. She took the elevator to her suite, locked the door, placed a pillow over her head and began screaming. In five weeks she had spent more than half the money Ramón had given her. Of course, there were the bonds and the jewelry. But still, this was finite. There was an equation of time and money. She had never realized before, not with such clarity and terror. And it had not occurred to her that patrones like Ramón might be rare. She realized she might have to work again, might have to scrub floors, might have to find another La Señora. She would have to assume the posture of subservience, she would have to live again as a silver platter, a lamp. And she had no papers, no passport or identification. And for the first time, her actual survival was in question.

The morning turned sharp and calloused with a sense of something persistently slatted and undernourished. It was like the palms, everywhere, the palms. The palm trees on the boulevards of Caracas, where American disco rattled the glass of the jewelry display windows. And the rows of gold chains and gold rings glared obscene and she felt as if all the sunken galleons, real and imagined, had simultaneously risen. Then she paid her hotel bill. There were no messages, no telephone calls, no letters. Then she took a cab to the outskirts of the city and rented an apartment.

"What I hate is not this city," she tries to explain. "What I hate is a certain scent, a certain shade of sky, a unique and complex texture."

She thinks of the rows of apartment buildings in San Juan, the projects with their protuberances of orange terrace. The worn sheets strung drying on lines. The air was steaming, greasy, stained, chaotic, mad.

She realized then that the region had been delirious for a millennium. And the women, always the women, standing overripe, trapped within the cycle of babies and constant abandonment. And the barefoot boys in torn t-shirts, dreaming of cars and knives and becoming boxers or film stars. The boys in packs, scratching like dogs at the edges of ripped sidewalks and in the dust of alleys that led nowhere.

She had seen the world as it truly was then. And the world was a shallow travesty, lacking even the theatrics of ritual. Bells rang, but they had no meaning. They were blank shots, bullets which could not kill. God did not come down from the sky with wings. He crawled out of a bar with a machete. And she realized there were no longer any sacraments, not in the jungle or the city, not in a pueblo or a capital. No, not in blood or marriage, words or rites or images or magic. There were no idols, no incantations, no combination of the elements which could provide solace. And she recognized then, with absolute lucidity, that the world had fallen apart. It had collapsed. And it was lying flat and one-dimensional, utterly broken, beneath a hot and abominable sun.

"Las latitudes de las palmas," she says.

Yes, of course, she realizes, it stretches from Mexico City and El Salvador, through Havana and Miami, across the islands of the Caribbean, from Caracas to Los Angeles. It is that particular air of slow rotting, that special scented steaming poison masquerading as emeralds, spice, clouds. This is illusion, a subterfuge of the elements.

Beneath this are cobblestone alleys of cassia and cactus and banyan and, always, the palms. Always the shadow darts of the slatted green hands of the palms. Empty hands which no longer know how to ask for anything, not absolution or grace, not even sleep. The supplicants with dead mouths. The unending profusion of gods who fail. The scorched parchments. The incessant ringing of church bells. The being naked only before God, who is harsh, unfathomable, alien, with his imported stones, with his contrivances of angles.

And, of course, the women. Everywhere, the women, fat from babies and abuse that is ingrained into the cellular structure of their flesh, embroidered on the inside, relentlessly duplicated, intricate as the wings of butterflies. And their eyes as they watch the horizon constantly collapsing in. As they watch from the windows of tenements. As they watched from tiled terraces above gated courtyards. As they watch from their silence, with stones growing in their mouths.

"You hate the lands where the palm trees grow?" the fat man asks. He has finished the second glass of scotch.

"Yes," she replies. She lets their eyes meet.

Yes, with their coconuts and frail legs, with their pinheads gutted by sun and by the callous stars which do not speak to them, which offer only inexplicable seasons of storms and mud which drape across their thin bark like a curse. The palms, with their tattooed legs, their inadequate skirts of straw and their guerrilleros. The palms, with their lashed bark flesh abandoned at the edges of ruined plazas, with the lost farmers at their feet, the legions of disappeared husbands and fathers and sons. The vats of oil, the plague of rum, the verdant wind twisting, always twisting their fronds.

The palms on the hills and in the capitals, on the boulevards, the corners, the palms alongside churches and neon-lit mango stands. The palms in the sand at the lip of the sea as if only an ocean could stop them. And the indolent mysterious soil which relentlessly keeps giving birth to itself, repeating the flawed and terrible pattern, in transitory configurations that call themselves cities and poise at the edges of deserts or livid jungles which swallow them. And La Puta de la Luna stands at her window, staring at the city park below her, at a park that could be any palm-draped plaza in any capital. She is thinking about las latitudes de las palmas even after the man seems satisfied and has gone.

PART TWO

I will tell you and only you because you ask with a soft voice erased of implication and you wear the white cloth, not the black. I know precisely what I have done, in this dominion and others. I could order my sins by hierarchy, transgressions of which the most intensely irredeemable require purification by flame. My sins are engraved within my flesh, permanent as the gash of a knife. After decades, such a wound remains, pinkening perhaps, razor-thin by burial, but the scar and what it implies last forever. Even maggots will not touch it.

You are surprised. I can decipher this effortlessly. The steady gliding movement of your pen has ceased. Your face has become still as a lake at dusk when the waters are in transition, their day bodies shed, their night disguises as yet imperfect.

I realize you thought me ignorant, inarticulate, unaware of the complexities. I did not learn English, read newspapers, or form opinions about Fidel Castro and the rise and fall of republics. For this failure to conform I was perceived as unnecessary and dismissed as slow-witted, a creature possessing an alphabet of only astringent winds, sand, rock and mud.

No one recognized the elegance of my resistance, my intricate immunity and certainty that the names of generals, capitals and film stars were irrelevant, trivial, an unexceptional expression of the ebb and flow. I am speaking of the subliminal tremors which make all nations, customs and artifacts of women and men temporary, obsolete from their conception. They are less substantial than the incidental patterns that waves etch and erase in sand. I always possessed this awareness. It was a gift, like women who can sing or paint or embroider opulent fabrics.

I kept my unique abilities shrouded and locked. Not even Marta Ortega, the bruja who lived directly across my street, suspected.

My family and neighbors on Flores Street surveyed the inexplicable layers of my silence and pronounced me rubble, a dead moon, useless. I was a curse that somehow walked. Their eyes were hooded and evasive in my presence, in my self-created solitary confinement and impenetrability. When they chanced to glance at me, they shut and locked the secret doors in their foreheads, in the channels and eddies of nerves and moss beneath their flesh.

You look at me differently. You are not blinded or deceived by parchments where the territories of acceptable behavior and those of trespass are neatly engraved, measured, outlined and named like actual countries on maps. You know there are vast dominions where mountain ranges and rivers are uncharted. You recognize that boundaries are illusionary. Borders have always been open to negotiation.

With you, I do not tremble at the possibility of the gas chamber or hell. Hell has a geography like any other. It is said that in hell there is an inexplicable juxtaposition, a river. Such a channel could be mastered and rafted. I am not without certain hopes, even now. In your eyes, clean gray American eyes, there is a distant sadness, like gray clouds or sails at the edge of an horizon.

Of course, I have always seen things as they are not. I automatically and instinctively improvised and invented. I was clandestine with my invocations, my deformed benedictions. I excavated continually, collected and polished shards. My life was a siege of recurrent and desperate rearrangements. This was the method by which I survived.

Perhaps this was a form of innocence. I did not fully recognize my idiosyncrasies and frailties until she came. Yes, Barbara Branden. The American. The dead woman. Before Barbara Branden, I existed as a chameleon, veiled.

I was undemanding as adobe, as yucca, as a plant in an interminable windless moonless season willing to wait a century or a millennium before I entered into blossom. I had the patience of agave. I was protected by the knowledge that my destiny would simply appear when it chose, open, a portal with abrupt channels and abnormal gravities. I was content to await in silence this magic arrow. One day it would strike me, and that which had been blood would be transmuted into poison or flame.

My world was Flores Street, my white cottage with its glistening orange-tiled roof, miniature square courtyard, sloping front lawn and terraced backyard with avocado, orange and lemon trees. I had planted beds of marigolds and asters, pink rosebushes, azaleas, geraniums and iris. I had memorized the appropriate postures and tones required of a mother and a wife. I had accepted these details, these anchors and binds which had no resonance, as inescapable. My personal realm was defined by the market on Alvarado Boulevard and my church, Neustra Señora de los Dolores, one short, slightly arched block beyond Alta Vista Street. This terrain was nearly unbearable, immense, with a turbulence and plentitude I could barely contain. I desired nothing more.

Number 6592 Flores Street. You know this already. My address is inscribed across the top surface of the numerous papers you have assembled and hold now in your file. My street numbers are etched in blue pen, yes, but these are descriptions of the surface, mere scrawls.

They do not note that my front-room windows were angular and wide and clean, opening like startled eyes. With my soft sea-pale-blue curtains pulled apart, I watched the sun rise and position herself in the center of the sky like a Spanish dancer assuming her pose on a stage. In the early mornings, she draped herself in subdued antique brocades and lace mantillas. At noon, her dress was the white of a postulant. By sunset, she was an outrage of yellow, vivid, furious, her gestures erratic, her gown the plumes of rare jungle birds thought to be extinct. They still exist, these birds that speak, but they are cautious, solitary. They possess a mastery for disguise. They might appear to you as sparrows.

I would stare at Flores Street below, Manzanita Street beyond and the gash of cement and insinuating rattle of metal and tin that was Alvarado Boulevard, and by implication I studied the whole city for hours each day. I surrendered to subtleties which are nameless in any language, without vocabulary, mouth or lips. They are limbless and leave no artifacts. I was hypnotized by that which drifts and vanishes before it can be identified. The hooded incongruity of the external was continuous. My hours accumulated, mated, formed their own subterranean structures. I aged, but I was oblivious to this. Calendars were irrelevant. I was compelled to decipher a process resistant to conventional increments. This was my purpose. I had taken a vow and married a trance. Obsession was consuming my life, but I was unaware of the slow devouring until Barbara Branden came.

Before the white woman, I lived concealed and morning astounded me. I noted that the palm trees on the sidewalk below my house were anchored as usual beside the streetlamps, rooted in poor soil, surrounded by the droppings of dogs, wind-scattered trash and ripped leaves. To the north, behind my house, the softly rising hills would not have altered their stature or contours, yet the composition was unsolid and divided.

I sought points of reference. The wooden house directly across the street from me was the first house built on Flores Street, the structure where Marta Ortega had lived since her youth. When we first moved to Flores Street, her house was painted blue, then it was beige and finally yellow. In the last years, I studied the house of Marta Ortega as if engaged in an augury. The house would be the same serene shade of lemon in sunlight or lamplight, precisely as I remembered.

Marta Ortega would be working in her garden, oblivious to seasons or weather. She had mastered the art of recombining the alphabet of nature. She created orchids which had never existed before. They were an anomaly, a conflagration of magentas and reds, lacquered and inflamed.

Marta Ortega would be potting or pruning, birthing the eccentric and unpredictable. She was a detail in the landscape which did not waver. She bent on her knees in the dirt as if taking communion.

Once, when I stood near her in the garden, Marta Ortega had suddenly risen from he dirt. She stared into my eyes, reached her arm around my shoulder and pressed me in a fierce embrace. "The ice is thin," Marta Ortega said that day. "We are all walking upon water."

My world was an anarchy of odd shapes, defective slabs with colors muted or deliriously vivid. Shadows obscured and tilted the shards in a windblown geometry I had each day to reassemble, rapidly, before it became apparent I was blind, dazed and incapable. My work was unceasing and exhausting.

When the sky turned exceptionally blue, seamless, untainted by even one stray cloud, I thought it would unravel and reveal a pattern, indisputable, ineluctable. It did not.

I thought the world was a dance of exquisite and complicated gestures I had by an inexorable force forgotten. There was a music, precise and measured, but I did not know why it formed a veil across Flores Street or what it intended. Perhaps, somewhere, a gitana wearing a red silk scarf and orbs of genuine gold earrings stuck a pin into the likeness of my head. This was possible. I have the head of a rag doll. Split me open. You would find ash and rust.

In my long silence, I was partial and unfocused as a woman with a head wound. Yet I experienced no release in this, felt only an occasional twitching, an agitation and the persistent sensation of falling. Perhaps I was not a woman at all but a leaf or cloud, beyond bone or flesh, that drifts where winds and currents dictate.

In the early mornings, bamboo stalks rubbed their slim shoulders together, impelled by a sea breeze in the corner of Marta Ortega's elaborate garden, across the surface of the earth she had planted, designed, arranged and perfected for more than fifty years. Her garden had been transformed, become a fabric, her plants stitches, her orchids designs in a fantastically intricate embroidery.

And the bamboo formed a veil through which I watched the palms and manzanita near the yellow-painted wooden fence marking her perimeters like hems and seams. Her front yard was a transparent green as if polished by stones retrieved from antiquity, rain-anointed. I would be momentarily reassured then, convinced that the paint of the world was intact, with its near-red geraniums, sudden eruptions of purple iris and the blazing yellow stalks of canna brazenly splitting the air, proclaiming their singular similarity to lava.

As I inspected Marta Ortega's garden, I realized that plants, flowers and trees were members of a randomly assembled orchestra. The yellows, ambers and reds were the reeds and the brass. The leaves which rocked and swayed were the strings, the violins and cellos. But the actual music was marred by the static of honking cars, barking dogs, wood pounded by hammers, radios, and my sons, who were in constant need of my attention.

Always, I was tightrope-walking between mutually exclusive domains. Winds stirred the cool-edged winter, hardened by the staked vertical weight of the city, an accumulation of neon-impaled clouds and the rampant sins of uncountable legions of women and men. I reached the verge of revelation when my babies began crying.

I lived as all domesticated beasts, assuming a posture of fraudulence, tethered and gutted from within, clawless, feathers shed. I had tiny teeth. My acts were trite, redundant, listless. They taught me nothing of the process. Always, there was sponging and polishing, baking and steaming, washing and mopping, drying and feeding. Relentless motion without meaning, a slow rotting.

There was an insistent geometry of objects inescapable as bars. The sterilized baby bottles dried on a tiled surface like a series of glass pyramids. The boiled nipples rested on sheets of paper resembling a blanched plain the color of bone where pyramids of soft rubber rose. I was surrounded by dense and solid assemblages. They formed a cell within a cell. I moved insignificant three-dimensional forms with care, scrubbed, dried, stacked and replaced them. My hands offered no resistance, yet there was a terrible lack of connection and the unremitting sense I had forgotten something vital to my survival. My days were shattered, the shells damaged, the embryos within dead.

Then, without warning, I found myself elevated into a state exceptional and luminous. I trembled at the beauty I witnessed below my windows, the remarkable craftsmanship of lawns and courtyards forming the composition called Flores Street. I was awed by the textures and shapes created momentarily by sun and shadow colliding and disappearing as wind washed across a lawn, as a door or a window opened or closed. It occurred to me that cities and nations, events, opinions and the artifacts of women and men were no different, were a temporary design, the process would take as cleanly as it stripped the fronds from palms, as it gutted Tenochtitlán.

I possessed exceptional clarity. I was frightened by this and the hypnotic power of the trees, continually shedding and swaying, each with a separate destiny, a distinct mythology dazzling with legends of warriors and gods, concubines, traitors, prophets and whores. I reached the edge of revelation when my sons began crying.

In autumn, I observed an old maple with leaves yellowing, pronged like hands gesturing in the intricate language of the deaf. The palms, the manzanita, the occasional maple and the displaced elm were joined in an elaborate conspiracy. They imparted sagas to one another, generous with detail and insight. Each leaf was a syllable, branches a phrase, trees formed paragraphs and barrios were a page.

If one possessed diligence, concentration and will, it would be possible to decipher the continent branch by branch. Of course the slatted fence perimeters of lawns, the gashes of concrete alleys, the boulevards and the monumental highways were irrelevant, minor obstacles the songs of trees floated without effort above. Always, they found one another, embraced, adding information, speculations and conceits. There were matings and betrayals. And they concluded each season in a cacophony of abundance and despair.

There were mornings when I saw the whole, unfragmented, motionless as a mural painted on a wall which does not bend or sway. I comprehended the interwoven fictions of the trees as indisputably as one hears church bells on certain Sundays in seasons when the air is a conduit and the flesh particularly vulnerable. And above were thin clouds that had escaped the pull of the sea which longed to drown them. They struggled inward, motivated by the insistent promise of what was verdant and indigenous.

These moments were brilliant, lucid, stripped of artifice, beyond pure and raw. I was a seed winds accidentally planted. I searched for a point to appear, a sense of shape or blossom, a hint of yellow, blue or red. I wondered whether I would be delicate or edible, scrub brush, lemons or moss. Or perhaps a rarity like the orchids Marta Ortega tended. Sun fell measured and assured across damp grasses and the backs of stray cats. I informed the air I was prepared for splendor, incandescence, a radiant green renewal. But spring ignored me.

At night the artificial lights of the city were the glistening perimeter of the shell, the streams of neon infestation a fragile assertion of order that one bombed power plant would negate. I had insomnia. Perhaps it was this deformity in my ability to sleep that distorted my perceptions and permitted me to evolve my mysterious X-ray eyes which were a gift and an affliction.

Continually, I struggled with a sense of concurrent tides, of a pull from a divided other which was unresolvable. I lived within a cell. Inside my bars there were no lamps, incantations or gestures to induce tranquility or soften the agony of the night. In my unremitting abscess of darkness, I considered hell, how brittle and hot it must be, parched, seasonless, incessantly whipped by winds pitted with the needles of cactus and the orbs of sharpened sand. I wondered what grew there, whether the inhabitants wore clothing, whether their flesh aged, whether there were radios, dinners, siestas, matings and divorce. I imagined horizons, sunsets, moons, plains and mountain ranges, beneath the earth, in the region of perpetual flame. Even there, in the ruthless and delirious latitudes of crimsons and bloods, nuances must exist, subtleties, a sudden opening, a river of liquid conflagrations one could navigate.

In this manner, I squandered the nights of my life. A quiet terror lived within me, like a seed or a nest. It was an entity, with its own history, desires and will. It stirred like the petals of a budding flower, gradual and tentative. It felt like the hands of sleeping infants when invisible winds blow through their translucent skin, making them shudder and twitch in their special darkness, which is not night but an otherness, a reflection of moon-draped water. At midnight, the world below me was suspended, malformed and not quite born. In autumn, I tasted the amber embers of leaves at the verge of extinction and I shivered.

My house was a kind of ship. Trees swayed without mercy, rose and dove like waves at my fog-grayed windowpanes. In the seasons of rain, the city of wet wood beneath my windows seemed like any pueblo, calm and undiscovered beneath a storm born in Mexico, wandered north, thunder still rattling in its mouth. The hills would edge closer, shudder and be sealed together, as if by a migration of prehistoric damp moths, enormous gray flying things with wings of heavy cotton or wool. They were creatures no saint had blessed. Yet they existed, somehow intrinsic, necessary.

Night chipped the lime-green lawns of Flores Street, skidded and yawned ink. Night offered me paradoxes, salt for my wounds, and there was no illumination. Night was resplendent with graveyards, saplings struck by lightning and the maniacal pools of neon which were the city, this illusion called Los Angeles that the ocean or desert would inevitably swallow. The sky was littered with dull banished stars that were less than pebbles. And I stood alone at my angular, wide front-room windows and let my ship drift.

I knew that my lucidity and agony were abnormal. But there was an intoxication within it. My sickness was like the night and the sagas of trees, forming its own seasons and terrain. I intuited I was unusual. I possessed powers which must be hidden and camouflaged. I was without fever. I did not cease eating, shrink or swell. My body was without remarkable eruptions. My illness settled in my eyes, in the dull orbs I wore embedded in my face. And my eyes felt aged, as if by a lingering disease or impossible yearnings.

I slumbered through warm mornings while my husband, Miguel, was working and my son José was at school. I wrapped myself in woolen

blankets which might have been the wings of the prehistoric damp un-
blessed moths of the rainy seasons. The creatures the saints had never
heard of. I pretended I was even older than Marta Ortega and being
wheeled in a chair across the sunbaked orange-brick patio of a mountain
hospital where no questions were asked and there was no writing in blue
ink on pages. Yes, like the papers you etch which now define my life. The
pages that serve as my borders, land masses and oceans. I dreamed of
being wheeled in a chair in a dominion of seamless silence where women
wearing the white dresses of practical angels sponged my flesh and not a
single syllable would be exchanged. There, in the realm of the invisible.

I suspected I harbored the seeds of a cancer or an equally virulent and
terminal disease your science has yet to detect and label. It spread, inexorable, soundless, eating at my molecular structure, the fibers of my nerves.
It consumed the marrow of my bones and created a dampness, hollows
formed, gullies, streams and wells. One day, I would open my mouth and
the ocean would pour out.

I prayed with intensity and desperation, motivated by terror. I was not
devout. On my knees in the darkened front-room, I beseeched all the
saints whose names I could remember to grant me strength and guidance.
My fingers were tightly clasped, blood drained from my hands, and nothing spoke. My prayers were stilted and conventional. They had the stench
of fish rotting on a pier in July. I was too insignificant and flawed to
bother any god. That was when I took my private vow of silence. I longed
to be still as a boulder on an undifferentiated and remote hill, shorn of
yearnings, mouthless, turning simply as the earth.

Increasingly, it was a struggle for me to leave my house, to force open
the heavy wooden front door. When I walked to the market, fevered,
secretly crippled, it was only the necessity to buy milk, eggs or tortillas
which propelled me. This action was fundamental. If I failed to purchase
food, Miguel might notice my infirmity, my erratic gestures, fraudulent
postures and profusion of cavities. I pushed my feet across the sidewalk,
and my body was numb. I willed myself to shed my terrors, my ancient
suffocating damp blue air. I told myself, This is the holy rain of February.
Your thoughts have been absurd and deformed, arrogant and unnatural,
but now you are absolved with the palms.

My state of grace was brief and irregular. Always, the season would be
turning recklessly fast, hurtling into the heat of spring with its sullen rows

of poisoned daisies, those odd yellow flowers barely breathing in a thick sea breeze swollen with ritual ambiguities. My comprehension of the earth flickered on and off like a candle in a village church in a month of unusual and compelling winds, when the raw elements are exposed and women and men whisper of omens and portents and the air is heavy with fear.

I never felt complete. I searched for myself on Sunset Boulevard, on Alvarado Boulevard, on Flores and Manzanita and Alta Vista Streets. At such moments, it was an unbending noon and still as the interior of a forgotten lake, comatose beneath centuries of dust and malevolent stars, where tiny fish were going blind and dying.

I went on expeditions to locate myself. I stared at liquor stores with iron grates across their doors and windows, with the paint of local gangsters engraved across their stucco sides like flesh which is an obscenity, a monstrosity of tattoos. I studied taco stands with their vats of beans and mashed avocados, a red and green glaring as liquid neon. Out the rock-ripped panes of windows came an assault of Mexican disco and the screams of children, startled, betrayed, as if they had recently been pinched or bitten. Cars honked, screeched and shattered the streets with a sharp metallic maliciousness which was blatantly deliberate. The cars were not vehicles, but weapons, spears and arrows.

I realized there was so little left of me. I was a somnambulist, an amnesiac on smoldering sidewalks of grease-stained food wrappings, torn newspapers, tar and glass. These elements were insufficient for an act of resurrection.

I became disoriented by the chaos of noise, the glare of color, the meaningless and relentless movement and the air which was confused and abusive. I sat down on a patch of grass, sensing the thin ribs of the world pushing up from below, from the derelict interior. I compiled a list of my fears. My hidden cancerlike illness, the symptoms I camouflaged which might erupt into lesions or gashes at any moment. My sons dying. The house burning as we slept. Earthquakes and madness. Miguel finding another woman and deserting me. The agitation I could not control. The scream which would eventually rise from my disguise of a barren mouth and tear from my lips like bullets. The scream which would never stop. Then, quite suddenly, I became calm. It was a stasis of noon, everywhere a form of yellow. And I realized that the creature stalking me would not come by daylight. It would not dare.

Still, in my unique fashion, in my series of mime gestures which meant nothing, I was not a bad mother. I never struck my sons or pronounced them flawed and inadequate. Such words can bruise the unformed and alter their destiny. I recited the expected phrases, postures and activities which were demanded. Each morning before Miguel left for his work in the central region of the city, I scrambled eggs, heated tortillas, poured coffee. Later, I walked José to his school on Alta Vista Street, north of our house. These rituals were an ordeal, a debasement, almost unendurable.

My life was an arc between darkness and irradiated clarity, an unpredictable and brutal journey. I felt as if I were a stranger to this earth. No, not merely this collection of angles, streets and alleys named Nuestra Señora la Reina de los Angeles. I was estranged not from a particular season or region, a climate or a barrio, but from the planet itself. I stood motionless on my front lawn, humbled by sun, wind or fog, a passing sparrow. I heard the sighs of trees in their inviolate dominion where the sky is pearl, glazed, a mesa of puffy clouds tracked by wild gulls that could, if they chose, shriek your name and the hour and latitude of your birth. I thought all women lived like this, in a torment of concurrencies.

You listen to my talk of lawns, trees, birds and vines and ask only whether I cry. Of course, even I sob at sunset when I sense the day closing like an enormous factory slamming its iron gates shut. Yet there is a sense of the familiar here. This institution is not unlike the office where Miguel sent me to work, where I processed invoices for keypunch. This prison is composed of the same substance as the edifice where I was employed in the center of the city where there were no windows and even the air was gray. There were no windows, not even tiny slats sealed with iron bars. In that horizonless room, the women sitting at their identical desks assumed the texture of clay and mud. Their dreams became tame. Even as they slept, they remained chained to the dock, severed from the unassailable necessity to drift across waters, to be one with the fluid other, to be as a shell or a sculpture of branches, the wooden arms and legs that float.

Actually, I prefer it here. I do not have to press my fingers into the keys of the adding machine that taunted me. I do not have to push my yellow rectangular card into the metal mouth of the clock which was a torment. Here, weeping is permitted. This geography recognizes the human deviations and indecencies, the gray clouds we wear in our eyes.

The hours are expressionless and demand nothing. It is seamless and immeasurable as an ocean. This is the gray of integrity and calm, an aged lagoon, static and content. I would be satisfied to remain within this structure forever.

My children recede from me. Their faces become indistinct. In my other life, in the late afternoons, I prepared dinner. Cornhusks and plates of sliced tomatoes, onions, chiles and grated cheese rested near my kitchen sink. Simmering frijoles filled the house with their familiar steam, the scent which provides the illusion of what is ordered and dependable.

Once I knew the appropriate rituals, the gestures which formed an artifice of sutures. My husband returned from his factory, and his presence, outline and voice were a kind of temporary stitch in my flesh, holding the rushing blood back, damming its craving to explode. Often I felt as if I were bleeding and my skin was merely a fragile shell that would one day reveal its contrived solidity and erupt like a flood. I would be slicing tomatoes, onions and chiles in a kitchen dense with objects of destruction. I willed myself to be careful with the knife, to remember that the red, green and yellow spheres I held in my hands were entities separate from myself. I was impeccable with the metal blades. Night passed and birthed another. I waited for Miguel at my front-room windows while one last translucent blue cloud streaked the darkening sky like the lane of a highway.

I sense you do not wish to record my recipes in the kitchen, my listless charade, my constant memorization of the ordinary details of that other world. You say you want to know everything, from the beginning. Which beginning do you wish to explore? And how can I tell you? I am a broken vessel, a ghost, singed and partial as wood after fire. I am ash winds take. It is always March and I am naked, boneless. We who have returned from the grave are dormant as cows with sheeted eyes. We reveal nothing. We are what worms discarded, too small for the pretense of resurrection.

In the beginning there was God, of course, and his meaningless accident of a world. God was an eccentric bandit. It is said God invented the hills and rivers, fashioning them from clay, air and the skin of infant clouds. Then he created moss and vines, women and men and the finely engraved wings of butterflies. He embroidered their mouths and eyes. Then in boredom and indolence, he invented sin, brutality and lies.

The intricacies of retrograde betrayal amused him. He was restless, with a short attention span. He arrived on this planet by happenstance, a random occurrence, a problem or confusion with travel arrangements, perhaps. The world was an experiment which failed.

Before God departed, before he abandoned us, God designed my village. The pueblo of my birth, Santa Cruz, in the north of Mexico, lies in the foothills of mountains which issue forth nothing but rock and scrub brush sharp as wire. Once it was Yaqui land, harsh and relentlessly miserable. As Marta Ortega said, it was an area bereft of ambiance. It was a place God assembled in mere seconds, without conviction, when he was already bored by this particular and unremarkable world. It was his final act of cruel indifference.

Santa Cruz was an outline for a region, a sketch no one bothered to fill in, color or shade, devise nuances or surprises for. The inhabitants had to invent themselves. They were fierce as the winds and rocks and cactus God gave them for reference points. They did not care for songs or artifacts. There was one theme and one theme only. It said feed the belly. I have my father's Yaqui blood. The Yaqui cut off the soles of the feet of their enemies. Torture was their form of art, their only sport.

It was obvious Santa Cruz was constructed from raw and angry ground, desecrated mud, stagnant waters, brutal sun, adobe and blood. I was born in a territory where the structure revealed itself, disparate, enraged, perpetually incomplete.

You ask for specific details of my childhood in this pueblo God abandoned. I sense I am failing you. I see this in your clear gray American eyes which resemble a monument or a highway with precisely constructed lanes that imply a final and permanent destination. You collect numbers. You are convinced the equation can be solved. That is the difference between us.

My memories are scattered like bones after vultures have engorged their black bellies, dipped their feathers in blood and left the residue for the winds which will consume anything. I remember our church, with its cruelly weathered courtyard walls, the plaza and the well, the persistent knowledge that God had fangs rather than teeth. The air was cactus and dust, barking dogs, loss and a callous indiscriminate wind that gnawed like hunger or fever.

My mother washed and braided my hair when we walked the dusty alley to our church for mass on Sunday. My father was not with us. He drank tequila. The liquid turned his eyes yellow as a field of wild mustard. His eyes were pools of encrusted caged water, beyond the natural cycles, beyond even dream. His eyes were a well where insects carrying disease came to feed. He slept all day Sunday, on the floor of the front room, on the bare earth, without a blanket, like an exhausted dog. There is nothing more.

Only his yellow eyes and easy fists, how he stumbled over chairs and created bruises across my mother's arms and shoulders. She wrapped herself in a shawl, even in the midst of summer. She hid her shame, the purple marks like dead flowers my father engraved into her flesh. That was the extent of his invention, his embroidery and vision, the arbitrary tattoos he punched into her skin.

Then, like a virulent storm which bellows and rattles and makes rivers flood, that hisses and studs the air with the sound of deranged cobras before it passses, he was gone. His name was Óscar Delgado. When you have inhabited an area of perpetually deformed skies, you are not quite certain, precisely, when they have at last ceased spilling their walls of black rain. But one day I noticed that his jacket and guitar were missing. The smell of alcohol and cigarettes remained within our house like the stench which fades with reluctance after a potent curse. My mother and I did not speak of his absence.

The curandera visited our house. She studied the corners, the walls, our floors which were raw earth. She lit a white candle and then another. For one whole month, at each dawn and sunset, she created a cross in the center of our courtyard with the blood of a freshly murdered chicken. Still, something lingered, resistant to cure, absolution or banishment.

The curandera recognized this. After a month of crucifixes etched in blood across dust, she suggested we move to another area. I was six. My mother was twenty-one. It was summer. My mother was not wearing a shawl. Her limbs were slender, sculpted, like carved mahogany. The curandera was whispering to my mother. Then my mother took us to her cousin, Elena Ramos, in Tijuana on the border of the United States. One afternoon I returned to the house and my mother was gone. I never saw her again.

Elena Ramos was a widow. Mourning was her passion, her one extravagance. She was generous but remote, childless, quiet. She did not even own a radio. We rarely spoke. Elena Ramos embroidered red, purple and yellow flowers across the sleeves of white cotton dresses. American tourists purchased them. Her hands were in constant motion like an agitated ocean. The name of my mother was never mentioned again.

Our life was unexceptional. When winds blew from the north, I could smell America. It was an odor of clean tin, clean metal, clean sun and tamed rain. America smelled like time structured and welded into place. It smelled like all of the future, huge, a colossal dead beast which does not decay but lies motionless, a mountain of flesh, perpetual. A carcass you could hack into bits and eat off forever.

You survey me with a blank expression. Your face is a just-painted wall. You say so little. You barely breathe or sigh. Surely the description of the pueblo of my birth is of no significance. It bored even God. Do you not want to hear the story of the white bitch named Barbara Branden?

You shrug your white-coated shoulders and say it is my choice, as if I held all power of decision. Understand, I cannot supply the numbers for your equation. I am not ignorant. The world of ordinary women and men is webbed with abstract symbols, formulas, exact combinations of substances. This is how metal and buildings and cities are formed. The texture and rhythm of your region is irreconcilable with my own. And I have told you I am nothing, am what winds have scattered and effaced. I am mud and dust after a remarkably intense storm, or less, a dead river, cracked clay, perhaps. Or a star or a child not yet born, that which exists only marginally, by implication.

No, nothing extraordinary occurred in Tijuana. After Santa Cruz, the city seemed enormous and the colors of the buildings blinding, spectacular, brilliant blues and pinks and reds like peeled flowers nailed to walls. The streets were dense with crucifixions.

Always American men crossed the border, soldiers, searching for the numerous women who sold themselves for dollars. Their dresses were redder than the storefronts they leaned against, fragrant and laughing. I thought their posture a form of crucifixion. And the air seemed strange and bloody.

Did I say I admire your patience, how your face remains unchanged day after day, as if you inhabited a climate of one season and one season only? I am grateful you do not chide me. There is a tenderness in your gestures, an elegance and grace. I observe how you slide your blue pen across the sheet of white paper. I hear you etch your secret script on the quiet surface, and the sound of this is a form of caress.

Yes, it was in Tijuana that I met Miguel. Perhaps it was on a street corner, in a plaza fragrant with flowers, in a market of melons and fish or at a traffic light. It was simply an intersection of chance and happenstance, simultaneously inexplicable and predictable. You take a certain bus or train, answer a telephone, a doorbell, cross a boulevard, climb a stairway, and the course of your life is changed.

I was fourteen. Miguel was seventeen. He gave me a medallion of Saint Anthony, guardian of lovers, to wear around my neck. Later, he encased my finger with a thin gold wedding band. This is the nature of women and men. Women are not chained with the obvious saddles and leather straps of pack animals. They are bound with a more subtle and corrosive metal, the thin gold of the wedding ring. Everyone knows this.

There were moments when I felt the metal eating the flesh of my hand like an acid. I longed to remove it from where it had been placed by Miguel, on the finger that burned. But I did not dare to do this, not in my bath or even in the hospital where I gave birth. The ring had grown into the fibers of my flesh, like an appendage, a deformity, an extra eye or toe.

I have never lain with another man. I laugh because the idea surprises me. I have no impulse to press my flesh into another. It has nothing to do with vows or the promises of marriage. There are no final destinations. Tenochtitlán was eradicated by a pathetic band of exiled renegades. Marta Ortega once said ther are no ports which do not change their names and contours, languages, gods, rituals and customs. And Marta Ortega said the love of women and men is similar, temporary, a trite recital of gray-worn tides that rise and die, come and go, mostly go. Even the most sacred words of women and men cannot form fences that are permanent, walls which do not weaken and stain with the atrocities of ordinary events and time.

I had small boulders for breasts, sand and cactus for flesh. A dead river, dammed with concrete, filled the juncture between my legs. I masqueraded as a woman. I memorized the tasks required, simmered frijoles, planted beds of marigolds and asters. My body swelled and I birthed sons. But this was pretense, an intricate net of lies.

Miguel was born farther south, in a village not far from the capital, from what had once been Tenochtitlán. The region where the Conquistadores came with their horses and cannon, priests and guns and uncountable varieties of plague, smallpox, syphilis, cholera, slavery, greed and the new God, with his penances and sins. Their diseases were legion. Miguel was warmer, darker. He looked Indian. His black hair was long and straight, his skin tanned a burnt umber from working beneath the constant sun. He was trained as a carpenter by his uncle. In the spring and summer, when he wore a white or pale-blue shirt, his brownness was startling, radiant as transmuted earth.

Miguel was proud of his Indian blood. He claimed to be uncorrupted Aztec, untainted by the seeds of Europeans. I laughed when he said this. So many centuries of blood and rot have passed, who could have the arrogance to assert such a thing? Still, I drank of his insistent southern heat and perhaps, in a midday July plaza laden with excessively scented flowers and ripening fruit trees, for that transitory moment I might have loved him.

Miguel was filled with dreams, with images igniting him from within as if he had swallowed burning candles. And all of his dreams were set in America. He spoke of the United States with intimacy, as a village priest talks of God, as if this enormous other was a distinct entity, embraceable, possible to fully chart and conquer. Miguel made the United States sound like his personal friend.

Miguel practiced his English with tourists. The simple task of providing a fat white woman and man with directions to the racetrack or the bullfights became an elaborate dialogue. He drank beer with American soldiers who had come to Tijuana hunting women they could purchase. Miguel assembled precise information, details, place names and descriptions of conditions, wages, occupations. He swallowed their English words like a wafer at communion. America had become a kind of god for him. He longed for this particular salvation, fevered, like a starving coyote.

It occurs to me for the first time that America was more than this for him. The winds from the north contained a form of perfume, a certain scent which inflamed him. Yes, America was a woman, although I do not think he recognized this. America was a woman who taunted him from the other side of the border, pulled up her coral and pink silk skirts, exposing the place between her legs, and whispered, Come and take me, I am waiting. Her eyes were blue, her lips red, and she said, I am the final answer. What you were born for. I believe this was the seductive allure of the United States, the subconscious intoxication Miguel felt in the northern winds, the irritant racing through his blood, the motivation buried beneath the surface.

When I became pregnant, Miguel said he knew the baby would be a boy. It was an omen. God had blessed our union. Then Miguel became obsessed with the notion that our son be born an American.

I was without interest in which patterned flag fluttered across our future. A cloth banner meant nothing. Tenochtitlán had been dismembered from the stone pyramids to the fragile definitions they contained, their music, poetry and mysterious procedures.

Even then I was without illusions. I did not crave antique brocades, lace mantillas or Spanish fans. I did not require wine for air. I was fifteen years old, my belly swollen, pregnant enough to feel the baby opening and closing his fists inside me. The boy baby, opening and closing his fists as if he were already angry and dreaming of spears, arrows, rocks which could be gathered, sharpened and thrown.

Then, one quiet and undifferentiated midday, we entered the United States. An American couple who demanded no money took us in their car. The American police waved us on without a single question. Miguel and I simply sat in the backseat of the car, crossed the border and penetrated the land called America. We were speechless with the enormity of what we had done.

I remember this as a moment of revelation and paradox. As we passed into the clean gray channel that was America, I realized the border was merely a line a lunatic had arbitrarily etched across the surface of a map. We drove north and towns and rivers, beaches and avenues, even gigantic cities bore the names of Spanish lords and saints. The avocado trees and bougainvillea, the slow blue coves and sea birds were identical with the lands we had left behind us in the country we called Mexico.

I drifted, unanchored and confused, convinced we had not actually crossed any border. It was an elaborate trick Miguel contrived for my amusement and bafflement and to prove his superiority with the external world of people and machines. Then San Diego and San Juan Capistrano were behind us, and then Vista Del Mar and Laguna Niguel. Palms embroidered the sides of the highway. Fat gulls perched on the rocks sheltering the beaches, taming the pale-blue waters, ordering the waves into coherent and predictable patterns. Then, in late afternoon, the American woman and man stopped their car in the center of Nuestra Señora la Reina de los Angeles, wished us good fortune in terrible Spanish, gave us fifteen dollars and drove away.

We stood on a boulevard, dazed, half expecting angels to appear. The air was laden with the caress of our language. Even the signs in the shop windows were printed in Spanish. There were textures I recognized immediately, a rhythm and a scent which were absolutely familiar. It did not seem possible that we had entered a new country.

We held hands as we walked. We bought tacos and fruit from street vendors. We crossed boulevards bearing the names of Spanish kings and saints, here in this land which had been an outpost of Spain and later a region of Mexico.

You ask what happened next. It was more than half my life ago. How can I recall precise events across the profusion of seasons with their gradations and nuances, the relentless, nonsymmetrical accumulation of shadows, the lime-green sloping lawns and sunbaked cement? There was only the incessant swaying of trees, the choreography of their branches and fronds and the dancing of the elements.

You deal with chronology, although you must suspect that evolution is not linear. Still, you are compelled to fill in your blue marks, to create an order where there is none. Your logic is strained through an impossible grid. Yet I attempt to satisfy you.

First, our son José was born. I lived with a cousin of Miguel's then, while he joined the American Army. Miguel was in combat in Vietnam for three years. After this, he was awarded American citizenship and several tinlike medals for valor. I remember this clearly, indisputably, because his citizenship document and honorable-discharge plaques hung in frames on the wall of our front room where the mailman or a passing salesman could see them and comprehend instantly that we were not illegals or refugees like these new Latinos who come from even farther south, from the wars beyond Mexico.

After the war, Miguel could speak English with authority and grace. He navigated the white bureaucratic maze of waiting lines, the completing of applications, the network of appointments and interviews. Miguel also thought the world was a set of numbers which could be collected and arranged into an equation that could be solved. Then we were given the money to buy our house on Flores Street.

We moved into the house on my nineteenth birthday. You will appreciate that detail, that shard of absolute precision. You can scratch those numbers in your blue ink on the white pages which are all that remain of my life. I remember that specific incident because the electricity had not yet been connected. That first night, the only lights in the house were the candles on my birthday cake, the amber streetlamps on the sidewalk below and the radiant white beams of the moon. It occurred to me then that our arrival on Flores Street was a kind of ritual, an initiation. My future would be measured in ambers and flames. Perhaps I intuited something then, and our first night on Flores Street was, in fact, a prophecy.

I was satisfied with simplicities, the raw manifestations of necessity, of plants in terra-cotta pots and the flesh of babies. Flores Street anointed and purified me. I craved neither genius nor grace. Summer afternoons were immaculate. Sun brushed the walls of stucco and wood cottages a white, the color of light itself. Heat asserted itself, bathed the leaves of trees in a pale yellow and caressed us in our siesta. There was the constant scent of lemon. My triumphs were private and intangible, were the pink rosebushes which reappeared in February, unexpectedly vivid and assured, reddening, profuse with buds.

I polished our wedding plates and trays although we used them only twice a year. I ironed the bed sheets despite the fact Miguel did not notice this refinement, this tenderness. I realized that the purity of my personal gestures was necessary, even if they remained invisible. And I could feel my heart breaking like waves, eating the shoreline. I was already becoming muted and small.

There were seven houses on our side of Flores Street. The hill rose and we thought ourselves superior, northern and higher. We shared a subliminal sense of stature. There were five houses across the asphalt gash dividing Flores Street in half. Their yards were larger. They were the original settlement and they thought themselves wise, closer to the south and the source.

Our distinctions were subtle. Everyone had come to Flores Street from mountain or coastal villages similar in substance and design to our own. Even the two white men who were lovers and lived in the largest house in the barrio, a two-story mansion next door to Marta Ortega, spoke a gracefully fluent Spanish.

When it was hot, we opened our windows to the sea breeze which was heavy with jasmine, the inexplicable lemon tinge of the orchids of Marta Ortega, and the thick pastel webbing of her roses and camellias. Radios offered ballads from my childhood. I could hum the melody and sing. Flores Street was its own pueblo. We witnessed births and deaths, marriages, an occasional divorce, desertions and betrayal. We were washed by an air of bluejays, gulls and the church bells from Nuestra Señora de los Dolores, falling like a veil across our street at sunset, a final blessing.

Our village was slow but not entirely static. There was the continual coming and going of visiting cousins, sisters-in-law, brothers. In particular, Marta Ortega, who had been the first resident of Flores Street, was relentlessly besieged by the returning of her daughters, Angelina and Orquídea.

Angelina and Orquídea were the scandal of our pueblo. It was said that, years before, they would appear at dawn or midnight, in taxicabs or moving vans, with cardboard boxes and suitcases. Later, they came with cribs and playpens for their children. Even after they had children of their own they returned to the house on Flores Street, to the labyrinth of drama and emotion they had created for themselves. They were simultaneously brazen and pathetic. Always they arrived on Flores Street with expensive, fashionable clothing and high-heeled shoes. Their faces were painted and their bodies laden with imported perfumes. They were cloaked impeccably. Their illness was beneath the cloth.

It was said Angelina had abandoned an American husband who owned four shoe stores in Santa Monica to run off to Caracas with a part-time dance instructor named Federico. Angelina had simply knocked on Marta Ortega's front door and handed her infant son Antonio to her mother. Then Angelina slid into the waiting taxicab and vanished for more than two years.

Angelina and Orquídea knew that the contours were fluid and unreliable. Still, they had atlas eyes. Their hands were passports. They thought their impetuous behavior artful and extraordinary. Yet in each man and marriage, in each exotic and distant country or territory, they discovered only confusion, disappointment and a grief so encompassing and profound they hastened back to the arms of their mother. Marta Ortega was their tree. She was littered by the debris of their numerous poorly constructed nests.

I studied their chaotic passage with fascination. They were similar to lost birds, gulls perhaps, who will circle the same steeple, disoriented, beating at a wall of wind, unwilling to alter their direction despite the blatant dictates of the elements.

Angelina and Orquídea lived as if they were characters in a television drama. They changed names, religions, accents and husbands, the shape of their bodies and the color of their hair at will. It was said Angelina and Orquídea had attended universities, yet they were irrefutably defective. Even the accumulation of knowledge failed them. Always, they attempted to construct themselves from the outside. They were adorned with fraud.

They visited American doctors and were given pills to moderate their appetite. In their purses they carried bottles of pills to help them sleep. They investigated new theories of fashion and behavior with the delirious conviction of women sensing themselves at the edge of absolute salvation. They chattered, raged, wept and howled. They scattered their dyed feathers everywhere.

When it was summer, you could hear them cursing and vowing, sending their syllables of loss and hate and extravagant need into the night like arrows. Even with the windows opened, the daughters of Marta Ortega screamed, oblivious to humiliation or discretion.

"You imposed your sophisticated values on children," Angelina raged. "You were barbaric."

"Would you have preferred falsehoods?" Marta Ortega countered. "Marrying that subliterate from Echo Park? A shack on Alta Vista, perhaps?"

"Don't patronize me," Angelina yelled. "But the Easter eggs, Momma? The fucking Thanksgiving turkey?"

"Not the litany again," Marta shouted back. "It gives me a migraine."

"Drink another quart of vodka," Angelina sneered.

There was silence. Perhaps mother and daughter were whispering. When I looked across the street, Marta Ortega was holding her daughter's hand. Later, I heard the sound of weeping.

Angelina and Orquídea often arrived on Flores Street in the summer. Their children were in summer camps. Then they spent weeks with their mother. Each night was an individual drama. In between the shouting and the weeping, Angelina and Orquídea bent on their knees, begging Marta Ortega for forgiveness. Often, her daughters kissed her feet.

"Forgive me, Madre. I have sinned." It was Orquídea. She was sobbing. Angelina typically accused her mother. Orquídea more often beseeched her mother for forgiveness. In either mode, Angelina and Orquídea were equally indulgent and ridiculous.

"It's your fault," Orquídea yelled. She stood in the front courtyard of the house on Flores Street. She woke up half of the street. "Compromise is alien for you. Compassion. Empathy. You are inhuman." Orquídea slammed the door. She drove her car into the night, blasting the radio, making her tires squeal.

"Always your garden," Angelina or Orquídea accused in one summer dusk or another. "Your stinking orchids, your ocean of vodka, your mountains of books. What are you growing here? A crop of diamonds?"

"Is it only jewelry which compels you?" Marta Ortega inquired.

"It is your stubborn resistance to the rudiments of convention," Angelina or Orquídea screamed, following Marta Ortega into the garden. "It is contrived. Why don't you move from this hellhole of ignorance?"

It was a hot dusk, They followed Marta through the garden. "You are the Queen of Flores Street. Surrounded by pagans. It makes you feel superior."

When Angelina and Orquídea had children who were nearly grown, they remarried and moved from the city. Still, Marta Ortega was deprived of peace. Suddenly she was invaded by her grandchildren. They were like their mothers, appearing without warning and impossible to ignore.

They pinned feathers and flowers in their hair and thought they looked like Indians. Some wore the clothing of soldiers, khaki jackets and high-laced boots. Often, their feet were bare and even the boys were adorned with necklaces. They carried guitars and flutes. They draped themselves in serapes and wrapped red bandanas across their foreheads. They called themselves Flower Children.

Of course everyone on Flores Street laughed at them, with their light skin and eyes, their army clothing and terrible Spanish. Marta Ortega let them sleep in her back garden. It was rumored she permitted them to grow marijuana between her rows of staked tomatoes. No one objected. Everyone in the barrio knew Marta Ortega was a bruja with powers rare and immeasurable. Her children and their children came to her as supplicants to a shrine.

The grandchildren of Marta Ortega were even worse than their mothers. These grandchildren with their beads and serapes, khaki jackets and sandals. They did not even look Mexican, some were freckled and blue-eyed, bearing the coloration of their many American fathers.

Once they insulted Miguel. They waited for him near the curb and called him a fool for having fought in the war in Vietnam. Miguel stared at them, amazed by their insolence and their ridiculous desire to burn American flags. He was speechless. He did not know whether he should strike the boy who spoke to him or simply throw back his head and laugh. He did neither. Later, Marta Ortega apologized.

She crossed the gash of asphalt separating our houses. She carried a bouquet of fantastic orchids, the corals, purples and reds of a sun setting. An extraordinary sun, sensing impending extinction. "It is simply a passing fashion," she told Miguel. Marta Ortega seemed saddened by this admission. "It means less than wind across palms."

The grandchildren of Marta Ortega were birds who feasted and then departed, like their mothers. In the autumn, when the air chilled, they rolled up their sleeping bags, packed their musical instruments and vanished in their loud and brightly painted cars and vans. Slowly, Flores Street calmed.

Flores Street was in a state of grace, intact. In between, a visiting sister-in-law from the Yucatán or Mexico City, from Tucson or Juárez dispensed advice and herb remedies. When a woman fell ill, had recently borne a child or a death, a savage betrayal or abandonment, she could expect bouquets of flowers with fragrant petals, stews in iron pots and baskets of tamales wrapped in cornhusks, ready to be stored or cooked.

Sometimes on Sundays, we who were Catholics and not lapsed, fallen, excommunicated or simply too exhausted, would walk together to Nuestra Señora de los Dolores. It was not an event we planned. It simply happened, spontaneously, the wooden front doors opening at precisely the same moment. The various washed and brushed children offering their tender, barely formed hands to their mothers. On summer Sundays, Flores Street surrendered to a squad of angels like an invasion of white moths or stalks of lilies that somehow walked.

Flores Street was a village defined by long seasons of quiet and tamed currents, a tranquility broken only by occasional spasms of violence. We were without politics. Even the boy-men who wore identical jackets designed to simulate the skin of animals and headbands like pueblo farmers were satisfied to engage in trivial acts of vandalism. They merely painted their invented names on our sidewalks. These Dreamers and Chicos and Charmers recognized we were content in our insignificance. We offered neither resistance nor interest in their rituals of cars and knives, in the territories they patrolled and guarded like dogs, moving in packs, marking the edges of their squalid domain. They were a wind that rattled in the night alleys and dissipated with the rising sun. In time, we became invisible to one another.

No, the war did not change Miguel. Or perhaps he was subtly altered and I failed to notice the rearrangement. We had both been anointed by blood. Miguel killed yellow-skinned men in the fields of rice and palm-draped pueblos of a land called Vietnam. I split my womb apart to birth a son. We had shared a passage simultaneously ordinary and unassailable. Miguel had risked his life in battle to make us safe from Immigration. We became citizens of the United States. In turn, I provided Miguel with José, a son who was our future, irrefutable, alive, growing, bearing the name of Miguel's father.

Perhaps America had been a woman for Miguel and he had seduced her, won her, stripped off her burgundy silk skirt and speared her. He returned a conqueror. But he was a man of moderate lusts. America had kissed him on the mouth, once. She had tossed him a flower, an orchid or gardenia perhaps. For Miguel, this was enough.

There was one tangible change in Miguel after the war. He mastered the language of English. He accumulated words and phrases like someone possessed by a passion for precision. He memorized the idiomatic, the colloquial, the nuances of the contemporary and the formal. He became fluent and assured. He had the *Los Angeles Times* delivered to our house each morning. Often the sound of the paper hitting our front porch or the brick of our courtyard made me start in my sleep, as if I had been struck by a rock.

There was something about the newspaper itself that made me angry, I admit this. I could not learn the English language. This disappointed Miguel and became a gulf between us. Perhaps it is inexplicable, but English cut at my eyes like barbed wire. It seemed composed entirely of razor-sharp angles such as the steeples of certain churches, the grand cathedrals in southern capitals that are twisted, aberrant, with an architecture which is unyielding, which will not compromise.

English hurt my lips, the soft fibers of my tongue. When I repeated English phrases, my mouth embraced unnatural American objects, appliances, concrete, steel girders and electric lights in abnormal abundance and force. I felt violated by traffic, pollution and the abuse of sirens and neon. English was absolute as a world where the forests have been felled, rivers dammed, and each inch of earth parceled, labeled and sold. It was an offense to my aesthetics. And I resisted the intrusion of these alien shapes and sharp-edged forms and what they implied.

Spanish flows like the ocean, aware of cycles, waves, completion and return. It sculpts the air with tenderness, with the fronds of palms, with moss and beds of vines. It is delicate and discreet, speaking in whispers, incantations and chants. Spanish dances across the tongue, intimate and accomplished, composed of moonlight, cliffs unnamed and lush, moist earth, dusk skies and the arcs inscribed by serpentine migrating stars.

English resembles a shore of pointed cliffs where the waves are reluctant, as if sensing contagion, and sea birds will not nest or deposit their eggs. A special rock, metallic, nonporous, frightening. English is a matter of edges, a severed tortured earth and transfigured fragments which are obscure, harsh, ungiving. The difference between the languages was one of intention, purpose and perception. The border did not lie at Juárez or Mexicali or Tijuana. The border sat in my mouth.

When I studied the books Miguel purchased for me, the pages disappeared into white patches like clouds or sails or perhaps bridal veils. I saw enormous white Easter lilies. Something within me refused. I could not concentrate on the letters etched before me. They were a series of twigs winds had twisted and spilled into the gutter. They were debris.

Each page seemed an entirely new continent. I thought of distant

countries where people measure time by dancing and the jungle is unspoiled, green without interruption, verdant beyond the concept of inter-
vention. Such lands are ripe with fabulous insects that sing and scented
flowers with elaborate petals that open like chanting mouths. The air is
recurrent with chimes and bells, the repetition of certain tones known to
soothe the gods.

I considered traveling to such a kingdom. Marta Ortega would aid me
in securing the documents necessary for departing this country and arriving in another. I would be clandestine, impeccable, discreet. While Miguel
was working, I would take the framed citizenship award that hung on our
front-room wall. I would decipher the forms and waiting lines and appointments. And one day I would simply disappear.

I would leave José with Marta Ortega. It was merely a matter of hours
only until Miguel returned from his factory, I would say. But in actuality I
would already be airborne, sailing, living in a metal shell hurtling through
the underbelly of clouds. Then the airplane would be touching the pavement of this distant realm. I would know instinctively where to go. My
cellular structure would direct me, would respond to what was remote
and uncalculated in the air. I would follow gulfs of fragrance in the green
veiled dusk. There I could learn the arts of dyeing cloth, steaming bamboo
shoots and singing from behind a carved and painted mask.

I thought you recognized my sophistication and elegance. I have a
capacity for nuance. I merely masqueraded as a creature of a wind callous
and indifferent. I had visions. A multitude of women simply vanish. They
enter a bus and chance upon the police or Immigration. They do not
return for dinner. They are placed in a cage near the illusionary border.
They are not permitted a telephone call. Later, they are flown south to
another land which does not want them.

Other women wander from the compound. With one inspired juxtaposition they scale the false walls. They become one with the air, the
avenues of amber and jasmine, and since they are drifting, they leave no
footprints. Not even dogs can find them.

But this was a foolish thought floating in and out of my gutted head. I
went nowhere.

I stared at the white-and-black printed pages Miguel patiently held for
me like offerings or a ticket into a world of stripped trees and wire fences
I did not wish to enter. I thought of Colorado, an American state where

Miguel had once taken me after he returned from Vietnam, we visited his friend from the Army, an American with red hair and blue eyes and a wife who looked very much as he did. In that region, everyone seemed as if they belonged to the same family, as if they were all cousins perhaps.

Miguel and that man from the Army and his wife laughed easily together. Of course they spoke English and I understood nothing. It was December. Winter spread itself across the surfaces, arrogant and white. Vain aggrieved flurries of snow fell like dust over boulevards simultaneously dry, brittle as a desert and yet stingingly cold.

Always, Miguel and the white man and woman were laughing. My bones responded and hardened. The trees were different there, stripped absolutely, mere wire. I became convinced English was a land of vicious sharp fences I did not wish to experience, ever. And the trees there were creatures of measured seasons, deciduous, American, with clocks embedded in their fibers. They obeyed.

Later, as the bus wound through the white hills, I longed to endure as they did, content in their silence. Although Miguel said nothing, I recognized he was disappointed in our visit. I had been as the landscape, remote and sheeted. And we did not see that red-haired man with his perpetually delighted white wife again.

Miguel no longer demanded my presence at his side while our dining-room table was erased beneath the pages of the English newspaper spread out like the wings of an enormous felled black-and-white eagle. An eagle tortured with the imprint of metal strips before it died, tattooed by a deranged American who inhabited a realm of silence and whiteness and trees which were naked, planted like stakes across a locked horizon.

With the birth of Carlos, our second son, Miguel accepted my preoccupation with the details of our house, the pyramids of baby bottles on the tiled kitchen counters, the cloth pyramids rising from baskets, waiting to be washed, dried, ironed. The necessity of my interior architecture was monumental and tangible. It was a web. I lived within it, camouflaged, safe.

Still, I had resisted Miguel's influence. My refusal was wedged on the periphery of his consciousness. It was a tiny crevice like a crack in pavement, a line thin as a scar but permanent. And the subject of the English language was let to drift out into the warm grasses and limed lawns of Flores Street, to mingle and spill its lost promise and sharp senseless edges in the air of neon and stalks of insistent yellow canna, across the fences adorned with branches which softened them. Then it floated farther, this terrible English thing, over the alleys of identically garbed boy-men, the vandals who lived in a terrain of nightness and blood and barking dogs. I was relieved.

I moved in a stupor between the objects which anchored and defined me. The glass bottles constantly drying, the clothing waiting to be washed, to be hung on the backyard line strung between the patio and the side fence, the perpetual acres of cotton demanding to be folded, mended. I stitched, stacked, polished and replaced. All that was required of me were my hands.

Angelina and Orquídea returned to the house of their mother. I did not need a calendar. When I heard their voices, I knew it was summer. In the hot nights, I listened as they cursed Marta Ortega, the bruja who read American and Spanish books alphabetically and redesigned the forms of nature. I wondered at their audacity and torment.

"You forced us to transcend convention," Angelina is accusing. It is airless, perhaps August. They are sitting in their courtyard with Joseph, the white man who loves other men.

"You regret this?" Joseph inquires.

Angelina is silent. They drink liquor by candlelight. Angelina has arrived with a suitcase. She has just returned from a vacation. Her expectations are extravagant. Always, she comes back to Flores Street in an agony of disappointment.

"I rushed into the jungle when he called," Angelina reveals. "I was molten, aching. Noon steamed. The wind in tea leaves and passion fruit." Angelina finishes her drink.

"Ah, the texture of passion, the density and danger you demand and imagine." Marta Ortega lights a cigarette.

"The bridge to his house," Angelina recalls. "Reaching through hibiscus and red ginger. The jungle decadent with embellishments, young, delinquent beneath inflamed stars. We mated wild."

"Blood leopard lovers?" Joseph muses. He pours himself another drink.

"You expect pain and receive it," Marta notes.

"I am your flesh sculpture. You created me," Angelina lashes back, her voice a howl.

Marta Ortega rises from the table. She carries a watering can and shears. She walks toward her garden.

"Wait, please," Angelina cries. "Help me, I beg you." Angelina runs after her mother. Marta pauses. It is past dusk.

"In each port, you are stranded and debased." Marta Ortega says. "You attract the fraudulent and transient."

"The wind is more intimate than my lovers," Angelina realizes, bitter. "More generous and specific."

"Your destruction is deliberate, predictable," Marta Ortega tells her daughter.

"I am careless," Angelina admits. "I have an absence of will."

"You are a tourist in your own life," Joseph points out. "You purchase trinkets and are, without exception, dissatisfied."

"What should I do?" Angelina shouts. Marta Ortega has walked into her garden. "What can I do?" Angelina repeats, louder. It is night.

"Summer in Paris, Madrid or Maui," Joseph says, "the shifting of exteriors and alphabets only. Your suitcases contain ignorance and accidents."

Angelina pours herself another drink. "There is not geography enough to fill me," she recognizes. Then she weeps.

Orquídea returns to Flores Street. She is carrying a large suitcase. As she parks her car at the curb, as she pushes the car door open, she is already pleading for counsel. Marta Ortega is cunning. She pretends she is losing her hearing. Orquídea follows her into the garden. Orquídea assaults her mother with details. It is summer. It is another loss.

"Are you saying you loved him?" Marta Ortega appears curious. She stares at her younger daughter.

"Yes," Orquídea says, her voice tremulous.

"It is the torn wind you love," Marta informs her. "The wreckage, the startled gasp of a reef ripped in half, a sunken galleon, a legion of condemned men, an inverted contagion beneath your feet."

Marta Ortega retreats into her terraced hillside. She knows that her daughters with their painted faces, their skirts of expensive silk and their high-heeled shoes will not dare follow her into the grasses and narrow paths of the garden.

"Mama," Orquídea screams.

And on one such afternoon or dusk, it occurred to me that nothing would substantially change. The weeping of Angelina or Orquídea faded into the night. I stood at my front-room window and, yes, I was profoundly pleased.

From my front-room windows Los Angeles was irrefutable in its enormity, its incessant rhythm and how it damaged the air, even in the sacred hours of invocations and private illuminations, prayer and communion. Still, the city was peripheral to me, our proximity merely accidental.

Los Angeles was terrifying, a wound hidden by poisoned air forming a grayish and impenetrable fence around it. At night lights were a piercing shaft, a form of metal emanating not from windows but from the eyes of legions of lunatics, the sort of men who would take the wings of an eagle and torture it with glass or metal. I could not bear the sheer weight of the city, its American vastness, and its assertion that the ground was insignificant, obsolete, and all breathing entities, from the tendrils if infant plants to things winged or limbed, could be eradicated. Across the radium plain, steel-reinforced structures clustered and rose, impervious to the possibility of earthquakes or enraged gods. They thought themselves larger and stronger than nature, more intelligent, devious, permanent.

I was protected from this distant disturbance by the objects of necessity which defined me. The city was merely the region where Miguel worked.

Once Miguel took me to his factory. He was adamant, he insisted. I had no idea why he wished me to accompany him. We rode a bus to a low brick building sitting beside a brutal gash of cement which was once the Los Angeles River. In past decades, there had been fish, currents, weeds and flowers growing profuse along its banks.

Marta Ortega had told me of a day in her youth when her brothers attempted to raft a tributary of el río de Los Angeles into the ocean. They planned to paddle their raft southward and sail back to Mexico. Marta Ortega said her brothers envisioned Mexico as a land of jaguar, coral orchids and trees which would drop coconuts, bananas and strawberries upon them like a kind of rain. I had laughed.

"It is not an anecdote intended to describe an act of foolishness," Marta Ortega had reprimanded me. "It was the one moment when they most clearly understood the nature of the world."

I was not certain what Marta Ortega meant. And Miguel was attempting to explain the intricacies of his factory to me. But I could not quite hear him. My skull was invaded by the image of the dead river, the murdered river. A chant formed in my mind, Forgive them, forgive them, they have deliberately and savagely slaughtered a river. They have denied it the caress of the sea and its unequivocal right of completion and return.

In the factory building there were no walls or partitions. It was cold. Here they manufactured pieces of metal necessary for the construction of certain vehicles and machines. Miguel became excited as he described the numerous varieties and purposes of these metal slats and plates. He took pleasure in their clever design and miraculous strength. He imbued with the qualities of a minor god this senseless process that birthed ugly objects.

I was introduced to men who worked with Miguel. Their eyes were flat, dulled gray as moths sucked into cities and stranded. Their eyes were dense with numbers and abstractions. And I did not peer where Miguel indicated. Something within me resisted as my mouth had said no to the language of English. My eyes refused this building and its crop of grotesque metal. I thought of the wantonly murdered river beside the brick factory building. Miguel did not mention the river. He might not have noticed it. And another gulf was forming between us, this time a crevice was rising across the surface of our eyes.

Then there were boulders in my ears, rocks that shut out Miguel and his chatter about the factory. I barely listened when he spoke with pride and emotion about the manufacturing of American objects. Obviously men who squandered their youth assembling hideous substances in a brick vault of a building bordering a butchered river were engaged in an unholy process. It was even possible that participating in this set of contrived occurrences was a form of evil.

But I said nothing. There were gullies between us, in our mouths and across the surfaces of our eyes, small cracks separating me from Miguel. The children were fed, were playing quietly, were watching television or sleeping. Night would be falling in a tapestry of grays and purples, turning at last into a blue which was startling, flawless as the folds of the dress of La Virgen de Guadalupe. It was enough that Miguel seemed satisfied.

Weeks and months mated and bled into one another. In the periphery, Miguel talked of quotas, contracts, promotions. My ears refused to hear him. The seasons were barely distinguishable. I could not remember why they were rumored to be significant. One morning, when it was unusually warm and undeniably spring, I planted lemon and avocado trees in my backyard, then a bed of marigold and carnation seeds. Canna and iris and geraniums appeared on their own accord.

When Marta Ortega was not surrounded by her daughters or her grandchildren, she instructed me in the tending of rosebushes. She was a brown nun, married to the earth. It was said she had been excommunicated, but I felt a purity in her presence. She was resplendent with detail. Often, we walked through her back garden, down her terraced hillside of orchids which were both her passion and her livelihood. Women and men journeyed from as far as Beverly Hills and Pasadena to buy them.

There were certain afternoons when Marta Ortega noticed me standing alone at my front-room windows and motioned me to descend my stairs and enter her house. She would give me a tendril or a green strand. I felt as if strips of flesh were being bestowed upon me. I was instructed to place these intricate fibers in a container of water until they issued forth fragile white roots, signaling their desire to penetrate the earth and their capacity to mate.

"To tend one garden is to birth worlds," Marta Ortega said softly.

She looked at my face. Marta Ortega was gracious and calm. She seemed constantly prepared for me to speak. But there was a channel between us I could not cross, a disrupted current like a rapid-laden river. I was different. I was not flamboyant and erratic like her Angelina and Orquídea with their dyed hair and midnight taxicabs, their plumage, psychiatrists, diets and astrologers. I did not have the blatant intensity of her daughters with their compulsion for risk and new identities, intrigues and rarities.

Marta Ortega offered me horchata, inquired as to the health of my family and plants. I longed to tell her of my discovery, of the music of leaves and their epics. Marta Ortega would understand this. But I felt myself dull in her presence, lacking in range, aspiration and scale. Angelina and Orquídea were brash and precipitous. Marta Ortega was accustomed to this form of tempestuousness. I existed only after the fact for her, in shadow. Or perhaps I was not yet fully formed. I realized Marta Ortega erased me from her personal landscape, her embroidery. She saw me as a chained thing, wingless, undecorated, a sparrow, a rain-spawned weed.

My trees and sons grew taller. Our house settled into the dirt. My shoots and tendrils with their dreamlike white roots began their dangerous and uncertain journey down into the earth, connected with the core and found acceptance. Then I entered into my silence.

I resisted memorizing the names of generals or capitals or the manner in which nations and territories changed their hypothetical borders. The extravagant behavior or sudden deaths of cinema stars and princes meant nothing. I was without interest in the invention of weapons, sciences which constructed human beings in glass tubes or hurled them into space. I knew this was an intrusion, temporary. The high tide would come and effortlessly erase the beach of its profusion of litter.

Still my anxiety persisted. I noticed that the sky never fully darkened or touched the earth as does a natural night when it is uniform and unmolested, embracing the dirt with an ease and a passion. The night I watched did not take the ground with necessity as it would a wife, with longing and assurance. This darkness was deformed, suspended, its flesh webbed with cables and the chicken feet of television antennas. It was scarred, continually frustrated and abused. I felt the night's wounds and unappeased desire for absolution and we shared this aching, this inexplicable pain.

Often I awoke on a chair in the front room or on the rug beneath the window. Days were damp. I was conscious of how heavy objects were, the unceasing acres of sheets in their basket, the plastic of clothespins, even the air. Continually, I felt as if I were walking through water. I was helpless, armless, like the representations of La Virgen de Guadalupe who is perpetually draped in a blue cape, as if she did not need fingers or hands at all, as if God moved the world through her eyes alone.

After Miguel left the house for his factory, for the brick vault bordering the murdered river, and José and Carlos had gone to school, I stood at my window and stared directly across the street at the courtyard of Marta Ortega. Her bougainvillea was beyond abundant, colossal in its layerings of burgundy, of a color in constant transition. Sometimes it seemed a shade of coral or fuchsia. It was the blood of the earth rising. I would think to myself, You are Gloria Hernández. You are staring at the wall of bougainvillea adorning the courtyard of Marta Ortega, the bruja who reads books unceasingly and transforms the elements of the earth.

Later, I studied the wild near-red geraniums claiming the blank sides of my front-yard lawn and told myself, You are Gloria Hernández. You are watching red geraniums rise like red clouds from their fraudulent sleep in the ground. They are like you, Gloria Hernández, brilliant with their disguise. They appear common and ordinary but are not. In this manner I ordered my hours and seasons.

I inhabited a region of constant repetitions and inconsequential variations. When it rained, the city seemed sullen, anchored beneath a grayish haze, colorless and acquiescent as the eyes of cows or clouds mirrored in deep wells. I would tell myself, Your name is Gloria Hernández. I reminded myself that Gloria Hernández was thinking about the eyes of cows and wells.

I remembered that other women and men assumed me erased of significance, vacant. They concluded I was devoid of intelligence and grace, but this was an illusion. I told myself, You are Gloria Hernández and you have contrived this. We know the reality of the buried creeks beneath the house, the invisible channels, the ways you are singular and rare. Then I smiled.

I was oppressed by a breathlessness, an anticipation, a sense of an impending omen, definitive. I lived awed, sheared, raw, at the shore of an enormity, at the lip of a monumentally cold and remote ocean which would one day open and the unutterable be revealed.

I was a city that time and occurrences had buried beneath dirt, rubber trees, banyan, palms and vines. I was a ruin the jungle had swallowed, as it laid its tendrils over the pyramids of the Yucatán, as it hung its green veils across the plazas, canals and gardens of Tenochtitlán, erasing the feathered capes of the lords and the images of the gods. Eventually I would be rediscovered, excavated, reassembled. The culture I had once been could be reconstructed based upon the coloration of my shards. If such a method were possible for a thing as complex as an entire city, certainly the rebirth of one woman was conceivable, perhaps even simple and inevitable.

Always, I was aware of a relentless other. It was ruthless beyond category or metaphor, a distinct entity, with a morphology, intelligence and purpose. It was real. And it sensed me. It was patient. It forgot nothing. In time, through a series of accidents, random chance and a confluence of events both in and outside of me, it would speak my name. At dusk, waiting for Miguel to return from his factory, I felt precisely as freshly plowed ground must feel, longing for resolution, shoots, buds, stray birds or a sudden mutation inspired by clouds.

Then, of course, the dormant bell in the buried chamber rang. The planet deserted its orbit, the climate was revised, the vegetation, the spectrum of recognizable colors, the lips and eyes of gods and women and men. It is strange that I, Gloria Hernández, who had been awaiting this cataclysm for decades would be astounded when the earth revealed herself, one partial syllable at a time, unmistakable, exactly as I had imagined.

Have I said it happened without warning, inexplicably, with an eerie simultaneity? A curandera might suspect magic in this series of unnatural events which stunned and severed me from the ordinary, which hurled me into an irredeemable exile.

One night when it was extremely hot, Miguel did not return from his factory. In the periphery, Roberto, Marta Ortega's youngest grandson, drove his loud green truck into the driveway of their house. I watched the young man unload the carpets he had not installed that day. They were fat coils he expertly draped across his shoulders. He looked as if he were carrying bloated boa constrictors around his neck. This in itself was abnormal. Ordinarily, I did not hear Roberto parking his noisy truck until after Miguel and our sons were seated together at our dining-room table.

But I resisted the portent in this. Even when I fed José and Carlos alone, I did not adequately perceive the absence of my husband. I washed the dinner plates carefully, with the exaggerated precision of a woman doomed. I returned them to their cupboards, their night graves. I was trying to erase the emptiness I intuited but refused to name with the architecture of the interior which was calming, the senseless moving of objects, the details, the tedium of repetition which protected me.

The incomplete night yawned. The moon was full. I reminded myself I was named Gloria Hernández. I told myself Gloria Hernández was watching the spectacle of an absolutely full moon sail above the city called Los Angeles. And the moon was a naked bitch, flaunting herself an obscene yellow above avenues of random jasmine, through bougainvillea-studded alleys and an idiot smog-blue summer night I suddenly realized I might not survive.

And because I was no one, I could be everyone. Do you understand this phenomenon? I watched Flores Street surrender to the thin darkness masquerading as night. Amber streetlamps appeared in unison, as if part of an intricate conspiracy.

Because I was no one, I was everyone, all women who stood at windows taunted by the terrible and too-hot moon, round as an open, screaming mouth. It was the time of my bleeding, my menstruation. I realized multitudes of women in the city called Los Angeles were simultaneously bleeding. Our bellies were planets turning on axis, in cycles immutable as the words of a god or the paths of a star. The women were smoking cigarettes on terraces, hanging clothing above stucco alleys, millions of them, swollen, foul-smelling and mourning what might have been.

They were leaning out of windows and terraces, staring down at miniature suggestions of gardens, alongside gashes of boulevards. They were waiting for their lovers or husbands, uncertain, agitated. There was no breeze against their faces, their polished cotton curtains, their white ruffled curtains, the acres of curtains of their lives.

I, Gloria Hernández, who did not smoke, found Miguel's cigarettes and lit one. The transformation was beginning. I was undergoing my undetectable surgery and becoming someone else. And I knew the thoughts of all waiting women. We posed with rouged cheeks. We stood in freshly washed cotton or silk, with bare feet or high-heeled satin sandals, our flesh perfumed. We wore the smell of lilacs and musks not to intoxicate, but rather to ward off the odor of terror clinging to our skin, the fear scent that men could detect.

I thought of Consuelo López who lived at the bottom of Flores Street in an obscenely pink house she had painted herself. She became my sister. Consuelo López in her absurdly pink house waited in perfumed stasis for her lover to come from Mexico as he had vowed. He reaffirmed his promise in weekly letters, but there were inexplicable obstacles, reversals, ambiguities. Consuelo López stood at the edge of the sidewalk even in rain, hungry for the postman who feared her as he did certain dogs studding his route.

Suddenly, I knew the lamentations and prayers, incantations and curses of Consuelo López and continents of other women. There were no divisions. We were thinking he would pack his suitcases this night. Or crash the car, drunk. He was in the arms of another woman or locked in a cage by the police. Perhaps he had forgotten his address and the reason why he lived there. He might have suffered a humiliation from which he could not recover or return. The possibilities of cataclysm were multifarious as the bougainvillea-draped alleys of the city, as the intersections punctuated by blanched palms. And we stood at our windows, on terraces above miniature implications of gardens, paralyzed.

Night smelled of abandonment, blood and betrayal, a heart rotten, broken. This was its secret underbelly. The telephone which did not ring, the empty letterbox, the doorbell no finger touched. We painted our fingernails and mouths. Our shoes would be pointed, shined, a fine leather which strapped at the ankle. Later, we placed our shoes back in a tissue-lined box in the closet. Then we would wash the paint from our cheeks and eyes.

Something was rising from our collective terror and misery. The air was charged. It was not clouds precisely, but tiny wounded sounds, collecting and forming shapes, omens, holes in the bruised darkness no incantation could heal or contain. Dreams were awakening, entering rooms, three-dimensional, real. They spoke our names. And even though it was August, the spine of summer, I shivered with a strange chill. I covered my shoulders with a shawl while the bitch of a moon rose higher and drifted like a lost ship, white as a flag of surrender above the apathetic palms.

Did I tell you it was August and the moon burned? She was blatant that night, first yellow and then a polished white like bone or a disc which could be strung and worn around the neck. The air was textured, embroidered and somehow solid.

I realized Marta Ortega could assist me. Her English was perfect, her memory unimpaired. Her tone would command attention and respect. She was, after all, a natural citizen.

Of course an unexpected doorbell would not startle her. Angelina and Orquídea often arrived in taxicabs at midnight. They left their children on the porch of the house on Flores Street and drove away to airports. They carried passports in their purses like appendages to their flesh. Marta Ortega would not be surprised by a sudden knocking of a fist against wood. There was the profusion of Angelina's and Orquídea's offspring, the children of their numerous American husbands, arriving in brightly painted cars and vans, carrying sleeping bags and musical instruments and holding the hands of their even lighter-skinned girlfriends and boyfriends. They spoke Spanish with terrible American accents. One could barely understand them. They wanted to burn American flags and build farms in the northern forests. They slept until noon. Their chickens would starve. Their hands were without calluses. It was rumored one of her grandsons had been arrested for possessing marijuana. There had been lawyers and telephone calls, judgments and fines. Yes, Marta Ortega could aid me.

I trembled and rocked back and forth in my bare feet, swaying like the fronds of palms in a storm. I was abnormally wide-eyed and indecisive. Then my body split into two parts, both of which were identical. One of me was on the outside. I could study the other Gloria Hernández as one can a character on a television screen.

I watched Gloria Hernández decide instead to knock on the door of her closest neighbors, Rico and Linda Almáraz. She climbed the stairs of their house, then her legs locked, refusing her command to continue. Gloria Hernández stared at the street, observing the lights which had been extinguished. She realized Rico and Linda Almaraz would be in bed, bathed in the soft radium glow of their television, in nightclothes, perhaps even in the act of making love. And we could not intrude upon their private acre of stillness, shatter their diminutive state of temporary blue grace or wake their children. We could not spill our terror into their hushed and unsuspecting air. We would not violate them, no.

It became darker, stiller, like the vestibule of a buried chamber or a tunnel leading to a metal-encased vault. Then Roberto, the young grandson of Marta Ortega, shut off their porch light. This was perceived as a meaningful signal by my legs, which were now composed of a strange substance, perhaps wood. I was a kind of worm. I thought in terms of inches. I crept along the immense surface of the sidewalk rehearsing my words so I would not forget them. I would say, My name is Gloria Hernández. My sons are in their bunk beds, sleeping. My husband has disappeared. No, he would not simply vanish without saying goodbye, if not to me, then to his sons. This is an aberration. The police must be called. Yes, it is safe, we are citizens. And I do not speak English. I am terrified.

I remembered Consuelo López. Once, I had thought the pink of her house repellent and sickening. It tore at my nerves as a pink-painted coffin might. I misunderstood her intention. Her house was the pink of an imploring mouth.

I walked halfway down the hill that was Flores Street, down the street I shall never see again, toward the house of Consuelo López. Lights blazed, intoxicated, specific as the yellow beams in a remote lighthouse in winter. We were sisters. She too never fully slept. She had lived two years in a state of constant and unbearable waiting. Two years, longer than it takes to birth and wean a son or regain one's senses after a father or a husband has died. I had dismissed her grief as inappropriate. Now I understood her.

My legs stopped like a machine which has exhausted its supply of fuel. My body was becoming useless. I was caught in webs of incongruent possibilities. Suddenly I realized that in her delirium of pink anticipation, Consuelo López kept her front-room lights permanently lit. It was a ritual beacon for her lost husband. Somewhere within the pink wound of her house, within her assertion of yellow light, she was probably sleeping. Or, worse, painting her fingernails now crimson, now apricot or lilac, studying her hands beneath lamplight, imagining their variations, how they might look by noon sun or the amber of candles. My knock would startle her, she with her fingers each painted differently and her hair uncombed. She would thiink it the fist of her husband. Consuelo López would open her front door. Her disappointment would be unbearable.

As I began climbing the hill I heard the church bells from Nuestra Señora de los Dolores. I counted them. It was 10 P.M. precisely. I had lived on Flores Street for fifteen years, yet I rarely heard the bells at night. I was struck by this oddity. Of course, the church had outposts everywhere and the bells reached into the darkness, subliminal, fundamental to the design.

It was 10 P.M. I heard the echo of the last church bell floating through the night, leaving a small wake in its path like the tender liquid scars boats engrave across the surface of water. The moment was seamless, immense.

It was 10 P.M. And the heart could not be calm.

As I walked up Flores Street I noticed that the lights were lit in the corner house next door to Marta Ortega. It was the Spanish mansion where the aged white men lived. The house was designed by an architect, the materials were ravaged but still asserted an opulence. Here the two white men had lived as lovers since they were mere boys.

When I forced myself to buy groceries, it was necessary I pass their house. Perhaps that was one reason why it was difficult for me to push my body across the enormous inches comprising the sidewalks of my awful journey. Always, they waved at me, called me by name, offered me coffee, juices or horchata.

I refused, even when Marta Ortega was sitting in their front-courtyard patio with them, at their round dining table which they draped with linen cloths at night. They would have sprays of Marta Ortega's orchids in heavy glass vases on their linen-draped table. Often Marta Ortega would eat with them. From my front-room windows I observed them laughing, half listening to records in English. It was the music of women who sounded haunted and broken singing in a kind of torment.

Marta Ortega treated the old lovers with the grace and fluidity ordinarily reserved for blood relatives. She insisted that her grandchildren refer to them as uncles. I did not comprehend her ease with them or why she sought their company almost daily. The two were similar in their aging: blanched, stained and featureless. I knew one was named Joseph and the other Bill. But they were like ruined walls in a deserted pueblo rains and winds have engraved with dust and veins of emptiness. I could not tell them apart, and this embarrassed me. I thought it necessary I address them by name and they would realize I could not distinguish which was Joseph and which was Bill. This would be perceived as yet another sign of my stupidity.

There was something more, yes. Their obvious proximity to death disturbed me. They were both dying, stubbornly, tediously. They coughed and spat blood and slept separately now, it was said, in different rooms. I could not ignore them as I turned the corner to the school on Alta Vista Street with José or Carlos. Always I was assaulted by the singing of the women in English. The composition did not change. They were drinking alcohol and, in the mornings, working puzzles in the American newspaper and arguing loudly, as if events in China or Chile had a direct application to them. They were ludicrous. I thought it more appropriate they consider the magnitude of the sin of their union and the climate of their future geography.

Occasionally, I imagined I was speaking with them. "Is there a river in hell?" I would ask.

"Of course," one would say. "It can be mastered and rafted like any other."

"And the flames?"

"Like all that burns, subject to variations, nuances. It is always relative," he would say.

"And it couldn't be worse than Houston in July," the other would add.

"We are, of course, bringing suntan lotion and asbestos with us," the first would say.

"We do not believe in hell," Marta Ortega might inform me.

"It is an antiquated kingdom. A flash in the pan," one of the white men who seemed identical in their bleached wornness would pronounce. "It disappeared like a suburb in Etruria. It was erased like the dragons that were once drawn across the oceans on maps."

Of course I could never actually speak with them. They were too polished in their quickness, too finely rehearsed, like Angelina and Orquídea, with their dyed hair, doctors and constant changes of religion and husbands. They bantered in code. They would think me provincial and immune to invention, with my hair not adequately trimmed or curled, with my low-heeled shoes and drab skirts, with my deliberate absence of color. Quantity and variety had muted them. They read only the clues of the surface. They thought this made them exceptional and smart.

My eyes ached as I looked at their house. It was an exposed nerve, raw, in visible agony. Their yard was a ruin. Bougainvillea thrashed the wall of their courtyard like a cancer eating a throat. Roots consumed the plaster and the bricks. Their roof leaked, rain etched grooves in what had decades before been white paint. Obviously, their names were being engraved by the elements which would soon claim them. They would wear the earth skin and their eyes would be clouds. If hell was a nonexistent country. If they found the river. If they were fortunate.

I was standing on the sidewalk below my house, leaning against the trunk of a palm. My name was Gloria Hernández. My sons were sleeping in their bunk beds. My husband was missing. And the bark beneath my fingers felt broken and hard, studded with tiny etchings, intricate hieroglyphics. The trunk was scratched, as if deliberately. There were elaborate symbols beneath my fingers where an entire saga had been tattooed. The flesh of the tree seemed familiar and intimate. Then I made a decision. Yes, the old men who were an abnormality of nature and yet friends of Marta Ortega would know whom to telephone, how to phrase the questions and translate the answers. They could pierce the deliberate static which was the expression of the English language, the words that dropped like rocks from white mouths.

I had been in their huge decaying house only once. One warm spring morning, motivated by courtesy, I accepted their offer of coffee. To refuse indefinitely was a flagrant insult. When I crossed the front-courtyard patio and realized my body had actually entered their home, I was frightened. They attempted to pour brandy into my coffee. They claimed it tasted like oranges the sun had caressed, made molten as a form of liquid spice. Of course I refused.

Then, without introduction or prologue, as if the ordinary proprieties did not exist, one of the white men began speaking in excellent Spanish. He was telling me a story about his youth. He was nineteen years old in a city to the north, San Francisco, where there was an enormous port and sidewalks crowded with sailors. He lit one cigarette after another as he recounted this anecdote. He poured more of the orange-scented liqueur. The orchids of Marta Ortega were fragrant with the implication of oranges and the air was strange and dense with a sense of pollens and filtered smoke, a glowing, foreign, alien. There was a dizzying excess of amber.

I sat down on their yellow sofa. It was frayed, I noticed, but recently dusted. This lover of other men was saying colonels had taken him in glass elevators to hotel rooms above a bay which was bluer then, with the water wilder, younger, more assured of its purpose and direction. He made the bay sound irresistible, as if it were a rare wine or holy water, pure enough to drink.

They had shelves filled with photograph albums. The other man, the one who had not been taken to hotel rooms by colonels, opened a book at random and pointed to a boy he claimed was himself. This irrelevent approximation of an earlier version of himself was smiling, the man explained, because he had just won a dancing contest in a place called Memphis in 1936. He still seemed proud of this. I realized vanity lingers. I said nothing.

They possessed an astonishing number of photographs. My eyes ached, assaulted by the fifty years of summer vacations stuck between cellophane pages. I was awed by greenery and avenues lined with statues of warriors, saints and kings and stalls of flowers, fish, cloths and flasks. The seashores, oceans and ports seemed interminable. I became disoriented, staring at water, blues and greens below cliffs burdened with red flowers. And there was the impenetrable scent of oranges in their house, the thick air, like a kind of incense perhaps.

"You don't have to really look at them," the man who had won the dancing contest said, indicating the book of photographs I held like a slab of stone in my hands. "We know they are boring."

"Like life," his lover said.

"Tedious as the photographs are, they are superior to the actual experience," the one who had won the dancing contest said.

"Indeed," the other had agreed. "In reality, the colors are muted and confused, the outlines less intense."

"We save them to remember how meaningless they are."

"Quite true," his lover concurred.

"It's all a ten-cent postcard gone in a flash."

"Gone the unmolested acres of mahogany that were the Yucatán," the one who had been taken to hotel rooms by colonels said, pouring more of the orange-scented brandy into his glass and the glass of his lover.

"Gone, too, the unmolested acres of orange groves that were Los Angeles," the other added.

"Gone the centaurs and the mermaids. Java Man, Peking Man and the young men of the innocent San Francisco Bay," the other said with a sadness that moved me.

Then they began dancing and laughing. They danced badly, erratically, without precision or grace. They crashed through the room with a raw passion which both intrigued and offended me. There was the disorienting fragrance of oranges in the brandy and in the numerous vases of orchids from the garden of Marta Ortega. And women were singing their haunted and savagely torn songs in English. It was the first time the language of English seemed accessible to me, vulnerable, sealike, gentle and bruised.

And the day dissolved into green, patches of river-moistened moss, strands of turquoise and jade, and the liquids which spill from split emeralds. Joseph and Bill were justified by green. Soft white sunlight brushed the walls of their collapsing house, cracking at the seams as the limbs of the earth reached out and called them by name.

Their strained extravagance was an attempt to banish the anxiety of death. This was why they danced. They were resisting the ordinary simplicities. I watched them, hypnotized. Their phonograph records were scratched. One of the white men was nearly deaf. He wore a soiled suit, more yellow than white, and a hat which might once have matched his jacket. Perhaps, years ago, this had been elegant attire. And the two old white men embraced as they danced, as they spilled glasses of the orange-scented brandy, merging with the green noon, changing the records, executing now the suggestion of a rhumba, now a waltz. And they danced until they fell down.

I was standing near the curb, staring at the house where the two dying lovers lived. The moon was indecently hot and full and white. She stalled above me, her message urgent but incomprehensible. The tattooed trunk of the palm tree I leaned against was also attempting to communicate with me. It was an unexceptional palm, frail-headed, prepared to bear another night when the stars would reveal nothing and the neon of the city deny it even the solace of sleep. My legs poised at the curb. I would cross the concrete that separated us. My hands were ready to cup themselves, to knock my locked fingers against their door. That was when I heard my telephone ringing.

My legs, which were short-circuiting, responded, startled. I ran up my front stairs. It was Miguel. He was speaking rapidly in a whisper. I could barely understand him. He was in the hospital. He had been injured in the factory. These facts sailed through the telephone wires and struck me in the head like arrows or bullets or meteorites which are still part fire.

I told myself, Your name is Gloria Hernández. Your husband has been injured, has been taken by ambulance to Queen of Angels Hospital. You must remember this. You will repeat these facts to Marta Ortega. She is a bruja. She will not be angry when you wake her. She will order her grandson Roberto to drive you to the hospital. This is the continent she has cultivated, nurtured. She is a deranged botanist. She inhabits a region of orange-scented orchids flaunting their exquisite beauty. But beneath these petals, her sculptures are inexplicable and unholy. Ring her bell. She is accustomed to this, the shattering of darkness with words of catastrophe. It is her secret pleasure.

But Miguel was saying no, I need not journey to the hospital. He was fine. I must listen closely. He did not sound like a wounded man. His voice contained an excitement, a crispness, like dusk in autumn when a wind rises raw, hinting of intrigue and discovery. He had spoken with an attorney. He could collect disability insurance. The United States government would pay him money for not working. Glass shards, objects of metal and concrete were rushing through the telephone cables and striking my head, my hand. Miguel promised to call later, when it was safe, he said. Safe, I repeated, wondering what the nature of his danger was. Then he hung up the telephone.

I slept or did not sleep. I woke or did not wake. I was Gloria Hernández. I was Consuelo López. I was all women who through an accumulation of accidents find themselves in a stasis of waiting. We atrophied in pastel rooms with vases of fading brittle carnations, brass-framed beds and windows with city views. From tiny iron spokes of balcony we stared at miniature square gardens beneath full moons where we ripened and went rotten, turned bitter, stagnant. The sea breeze gnawed our sheen.

The morning was extremely blue like an ocean or a winged jungle predator, certain, strong and deliberate. A creature of dream, presumed in error to be extinct. José and Carlos were in high school on the other side of Sunset Boulevard. They no longer permitted me to walk with them. As they turned the corner at Manzanita Street, I waved a goodbye into the air, but they did not deviate from their course, glance back once or notice. I was insignificant, a part of the landscape, a lamppost, a vacant yard. My sons thought me ignorant. They were ashamed of me. Other mothers spoke English, styled their hair and drove automobiles. Then I forced myself across the enormity of asphalt to the market as if the day were typical, merely an agony of blue, a morning like any other.

Miguel had cautioned me to say nothing to anyone. Surely my neighbors were aware of his absence, but no one directly confronted me. They responded to his disappearance with respectful distance. I was grateful. A vanished spouse is a tangible manifestation of disturbance, a severing of the ordinary, a potential disaster. Such events must be sealed shut behind lips that are metal. Words can be brutal and dangerous. They can strike with ferocity. What remains unrevealed is hidden for a reason.

Then Miguel was stepping out from the backseat of a taxicab. I had never seen him in such a vehicle. Taxicabs were an anomaly on Flores Street, a rarity like orchids, a method of transportation employed only in irrefutable emergencies such as childbirth. Taxicabs were the glaring yellow vehicles used by Angelina and Orquídea and no one else. The taxicab was an object of their exclusive domain, of the lavish and precipitous. And

Miguel was limping toward our house, bent, like a man beaten and aged. The taxicab was enormous, a conflagration of yellow behind him.

My husband stared at our front room as if it were a vestige from an earlier life in which the details had faded into a vagueness, an obscurity, like the out-of-focus backgrounds of the countless photographs of oceans the two old white lovers, Joseph and Bill, had stuck between cellophane pages. Miguel sat down on the sofa. When I brought him coffee and pastries, he smiled. The shape of his lips seemed oddly inappropriate, a juxtaposition which seared like the raw yellow metal of the taxicab. There was an aberration of yellow and incongruencies. The glare of his lips, the implication of the taxicab and the cane which he now leaned against the sofa near his leg. The cane was a kind of appendage or deformity. And the smile twisting the contours of his lips, like a sudden explosion of rain flooding the natural channel of a river.

"Your leg," I began, staring at the sofa, the cane.

Miguel swept my fears away with a flick of his hand. My terror was no more significant than a stray insect, something to be brushed aside, automatically, without effort. Even his eyes seemed to be smiling. "This is nothing," he said firmly.

As if to demonstrate this reality, he tossed the cane across the room. It clattered like the severed limb of a tree, a branch crashing against a wooden porch. Then he walked without a limp to my side. He embraced me. "This is a fabulous opportunity, a new beginning," Miguel said with conviction. Then he was walking past me, explaining that the United States government would send him checks every month forever. He would never need to work again.

I did not understand his happiness, not at that moment or later, when, with a paper and pen, he assembled a list of numbers. He motioned me to sit next to him as he explained the significance of his carefully written numbers, one by one. They proved we would have as much money with disability insurance as we had when he worked at the factory.

It was a miracle, he shouted. We should celebrate. He instructed me to buy beer in the market, changed his mind and told me to purchase tequila. Then he turned on the radio.

Miguel had dispatched me, had given me a direct command, and yet I did not obey. Instead, I stared at his cane, his leg which was undamaged and the numbers he had embossed across the paper. They might have been the scrawls chickens leave in dust. This is a mere design of ink, a series of symbols without resonance, I thought. The numbers might have been the addresses of strangers.

His joy was incomprehensible to me. I believe it was then, on the day he returned from Queen of Angels Hospital, that he began to think me stupid. The crevices webbing the surface of our eyes were finally visible to him. The gulfs and channels separating us, yes, he could sense them at last. He did not say this with words. His eyes said it, his lips and the texture of his skin. He was viewing me from a slightly revised angle. It was as if he had suddenly realized I was a grazing animal, a cow perhaps. Or a goat on a muddy rut of a road in an abandoned pueblo. It was even possible, as he surveyed me from his altered vantage point, that he thought me less, perhaps a hedge or a lawn or a wall.

Sun hung without mercy, bloated, seething with poisons, rancid and dangerous. An excess of yellow. And the sun was the color of the eyes of a man who has transformed his blood by the constant drinking of tequila. A man who will one day take his jacket and guitar, leave the house and never return. A man who will vanish except for his terrible smell which even a curandera will be unable to release from the air.

Summer was suspended and Miguel was always with me. He cast shadows like nets where he walked, where he sat. The house shrank. The relentless density of him made me tremble. The sheer weight of him shifted the balance of our rooms, the orbit of the house, the quality of the light and our private climate.

When I returned from the market, Miguel was lying in bed, staring out the window. His eyes lacked focus or conviction. He draped his legs across the front-room sofa and watched television programs indiscriminately. Later, he read the American newspaper one interminable page at a time, as if he had an eternity for merely sitting, as if his fingers had been devised merely for the turning of paper as a great Spanish lady is born to hold only lace, pearls and a fan.

Miguel reread certain newspaper pages, tenderly, savoring the black-and-white embossed symbols, as if he were on the verge of a monumental discovery. He spent entire afternoons engaged in an activity he described as studying and thinking. He said ideas were growing in his head, structures and networks were emerging like cities. The forms were not yet solid and connected, the highways and cables not functional, the paint not dry. He was determined to force these pieces into place.

Of course I perceived the disguised implications Miguel had yet to recognize. He was designing a continent in which I was unnecessary. I was aware of this as one with a terminal disease cannot ignore its ravagement. Miguel could compile lists of numbers and names of capitals until his fingers bled. I already possessed the answer. In time, he would realize he did not want me. This was inevitable.

The first summer after the accident which was not an accident, Miguel fixed the front-porch railing and steps. For an entire hot season, he hammered incessantly, trying to penetrate the silence between us with the hard and tangible, boards and bricks, cement and nails, the elements men designate as solid and unassailable. Miguel measured, carted lumber, sanded and painted.

His acts were a transparent subterfuge. Obviously, his embellishments in our house on Flores Street were metaphors for the city he was erecting in his head, that as yet unformed realm which excluded me absolutely. And the silence between us could not be hammered into order. It lay between us like a mountain range or an ocean.

Then Miguel stopped his senseless hammering. He slackened and fattened. He wore nightclothes all day. He seemed drugged, adrift in a private latitude, a density which was transforming even his morphology. Perhaps he thought he could make his body as large as his purpose. Or that his flesh could become a kind of sail. But the wind rejected him. His stacks of blue-inked chicken scrawls rested like a blanket across his expanding lap. The sofa bore the constant imprint of his sitting. Miguel was becalmed.

My husband awakened only when our sons returned. The three of them leaned over their English textbooks, the books I could not read, as if they were engaged in a sacrament. Later, they spoke with excitement in English about American sports.

Their conversations were unfathomable, studded with English words for animals and machines. They pronounced these words as if they were an invocation, a spell containing magic. And our house was invaded by rams, tigers, bears, dolphins, cowboys, cubs and raiders, eagles and redbirds, steelers and jets and rockets. It was impossible. These birds and carnivores, fish and thieves were various teams emanating from distant American cities. There were subtleties within this chaos. My ears dulled. A hill formed across the side of my face.

In the mornings, they read the reports of these sporting events in unison, animated, sharing information, engaging in speculations and predictions. It was a form of communion. More English words, each syllable a rock, their mouths were avalanches.

I spooned food onto the plates in front of them, deciding upon the size of the portions, the textures and colors which formed a composition only I perceived. They received my offerings in silence. I did not appreciate the intricacies of American sporting events or understand why, fundamentally, such displays were important.

I created the illusion I was necessary, if only in a rudimentary fashion. I rattled plates and utensils in the kitchen. I constructed a geometry of foods on their plates, pyramids and rivers. They would starve without me, I tried to insinuate. My acts were fraudulent, trite and listless repetitions. And only my hands were required.

I sat alone in my backyard garden scrutinizing the shifting of shadow and sun across the wooden railing Miguel had hammered, sanded and repainted. Sun and shadow engaged in unrepeatable and complicated rituals. The wind was an incantation, a chant. The air formed patterns like waves painting dawn shores in nameless coves where the jungle rises from mists, verdant, fragrant, colossal.

Houses perched as if they bloomed in annual cycles or paused on the soft ridges of cliff like certain ocean birds. Goats pushed up puffs on coconut-palm hills. Flamboya was a liquid red, framing a port with petals and flame. The edges were thermal. One could navigate by heat beneath an undivided sun.

Farther, rivers were crowded with thin men in boats close and white as strung skin. Women arranged flowers at the ritual birthday of a god. The air was hot, opiated, sullen with experience. In such regions, women were draped in gowns of flower petals. One shed excess, became lean as a new moon, a bamboo sapling rising after rain. Flesh was unnecessary. One exposed the raw architecture of bone, kneeling at a ceremony of green tea at dawn.

Sometimes I did not hear my sons and my husband when they shouted demands through the windows. I was an appliance they were switching on. They were hungry. They wanted food wrapped in plastic to take to the park with the lake surrounded by palm trees where they practiced sports. Their voices were commands.

When my husband or my sons verbalized an enthusiasm, an interest or an idea, however banal or transitory, I was expected to encourage them. They were unaware of my boredom, my rage born from constant exclusion and their unshakable assumption of my invisibility upon request. I could have been a potted plant, sturdy, requiring only occasional watering.

They informed me that they would not return before nightfall. Or they were yelling that they were cold. They wanted me to bring their jackets. Failure to respond immediately resulted in blatant annoyance. I observed the faces of my husband and my sons, their expressions of anger and contempt, their lips barely concealing a snarl.

I knew what I was. The details defined me. I was an insignificant moon, remote, unnamed, too barren to conquer. I was a refrigerator that walked, a closet with arms and legs. I was a vacant city lot where bamboo rots, cats stalk occasional moths and the desert stretches and threatens. I lived my life as if dying, modest in my taking, weak in my grasp. A self-proclaimed terminal woman in my private ward, satisfied with a slat of cloud-ridden sky, one palm with a skirt of straw stripped by winter wind. I lived by implication, waiting for purpose and clarity to descend from the sky like a hurricane. I was numb from limbo and failure. Days passed when I did not say a single word. No one noticed this.

José and Carlos left the house for their schools. I handed them their jackets and lunch bags. They said nothing. It was suddenly autumn, the winds howling and rattling like broken shells at the millennium when the sea floor has at last been swept. I was an empty husk winds had left. My umbilical cord of fresh dirt and flat worms was cut. I was less than leaves lying curled like angry fists in alleys and gutters. They had substance and form. You could hear their bones cracking as you stepped on them.

Miguel was sitting with his American newspaper spread across our dining-room table. He was wearing pajamas and slippers. This was usual. The trees beyond my kitchen window were jettisoning leaves like birds divesting themselves of excess plumage before a storm. I was thinking of the necessity of flight and the principles of aerodynamics, of rubbing my flesh into the gray sides of purposeful clouds. I wondered whether Miguel no longer dressed because he too was convalescing. Or perhaps our life together had become a form of sleep or disease for him. Then Miguel said, "I think you should get a part-time job."

I was heating tortillas on the stove. In my confusion, I burned them. I glanced out the kitchen window. The sky was crowded with clouds of unknown intentions. The sun I once despised and cursed had abandoned me. Miguel said, "You should leave the house more often."

I stared at my husband, openly, struck by this oddity. This man who spent entire days in pajamas wanted me to leave my house with greater frequency. He was saying he could manage our sons, he enjoyed this and they required little now. Our sons were trained dogs. They knew their territory and limitations. They returned to the house only when the darkness was indisputable and their bellies signaled the pain that was hunger. They returned if they encountered more formidable predators or if they thought their father would take them to the park surrounded by palms to practice one of their American sports with them.

Miguel was saying it would do me good to work three days a week, to work part time. He kept stressing the part-time aspect of this. "It will open your eyes," he said, his voice neutral, deliberately casual and false.

Miguel spread out the American newspaper. It covered the table completely, like a cloth, and I thought, So this is the mantilla of the twentieth century. He was doing something with a pen. He was circling tiny black-and-white boxes with a heavy-tipped blue pen, thicker than the pen you use. These circled boxes represented possible employment opportunities for me. I watched as Miguel made telephone calls, smoked cigarettes and drank a third bottle of beer.

"There is a world you never see. You should broaden your horizons," Miguel informed me as he held the telephone, as he dialed one series of numbers after another, as he spoke in English to strangers. "Broaden your horizons," Miguel repeated.

He was demanding a surgery of the eyes for me. A correction of my vision had been deemed necessary. I did not know whether such operations were possible. I wondered whether such a procedure would be expensive and painful. No, I did not understand what Miguel meant. Clearly, he was speaking in code. His intentions were obvious. He could not tolerate my presence in the house with him each day. I was unnecessary, an affliction. Even my sons abhorred me. I was holding tortillas over the blue flames of the stove. They turned to black scraps in my hands, like the parchments of the Indian wise men, the histories and science and magic the Spanish soldiers and priests burned in the chambers of the pyramids.

I longed to explain to Miguel that it would be a torment to leave my arched front-room windows with the sea-blue drapes we had purchased the previous Christmas, store-made curtains which erased the irradiated plain called Los Angeles with a single pull of their fine strong cord. I wanted Miguel to recognize I was without interest in this broadening of my horizons. Did he not intuit that from my front-room windows I could see beyond the low hills, the sea and the harbors?

Miguel was constantly with me. He noticed that my hair was uncombed, I rarely bathed and night haunted me. I awakened on the front-room floor, on the border of darkness and that gaping other. I was afraid of sleep, the journey down to the sea floor of sharp corals and the struggle to find the surface again, to force my lungs to receive the air, one alien molecule of oxygen at a time. And always, I sensed the thing within. It agitated and wanted. It said, Surrender, come to me, now. It will be effortless, like returning to a city in which you once lived. Let the streets move you as they would an army or a leaf. You will hear the river, see the steeples. You cannot get lost. Trust me.

Miguel was determined and my silence was an acquiescence. I stood in the backyard letting the wind bite and whittle me. The hiss of wind which has recently ripped sagebrush and thistle lashed my face. I wanted it to tear out my useless ears and mouth. Then winter erupted in gusts of cold and veils of rain. A storm like an exploding shell. The air sharpened with detail. Miguel finally saw me as I was. My heart was a rotting stump. I bore the cold rain while he made telephone calls. I was accepting as a manzanita or a palm, amputated by lightning.

Then it was arranged. Miguel wrote down the specific times and the address of my place of employment on a piece of white, blue-lined notebook paper. The details were like the elaborate machinery of a lie memorized in a foreign language, one tortured and meaningless syllable at a time. I would leave the house on Flores Street at eight each Monday, Wednesday and Friday morning. I would walk to Sunset Boulevard and take any eastbound bus into the center of the city, to Seventh Street.

Miguel described my duties. He offered me a beer which I declined. My future task seemed without nuance. I was to be a clerk. I would fill numbers in on sheets of differently colored papers. The papers proved to be blue, pink and yellow. They were thin and moist in my hands like patches of severed skin. These pages were invoices. I was preparing them for a process called keypunch. Miguel stressed the simplicity of my work, as if in my irrefutable inadequacy the absence of complexity was an inducement. Miguel assured me repeatedly that I would board the three-o'clock bus and leave the terrible wound of the city, walk up Flores Street and be inside my house before José and Carlos returned.

I had served my limited purpose. I was no longer necessary. In fact, my presence was not even acceptable.

That night I lay by my husband's side, but I could not sleep. The wind bellowed and the tree branches and the dogs answered. There was a plenitude of information, complicated and interwoven. I could smell my fear. I silently repeated the details I had painfully memorized. The time of my bus. The address of the building on Seventh Street. The meaning of the papers called invoices.

Miguel walked me to the bus stop as once I had accompanied my sons who were no longer aware of my physical existence to their school on Alta Vista Street. Perhaps my husband supervised my journey to the bus stop because he suspected I would run away or, at the final second, fail to follow his instructions. My hands were shaking, but Miguel was not aware of this. The winds were tearing at the trees, eating the aberrant surviving leaves and, insatiable and redundant, tearing the twigs and the bark. The air was everywhere alive and chaotic, charged, rustling the fabric of the world, the fronds of the palms, the hair and the scarves of the other waiting women. Even the bus seemed to sway as finally I entered it.

The bus pushed its arduous and uncertain way through wind wild as an ocean current. The bus was more a ship than an object with wheels. I was driven past Nuestra Señora de los Dolores, the church which had once been ours, years ago, before American sports became our sacrament. Then the bus passed the market and finally the park with the lake surrounded by palm trees where Miguel and our sons sometimes went on

Sundays in summer, when the sun was fierce and the miniature lake provided the illusion of shade and cool. The park where Miguel now often took our sons to practice American sports, the goals and rules of which I could not master, like the English language and the machinations of politics, the names of disco singers and the proclivities of film stars. The part of me that resisted.

The bus turned up into the city and I gripped the side of my seat like a woman on a boat in a storm. I had not entered the center of the city since Miguel took me to his factory, when he explained the diversity and durability of the metal slabs he welded in a low brick building beside the gash of ugly cement, the carcass of a butchered river. The building where Miguel no longer worked.

Then I was transported across a border into a land of glass and steel, metal spears, fields of pavement where nothing grew, not even geraniums or oleander, plants which require virtually nothing. I realized there would be no stray palms here, patches of wild iris or occasional birds. Billboards assaulted the slow-rising hills, shattering their calm green with gigantic white faces with teeth like ridges of pearl and eyes liquid and blue as the waters of glaciers. I was awed. Days passed before I realized that the billboards with their azure-, sapphire- and emerald-eyed women draped in jewels and the furs of rare animals were actually advertisements for liquors, automobiles and resorts.

These women stood at the invisible gates of the city, formidable as the wild dogs and the winged men of legend. These women were the sentries of this land, the guardians. Their perfection was unassailable, magical. I trembled in their presence as if they were not models or the creations of painters but more profoundly potent, like the images of saints.

I stepped off the bus, shocked by the stench of cement and automobiles. And although the wind was fierce, I felt as if there were no air. Here, the lungs would learn to breathe asphalt, fumes and glass. I could barely walk. My legs had become unreliable, entities distinct from the rest of my body, appendanges which seemed merely glued on. The thin strips of sidewalk swelled with Latino and white women and men, rushing frantically. Their synchronized limbs drove them relentlessly. They had invisible metal clocks embedded in their flesh, and these machines were constantly ticking. Here, in the center of the city, the increments would be precise to the second. I was embraced by a chaos of strange arms and legs, a turbulence, a liquid riptide. I was without a sense of direction and walked twice around the building which was my destination.

I was instructed to ride an elevator to the sixth floor. The elevator was old, with iron bars across the door. When the black grate unfolded like a terrible black metal fan, I entered a room so vast it seemed edgeless, and I began to sway. Gradually my eyes responded, made tentative approximations of distance and objects. There seemed no path to walk, no obvious indication of navigation.

There were hundreds of desks in perfect rows, neat as the fields of a just-plowed farm. The rows were measured and tamed. There were no deviations. At each desk, an adding machine sat bolted into the center of the thin metal surface. The desks and the machines were a uniform seamless gray. It was difficult to invent or remember distinctions.

The white woman supervisor, Mrs. Hathaway, told me where to sit. Her Spanish was terrible. It was a gray metal chair bolted into the floor. I sat. The gray metal was thin like a kind of tin. Four huge round clocks were planted firmly, squarely into the center of each featureless wall. The room was incomplete. It slanted at an odd angle. The floor beneath me seemed unsolid.

Days passed before I realized the room contained no windows. That was an intrinsic detail to this geography. In a terrain where there is neither sky nor ground, windows are irrelevant, an unnecessary distraction. A window might tempt a woman to look up for an instant from her work, glance at an escaped sunbeam, an aberrant passing sea gull or a falling brick. A window could beckon for attention. They were a danger. A woman might leave her thin gray metal chair, smash the glass with her fist and scratch an opening wide enough for a body to jump through.

Mrs. Hathaway instructed me to place my purse in the bottom desk drawer. I was given a stack of yellow, blue and pink pieces of paper. I added certain numbers and, depending upon their ultimate sum and the date inscribed on their top surface, I determined which of several letters they should bear. I was preparing the invoices for the next process, keypunch.

Keypunch occurred on a different floor of the edifice. I was never told which floor. It was not important. Keypunch was reserved for white women. I saw them in the lobby with their short, colored print skirts, high-heeled shoes and hair which had been professionally dyed and styled. I simply marked my blue or yellow or pink papers with one of a series of letters, and, although the entire system was neither intricate nor complicated, I never fully understood it. The process was like the American sporting games Miguel and our sons watched and played. The rules were outlined for me, yes, but my mind pronounced the information too insignificant and alien to accept. Something within me resisted.

Each Monday and Wednesday and Friday, I sat at my desk in a room with ninety or one hundred women who looked as I did. The women on the billboards with their glacial blue eyes, fur-draped bony shoulders and pearl teeth did not apply to us. The young white women with pink or blue or lilac high-heeled shoes, painted smiles and easy chatter spilling from their glistening lips were a different species entirely, glorious with variation, inspired eddies of color, gold chains around their thin necks and hair that cascaded like a yellow or red waterfall.

We were uniform as our room, as the gray metal desks and chairs, as our environment of gray and brown only. We added numbers. We placed letters on pieces of paper. Only our hands were required. When a bell sounded, I gave my blue and yellow and pink invoices to the white woman supervisor who passed each identical desk, carrying a large metal basket. The completed invoices were clipped together. They would be counted later. One was expected to finish seventy-five invoices each day. Failure to compile the correct amount resulted in immediate dismissal. There were moments when I longed for this.

When the second bell rang, abrupt and vicious as a dog bark or an unexpected slap, my body jumped, startled and frightened. My nerves were the frayed cord of a worn-out appliance, subject to eruptions and sparks. I was obviously short-circuiting. I dared to glance up from my gray metal desk wondering whether this was the moment when we would be stripped, beaten and degraded. Would we be asked to produce green cards and visas? Would some among us be dragged from their gray metal chairs, incarcerated and deported?

But no, the second bell signaled the beginning of our ten-minute coffee break. It was a law in the United States, someone told me, the ten minutes away from the desk and the opportunity for coffee. With the second bell, all the women left their desks like a flock of birds sensing an impending storm and exiting a tree in exquisite simultaneity. We were birds without decoration or pattern. We were muted and common, without wings, grounded, atrophied, the clouds lost.

We entered another gray cubicle, small and square as a cell. There were several of these cubicles and they too were absolutely identical. Here machines dispensed coffee, candies and American pastries. I was shown how to put the correct coins into the metal slots. We ate rapidly, oblivious, watching the movements of the clock as an animal at a dusk water hole searches the shadows for predators. Chocolate and crumbs of sugar stained our fingers. Later, when we sat at our adding machines, we licked the chocolate off. The third bell broke the air like a bullet. Our invoices were again collected. Then the fourth bell tore at the afternoon and it was finished.

With the fourth bell, we opened our identical desk drawers on cue. We removed our similar gray or brown simulated-leather purses. We stood at the edge of the enormous windowless room, waiting for the elevator with the black metal bars to take us, in groups of fifteen or twenty, down to the lobby where the women who were keypunchers or secretaries seemed to be perpetually laughing. They ignored us.Then we pushed our way into the crowded midafternoon street, found and boarded our buses.

After the second week, the other women ceased assaulting me with their tedious questions. I was grateful. I spoke as little as possible. I had no interest in viewing the photographs of children and lovers they removed from their wallets and passed from one sugar-stained hand to another. I cared nothing for television programs or discos, the details of a sister-in-law's illness, or a birth or a death. I had no clothing on layaway, no recipes to exchange or recent visits to Mexico to describe. I did not dream of owning a car or personally seeing Julio Iglesias sing in a theater. Their chatter was incomprehensible, a distraction without focus, noise without direction.

I remained in the corner of the cubicle where the machines dispensed their American foods. The women who meant nothing extracted photographs from their worn plastic gray or brown wallets. They showed one another pages they had cut from magazines. They discussed the comparative attributes of various hairstyles and nail polishes, sensitive to color and sheen, as if such a refinement mattered, as if it could somehow alter the fabric of their destiny. Inevitably one of the sparrows displayed a glass ring she claimed was a genuine diamond. Another, predictably, asserted that the medallion she wore was actually gold and given to her by a boyfriend. This gold disc was merely a token. A car would follow, an apartment and marriage.

I pushed my back against the hard cold wall of the dispensing-machine cubicle. Ten minutes of this incessant babbling was unbearable. I asked no one where they lived, how many children they had or what village in Mexico or Central America had birthed them. I did not inquire what had become of their husbands or what series of atrocities, exile and horrible miscalculation had deposited them in this windowless American structure to place letters on sheets of pink or yellow or blue paper thin as tissue.

I was a blank they could fill in at will. It is common sense not to ask a rock to speak. It can tell you nothing you do not already know. The rain is cold and maniacal, the sun malicious and the stars a constant humiliation and abuse. Perhaps they assumed my husband had deserted me, been imprisoned or deported. Our stories were variations on a theme of isolation and loss. We were born in meaningless villages. We were defective, fattened by tortillas, children, American doughnuts and lies. We ate ferociously, in response to a bell, like a herd of trained animals. We wore shoes low to the ground which we resembled. We carried handbags with torn straps which we pretended were made from leather. Obviously, the gods had abandoned us. Words were unnecessary.

When I rode my bus home, when the bus listlessly forced its way out of the mouth of the city, the stifling labyrinth, the monotonous configuration that called itself Los Angeles, I would see the sentries who guarded the invisible gates. The billboard women advertising American cars silver and sleek as spaceships or pumas. The liquors were painted the amber of rivers that flow across remote stars, molten, yellow as a bleeding metal. And the beaches, with their brazen blue seas, their coconut palms rising, their signs saying Mazatlán or Maui. But always, these objects, even the oceans, were in the background, behind women who rose and posed exquisitely across the sides of the hills. The women, impossibly thin and radiant with whiteness, starved, sculpted down to raw bone. Their teeth glistened like ivory tusks on vanished species larger than elephants. Their eyes were huge, always blue or green, like the eyes of cats or gems. They did not resemble human beings at all.

I could not make sense of this geography. Nothing I saw from the window of the sluggish barely moving bus had anything to do with me. I realized this was the secret of the word *alien*. It had nothing to do with borders or languages. It was a matter of vision and perception. I was attracted by trash spilling across gutters and sidewalks, the newspapers and pamphlets, the stained food wrappings. These seemed to be the only human artifacts, the only remnant of something alive, lying on the surface of the vault of steel and cement. I sensed something darker beneath the artificial lid of ground, the premature burial, an entity struggling to push its way up.

The bus veered away from the abscess of the city, with its terrible smell of hurry and stone and insomnia and money, with its erased sky and the obscene absence of birds, trees, clouds. Only then did the shaking within me lessen, but it never completely ceased. I had a persistent trembling, as if I had somehow swallowed particles similar to wind. Bits of ripped leaves lived inside me, poked at my eyes, swirled in what had once been my mouth.

The bus curved down to the park with the lake surrounded by its stilted palms. The bus always slowed there, at the corner of Temple and Glendale Boulevards, the corner where the insane whore sometimes stood, even in the afternoon, pacing the sidewalk, taunting the cars. One day she had simply appeared. She was always alone, flamboyant in purples and magentas. Her mouth was an indecency of red. Even her skin seemed webbed with red fibers. You could not ignore her.

She was a demented prostitute, flagrant and inflamed. She was a brown bird who had somehow discovered decoration, fragrance and textuue. A brown bird with a raging fever. She was a predator, a draped-in-silk vulture of the rubble.

Yet she contained a kind of intricacy, an assertion of confluences and wounds, of concurrent and random impulses which had deposited her at this particular intersection of necessity and chance. She was a set of red hieroglyphics. Increasingly, I was afraid to look at her. I sensed her eyes searching mine, evaluating, pronouncing me useless, nameless, mud. I intuited she somehow wished to speak to me, to explain the nature of her torment and mine, our similarities. She was trying to call to me with her eyes. I ignored her. Still, I felt her brilliant hot power, even after the bus passed the park and stopped at Flores Street. I wondered why would she wish to speak to me. No, she was merely a brown bird who had chanced to learn how to sing and longed to impart her strange and bruised melody to any passing stranger, that was all. Then it was three-thirty. Then I was stepping down from the bus. Then my ordeal was over.

I had been working each Monday, Wednesday and Friday for two months when she came. Yes, the dead American woman, Barbara Branden. It was winter, winds were stirring. The Santa Anas which come from the desert beyond the city, unpredictable and fierce, scented the irradiated air with sagebrush and sand. I took pleasure in the way the wind howled through its broken Spanish mouth, shattering leaves, breaking branches, etching its insistent southern story in wisted fronds.

I enjoyed the stillness in the afternoons, after the winds passed, after the winds ripped the palms, made confetti of the pale listless fronds. Then the city was purified. A sense of salt and chips of quartz lingered. The calligraphy was obvious. I understood exactly what God was saying. His voice rose with the clarity of church bells above the debris of fronds and leaves. And God was saying, Behold, you are insignificant and flawed.

It was a cold afternoon. I wore my dark-gray coat. My hands were folded up tight in my pockets like two meaningless pebbles. It was early December, I remember. The oxen and mules in the citadel of invoices rambled incessantly about Christmas. They behaved as if this occasion were a phenomenon of nature. My ears were brutalized by their trivial rustlings, how they debated the selection and wrapping of presents, the relative merits of various brands, the intricacies of recipes. They compared tree ornaments and scurried to retrieve their gifts from layaway.

Their excitement was absurd. They planned their menus, recited lists of who would visit them and wondered whether they dared cook American foods such as ham or turkey. They were pathetic, convinced that on this particular day they were not common carriers but the sort of women who adorn billboards. On Christmas they believed that their skin would turn white and their ordinary cotton and chenille bathrobes become gowns of silk. They were sickening.

There was an intimation of a somber tone beneath the rustling of their hyperactive feathers, an implication of danger. It was in the midst of a feasting season, on a night such as Christmas, when you least expected, that men left. As you stood at a window, certain you had transformed your skin, your robes, and you glowed, it was at that moment men deserted you.

I was walking up the low hill of Flores Street from Sunset Boulevard. I noticed new pink curtains in the front room of Consuelo López's house. I nodded to her as I passed. She was sitting on her front porch, her long hair brushed, her dress a light green which seemed as if it had just been taken from a box. She was arranged like an offering beside invisible candles and flowers.

She removed her eyes from mine. She studied the gash of pavement that was Flores Street as a moth will flame. Soon it would be Christmas. She would bear the weight of yet another feasting season alone. The lover she had invented, had imbued with the qualities of a minor god, would or would not come. He might arrive draped in the skin of jaguars, with the teeth of sharks and the claws of eagles strung around his neck. This would be irrelevant. There is a certain stasis from which one cannot return.

Then I was passing the Doberman pinscher Juan Martínez kept as a guard in his front yard. The huge black dog was chained to an elm tree in the center of the lawn. The dog was actually sick, deaf it was said, and purely symbolic. Juan Martínez kept the dog because he was old and alone. Despite the fact that he had lived on Flores Street longer than I, he suffered from the constant terror that Immigration would find him. He too inhabited a realm of tortured expectation. He thought it inevitable that the police would appear, shoot his dog and send him in chains back to Mexico, to die amongst strangers in a village which had ceased to exist.

As I was thinking this about Juan Martínez, as it occurred to me that the holiday season was a poison turning Flores Street rancid with fear and self-pity, I looked up and saw her. One of the creatures from the billboards had slid off, left her hillside perch and landed without warning on Flores Street. Or perhaps it was the huge red moving truck I first saw, then her.

It was cold, and she was standing on the porch where just two weeks before Rico and Linda Almaraz had lived. She was wearing blue jeans tight as bands of blue elastic around her legs and a bright-colored blouse that accentuated her bare white arms. The sky was a metal-veiled gray. The clouds were insidious and fat with certain rain. But she was oblivious to this minor detail. She was pointing to boxes and cartons, sofas and chairs, giving instructions to moving men.

As I climbed my front steps, she waved to me. She greeted me in formal and acceptable Spanish. The words seemed bizarre coming from her white face with the wind blowing her yellow hair like a field of wild mustard. My hands were frozen in my pockets, my fists were mud and pebbles. I could not wave back but merely nod my head and walk quickly into my house, feeling her yellow presence behind me, lingering.

Miguel kissed my mouth. This startled me, almost as if I had been slapped. Something was different about the house, the texture and scent were abnormal. Miguel was buoyant with energy. I hung up my coat. I noticed he had set the dining-room table. He had placed geraniums in a vase in the center of the table, as if this were the birthday of one of our sons or already Christmas.

I washed my hands and face. There was a pounding in my head, like a series of demented angry waves rising and crashing against rock. I had navigated the elevator with its black metal mouth, the boulevards, the bus, the walk up Flores Street. I was home, but still the floors and walls were swaying. And Miguel had cooked rice and chicken. He had never prepared dinner before, not even on the nights when I first returned from the hospital after birthing our sons. I was surprised that he knew how to operate the oven.

This is so unusual, I kept thinking, so unusual, while I watched him place salad he had made himself on first my plate and then the plates of our sons. And Miguel was not wearing pajamas. He was dressed in his old working clothing, the white shirt and light-brown slacks he had once worn to his factory. He was smiling. He was saying, "We have a new neighbor. Her name is Barbara Branden."

I nodded, as if the motion of moving my skull would somehow clear it of the clouds and gray patches nested within. Perhaps microscopic gray birds, some thought-to-be-extinct variety of dwarf sparrow, was actually living in my brain. That would explain the feathers and twigs I felt rustling in the empty chamber of my head.

"Barbara Branden's Spanish is excellent," Miguel informed me. "She was going to be an actress. That's why she moved to Los Angeles. Now she is a social worker." Miguel was explaining the specific duties of a social worker in elaborate detail, but I did not hear him. I was a mural, fragile, aged, crumbling. I willed my numb mouth to receive food. It opened. It closed. I had cement in my ears, birds flapped their wings behind my eyes, leaves drifted brittle, sharp as claws. There was a purpose in their movements, their etchings, their constant demand for definition.

Yes, I was surprised by his behavior. I was shocked that he had already spoken with the white woman, that he had learned so much of her personal history. Perhaps this was their nature, I tried to convince myself, they kept nothing hidden and offered their chronology without hesitation, opening themselves up like maps.

She had been born in Wisconsin, an American state far to the north where there were numerous lakes and exceptionally long winters of unremitting snow and a fierce cold which made the bones ache. Her ancestors had journeyed across the Atlantic Ocean from a region in Europe called Norway, a land encased in white ice. Her people were white, yes, but skilled hunters, sailors and warriors. Her ancestors had fought the Indians who once lived in America.

Miguel had already transformed her whiteness into a masterful and unique climate. He had given her whiteness roots and history, an implication of blood possibilities. He offered me more. Barbara Branden had been divorced, twice. She had no children. She had studied Spanish in a university and then lived in Spain and Mexico.

Miguel was speaking in code. Each phrase was a concealment, a shallow veil which would not confuse a village idiot. He was actually saying that this white woman was extraordinary and rare. She was not pale and severed, an erased thing, bleached, with ghost skin. This white woman transcended the world as we knew it. For Barbara Branden, Miguel was devising a new hierarchy.

Miguel was proud of his accumulation of knowledge. He considered his words valuable, as if he were holding a string of pale jewels in his hands, opals or pearls perhaps, and we should stand together, breathless and awed, admiring them. He looked like a man who had been pulling weeds in his garden and chanced upon a buried treasure, parchments and feathers and stone necklaces of magnificence and antiquity. He was already justifying her.

Miguel came to me later. He had not spent the evening with his newspapers and American television programs. Instead, he had bathed and shaved. I was startled by his clean-shaven face, how soft, how like a child the skin of his face was. He told me the boys had gone to bed and he had washed the dinner plates. He kissed the place which would have been my face had my face not disintegrated, had it not been blown away and scattered by high desert winds. He made love to me almost delicately, then with urgency and groans, as if he had completely forgotten José and Carlos and our inviolate ritual of quickness and silence.

In the near-darkness, when it was over, I realized that Miguel had become an absolute stranger. I might sit next to him on the bus and not recognize him. Of course, I immediately understood that his sudden tenderness and passion were born from his desire for her, for Barbara Branden. He could not admit this forbidden impulse within himself and transformed it into a longing for me. It was a terrible act of fraudulence and I felt stained by it.

I was awake and thinking of his banal subterfuge when he entered me a second time, when he climbed upon me, strong and purposeful. He did not take me from behind, from beneath the blankets on the verge of sleep as was our custom. He took me from above, where he could cruelly look down at me. And I thought, this is so unusual, so unusual, as he spilled himself into me without asking if it were a dangerous time of the month. When he emptied his manhood into me, he emitted the grunting sounds of an exhausted dog. And I thought, This is so unusual. But I was not deceived. I realized it was not me he was embracing. By some process of the imagination, when he closed his eyes, my flesh became the flesh of Barbara Branden. It was obvious. The only surprise was that Miguel thought me so ignorant I would not decipher this.

O f course, that was simply the beginning. Then Miguel was helping Barbara Branden with her wind-ravaged backyard fence. He could not believe the Santa Ana winds had dared to violate her property. He seemed to think her immune to the vicissitudes of fortune. Then he was driving stakes into the dirt for her, terracing, digging, building. He was hammering nails into the lumber she ordered. Always, they spoke in English.

When they saw me on the other side of the bamboo fence which no longer adequately divided our houses, which was a mere symbol without resonance, Barbara Branden would call to me in her fine and formal Spanish, "Come join us, please." I was hanging clothes or bending in the rain-soaked earth, pulling weeds from my marigolds and carnations. I would look up, startled and frozen in place, transfixed by this billboard that talked, this creature standing next to my husband with the blood familiarity of cousins.

"You don't mind," Miguel said to me in our bed. It was a statement rather than a question. It required no answer. His voice was soft, as if the shape of his mouth had changed. Now he sought me in the darkness often, as he had when we were sweethearts in Tijuana, and when he returned from the Army. He entered me constantly, every night, as if we had not been married seventeen years and birthed two sons together, but as if we had just chanced to meet. He forced my flesh into strange postures, draped my legs over his shoulders and arranged my body in angles I had not imagined possible. I recognized that these gestures were intended for Barbara Branden. It was possible he was practicing these obscene positions, perfecting them on my insignificant flesh until he felt assured enough to take her.

"She's alone and I have the time. You don't mind, do you?" Miguel was asking.

In the space where I might have replied, Miguel recited the litany of facts he had assembled and memorized about her. Barbara Branden was to be pitied. Her family of yellow-haired, glacial-eyed warriors no longer spoke to her. They shut their white hearts to this daughter who had divorced two men and refused to bear children as convention demanded. She had dared to take an apartment in Madrid, and later lived for sixteen months in Veracruz. She had outraged her family in her youth when she was an actress for one summer in a theater near Chicago. Barbara Branden was almost simple, Miguel concluded, trusting and generous. Invariably, she chose men who used her, took advantage and behaved without honor. Men broke promises and deserted her at moments when she least expected.

Miguel seemed to think this exceptional. He was convinced her whiteness elevated her beyond the ordinary fate of all women. She was somehow beyond wind, lies, the natural cycles and abandonments of men. His voice became hushed when he spoke of her, as if she were a nurse or a nun. Then he was above me, touching me with intensity, staring directly into my eyes which were not my eyes but the eyes of Barbara Branden. Then he was pushing himself into me as if I were a bride.

For Christmas, Miguel presented to me a bottle of perfume. From my bus window I had seen this product advertised on a billboard. The liquid was depicted as the yellow of intoxicated candles. The woman who demonstrated this fluid, who was pasted across the surface of a billboard that strangled a hill, held this perfume in her white sculpted hand. She had enormous green eyes, a coral-painted mouth and a white fur tossed across one of her feline shoulders. No saint had ever been as beautiful. She was delicate beyond grace or absolution. My sons presented oils to me to pour into my bath.

I could effortlessly translate the significance of these gifts and what they implied. I was unacceptable. It was Barbara Branden they craved, but they feared they could not have her, or perhaps not quite yet. There was a limbo. They were attempting to form me anew, to cloak my dull flesh with appealing scents which might make my body glisten, pearled, glazed with promise.

I was a failed crop to be ripped out, root by root. I was less than a weed. I was a stain upon the earth. I was to be replowed and replanted. I was to emerge with splendid jungle-green leaves, damp vines exploding with petals startling with fragrance. I must sing now, improvise and amuse. They would no longer tolerate my simplicities. The perfume bottle glared at me. Their message was indisputable. Miguel and my sons were giving me one last chance.

Then the fourth bell rang. Then the bus slowly pushed past the insane red-silk-skirted puta of the lake, the delirious brown bird who had transformed herself from a sparrow into a vulture and thought herself invulnerable and exceptional. She was the product of an ordinary sort of surgery. She was a thing contrived, like a machine. She searched for me with her eyes. She said, Join me. We will eat lava. The span of her painted wings was exaggerated, aberrant. She knew only the spectrum of red. She was incomplete and resistant to this knowledge. The bold design of her wings was a subterfuge. She was a vulture of the rubble. The sky would remain locked for her. I turned my head away.

The bus was passing the park with its lake surrounded by a legion of banished and tattooed palm trees. Then I was walking up the low hill of Flores Street, waving a slow hand to Consuelo López. She responded with the lethargy of one encased in a state of terminal waiting where the ordinary increments of measurement have lost their meaning and the air itself is a corridor of cells, each molecule locked and barred.

I found myself standing in the courtyard of Marta Ortega, on the patio of her yellow wood house which gleamed like rain-washed lemons. She had lived in that house for half a century. Her garden had become an extension of her body, a womb. And the dirt she touched was more than earth, was a sacrament, a testament.

I watched Marta Ortega on her knees, digging and planting, cutting and pruning, watering and ceaselessly perfecting. She called the earth a kind of caress. She studied the dirt as one might an ocean, aware of nuances and subtleties within what appeared to be a seamless brown. She stared at her orchids, fuchsias, camellias and roses as if looking beyond the plants themselves, beyond their leaves, petals and roots and farther, into the submerged regions beneath the surface. She dug in her garden as if she expected to uncover the pulse of the universe, there beneath her aged fingers, there on Flores Street. At certain moments, I thought this was possible.

On this rare afternoon, Marta Ortega was not gossiping with the old white lovers, Joseph and Bill. I drank horchata with her. Marta Ortega was gracious, empathetic, but there was a veil between us, a formality. as if we were characters reciting dialogue in a play which exhausted and bored us. Marta Ortega did not actually see me.

I was not like Angelina and Orquídea. I did not change my name, carry a passport in my purse, arrive at midnight with my mouth a wind of curses or vows. Now both Angelina and Orquídea had married men of wealth and stature and this, at last, soothed them. Still, I was too simple and common for Marta Ortega. She was the Queen of Flores Street and I was a boulder, oleander, geraniums.

"Your tension is unnecessary. She's a silly girl and pretentious," Marta Ortega informed me. I had said nothing. Of course, Marta Ortega was a bruja. She was permitted to speak of any matter she chose. I was surprised she had observed my agony.

"Angelina and Orquídea took her to lunch. She could barely read the menu. She's a fool. She will marry and move. She is a temporary configuration. Forget her," Marta Ortega ordered.

I nodded in agreement, but no, I did not believe her. Miguel was sitting on the front porch of the house where Barbara Branden, the pretentious fool who could not read a menu and would marry and move, now indisputably lived. When my husband noticed me approach, he returned to our house immediately, like a dog who has heard the sound of food poured into his bowl. Or a dog who has been told not to venture across certain boundaries and has done so.

He was asking whether I wanted coffee. He was inquiring whether I was tired, whether I wished to bathe. He offered to slice tomatoes and chiles for our dinner, to grate cheese, to water the backyard marigolds. He was obviously not speaking to me. He was practicing the phrases and attitudes he would employ when greeting Barbara Branden. And I would be submerging my numb useless hands in water that burned. My hands were tinged with red like a leaf in autumn, and still I felt nothing.

"You're jealous of this fat old Mexican, aren't you?" Miguel accused me one evening. He made his eyes appear incredulous. He patted his belly and laughed.

It seemed strange that he referred to himself as a Mexican. He had fought an American war and he read the American newspaper each morning, page by page, with the patience and indolence of a great Spanish lady, the daughter of a duke or a count perhaps, unfolding her hand-embroidered white or black or red lace fan. Yes, this was odd from a man who left the house at 7 A.M. to vote in the polling place in the school on Alta Vista Street, saving his election pamphlets as if they were sacred, vestiges from antiquity or religious documents.

Invaluable information was being imparted to me. Miguel was still cloaking his words in code. He thought that in my inadequacy and ignorance I could not recognize artifice. There were hieroglyphics in his words like the glare of numbers forming an equation. I reached the edge of revelation when our sons pushed the door open, hungry, muddy, needing to be fed, tamed. My interior architecture claimed me, the details I submitted to as unassailable. The blue jeans to mend, plates to be filled, washed, dried, stacked. The mouths which rarely said thank you. The details defined me. I was an appliance which existed only when it was plugged in. A refrigerator that walked. A closet that responded to verbal commands. That was all.

We settled into our familiar night pattern. My sons sat near their father, his miniatures, his legacy with arms and legs. They formed their own circle, a nest, passing the American newspaper from one to the other, sharing their exclusive sacrament. Their conversations were interminable and incomprehensible. I understood the English words. It was only their excitement which eluded me.

And the night was studded not with stars but with rams and dodgers, steelers and cowboys, raiders and mariners, dolphins and eagles, bears and cubs and colts and broncos. The nights were littered with the names of animals and bandits, batting averages and rushing yards, fast balls and field goals and sky hooks. Nights of the redsocks, the redbirds, tigers, falcons, braves. They inhabited a kingdom of predators and killers. They even spoke of angels, padres and cardinals. I wondered whether the church itself now participated in these sporting events.

I did not inquire about this possibility. All of my questions made them laugh. It was better I remain camouflaged, with my mud-brown eyes, with my sheets of rock skin, with the mule breath they wished to eradicate with oils and scents as if I could be rebuilt from the outside in. Frijoles would be simmering, and I was sinning, standing at my kitchen slat of window, regretting I had borne only sons.

Of course they would leave me as all sons left their mothers. This was natural. In fact, they had already departed. They remained merely as boats chained to a rotting dock. One day, the wood beneath them would shatter, the rusted chains unlock. Then they would drift into the sea of chance, war and women, distance and circumstance which was their destiny, their necessity. They would beget more of their own. The talk of American animals and birds and renegades would perpetuate itself indefinitely. It was like the steel-encased edifices of the city, the metal slats Miguel had once manufactured, an entity which would outlive me. I had served my minimal purpose. I was an empty vessel they permitted within their borders because of their lethargy and indifference. I did not merely exist peripherally, but, rather, after the fact.

The world began to blacken then. The deterioration was subtle. It took months. First, the outlines were smudged as if with rubbed charcoal. Gradually, the darkness spread like a virus which has found the precise environment it requires to prosper. I birthed foul blooms oblivious to proportion. Darkness pulled apart like petals. Black roses grew. Crows wet with rain flew, their night eyes savage. They were birds that did not sing. They had elaborate claws beneath their wings. Their throats were corridors of nails. Their vocabularies were limited. They knew one word and one word only and the word they knew was *blood*.

But understand, it is not forgiveness I ask. I descended as all others, in terror, without map or compass. I entered a region without name or lines of demarcation. It was as if I had simply opened my front door and the lawn was a well, aberrant and alluring. The landscape deceived with fences of random purple iris and the constant dense scent of jasmine. There was an unremitting radiance of rain-draped glistening ravens, their bodies obsidian. My body narrowed. I was mole-small in a corridor of harsh brown dirt. It pressed down upon me with the weight of an ocean.

I knew that a disease was breathing within me, poking and flapping, spreading its wiry wings, moving from bone to bone as if they were tree branches. It was preparing to force its way out. It was insatiable and clever. I still believed salvation would intercede. I was convinced of this the way a terminal woman will wait until the final seconds, still expecting a cure. Perhaps a passing saint would sense my distress, hear the desperation in my prayers, imbue my invocations with an imagination they did not have and, out of sheer random chance, offer me grace. Certainly, a saint would notice my chaos and delirium and press a cool hand across my forehead, take me against his flesh as a woman does a child with a fever and gently rock me into a sleep of absolution. Or perhaps, somewhere, on the banks of a dusk river, a prayer would be offered in my name, a candle lit and the long and unreasonable season would lift. It did not.

It was as if a wrong door had been opened by accident. I stepped across an intangible threshold and entered the vat kingdom. It was deep as a poisoned well. Night was a tunnel for my fist. The sky was welded shut as if by a metal lid. I heard the pin being pulled on the hand grenade in my head. I could not sleep at all, or slept and dreamed of scorpions stinging with countless unclean spines.

Ask me what the idiot dreams. She dreams of a thick seamless blue, the same frozen blue frame again and again. She dreams of mice, blue-breathed, with blue feet sharp and bloody. She dreams she is pouring blue acid into the mud pools of her eyes. She measures survival in decreasing increments, sometimes only in minutes. She dreams of ice and the rocks engraved there, above the cold waterline where the blue sheets slide up, perpetually up, reaching like a knife for the throat.

The fabric of this night was pitted and worn, ancient, scarred. I was not the first to walk upon its shores. There were water holes where the half-dead, the mad, creatures who no longer belong to this world or any other, come to feed. I sensed a crowd of scales with amphibian breaths, clustered, just behind my shoulder, their shapes deceptive. All could fly and bark and sing. They were the devil's personal icons, his bastard sons with lethal shadows and razor tongues, his version of tigers and bears and broncos and colts. But they were infinitely more unpredictable and dangerous. And they had found me, precisely as I had imagined they would.

I shivered, wrapped in a chill that acres of wool, gallons of herb teas and a sea of hot baths with fragrant oils would not cure. I inhabited an internal winter, callous and glacial in impact. I was sheeted, a pond under ice where rocks are tossed and lost stars fall, jaded and degenerate, burning to death. Night of coal-wings and asps. Sleep brought no deliverance. My dreams were small zoos.

I feared the drain of morning, the affliction of dawn birds and the weak winter sun, pale as the sun on a planet surrendering to clouds laced with metal and dying. A world inhabited solely by women wearing the names of film stars and saints, standing in stained slips on terraces overlooking miniature suggestions of garden, with the canna rising and the dogs barking, waiting for the Apocalypse alone.

In the night I called out silently. Come to me, Saint Francis, tender of the birds. Forgive me my envy, terror and nests of hideous blood birds. Forgive me my streams and rivers and oceans of malice. Come to me, Saint Anthony, beloved of the unions between women and men. Come to me, Saint Simon, keeper of the cloth. Cover me in this cold and sheeted-with-ice winter, in this infirmity of the soul.

Miguel began reading books. Barbara Branden had given them to him for Christmas. They were in Spanish and English, and Miguel purchased a dictionary. The books were difficult, he read each page carefully, circling the many words he did not know and underlining certain passages with a yellow crayon. The pages seemed heavy in his fingers, as if they were not paper but metal or brick. He became agitated, restless and excited. He slumped above his books and his dictionary, a cigarette in one hand, a yellow crayon in the other.

"Does this threaten you?" he demanded one evening. He was yelling. "Everything new terrifies you." His tone was so loud and enraged that José and Carlos rose from the floor near the television to stare at him.

I had been standing alone in the kitchen, in the vault of darkness where I masqueraded as an inanimate object. I had been staring at the stove and, without realizing this, weeping. I turned the place that might have once been my face toward my husband. His eyes were yellow with intoxication, fever or fear. He looked like a man who has just realized he is less than a trapped and caged bird.

We said goodnight to our sons. Our sons, who were chained to the illusionary sides of a wooden pier which was rotting. Soon, they would drift on the oceans, their home port becoming vague with waves and distance. They would remember nothing. Already they dreamed their spines were sprouting metal riggings for sails and their flesh turning into canvas.

Later, when we were in our bed, Miguel pressed his hands into my shoulders, shaking my body as one does an old rug thick with dust. "There is nothing between us," Miguel cried as he rattled my body of wind and leaves and birds. "She is courted by men who drive sports cars and have theater tickets. My ignorance amuses her. We only talk."

When Miguel was calmer, he told me what he discussed with the American social worker, Barbara Branden. She was teaching him of revolution and a man named Che Guevara. He was learning about the patterns of history.

Miguel's voice was serious, measured, as if he were reciting a formula and each syllable must be placed in an exact order, like numbers in an equation. Or perhaps each word was a stone and Miguel was constructing a kind of pyramid. There was a fantastic conspiracy, an almost indescribable subterranean architecture of deception, malice and fraud. It was interwoven, deliberate and hidden.

Miguel was speaking in a frantic rush like a man who has deciphered the code of the universe and must share his vision before the walls fold back and the winds and dust cover the plazas, temples and aqueducts, the canals and gardens and holy books.

It manifested itself in Mexico and in the countries farther south, El Salvador and Guatemala where the farmers had armed themselves and were fighting the troops of the government. No, they were not common bandits, Miguel laughed at me. The peasants were right. The government was decadent, evil, demented. And the Church was a whore of the President, his mistress, almost a wife. She sold her body in all climates and centuries. She would give her flesh to a vulture if it carried a strand of diamonds in its beak.

Then Miguel removed his framed plaque of honorable discharge from the war in Vietnam where he had killed yellow-tinged men in the rice fields and palm-draped pueblos of Asia. Then he unhooked his citizenship award from the wall, solemnly, like a man taking down a flag. The moment was profound as the conclusion of a graveside ceremony. We did not speak.

From then on, Miguel was erupting with details of the conspiracy. He was a kind of volcano, clouds and smoke spilled from his mouth. The conspiracy stretched across the demarcations between nations, continents and oceans. Distance meant nothing. It spoke all languages. It had the agility of a chameleon. It could camouflage itself in any terrain. It was ancient. It lived in chandeliers and masqueraded as maize. It inhabited the steaming green mists of the jungles and the regions of ice and tundra.

When Miguel spoke of the conspiracy, his eyes opened abnormally wide, as if the intricacies of this revelation were transforming his face. Or perhaps the alteration was deeper, within the structure of his cells, within the blood and bone and atoms comprising him. He was speaking with deep conviction about animals. He was saying, "They massacred everything. Here, they slaughtered the buffalo. In Mexico, the jaguar, puma and eagle."

I realized I was expected to respond to this information. Miguel had pronounced the church which had married us and blessed our children a whore. But I did not know why he mentioned these animals. I assumed he was merely talking of sporting teams again.

I had not seen Miguel consumed with ideas and purpose since we were first lovers, in Tijuana. America had been his passion then. She had beckoned to him like a face, a canvas in which a delirious sun rises and sets in ice-cream yellows and pinks, translucent, glazed as the underbelly of abalone shells, otherworldly, a child's vision. He had been a boy-child and America had been a kind of woman for him. He ached for her as a man in prison suffers the absence of his wife. He had been eager for the fever of her, for her limbs which he perceived as highways, for her womb which he called a city, for the orange and scarlet layers of her skies which were actually skirts he longed to lift, strip, take what was beneath. He had been dry twigs, and she the torch in August.

Now he was speaking of a conspiracy stretching on a series of invisible bridges and interwoven nets across the surface of the planet. It lived in the telephone wires and in the print embossing newspapers. It poured its invisible poisons into the classrooms and spilled out of radios and televisions. It nested in the deformed cathedrals and tiled plazas of capitals, in the marble halls of parliaments, in the palaces of presidents and in the apartment tenements of stucco and tin and brick, from Buenos Aires through Caracas, El Salvador, Havana, the West Indies and Los Angeles.

I was aware of the personal implications in what Miguel was saying. Through his circumscribed arcs and subterfuge of enormities, he was evaluating our marriage, the purpose and future of our union. This was obvious. He was recognizing that the world had divested itself of orange. This was fire's end, the ritual completed. The lovers of our youth were lost. Now we met above soft gray mounds of singed moths with blackened wings. Rain fell, we coughed dust and it worsened, became starker, harder, more poisonous, with each room gutted, infested and locked. Between us were gulfs, seasons of mudslides and floods, avenues of orange-tiled roofs and uncountable lawns strangling beneath near-red geraniums. Miguel realized it was not enough. I could decipher his code effortlessly. He was saying our lives had become the texture of watercolor paper rubbed thin by careless thumbs. He was saying our marriage meant nothing.

After that, there was always more. Miguel was excavating a buried city. Each day brought him sacks of shards and pottery, feathered capes, intact artifacts to assemble and analyze. It began with the Conquistadores, bandits and renegades whom locusts would scorn. Even Spain, that bitch, that colossal whore, could not abide them and sent them into exile. They chanced upon Mexico, their brains decaying with syphilis, their hearts stinking with greed and gold lust. They had no vision, no capacity for song or grandeur. They raped the women, savaged the land and made slaves of their children.

I removed my shoes, washed my hands and face with scalding water, and still I felt nothing. Miguel followed me from room to room like a haunted barking dog. The Conquistadores were extravagant with destruction. It was their only form of expression. They desecrated the true gods who had been Indian. They burned the books containing the solved equations of the ages. They looted and razed the temples where magic indisputably existed, astronomy, surgery and art.

I was filling plates with frijoles, rice, beef. Miguel was informing me that the United States government was paranoid and racist. The Mexican government was worse. The Spaniards, the priests, the elected rulers and the born kings were incompetent and perverse. The conglomerates and corporations that strung their invisible bridges and nets and webs across the oceans and earth and owned all that dared to breathe were sadists without souls. Everyone was wrong, it seemed, but Miguel and Barbara Branden.

I washed dinner plates. I knew the history of Tenochtitlán. I wondered why I was subjected to this abundance of information, this relentless barrage of detail, these words which shrouded, veiled and confused. Why did Miguel not say that he no longer loved me or wanted to continue our passage through the meaningless rubble we called our lives as my husband? Did he feel it necessary to justify himself with layers of memorized facts, with the recitation of theories other men had designed? Would he never tire of this charade and understand the simplicity of his motives?

Eventually he would shed his subterfuge. A man who could change his nationality by removing a plaque from a wall could as easily strip a wife of her wedding band. It is the gestures which define us, the symbols we imbue with meaning or erase of significance. I did not need the weight of history and shelves of books with underlined-in-yellow-crayon pages to comprehend this.

That weekend, my husband and my sons settled into their familiar circle on the living-room floor in front of the television. Their day would be measured in increments of sporting events, one such spectacle of uniformed chaos bleeding into another, uninterrupted, until they were dazed and exhausted. This activity had replaced church for us. They did not ask me where I was going. I was so peripheral to them, I do not think they even noticed when I left the house.

I walked alone to Nuestra Señora de los Dolores. As I crossed the church courtyard, as I breathed the special scent of fading white-painted walls stained by the abuse of seasons and the lips and fingers which had clawed or caressed them, I was seized by a desire for absolution, however temporary and partial.

In confession, I ordered words to spill from the wound of my mouth, to say, Forgive me, Father, I know you are a passing configuration, but in your transitory fashion, with your random hands, absolve me of my envy, jealousy and embroidery of blasphemies and lies. I curse the birth of my sons. My husband wishes to abandon me and take a white woman, but he lacks the courage, speaks instead in an atrocity of irrelevance given to him by this Barbara Branden. When he embraces me, it is her flesh he is holding. He surrounds himself with ancient cataclysms which are a blatant metaphor for our personal disorder. I imply this and he is righteous with denial. It is impossible.

But my mouth resisted, refused to open, to form syllables and words. I was mute in the wooden cubicle, aware of the many women and men waiting. I finally rose from my knees and, still silent, walked out. I had failed everyone, even God, who was so patient, who asked so little.

Marta Ortega was drinking coffee on her front-courtyard terrace with Angelina and Orquídea. I could not avoid them. Angelina and Orquídea with their tailored silk suits, their pastel matching shoes, their imported handbags and expensive smell, their self-indulgence and extravagance, styled hair and impeccably refined chatter. They were choreographed. They had practiced such conversations their entire lives. They were born for this. I sat my pack-animal body in a slab of shade. Fuchsias and delicate ferns spilled above my shoulders like a soft green rain.

"She is insignificant," Marta Ortega pronounced. "Common, less than geraniums or ivy."

Perhaps that is true, I thought, but what if this were the first plant a man ever beheld? Would he not proclaim it spectacular, a phenomenon, magnificent in complexity? Would he not fall upon his knees and worship this profound discovery with reverence and intensity?

"Her ideas are less than conventional," Angelina pointed out. "She is shallow and subadequate."

"Dated and predictable," Orquídea agreed.

You talk of her ideas, I thought, but not of the body which issues them. And if this were the first flawless female you had beheld, a creature of marble and pearl, would you not think it the mouth of a saint, an angel, an oracle?

"Your grief is a disturbance of the elements," Marta Ortega cautioned me. "The substance, the ebb and flow are delicate."

"Always, women wait, masquerading as potted plants, recognizing they are inconsequential, interchangeable," Orquídea revealed.

"To demand more results in being discarded," Angelina seemed to remember.

"In short, you are courting disaster," Orquidea said.

"You are deliberately chasing bad weather," Angelina concluded.

I tried to find solace in their words as I rode my bus to work in the citadel of blue and yellow and pink pieces of paper so thin they seemed to be patches of severed skin. Or perhaps they were the petals of flowers. Perhaps I should fold and arrange them, there in the center of my thin gray metal desk, I could fashion a bouquet. The invoices refused the structure of my fingers. They drifted from my hands like leaves, butterflies, tossed rocks, bullets. She is insignificant, common as geraniums or ivy. She is shallow. She will marry a dull blond-haired man with a sports car and move. She can barely read a menu. Her ideas are dated.

I remember that day with clarity. It was a Monday. It was hot. It was an exceptional spring which came suddenly, with the strength of summer. It was bold. It simmered and boiled the air. One could not determine seasons in the horizonless gray room without windows where I sat at my thin gray metal desk, always the same desk in the same section in the same row, as if I were planted there. I could sense, somehow, that the day was abnormally virulent, hot and unnaturally yellow. The glare of the yellow metal taxicab. The inexplicable abundance of yellow. The portent. Her hair. The excess of yellow.

I was thinking of the slain rebel leader, the Che Guevara, whose likeness was printed upon a poster the size of a window. Miguel had hung this in our front room. The man who looked like a bandit was now tacked across the space where Miguel had once displayed his documents of army service and citizenship. I wondered whether he had thrown the plaques away, discarded them as vestiges of a past which was embarrassing and unnecessary, like his wife.

Miguel was growing a beard, as if in tribute to the man on the poster, his new icon. Miguel wore a bandana around his forehead. He resembled a farmhand from the provinces. He looked as the grandchildren of Marta Ortega had, years ago when we first moved to Flores Street. I told him he could be mistaken for a barrio hoodlum. Miguel smiled when I said this, as if it were a form of praise. Then he asked me to stop buying lettuce and grapes from the market. There was a boycott on these particular plants, dug from the earth by ill-treated workers Miguel now called brothers.

"The grape boycott ended years ago," Angelina had informed me.

"It's a midlife crisis, male menopause," Orquídea had offered.

Marta Ortega poured coffee and said nothing. The ferns and fuchsias above my shoulders, hanging from pots on the beams of the terrace, were tranquil above me, like a green rain, an inverted forest, a channel into a beginning. Angelina suggested marriage counselors and psychotherapy. Orquídea spoke of her husband and God, her church near the ocean in San Diego, how she lived in a state of constant absolution. Then, with the same tone of reverence, she offered me the telephone number of a hair stylist. They babbled until Marta Ortega raised her hand once and told them to cease. With one command, they closed their painted mouths.

And pieces of yellow and blue and pink papers kept appearing across my gray metal desk. They were inexhaustible and meaningless as waves which have forgotten their intrinsic purpose, that spill themselves on the shore indiscriminately, without conviction. I could no longer bear adding their numbers and forcing myself to determine which letter they should receive. The task was simultaneously too tedious and too intricate. I touched my stack of peeled skins and coded them arbitrarily, now an "A," now an "R" or a "K."

I could no longer serve as a conduit for their destinies. They were leaves or butterflies. I was unnecessary. Anyone could see that these papers had their own lives, their own unique circumstances and fate. It was at that precise instant the supervisor, the white woman in high-heeled shoes, Mrs. Hathaway, appeared at my desk.

"Do you have your time of blood, María? Your period? Are you pregnant?" she demanded in bad Spanish. Her voice was loud, indiscreet. "Did you get beat up?"

The white woman supervisor addressed me as María. She thought everyone who worked in the gray room without windows, with its rows of gray desks like rows of a diseased plant, a crop that meant nothing, was named María. We were identical, brown as the earth, a flock of sparrows, a herd of mules, indistinguishable. And the concept of dignity did not exist within this room, within these gray rows with their crop of brown-bird women, with their harvest of pastel slabs of square pages the texture of skin.

We were all named María. Our world consisted of predictable disruptions, our menstruation, our dumb bellies which might erupt with blood or babies. Our men bruised our flesh, went to prison or deserted us. There were slight and insignificant variations. A child in a hospital. A death.

We had no other possible dimensions. We thought nothing, dreamed nothing, knew nothing. We were similar to the palm trees with their frail legs and their pinheads gutted by sun and the callous stars which do not speak, which offer only inexplicable seasons of storms and mud which drape across our bark like a curse. We were common as the palms with their inadequate skirts of straw, their lashed bark flesh abandoned at the edges of ruined plazas.

It occurred to me that there was another conspiracy, invisible to Miguel. It stretched from Mexico City and El Salvador, through Havana and the islands of the Caribbean, from Caracas to Los Angeles. It was a particular air of slow rotting, a scented steaming poison masquerading as spice, jade, clouds. This was a subterfuge of the elements.

And I said, No, I was not ill.

Later, I would not be permitted to enter the elevator with the other invoice clerks. My crop was pronounced inadequate. I was informed that I had not yet worked the necessary months to qualify for medical or unemployment benefits. It would be explained to a woman named María that were she to fail one more time with her slabs of severed skin, she would be dismissed immediately. There would be no compensation or appeal. The sentence would be absolute and final. A woman named María said she understood this and thanked them.

As I stepped from the lobby, from the cluster of pastel-skirted white secretaries, the street coughed hot and brutal in my face. The bus edged out of the city, apathetically, doubting it had the strength to free itself from the brick and mortar and glass web that trapped it. The bus was not a ship but a gigantic moth and the city was its light, its fire, its intoxication and death. The bus was a kind of carcass. It also existed after the fact.

Did I say it was spring but unusually hot, intense and focused as summer? The streets were dazed, hopeless, static, prepared to surrender without struggle. I said silent Hail Marys, but billboards continually intruded. Hail Mary full of grace. And I would find myself staring into the sapphire eyes of a billboard woman, her skin the color of cream, her neck thin as a tree contoured by the constant caress of a tender wind. But the ocean was never as blue or green as her eyes. The beach with its obligatory palm did not glisten like her skin. And the sign in the corner was advertising Maui or Mazatlán.

Hail Mary full of grace. And I was staring at a billboard woman, sleeker than the car behind her, the silver car fantastic as a spaceship. But she was swifter, incredibly agile, alluring and gifted. Her flesh was composed of starlight. Hail Mary full of grace. Your name is Gloria Hernández. You are different. Worms mate in your brain. Legions of horned beetles etch their trite histories of dirt and rock and rain across the remnants of your flesh.

The bus managed to escape the hypnotic pull of the city. It slid down the hill to Temple Street, with its park, its palm-encircled lake of grease and trash, its wooden boats chained to an unsolid dock. The lake looked as if it had been engraved by a fist. And the cement finally stopped for an acre of scorched grass embossed by the glass from broken-in-half beer bottles and the blood of boy-men who engaged in night rituals with knives.

The crazy prostitute stood at the edge of the park, radiating her special red heat, causing cars actually to stop as they do for traffic accidents or disasters. She was a spectacle, a wound calling itself a flower. For a moment, it seemed our eyes met, connected, merged. She was trying to tell me something simple, elemental. The bus is an illusion. You can step off it. Your chains will drop from your ankles. And the dense air can become green as an ocean. Your flesh can be transformed. Identities can be rearranged, created, shed.

But the bus was moving again, curving beyond the park of brittle grass with its man-created lake which sat static, irredeemable, beyond lost. It wished only to enter the clouds and die. The lake dreamed of this in the incomplete nights, lashed by the headlights of cars, there, beneath a sky erased of stars. The lake longed to seep into the air, to drift, to be reborn in a sea storm or a sudden warm rain above wooded groves, jungle gullies, cliffs of succulents and gulls, anything but this purgatory at the periphery of the steel-and-glass angles which had somehow risen, mated, assembled their sharp edges and called themselves Los Angeles.

Barbara Branden was sitting with Miguel and our sons at our dining-room table. It was spring. Marta Ortega was carrying pots of orchids from her terraced back hillside into her front courtyard which she had strung with sheets to provide shade. She had been digging in her garden, furiously, impassioned. She paused in her work to note that the heat was exceptional. It was disturbing her flowers, particularly her orchids. She admitted she feared for their safety.

The late afternoon was indecently warm. Barbara Branden sat with my husband and my sons. José and Carlos were no longer consumed by sporting events. Barbara Branden was more exciting than games played in a park or trivial acts of vandalism. For all intents and purposes, she was naked. She wore white shorts and a light-colored blouse, thin as petals, as the tissue of invoices. It barely covered her small breasts. The ridges of her ribs were exposed. They looked like two firm hands holding her flesh in place from within. Even her body embraced itself.

I washed my hands and face in the kitchen. It was spring, an extraordinarily hot April, even Marta Ortega said this. The planet was making its ineffable journey toward the sun. I felt a stirring in my bones which were metal corridors. I experienced a kind of cracking or melting. And I thought, So this is how oceans are born, after millenniums of burial, deep in the cold black liquid chambers, microscopic forms hatch, invent fins and the desire to live. And they begin to push against the edges of the vault.

Beyond my kitchen window, in the patch of garden between our two houses, a colossal white moth hovered. Hail Mary, full of grace. I will be a coastal sea breeze grazing wild barley and the soft clouds brushing grasses in fields adorned with orange poppies. Saint Simon, cover me in this altitude of madness and vertigo. Saint of the red zone that burns, save me. Saint Francis, grant me the solace you would a sparrow. Am I less than this to you?

There was one unoccupied chair at my dining-room table. Barbara Branden beckoned me to sit beside her. The sun was a form of curse, even Marta Ortega feared her orchids would not survive. But the skin of Barbara Branden was untarnished, absolutely white, precious as porcelain. The sun could not tan her. It would not dare. She was the white of granite in moonlight, impervious. Snow had formed her, a purer air that did not know of loss, charred parchments and feathers, gutted temples. Her original alphabet was intact, without deformities, invasions or erasures. She would remain perfect forever.

"Just in time," Barbara Branden said in her surprisingly fine Spanish, contriving her tone to imply she was pleased to see me. "We were just discussing the Spanish-speaking poets."

Gloria Hernández was unstrapping her tight shoes which seemed wrapped around her flesh like stained bandages. Barbara Branden was talking to her, or near her, sending syllables out across the space where the someone who had once been named Gloria Hernández was painfully removing her worn-out shoes which were no longer white, were a ruined beige, like her skin. She no longer wore these shoes on Sunday. Now Gloria Hernández did not go to confession or mass at Nuestra Señora de los Dolores. Even God found her repellent. Now she wore these shoes to her work in the cluttered ungiving center of the city. They concealed the stumps which had eaten her feet. No one asked Gloria Hernández for a description of her day, any more than one would bother to ask a horse how the hills of scrub brush and rock had been, whether the pack strapped to its flesh was particularly heavy that day, whether the sun had burned.

"Lorca and Neruda you know," Barbara Branden was saying, "and Octavio Paz, of course. And Ernesto Cardenal."

"He's a priest," my oldest son said.

"And Minister of Culture for the Sandinista government," my husband, who wore a red bandana across his forehead, said.

"In Nicaragua," Barbara Branden hastened to explain, as if I, in my mulehood, had no concept of this event.

They spoke almost in unison. They were synchronized, like parts of a clock or a machine no one had bothered to explain to me. I half-expected them to tell me what Nicaragua was. There was a subtle but unmistakable choreography between them.

Hail Mary, full of grace. I will be patient and calm. Your name is Gloria Hernández. You are thirty-three years old. God finds you repellent. You did not complete an adequate amount of invoices today. You will soon be dismissed and walk in the hills with a saddle strapped to your back. Hail Mary, full of grace. People think you are absolutely empty, erased of intelligence and imagination. You keep your powers hidden. Hail Mary, full of grace. The dust and clay of centuries of lethargy and slavery coat your flesh, have become ingrained in your skin, have become the grain itself. You have no eyes, no mouth. You are a rock, a goat. Lies have turned your skin brown. You survive by the nuances of the earth tones which comprise you. You are deceptive, magnificent. You could surprise them, even Marta Ortega. You are calm as mud, tranquil as a dead river, dried, the clay sun-baked, wind-eroded, dust-eaten, a feast for maggots or less. Mule woman. Dead river. Sleep fever. You could astound them. Dead river. Dead river.

"Your husband has quite a feel for verse," Barbara Branden pronounced. She laughed, making the air part its waters and dance around her mouth. She was the cove where the white-sailed boats come to dock, to drift in the tender water at her feet. My silence made Barbara Branden tentative and uncomfortable. I was a storm cloud where there should be none. I spoiled her flawless skies. She pretended she did not notice that the woman named Gloria Hernández despised her. Then she stood up. I noticed that her feet were bare and the nails of her toes painted lilac.

"It's late," Barbara Branden noted. She stared at her gold wristwatch for a long time, as if expecting a definitive discovery. "I'm going out for dinner at seven."

Then Barbara Branden executed an elaborate gesture involving the crossing of two of her sculpted fingers together. This was perceived as significant by my husband and my sons. They responded instantly and also crossed their fingers, the imitation precise as a mirror. There was an innuendo in this, something sexual perhaps. Then, with undisguised reluctance, Barbara Branden finally said goodbye.

Yes, she would be bathing. In the late afternoons, Barbara Branden bathed and perfumed herself. This was her inviolate ritual. In her long yellow hair she created curls. On her skin, a further coating of oils. Men in silver- and cream-colored automobiles took her to dinner in restaurants and then to theaters where actors appeared personally on stage.

When she stepped down her stairs to the street, she was high-heeled, ambered by lamplight, her head held centered like a rare jewel on top of her shoulders. She walked with the stride of a woman certain she is the favorite whore of a powerful lord.

"She isn't even a social worker," Angelina had explained. It was the Sunday when I sat in the front courtyard of Marta Ortega and the fuchsias and ferns were an inverted forest and the tendrils fell above my shoulders like an intimate green rain. "She's a part-time clerk. She merely types reports. Haven't you noticed? She hardly ever works?"

"She's a fraud," Orquídea had agreed. "A pseudo-intellectual."

"She's marginal at best," Angelina said. "She hasn't read a book since college."

"She will marry a dull yellow-haired man and move. She will only speak Spanish in the kitchen to her maid," Marta Ortega had said, dismissing Barbara Branden from the landscape.

In my backyard, breezy folds of sun glanced off the yellow flowers of broccoli I had planted and forgotten, let ripen and run wild, sun-savaged, inedible. Next door, across the bamboo fence which no longer separated our houses, I could hear the water running in the bath Barbara Branden was leisurely taking. She would anoint herself with imported oils, nectars, the fluids of tender purple petals, alluring, a form of cure. She had revealed the secret conspiracy to Miguel. The Church was a deformity. The presidents of nations were corrupt, savage and perverted. Of course she was more intelligent than God or governments. She would scent even her crevices.

My hand were trembling. I was startled by a profusion of blue wildflowers appearing beside the wooden fence at the back of our terraced rectangle of yard. Their unforeseen arrival seemed important. Now there are blue gulfs, I thought, soon there will be rivers.

It occurred to me that if I touched the earth, I might become connected to a root or an anchor. My fingers craved the dirt and mud, a sensation Marta Ortega had described as a subtle caress and a kind of love. I bent into the yawning sun and the air was sweet, as if spiced with nutmeg, ginger or marjoram. And I realized that the earth was alive, irrefutably feminine, vulnerable, a mistress of infinite disguises. And I was gentle as I pulled foxtail weeds from the green warm flesh of her belly.

Next door, the bathwater ceased. Barbara Branden would be selecting her clothing, posing in front of her full-length mirror, evaluating the folds of her pastel clothing from a variety of angles. Then there was the matter of which pastel high-heeled shoes, of course, the beaded or embroidered evening purse, the lace shawl or the crocheted jacket. Then she would ponder her perfumes, selecting which fragrance to spray across her throat and wrists, to dab between her breasts and thighs.

Dusk brushed the prematurely browned mountains like a charcoal smudge signaling the sun to sink. It obeyed and collapsed like a slaughtered animal, a complex beast with eons of history within its skin, a creature like a whale or a woman. The sky was bloody. Then I noticed the fires above the city. Dogs barked. The church bells from Neustra Señora de los Dolores slung themselves low as arrows across the darkening intimidated hills. The air smelled of cooling tamales and flames in brush. And I was afraid of the night with its endless stairs down to the final unabating stone heart where sin is spontaneous, fluid in its mystery and demands.

Hail Mary, full of blood, brush fires and dust, with your sky that slopes at unbearable angles, strangled with brutal confused clouds. Hail Mary, with your fever of sunsets and your translucent chill above lawns hooded, rubbed with limes and acid. Hail Mary, with your hands that rip the raw fibers of dusk, exposing them like the ribs of starved children. That is one of your ordinary pleasures. Hail Mary, full of grace, with your toothless men whistling obscenities in alleys of stone, in plazas of centuries of rubble. Hail Mary, creator of chaos, cataclysm and the exotic unexpected betrayal. It was your indolence and boredom which created sin. And you are insatiable. Still, you are not filled.

In the street below the house where Barbara Branden lived, a man parked a car the color of a star. He climbed the steps and rang her doorbell. He was tall, yellow-haired. He might have been her brother. He offered her a bouquet of small pink roses. She accepted them as if they were less significant than the evening newspaper, a mere token for a thing as grand as herself. Then they walked down her stairs with their hands entwined.

"She is common as geraniums or ivy," Marta Ortega had said. "She will marry a man dull as herself and she will move."

Miguel was sitting at our dining-room table studying a series of words he had inscribed across the surface of a white paper with a thin blue pen. My voice startled him. He had forgotten that the pack animal could speak.

"Why didn't you tell me you wrote poems?" the woman named Gloria Hernández inquired of her husband.

"You never asked," Miguel replied, not looking up from his papers.

We had been married seventeen years. Still we were hooded, remote and concealed as strangers. Miguel wrote poems. Birds nested in the gutted cavity of my head. Perhaps that was the intrinsic nature of events between women and men, I thought. It is the gifts one keeps hidden.

The season turned alarmingly warm. Both the Spanish and American television programs proclaimed it the hottest May in a century. Fires burned in the hills just beyond the city. At night, the circle of flames seemed uncontainable, staining the air, creating bridges and gulfs of red. Everyone on Flores Street stood outside, awed by this spectacle of deranged elements. It was said the palaces of film stars and become rubble and many coyote and deer had died.

Then ash fell from the skies, thick and gray, like a hideous snow across sidewalks and cars, the petals of flowers and sheets strung on lines to dry beneath the shredding sun. It was clearly a portent. I expected locusts would soon appear, the ground shatter and the molecules rise and rearrange themselves. There would be a brief void, a kind of womb and then the new configuration would be born.

In my kitchen, arrogant and confused ants paraded in formation all morning. It was 98 degrees. Fires raged in the hills. The day turned veiled and gray. My mouth was shut tight as the lock of a ship. The clock said it was ten after two. The clock said, You are mad again.

I stood at my front-room window, trying to dissolve my grief selves, my fear selves, and inch into the inexplicable summer paradise of yellow buds on the ripening tomatoes I had staked in rows across my gentle sloping hill. Bluejays scarred the air, drunk on nectars and anger. The heat intensified, became excessive, lethal. Streets seemed filled with the spilled intestines of something rotting forgotten beneath a relentless sun in a region where time curved, bent and lost its sense of purpose and proportion. The world was a failed experiment, begun without conviction and then impatiently and irrationally abandoned.

Hail Mary full of grace, with your fingers of napalm and flame. You have secret manicures. Beneath your carved wooden gloves, your nails are painted crimson and ruby, lacquered, designed to stimulate the flesh. You take men for money. You are in love with blood, I thought as I washed plates. Hail Mary, with your eyes which are the embers of consumed stars.

You ate them for breakfast. You have a marble mouth with lips that burn and scorn. Your codes of acceptable behavior are impossible and bizarre. You stinking bitch, admit this. I dried plates. I thought, No prayers are enough for you. Hail Mary, full of grace, with your scrub-brush-singed hair, cactus ears, your veins which are rivers of butchered concrete. You stare at yourself for hours in the mirror. You think yourself beautiful and young. You are bloated with delusions. I stacked the plates in their pyramids in the cupboards. Later, I heard the sounds of cracking and breakage, as if pieces of the world were falling apart.

I lay next to Miguel in the seared darkness. Hail Mary, full of grace, you work in a botánica on Sunset Boulevard. You offer potions of eternal youth for three dollars. You sell cards promising to predict the future. You wear a red scarf in your hair, sift tea leaves and think you are brilliant. You are banal. Hail Mary, you stand at the counter surrounded by crucifixes which plug into walls and glow, electric. You would undress yourself for a vulture if he came to you with a strand of emeralds in his beak. Hail Mary, full of grace, greed, a propensity for the garish. You son was a mutation, a deformity. You lacked the vocabulary for this distinction and proclaimed your monster a miracle.

These were my thoughts as I lay in a darkness more red than black, smelling the fires, sensing the trees shudder with horror. The scarred air, the wind, the red contamination filtering into the dreams of women and men.

That night, at the bottom of the hill of Flores Street, on the front-yard lawn of Juan Martínez, his ancient elm snapped off from its roots. It had severed itself, leaped up, airborne, winged, like a suicide in reverse. In the morning, everyone on Flores Street gathered near the tree. The elm had defied logic and gravity. It lay on its side like a gigantic slain beast, a creature of legend thought to be extinct. Its proportion was monumental. It lay dazed, its parched grandeur raw and exciting. The implications of its act, its daring and possible motivation left us breathless and trembling.

Juan Martínez and his old deaf dog sniffed at the tree as if it were an immense bone. Consuelo López woke from her stupor to pronounce the risen elm an omen of imminent destruction. She held her rosary, and her hands were shaking. We waited for Marta Ortega. She had known the tree for half a century. The elm had been resplendent even before her house was constructed, the first house to perch on what was then an unnamed hill.

Marta Ortega inspected the elm briefly and noted with a soft voice that it suffered no apparent ailment. Marta Ortega touched the leaves and said she detected no sickness in the branches or the bark. She pronounced the enormous roots that lay exposed to the hot air and the gray ash as still healthy, without decay or the usual ravagement of age.

The death of the elm had been swift and inexplicable. It was similar to stories I had heard of great whales who deliberately beached themselves, who left the sanctuary of the ocean to die slowly, painfully, on alien sand. And the fallen elm resembled a sea creature, blanched, with a skeleton, a structure. Surely there was a purpose in its singular feat, in how it had chosen to separate itself from the earth which bound and caressed it.

I experienced a terrible sadness at the loss of the elm, at the history it had known, the seasons, songs, nests. I wished it could somehow right itself and return, root by root, back into the ground which mourned its absence. Or perhaps in the sheared red-tinged darkness it might simply rise even farther, enter the thin brittle veil of camouflaged sky and become a cloud or a star or even less, a leaf or a moth, something no one would want. Then it could finally be free.

We were released from work at noon. The air was poisonous with static fumes and the contagion of the strange ash from the brushfires still burning the hills. Everything was bathed in a gray luminescence. At noon, an unexpected bell rang in the citadel of invoices. I assumed that the supervisor was going to announce the end of the world. Instead, we were informed that the government had ordered the center city shut. Then we took our imitation stained plastic purses from the bottom drawers of our thin gray metal desks. Then we waited for the iron-grated elevator to take us down to the confused lethal streets in groups of fifteen or twenty.

On the bus, where the common carriers and sparrows ordinarily sat mute within their fear and misery, strangers turned to one another, anxious to chatter about this air which seethed and birthed fires and ash. The world was a red inflammation. The bus was a ship caught in a web of red kelp, a steel net strung across an ocean. The sparrows coughed. Water ran from our insignificant eyes. And I thought, Your name is Gloria Hernández. You must pray for safe passage, a storm-free crossing, stars docile.

Then I was staring at the dead elm lying on Juan Martínez's front lawn. It stuck in the ground like a spear, its trunk whitening like bone. It had contrived to rise as Jesus had. It was a kind of resurrection. I studied its blanched bark, its trunk like the hide of a carcass, its roots like legs which might still move. I stood and waited like a mountain peasant who has journeyed to a shrine, a house where a saint was born or a certified miracle performed. I thought, let it rise into the air, born from ash, mysterious. Let us pray for safe passage, a storm-free crossing, stars docile. And the speared trees turned on their dead sides are holy. And holy, too, the rivers and uncharted currents we float in seasons of random necessity. I imagined the dead elm, its excruciating struggle up through gulfs and eddies of worms and pebbles and rot, into an air brittle and calloused, with spontaneous remission denied. Let us pray for safe passage, a storm-free crossing, stars docile. The elm struggled for transformation and failed.

I waited, but it said nothing. I was not surprised. It was simply one more predictable event in a season of irrevocable and recurrent betrayals. I considered the redundancy of blood and the tedium of being used. Once, May had spoken to me with delicacy and tenderness. That was before my interior regions became a slum, infested and abused.

On Friday morning, the telephone rang at 6 A.M. We were told not to come to work at all. They would not be collecting and counting the pink and blue and yellow slabs of severed skin this day. Cars and buses were barred from the center of the city. Radios cautioned women and men to avoid contact with the toxic sun.

Later, in the interminable gray day which had lost all increments of distinction, Marta Ortega waved to me from across the street. We sat on her shaded back patio. She was taking a brief rest from her garden labors. She poured horchata into tall glasses. She was wearing a damp bandana around her head, trying to shield herself from the contamination hanging above everything, blazing, scorching and raining gray ash.

Marta Ortega said it had never been so hot in what was not yet summer. She admitted that her orchids were ruined, her fuchsias and ferns; her white camellias and rosebushes were ash-covered, singed, unrecognizable. She was replanting, improvising, inventing moist areas and shade. In the early mornings and at dusk, the aged and interchangeable Joseph and Bill helped her.

Then Marta Ortega said it was possible the sun had grown bored by the follies of this world, had rebelled, veered from its course and set itself free. She said many planets and stars simply abandoned the arc they had been instructed to inscribe in the skies and became renegades. Or the sun might be another suicide, like the elm that had sprung from the earth on the front lawn of the house where Juan Martínez lived. Marta Ortega had heard a theory that volcanoes might be responsible for the disruption of the elements, radiation and the fumes from American deodorants and hair sprays. In their longing to produce bodies of artificial fragrance, the Americans were murdering the clouds. It was not a configuration born from sin, Marta Ortega clarified, but rather an accumulation of accidents, ambiguities, a mysterious geometry, human in origin, an expression of the heart in transition.

"The earth sways because it is all always in motion," Marta Ortega told me. "There are no stars which are permanent, no harbors where the languages, rituals, gods and contours do not change. Navigation is an illusion. Women and men drift between mutation and ruin, less than lost, unborn."

Then she took my hand. She cupped it gently in her weathered palms as one might hold a just-hatched bird. She stared into my eyes. And even though we were alone, she whispered, "Gloria, you do not look well."

Then I was walking across the gash of asphalt stretching like a gray stream between our houses. The air was red. Volcanoes and aerosol cans, torn layers of clouds and mutinous suns, trees which defied logic and gravity and committed suicide. Clearly the planet was possessed, steaming, greasy, stained, chaotic, mad. In the reddening siege in the low foothills, I sensed demented rabbits and impassioned farm dogs flinging their fur into strands of barbed wire, their blood seething, their flanks on fire.

At the edge of the gutter, on a thin slice of sidewalk, a jacaranda was ablaze, layered with purple, a lavender infidel. The tree was a woman, brilliant and pagan, an Indian maiden in a village which existed before the concept of plunder, increments, monetary units, conspiracies and sin. Even the jasmine smelled singed. Night was a liquid, hot and red as the neon spears and fluid bands leaping from the walls of bars and motels like the arms of love-starved women.

Dogs barked incessantly, taunted by the heat and the moon which was absolutely full, gleaming shamelessly, bright as a sun. The moon was wide as an open mouth of startling teeth. She hung in the sky, intoxicated, wanton, fearless. Somewhere, she had removed a veil.

• • •

Miguel had fallen asleep on the front-room sofa, a book open, pressed against his chest. As he breathed, the pages swayed like intricate black-and-white sails. His face appeared unnaturally yellow beneath the lamplight. Yellow flowers were growing along his blood canals, stalks and vines and blossoms would soon push through his flesh. He had invented a kingdom of amber. He inhabitated this amber other. I was excluded.

Once a curandera told me a husband could be bound by a mixture of mud, the ground wings of a young grasshopper, fresh jasmine and a teaspoon of menstrual blood. The potion must be collected beneath a full moon on a night exceptional and hot.

There was no breeze in my backyard. It might have been noon, a pitch-black noon on a planet of only singed darkness and virgin water. The moon was inordinately flagrant, elegant and purposeful. She was polished and unconcealed. I felt her heat, her rhythm, how sultry she was beneath her pretense of rock and oceans of dust. Tonight she did not hide her verdant gullies and banyans with trunks embossed by night-blooming luminescent moss. She was a woman, my sister, thinning and going fat, whitening and dimming, pursuing her own version of events. Men wished to trap her, have her stall, tread water, drown.

The moon was ancient and wise. She survived them, pitted herself with the holes of craters which were merely superficial wounds. She buried her strands of sapphires, her lagoons of violets and fuchsias. She deceived them with abundant offerings of inarticulate rock. She said, Behold me, I am infertile. I have no interest in your questions of mortality, prices, evolution or inventions. I do not care which latitude bore witness to your unremarkable nativity. I was busy that night. Do not beseech me with your platitudes. You would bore even a senile god.

I was searching for grasshoppers, yes. They slept in the leaves of the tomato plants I had staked beside the bamboo fence which formed an inadequate border between my house and the other, the house where the white woman lived alone. The fence was stripped of purpose and a shared context. It meant nothing. In this world, a man changed his nationality by removing a plaque from a wall. Such a man could take the wedding band from the finger of his wife, the thin gold metal which was also a mere metaphor.

Sun had stunted my plants. Their leaves were yellow and crisp as the hands of a burned woman. I knelt in the dirt, startled by an unmistakable connection to the earth. The pull of it was tangible as a riptide, electricity or flame. It left a red burn across my fingers, indelible. I will never be free of it.

My sons had recently watered the yard. The ground was unexpectedly damp. It lingered on my fingers like a glove or skin. I recognized that the substance was a chaos of confluences, happenstance, inexplicable intersections. Why you chose this barrio and not some interchangeable other. Why this stucco bungalow on Flores Street and not some interchangeable other? It was not coincidence. And I realized that certain forms of ecstasy and intensity often mistaken for insanity are not expressions of madness but revelation. It is not despair which births them, but an intoxication with what is lucid and pure, absolute, recurrent and irrefutable as the bones of the earth.

Then time dismantled herself like a woman slipping off her sandals, her nylons and her burgundy slit silk skirt. I saw beneath the robed illusion. I was as large as history. I knew what the speared suicidal elm longed to say, the elm which had risen from the earth. It said, Return what has been taken. And the moonlight above me was intense and specific as the eye of a god.

The dirt between my fingers began moving. Of course it had a life of its own, a history, a language of shadows, moisture and wind. And the earth I held in my hands was, at that particular instant, the final and fundamental punctuation, the last chord of the song. I experienced a joy then, profound, rare, celebratory. There were white butterflies in the white moonlight. My hands were charged, edged, infused with power, no longer flesh but the sides of stars, quartz, chipped flints and points crafted from obsidian.

Or perhaps what happened was purely magical in origin. It is possible that I was struck by a species of celestial lightning, an aberration of the elements your vocabulary has yet to identify and define. Your eyes widen with surprise. You know the stars speak but their language remains elusive. You fail to decode the alphabets of dolphins and whales with their insistent elaborate epics. You realize there are nuances which defy you.

I understand you cannot accept this. Then believe what you choose. It is of no consequence to me. I looked up and saw the light in her kitchen. It was a juncture, an opening, and at that precise instant the horizon stopped swaying.

Barbara Branden was sitting on her back porch, her sculpted legs draped across the side of a rattan chair. She was smoking a cigarette and watching me with indifference. I might have been a stray cat rustling among bushes. Her face gleamed like alabaster, a carved madonna, a cameo or a vase a king ordered buried in his vault, beside his gold dagger. He would desire her exquisite form in other lives. Of course she was the secret pearl all divers seek forever, their unspoken motivation, the incarnation of their compulsion to claw down to the floor of the sea. She was marble, lace, lilies, orchids, the ivory and teeth of sharks men are willing to die for.

She had not yet removed the clothing she had worn that evening, washed the rouge from her cheeks, the paint from her lips, or bathed. Her blue eyes were circled with green like grasses surrounding the lip of glacial lakes in summer. Her dress was pink as a tongue, a mouth. Her arms and shoulders were bare, as if any cloth, even silk, would be a violation. Her inhuman lips smiled.

The world stalled. The planet dropped its anchor and sat motionless. The earth was stripped. I stared at Barbara Branden and thought, From your mouth civilizations are created or fall.

I was the spine of the earth, wood, mud, dust, flame. She was an assemblage of cardboard and paint, one-dimensional. Of course Miguel would never touch her, Gloria Hernández suddenly realized. Barbara Branden was too delicate and fine. She was an excavated artifact of incalculable antiquity, completely intact. Barbara Branden was to be polished and placed between glass, protected, an object of admiration and awe, a thing to which one knelt and prayed, constructed altars, offered flowers, the first melons of the harvest or an infant son.

Miguel could no more embrace this white woman than he could the moon. Barbara Branden was a sealed-shut impossibility, unobtainable like certain mountains in the Andes which are perpetually shrouded in snow and remain inaccessible, permitted their uncorrupted sleep.

And Gloria Hernández was earth and sun, was the volcanoes of the southern lands which had birthed her. She was terra-cotta, adobe and thunder. She was deserted dust-covered plazas tracked by vultures and goats. She was the lost magic and poetry, the erased alphabets, murals and songs.

In Tenochtitlán, so many hearts were offered to the gods, the walls of the pyramids reeked and stank with blood. The uninitiated fainted. In the northern mountains which God created in indolence and apathy and then forgot, in the terrain of cactus and wind-beaten rock, the soles of the feet ˉˉˉˉˉ were cut off.

ˉe standing in her kitchen. Straw baskets of avocados and ere ripening on her windowsill. Postcards of cathedrals, boats were tacked to her walls. A philodendron hung from a ceiling near her sink. A knife for cutting meat rested on a tiled ˉeath the green leaves. And we are not all named María. That is ˉa Hernández was thinking as she stuck the knife into Barbara chest.

ˉhite woman was surprised, heavy, frightened and stronger than ˉrnández had imagined. It was hard to drive the metal into her flesh. ˉˉˉˉˉ ˉrnández imagined she was a man having sex, in cars and alleys and backyards, pushing into Barbara Branden until she bled, until she went hoarse yelling harder, more, like you wanted to break me in half. Call me slut. Slap my face. Come in my mouth. I knew what Barbara Branden said to her men. She said, My flesh is tissue, brand me. Make me say please. Bring a friend, then call four more. Show me what teeth are for.

Barbara Branden struggled, terror fed her, the snows and lakes and storms of her youth, the tricks of her tribe's survival. They were skilled hunters and warriors. They had slaughtered the Indians who once inhabited the region they desired. But in this sudden opening, in this liquid anomaly, her knowledge was useless. We looked into each other's eyes and we knew everything, the currents which inexplicably open in oceans, clouds and women. Happenstance and chance. Why this house and not some interchangeable other? Why this night, this particular design and not some interchangeable other?

We understood the fluid junctures, the confluences of lilacs and scrub brush, the dammed rivers, the gulfs where we are born and drown. We shared an intersection of cactus and orchids, an astonishing clarity. We embraced in the end. We were kin then, sanctified by blood.

Did I say it was difficult to force the blade into the white marble skin of Barbara Branden? The texture of her world was sharper, the outlines distinct and edged. It was harder than pounding a stake into the sunbaked unyielding ground of a field in a drought in July in a parched decade. It was like giving birth in reverse, returning what had been taken.

Then the air was clear acres of unmolested moonlight, strands of sea-scrubbed pebbles, strings of dwarf eggs and infant stars. There was a clarification. The erasure was absolute and pure. And I realized that the screeching had stopped. The chaos of black petals which had etched their demented chant into my ears, battered me as the sea lashes her history into a shell, ceased. The liquid enormities and weight, the deforming waves with their tide greasy and thick, receded. My bruises dissolved and flew from my flesh like freed birds. Then the brown-and-gray miniature sparrows crawled from my eyes, their twigs and feathers, their nests and debris, all of this left me.

Blue buds bright as sapphires, as lapis lazuli, erupted on a branch near my back-garden gate. They burst and fell, drifted soft as moss, as a purple mist, as a veil of petals floating from clouds across my marigolds and carnations. I was tired. I returned to my house and slept.

No, there is nothing more I can tell you. The details of my personal architecture of disaster are insignificant, are mere approximations of that which is more intimate and complex.

You assemble the pages which define my life. You cannot resolve that which resists definition, that which is raw, unknowable. It has always been like this. And there is little difference between an eye opening and closing, a window shade, a door, a fan, the life of a woman or a city or a world. Such distinctions are quantitative, not qualitative. They are negligible.

And I am pages in a file. My life is blue ink marks on paper like the chicken scratches sometimes left in dust. It is more than enough.

In the jungles of the Yucatán, jaguar are killed by wooden spears. When I was a girl, in the pueblo of Santa Cruz, in the northern mountains of wind and cactus, coyotes were murdered with wooden stakes. Such acts were considered an ordinary sort of surgery.

Yes, gather the blue-ink chicken scratches of my life. You are precise, graceful as you place my pages between a metal clip and slide my file into your briefcase. I know we will not meet again. You will walk from this room into another region and dimension. You will need a passport.

Do I imagine your eyes grieve? Remember, I am unrepentant. I am speaking about an other, a texture of intoxication and terror. There are gulfs which cannot be charted or rafted. They flow as they choose beneath skies molten, livid, outraged by birds blazing between stars. Always, there is the sudden severing of the ordinary and the impulse which insists upon manifestation. Beside the enormity and complexity of this, the interwoven and incandescent fibers and strands, all of your concepts are inadequate.

Understand this, if only this. I am completely convinced that in a tender and less recognizable region, where your compulsion of absolute angles and linear evolution has been ignored or rendered obsolete, my blood gesture will have an acceptance transcending explanation. In an undefined latitude, verdant, hot, pagan, rooted with orchids and rocked by green thunder in raw banyan hills, my personal geography will claim me. In a land vivid with green wind where noon is liquid and night exaggerated, the moon unmolested and wooded, my separate elements will be reassembled. In a dominion inexhaustible as the earth, as her oceans, as her cliffs of unceasing and languid palms green above lime and jade coves, calm and undisturbed, perpetually summered, I will find a dialect in which I am fluent. In ports green winds have erased of name, my heart will be calm. In a juncture dense, passionate, excessive with green cadences, green chimes, flesh, gulfs and mouths, I will without question be absolved.

PART THREE

It was a season of indisputable omens even before Gloria Hernández went insane. Gloria Hernández, the young and proper Mexicana housewife who walked her sons to Alta Vista Street School each morning and then stood transfixed at her living-room window, staring with eyes listless, vacant. She existed encased in an impenetrability Marta Ortega had mistaken for stupidity. Gloria Hernández was not inarticulate. Rather, she was engrossed in an elaborate hallucination and embraced by an impulse which spoke no intelligible language. It was not an absence but an intoxication of abundance and raw passion which rendered her mouth useless.

On the periphery, Marta Ortega observed the young woman growing increasingly haunted and silent. She seemed skeletal, ghosted and partial. But Marta had little interest in her. Gloria Hernández was dull, bereft of imagination, a minimal woman without significance. Marta Ortega had failed to recognize and identify the symptoms, to detect the rare punctures opening like eyes or precious stones in the woman's forehead. Gloria Hernández kept her gift hidden. Her disguise was masterful. And Marta had been satisfied with the surface.

Marta Ortega had witnessed the arrival of Barbara Branden. She meant nothing. Marta Ortega observed Barbara Branden descend her wooden stairs. She was ordinary, a dilettante, defensive and arrogant. She inhabited the exterior only, the predictable and conventional. Even within her own limited context, her triumphs were small. On one evening or another, a bland blond man opened a car door for her. On one evening or another, the car rolled down the hill that was Flores Street, erasing the occupants from the landscape effortlessly. There was no debris or lingering.

Then Gloria Hernández, demented with heat and a private fever resistant to definition, stabbed the white woman with a knife, drove the blade through the woman's breast. And then again. Gloria Hernández, a creature of the sea floor and corals, penetrated the metal blade on four-teen separate occasions into the silly clerk who called herself a social worker. Barbara Branden, the shallow and subadequate typist who had, in ignorance and indolence, flirted with Gloria's husband.

Fires raged, ash fell from clouds, the elm sprang from the ground like a suicide in reverse and Gloria Hernández had committed a blood act. With her mouth useless, a well of unresolvable impulses, she had brought ambulances and police cars to Flores Street. Morning was ripped apart by sirens and white men in blue uniforms with questions, clipboards and tiny notebooks which issued without warning from their pockets. They wore pistols. And Flores Street shuddered and quaked.

Perhaps it began with the fires in the hills just beyond the city. Flames spawned their own, litters of lava-tongued monsters born to feed their insatiable hunger with scrub oak, manzanita, wooden sheds and the skin of disoriented coyote, rabbit and deer. The fires were indiscriminate, as if knowing instinctively they were doomed. They would be judged by the heat of their emblem, the intensity of their blaze, and not their duration. This intuition of their mortality made them decadent.

Attendance at Nuestra Señora de los Dolores noticeably swelled. Even the notoriously lapsed and fallen of Flores Street were seen in the confession line. At mass on Sunday, the pews were entirely filled and many had to stand in the back of the church. Some were surprised to discover that the ceremony was now in Spanish and finally, as if magically, comprehensible.

Rosaries were taken from drawers where they had languished for years beneath nightgowns and socks. Photographs of saints were dusted, polished and placed conspicuously on living-room and bedside tables. Marta Ortega watched the residents of Flores Street returning to the church with the conviction of heathens to a mountain altar when a vol-cano rumbled. This analogy pleased her. She repeated it to Joseph.

Marta Ortega did not consider the impact of the flames on the dis-guised interior of the woman named Gloria Hernández. She noticed Gloria walking to and from the bus on Sunset Boulevard which transported her to a part-time job in the center of the city. Marta Ortega did not ask the young housewife to describe the specific nature of her employment or sketch the area she inhabited three days each week. Gloria Hernández was obviously a menial. She sewed or assembled, her task repetitive, without variation or nuance. Gloria Hernández was shrubbery, oleander, a strip of sand or gravel, a part of the landscape, unremarkable. Gloria Hernández was density without vision, like an object. And Marta Ortega had dismissed Gloria from her exclusive domain.

Then ash fell from the sky and lay on sidewalks and lawns like a thick gray snow, brittle and ugly as the final winter on a dying world. A planet imploding, opening up delirious with juxtapositions and rare intersections of incongruent elements at the precise instant of inflammation, of becoming nova, of careening into extinction or infinity.

The ash settled across the petals of magenta bougainvillea in courtyards and alleys. It coated cars and sheets left to dry on clotheslines strung beneath the deranged and erratic sun. It was clearly a message from God, Marta Ortega's neighbors maintained. Was she blind?

"Now, Marta," Joseph chided from his patio, "must God write your name and Social Security number across your garden before you accept the obvious?"

"Yes," Marta replied. "I have often wondered at the nature of his hand. I expect calligraphy at the least. Block letters would be a disappointment."

The stagnant air grew denser. Factories were ordered shut. Cars and buses were barred from the hideous wall of unbearable noise and misery that had become the center of the city. A ruined city, Marta Ortega noted, with a center and not a heart.

Once Los Angeles had been labeled the city of the future. But it had no core, it rotted at the edges and asserted a splendor which proved hollow, stillborn, its roots an illusion. The ground refused this alien configuration. Los Angeles was no longer described as a model to be emulated and duplicated. Of course, the trade routes always shifted.

Now Los Angeles was an elaborate series of diversions for tourists, an immense souvenir stand. The future was rumored to be in New Mexico or Alaska. Or perhaps it was no longer in the United States. London reclaimed the Thames, freed the river from pollution, and men fished on the banks at dusk again. Or perhaps Tokyo, where railroads were a marvel and, within the chaos, order was preserved.

On Flores Street dogs barked in an unbroken frenzy. Perhaps the belly of the earth would dissolve, her battered skin collapse like a wound or a well and swallow them. Or the canvas sail stall, flatten listless and becalmed. Marta Ortega worked in her garden. Always the trade routes shifted, she reminded herself, oppressed by the heat. And this season was like any other.

Both *La Opinión* and the *Los Angeles Times* proclaimed it the hottest May of the century. Scientists discussed inverted layers of air, the failure and confusion of currents and winds, eruptions of volcanoes, nuclear radiation and toxins. A clergyman alluded to the accumulation of evil and narcotics. An American expert claimed the clouds were shrinking, punctured and torn like bed sheets, ravaged from the fumes of aerosol cans.

Marta Ortega assimilated information from newspapers, the radio and the incessant flapping chickenlike mouths of her neighbors. She was particularly fond of the notion that the clouds were ripped and suffering. They were similar to linen. They too could wear out, become stained from relentless abuse, infidelity, lies, spilled tequila and passion stolen or contrived.

Marta Ortega had always imagined that space was not empty but populated by legions of women hanging clothing to dry on lines strung between a series of various-sized and-colored worlds. Planets of magenta and fuchsia where the air was purple as a flock of wine-plumed jungle birds, their nests lilac petals, their eggs violet. Or planets of green, where the boulevards were gullies, perpetually moist, overgrown by a millennium of ferns and moss and palms. There the air was lime and it rained leaves.

Men believed the glue of the world was steel, nails and concrete, edifices and machinery, highways, citadels and pyramids. Marta Ortega knew the planet was actually held together by entirely different materials. Linens, for one, and orchids, cymbidiums and cattleyas. And stringed instruments, the fronds of palms, the arcs of subtle transformed light created by candles and streetlamps in autumn, antique laces and brocades, the skin of infants and the cool caress of jade necklaces across a throat in August. Men could sit in their metal vessels at the bottoms of oceans or on what appeared to be the surface of the moon, but the earth was an assemblage of hand-painted parasols and fans, books, discs of music, parchments and feathers. The fragile antiquities contoured by inspiration, personal lyricism and obsession. Such delicacies were, by their intrinsic nature, impermanent. Shells and the teeth of sharks, steel girders and rocks remained, artifacts without illumination.

Suddenly Marta Ortega remembered herself as a young woman, fifteen years old and pregnant. She had experienced a sense of the fundamental liquid substance then. She stood alone in her backyard, staring into the sky with intensity and longing. The sky had returned her gaze. There was a communion. Marta realized planets were not built, not by the hands of men or gods. They were formed molecule by molecule. Space was fertile as the sandy loam alongside deltas, a womb. The void was not empty but merely waiting. What men called space was simply the belly between barren cycles and abundance. All women knew this, thinning and going fat, condensing the possibilities, weaving the fabric of all things, committing the ultimate sorcery and letting it flow between their legs like rain or waves. Oceans were born this way, snakes, and comets, rituals and science, lava, infants and stars.

"Marta, mi amor. You are looking muy india tonight," Joseph observed. "Are you contemplating a pilgrimage to our local shrine, perhaps? Have you polished your beads?"

Marta felt herself responding in kind. Her lips curved into a partial smile, and then she heard herself laugh. Their voices were physical, a form of caress. "It is a remarkable spectacle," she noted.

Marta Ortega stood near Joseph in his courtyard. The hills seemed inordinately close. The flames were brutal in their torture, consuming the scrub brush in slow motion, with pleasure.

"It is indeed extraordinary," Joseph agreed.

"It requires acknowledgment," Marta Ortega said.

"Tribute. Vestal virgins. Fresh human hearts, flutes, brass gongs. A real celebration." Joseph was excited. "I'll make piña coladas."

They sat in Joseph's courtyard at a round table impaled by a red-and-white cloth parasol such as she had seen in postcards of cafés in Paris, Spain, the cities of South America, Italy and Mexico. It was in such cafés that Angelina and Orquídea sat, drank, dreamed, wept. Beneath such parasols they were deceived and betrayed. Joseph and Marta drank a pitcher of piña coladas and then another.

Upstairs, Bill was playing phonograph records. "Was it in Tahiti, was it on the Nile, Just an hour ago when I saw you smile," the black voice seemed to float and cut the night, a deeper burning within the darkness. Her voice was raw with a transcendental personal anguish, as if her mouth was being singed as she formed the words with her lips.

Of course Angelina and Orquídea should be with me now, Marta thought, watching the flames in silence. Angelina should be here on this night, accusing. Angelina, with her voice venomous, screaming. "We be-came strange, Madre, idiosincráticas. You insisted we drift gossamer, mar-ried to the air."

"You instructed us to work without a net," Orquídea would insist.

"Without a fucking rope," Angelina would add, after a pause designed to sting.

Her daughters should ring her doorbell on this night of flame and ash. Angelina or Orquídea yelling, "You taught us to flaunt our triumphs, to sentimentalize our defeats. We learned to demand both awe and pity."

Their interactions were stylized, a form of ritual. Marta Ortega would deny this.

"Mamacita," one of her daughters would say softly, "You did. We became bad winners."

"Bad losers," Angelina or Orquídea would amplify, pointedly.

Then her daughters would recite their standard litany, the ways in which she had failed them, the ways in which she had deformed their personalities, made them neurotic, desperate, flawed. After the recitation of their despoiled childhoods, one detail, one example, after another, they would fall to their knees and beg for her forgiveness.

"I don't care if they blow the whole thing up," Joseph told her. He was drinking the last piña colada in the second pitcher. "As long as they've put Billie Holiday on tape somewhere."

"They've buried everything in vaults and time capsules, haven't they?" Marta was interested.

"Only the speeches of presidents, I imagine," Joseph said with sad-ness. He stared at her face. "Mi Reina de la Calle Flores, your eyes are absolutely obsidian tonight. You haven't, by chance, been taking bella-donna?"

Marta Ortega was thinking about the vaults. "They have not saved photographs of orchids and butterflies? No films of waves, infants or women giving birth?"

"Lo siento, pero no. All they put down there is nerve gas and the Bill of Rights," Joseph laughed. His chest shuddered in a spasm of dry cough-ing. Then he knocked his glass off the table and collapsed, his face nestled into his arms. Marta wrapped her shawl across his shoulders. Joseph was slumped across the table, snoring softly. Bill would carry him to bed.

Now, as Marta Ortega stood in her back garden, as she stared at the night sky which was webbed with red and smelled like seared human hair, she was assaulted by an inexplicable and profound intuition that the fires, the smoke and the ash were mere metaphors, symptoms of a complicated and irrevocable rearrangement, an impulse demanding physical manifestaion.

Marta Ortega was not superstitious. She was pragmatic and eclectic. After all, by nationality she was an American, by texture and choice a Chicana. She had been born on the edge of the central village which would eventually become the infestation of spires and steel citadels called Los Angeles. Her home was just beyond the original pueblo of Nuestra Señora la Reina de los Angeles, in a green pocket which would later be eradicated by tractors and bulldozers to form a home for the American baseball team the failed city lured from New York.

The barrio of her youth was a composition of greens, tamed fields, sloping hills constant with wildflowers and family plots of maize, tomatoes and melons. In the long afternoons, women fed chickens, leaned across whitewashed or stucco courtyard walls and gossiped between their scrubbing and their cooking. They watered terra-cotta pots of whatever stalks or leaves they had brought with them from Mexico. The ground accepted these seeds and cuttings with familiarity and recognition. Then the women dispensed advice, traded and embellished herb remedies, treated the afflictions of illness, mourning and childbirth with the juices of healing plants, with the vestiges of the antique magic and science that had somehow survived the Conquistadores.

Their pueblo seemed too insignificant to attract the attention of any conqueror or collection of warriors who were presently referring to themselves as governments. Time moved as slowly as a thing betrayed, shellshocked and paralyzed. This was collectively perceived as a phenomenon for which one should be deeply grateful.

Occasionally current events were discussed with an excitement Marta Ortega dismissed as desperate and contrived. These conversations were the exclusive province of men. And when she heard the men speak of revolutions, she assumed they meant the spinning of the planet, the arc it had been instructed to inscribe in the sky. When the men pronounced out loud the names of legendary capitals and nodded their heads as if the words Moscow or Paris actually affected them, Marta Ortega felt it was the preening of peacocks only.

Of course new lines would be drawn across maps, she thought, ignoring the pomposities of the men as she did the clacking of chickens. It was the nature of territory to change with regularity. Always there were documents to etch, emblems to design and seals to affix on various scrolls or parchments, depending upon which tribe, empire or warlord had won the most recent of their redundant, relentless battles for pueblos and land. Marta Ortega recognized that these conflicts were waged from habit and a vast irredeemable boredom, intrinsic to the cycles, the process.

Every two years, American government officials visited the village. They made no attempt to shield their disgust at the lack of interest the women and the men displayed in currently approved methods of hygiene, styles of education, roads and telephone poles. Still, government representatives appeared just before elections. The opposing delegates offered increasingly extravagant rhetoric and promises of American inventions which they described as marvels, as if they were objects created specifically for them by God.

The outlines of the future the Americans proposed were perceived as incomprehensible and aberrant, encased in cement, steel and wires, in patterns blatantly hostile to birds, trees, winds and clouds. Were it in their power, the Americans would erase the seasons, amputate the limbs of God, the interwoven and indigenous. Man would become peripheral. It was obvious these Americans were bereft of aesthetics, imagination and sensibility. Their religious education was defective. It was also possible they were lunatics.

Their banner was crowded with stars as if they already owned the heavens. If saluting their flag would appease them, the men of the pueblo would remove their sombreros, place their right hands across their hearts and repeat the required oath which was distributed on sheets of paper in phonetic English. Of course they would salute this arrogant flag which asserted a claim to the skies. They would stare at it with the devotion reserved for religious objects, retablos and bultos. This pose was not deemed offensive or fraudulent. It was simply an act of common sense.

Once, her father, Víctor Ortega, had been selected pueblo spokesman. This was not an honor but a matter of burden passed from one man to another by the drawing of straws. Her father removed his stained felt hat, the last article of clothing from Europe he still possessed, scratched his head and asked, humbly, "Why would we want you to build roads for us?"

"For travel," the American official replied, staring at her father, who had been born in Madrid and educated in Paris and Vienna, as if he were the village idiot. Or perhaps the entire pueblo was populated solely by people of subnormal intelligence and this particular spokesman was, in point of fact, absolutely representative. This distinction was of no interest to the American delegate.

Her father said nothing. After a long while, in which leaves swayed and fell like a green rain and exotically embossed butterflies fluttered, their wings an orange and purple enamel, the American candidate explained that with roads everything would happen faster.

"Why would we want it to happen faster?" her father inquired, after a discreet pause. "Or even to happen at all?"

The pueblo was considered backward, recalcitrant. The inhabitants were stupid as children. Or perhaps, by blood, congenitally moronic, incapable of grasping even the bold print of reality. This was noted on numerous reports which were filed in the archives of the edifice now called City Hall. City Hall was an effortless walk up the worn footpaths of the valley of green which was the village of her birth. But the city which was inexorably growing there, rising up and pushing out like a demented plant, rootless, with patches of mismatched and useless foliage, seemed remote. A weed, really, and visually abusive to the eye.

It was said the Chinese who had come to build the railroad remained within the city, living in catacombs beneath the train station itself. These Chinos were respected for their mastery of herbs. But it was also known that they smoked drugs which induced a trance and rendered sleeping and waking indecipherable. Once a man experienced these special pipes, he was enslaved. And these drugs could be purchased with ease.

There was also considerable speculation about the white women and men who were every day arriving in increasingly alarming numbers. These white women and men came with trunks and crates. They were not tourists but clearly intending to become permanent. It was rumored there were now entire streets near City Hall where women sold their bodies.

Now, as Marta Ortega stands alone in her back garden, studying the fires eating the hills, she remembers the village of her birth as seeming tentative. It was not built, she decides, rather it perched. Even when tomatoes and maize appeared on their own accord, rising like red- and yellow-winged things at one with the air, the land appeared muted. It flattened and darkened as if it bore a defect, a self-limiting factor, a hidden inability to be more than what it was.

"At least it wasn't pretentious," Joseph once pointed out.

The village of her birth had a random quality, as if its original settlers considered it temporary and insignificant. The pueblo straddled a creek, un tributario del río de Los Angeles. Crossing the village was a matter of mud or dust. In seasons when there was too much rain or not enough, nothing at all pushed up from the earth and the area seemed enormous then, directionless, abandoned.

This is ridiculous, Marta Ortega decided. She had witnessed countless fires in the hills surrounding the city. They were common, like mudslides and streets that flooded. Then she walked into her yellow wooden house, her second skin. It would clothe and protect her in this season of conflagrations and ash and rambling neighbors, mouths laden with Apocalypse and penances. As she entered her house, the black woman was singing, "Now you say you're lonely, say you cried the whole night through. Well, you can cry me a river, cry me a river, because I cried a river over you."

There was still a river then, Marta Ortega remembered. In the summers, she swam in the warm weed-colored waters with her brothers, Enrique and Vicente. She was closer to Enrique, the second-born. Only one year separated them. Her brothers cut wild bamboo with a machete and fashioned fishing poles. Once, after weeks of elaborate discussion, her brothers constructed a raft. They would paddle from the pueblo to the ocean and then turn south, back to Mexico. They envisioned the Mexican sea as a steaming green gulf, bands of turquoise and jade studded with gigantic yellowfin and marlin. They would hunt eagles in the coastal mountains and stalk tigers in fields of wild orchids and strawberries beneath coconut palms, mangoes and trees of papayas and bananas.

It was said that in Mexico gigantic insects with stingers like metal daggers nested in the fronds of palms. One could saw off these daggers and sell them for substantial sums of American money. Birds with gold-and-purple plumes and wingspans wider than a tall man with his arms spread flew in flocks at dusk. It was rumored these birds could speak in the language of antiquity. Perhaps after her brothers speared enough yellowfin and marlin, collected bags of eagles and the daggers from insects, after they had spoken with the birds and then murdered them for their rare plumes, they would venture into the interior, south, where mountains stood like sentries and the ground was a dominion of vines and brilliant yellow petals that hummed and glowed. Vultures were fat and numerous. Jaguar thrust orange heads silently, telepathically, perpetually hungry, almost invisible in the coral orchid underbrush. Their skins could be bartered or worn for protection like armor.

Vicente and Enrique packed little for their expedition. They would eat fish as they sailed. Then there would be the coconuts, strawberries and mangoes. Their raft had capsized immediately. Her brothers swam back to shore, ruining their clothing, scratching their arms and cutting their fingers.

She was held responsible. She was the firstborn of what would eventually be six children, nearly a woman and fully capable of evaluating danger. That night her father beat her for the first time. He would strike her once more, but that was later, after she announced her decision to divorce her husband and sometime shortly before the Americans voted to twist the natural channel of water which was el río de Los Angeles into an ugly scar of concrete gullies they labeled flood control.

After they chained the river, even when it rained opulent and torrential, the water was tamed within the terrible cement borders, the hideous gash that now severed the city in half and cut the river from its inalienable connection to the ocean, rebirth and absolution. Marta Ortega thought again of her brothers, Vicente and Enrique, and their raft. It was possible they had sensed a hidden channel, a portal beneath the illusionary ordinary. They had responded to the pull of an enormity which was liquid and irresistibly alluring, a magnet, a sudden intoxication with what defied increments and conventional divisions. It was possible that at that moment precisely, her brothers had most clearly perceived the fundamental nature of the world.

There had been a river then and seamless acres of orange trees, groves of lemon and grapefruit where bluejays dived drunken between branches, bewitched by summer heat and the sweetness bloating their bellies. Berries on vines climbed without effort from the dirt. Cars were a rarity, cubicles of thin metal crawling on wheels. No one took them seriously. It was merely a silly American fashion which would quickly run its frantic and excessively publicized course and pass, like any other aberration.

Certainly even the white men in City Hall understood that such vehicles implied an altered universe. They were men who preferred massacre to the taking of slaves, but they were not uniformly deranged. Some among them could recognize that the future they were feverishly designing would become one vast series of concrete gashes, interlocking, insatiable, a kind of fungus which would eat the skin of the world. She had been wrong then, underestimating the dimensions and implications of the situation. Perhaps she was failing to grasp the intimations now, denying the evidence, refusing to acknowledge the separate details of catastrophe forming a message from one end of Flores Street to the other.

Marta Ortega had come to Flores Street as a bride and a Catholic. She was fourteen years old when her father decided she would marry Salvador Velásquez, the son of his business partner. Her father and the father of Salvador Velásquez had built the one store in the village, el mercado del pueblo. The continuity of this structure would be solidified not by contracts or documents but by blood and heirs. That was the unassailable purpose of marriage.

Marta was strong rather than beautiful. There was a faint slackening of her skin, as if she were holding her girl's body in place only by an act of extraordinary will. It was also suggested that she spent an inappropriate amount of time sitting.

"You will look like an ox by twenty," her mother pointed out, shortly before she was forced to marry. This was in her large white bedroom in the back of her father's house. Arched windows faced the backyard lush with pink and white camellias.

"He's a drunk and a fool," Marta wailed. The backyard rolled across her bedroom, green as a bolt of velvet, acres of moss, waves, all that was lavish, scented and relevant. "I despise him."

"Be realistic," her mother offered. Her mother had not, in her own life, been realistic, had surrendered to a transitory impulse which propelled her into an exile that was physical, geographic, psychological and permanent. Her mother had lost the boulevards of Mexico City, the mahogany-paneled rooms of her home, the ocean, the jungle, the opera and even her leather gloves. Her mother knew the consequence of incaution, the turbulence of veering from the obvious path.

Between them they understood that Marta had failed bitterly, almost blatantly, the lessons of her womanhood. Her father wanted her to play the piano. He paid a man to come from the center of the city, to instruct her. But her hands were not nimble. She could not caress the keys, merge her flesh with the ivory and be one with the music.

"Touch them like flesh," her father commanded when she practiced. This made her hands tremble. "They are white faces, cameos. Blancos como ángeles y santos. Are you blind as well as deaf?"

But she could not seduce the instrument or perceive its glaring white rows of teeth as skin. Her father dismissed the music teacher. He looked at his daughter as if she had deliberately betrayed him. Let those stumps of fingers do the ordinary and useful, he decided within himself. Let her bathe children and scrub floors. They ceased speaking.

The separate elements of her failure were accumulating with an indisputable force. In the kitchen, she burned even tortillas. Such a lack of focus was clearly deliberate, a flagrant act of rebellion. She was relieved of dishwashing duties on the basis of the number of glasses and plates she had broken. It was noted that her menstruation always seemed to arrive with a debilitating violence on Sundays when the entire pueblo went to mass. She was struck by influenza and fevers on confession days. Her pattern was becoming obvious and tedious, even to them.

In her bedroom late at night or on rare afternoons when she convinced her parents of yet another virulent and perhaps contagious illness, Marta Ortega read incessantly. She began with the classics in Spanish and English, then magazines, novels translated from Russian, French and German and slim volumes of poetry. Her parents were stunned by her ability to collect these books and by the perversity of her selection.

"A trunk heavy with books like a chest of rocks," her father thundered one afternoon when he returned from confession at the village church, Nuestra Señora de la Soledad. With rare indiscretion, he entered her room without knocking, flung open her wooden trunk of books, the box which was supposed to contain bridal ornaments, and scattered the books one by one, as if they were feathers or straw.

"Baudelaire. Melville. Dickens," he raged. "A thousand books and not one of them is about God. A treasure chest of rocks without a single nugget of gold."

Marta Ortega read alphabetically. On the afternoon her father burst into her bedroom, she had just completed Cervantes. According to her plan, she would read Dostoevsky next.

She slept poorly. She spent hours staring out her arched bedroom window. Moonlight draped itself across the skins of the plants in a manner which both calmed and aroused her. She listened to her mother and father whispering. They were discussing methods of disposing of her.

She was subjected to a traditional courtship. Salvador Velásquez accompanied her to church each Sunday morning. Mass was now compulsory. Nothing less than a severed limb would serve as an excuse, her parents informed her. After church, Marta and her betrothed sat on the patio of her father's house. Her mother punctuated their silence with glasses of lemon or orange juice, pitchers of ice water or horchata. Marta Ortega's conversations with her husband-to-be were mechanical, without an implication of depth, as if they were already utterly bored with each other.

"I recently completed the essays of Ralph Waldo Emerson," she offered. She was on E then.

Salvador Velásquez stared into the distance. He had, of course, never heard of Emerson or read an essay, a novel or a poem. After a longer silence, he said, "I went to the cockfights last night."

Marta attempted to contrive a reply to this trivial and barbaric information. She found that she could not. Her mother refilled their glasses.

Marta Ortega hated their enforced Saturday and Sunday afternoons in the walled courtyard patio of her father's house. The yard was a kind of prison, she realized, and later she would inhabit another cell with this man. She had been condemned, she thought with rage, choosing to watch the fronds of the palms sway in a slow sea breeze. They were dull but preferable to the face of her future husband. She longed to be free of artifice, back in her bedroom where the white walls caught the sun as canvas sails trap wind. In her bedroom, wind insinuated a rhythm across the bougainvillea and camellias, an intimation of music which was tranquil and cleansing.

"Face it, Marta," her mother informed her, "it is Salvador Velásquez or the convent."

It was early afternoon. Marta was reading Edward FitzGerald's translation of the *Rubáiyât of Omar Khayyám,* exulting in what a wonderful selection she had chanced to make for F.

Marta Ortega considered the two possibilities she was permitted. They were both grotesque but were oddly similar. "Can one read without restriction in a convent?"

"No reading whatsoever. Just the Bible and that only occasionally," her mother replied with authority.

"I will never forgive you for this atrocity," Marta Ortega told her father when he announced the date of her marriage. Víctor Ortega did not respond. He had not heard a single syllable she uttered since he dismissed the piano teacher. She had become invisible to him then.

The village seamstress arrived with silks, white laces and spools of thread. Needles jutted out of satin pincushions like horribly deformed miniature porcupines. Marta Ortega perceived this invasion as an abominable intrusion. She was considering Persia, wine, sultans and the concept of time, drunkards, gods who scorned, mysteries and pleasures.

"If I must be subjected to this senseless ritual, this butchery of the soul, could I not at least have a green dress?" Marta asked.

Even her mother did not answer. There were other children. The youngest was not yet three.

"You are treating me like chattel. I think it is illegal," Marta Ortega informed her family. She bolted her bedroom door shut. Five years had passed since women were granted the privilege of voting. Now the implications, the labyrinths of ramifications and the literal logistics of women as property were being debated in one legislature or another. It was men who were doing the talking, of course. And Marta realized that the decision, should it come at all, would arrive too late.

Marta Ortega felt as a woman might in 1941 or 1963, perhaps, who is pregnant and does not wish to birth the unformed growth which time will transform into a baby. Her only alternative is to seek out a midwife in secret. An old woman, speaking with an accent and a mouth dense with garlic, perhaps. A furtive woman with a coat hanger and no anesthetic. They would exchange money but not names. Perhaps the young woman would bleed to death on a floor scattered with old newspapers or later on the seat of a Greyhound bus.

In a broader sense, Marta realized she was simply a victim of circumstance. The nature of life was a juxtaposition of accidents, of veils which could not be pierced, drawn straws, missed trains and chance. It was all a kind of lottery. Her name had been arbitrarily picked in the total-sacrifice department. She recognized the random horror of her fate and decided to accept her situation with strength and dignity. She discovered she possessed neither quality. And she could not stop crying.

"This isn't forever," her mother said, cheerfully, the night before her wedding. "Compromise is the basis of civilization. Profligates have a way of dying young. You will return here with your children."

"No," Marta said softly, her heart blank and dull, duller even than Oliver Goldsmith who had been her unfortunate choice for G. "I will never live here again." Marta said this with certainty.

Bells were ringing in Nuestra Señora de la Soledad beyond her parents' garden, beyond the house with the arched windows where she would never live again. Salvador Velásquez was rushing her into the early afternoon like a man pursued by maniacs with machetes. They were racing from the pueblo of their birth toward the new barrio which was forming three miles to the north, to the lone house on a hill which would become Flores Street.

Her father built the house as part of her dowry. Of course they had to pay to get rid of her. Marta asked her father to paint the house green. She implored, threatened and wept. Her father ignored her. Víctor Ortega had decided that the new amendment to the United States Constitution which gave women the right to vote did not alter reality. Women were still undeniably inferior in all respects. Then Víctor Ortega ordered her brothers to paint the wooden structure yellow.

Almost immediately she realized why Salvador Velásquez had agreed to marry her despite the fact that she had inherited her mother's dark skin and a body which few considered delicate or alluring. Salvador Velásquez wanted tall sons with good lungs and strong shoulders. And she came from an impeccably fortunate family, without a trace of insanity or consumption on either side, no webbed feet, hunchbacks or idiots, no withered limbs or obvious defects. She was to serve as breeding stock. She was flooded with rage.

Marta Ortega would give birth to two children in the yellow wooden house on what would become Flores Street. Across the decades, there had been brief flirtations with pink, longer sieges of beiges and blues, but now it was yellow again. Marta Ortega possessed an unequivocal sense of cycles, of completion and return. She could not ignore the fact that the house was the color it had been fifty years before when she and her eighteen-year-old husband were its first inhabitants.

So this is what the incessant chatter of omens, displeased gods, and torn ozone layers is doing to me, she thought with revulsion. Cataclismo y catastrofe. The hills are embraced by flame and I am reminiscing about Salvador Velásquez. She almost laughed out loud.

She calmed herself. She bore his memory without emotional impact. Since their divorce time had erected freeways, airports, forests, cemeteries, missile silos, and spaceships. A profusion of infants and taxicabs, cardboard boxes and cribs, orchids and hysterical telephone calls blocked the path between who she had once been and what she had become.

Salvador Velásquez was beneath the debris. Marta Ortega would have to perform an act of psychological excavation and she did not consider her child-husband worthy of the effort of digging and restoring, polishing and examining. One went on such archaeological expeditions of the soul to salvage magnificent artifacts, the memories of how her daughters' hair felt like moss against her lips, how pink the infant fingernails were and how they tossed in their just-born sleep, still part liquid, bound to the sea.

Salvador Velásquez drank too much and held his liquor badly. Often, he fell down and injured himself or the furniture her father and brothers had built for them, the tables and chairs which were part of her dowry like the bales of hay that accompany a cow.

Salvador Velásquez wanted sex constantly but often fell asleep before adequately completing the act. He blamed her for this failure, claiming her body was unyielding as a field in August. They rarely spoke. She ignored him effortlessly. She was on H then. She was reading Homer.

Her husband possessed a streak of cruelty which did not become apparent until she was pregnant. This surprised her. She did not think him capable of any sustained emotion. Yet as her body expanded he began to despise her. He mocked her when she was ill, when she retched in the mornings and her feet began to swell. When she admitted that the heat made her dizzy, he pronounced her spoiled and weak.

"If you behaved as a normal woman instead of a nun married not to God but to books, cooking breakfast for your husband would not be an ordeal," he scorned.

Of course it was not her confusion in the kitchen which infuriated him. Salvador Velásquez consumed too much liquor the previous night to eat anything in the morning. It was the books themselves which enraged him. She perceived this with astounding clarity, since she was, at that precise moment, on I and reading *A Doll's House* by Ibsen.

When her husband chanced to glance in her direction and noticed the book she was holding, the climate of his face shattered. An anger settled across the centers of his eyes like a certain species of black cloud which will sometimes hang suspended, motionless, threatening.

He waited for her to make mistakes, to create a pot of coffee too strong or weak, to fail to iron a shirt cuff or forget to buy milk. Then he sprang, calling her inadequate and defective. The baby within made her enormous, almost immobile and absolutely vulnerable. One night, Marta Ortega realized she had finally become a large and slow-enough target for him. This recognition of his miniature stature filled her with a contempt which was pervasive and permanent.

Salvador Velásquez's absences became frequent and prolonged. She suspected he was unfaithful. She felt simultaneously degraded and grateful. When her husband was gone, the yellow wooden house was tolerable, almost pleasant. And she had unlimited time for reading.

On the lip of the hill, on what would later be designated the corner lot, another house was being built. Marta Ortega observed its exceptionally slow construction. The house was a rarity, two stories, and remarkably elaborate in design and intention. Marta recognized that it was an assertion of solidity. There was an intimation of a sensitivity to the combination of elements which were intangible, like scents and shadows and those which were indisputable necessities like plaster, beams and tiles. The house demonstrated an awareness of aesthetics and definition. It was an interesting configuration indeed.

Marta Ortega watched the house form as she lay in bed for weeks, gigantic and deformed, motionless between the wedding linen, a wounded animal. She might be laying eggs. She was no longer human. She lumbered and swelled and stared at the clock, measuring seconds like a woman condemned. She began the alphabet again. Jane Austen. Emily Brontë. Coleridge. Dickens.

There were erasures in her memory as if, while her body expanded, pieces of her head drifted away, becoming air or clouds or steam. She could not recognize the earth. It was not a planet but the shell of a fantastic tortoise inching a tedious path through pitch-black gulfs, an aged thing, crippled, senile, deaf and tormented by sins and time which would not allow it to die.

Often Salvador Velásquez did not appear until noon in the store owned in partnership by their fathers. Someday the store would be his, theirs. But Salvador Velásquez intimated that the store with its dusty shelves of unfashionable cosmetics and the endless sacks of pinto beans and rice was confining. The loading of crates offended his sensibilities. The calluses on his hands defiled his unformed concept of himself. He wanted to go to sea, he mused, or to northern California where gold could be mined. Or perhaps he would journey farther north, to the perpetual snows called Alaska where bear and wolves and pelts of all varieties were still abundant.

Herds of polar bear and packs of wolves, Marta Ortega thought as she read Euripides, but a definite absence of cantinas and tabernas. How would her husband survive? South was a greater fascination, Salvador Velásquez soon admitted. Back to Mexico, to hunt jaguar and build a villa at the shore of the sea.

She experienced a constant sense of stain. An inviolate part of herself was being demeaned. His smell lay on the bed sheets, her nightdresses and linens. It was an odor which was rum and dusk, sweat, fear, sun, tobacco and flesh which was not her own. One night, with wind whipping the house, grating and pounding and moaning like a woman being brutally raped, Marta Ortega realized she had married a base man because she lacked the courage to say no. She permitted herself to be treated as chattel, and for this her life would be as a grazing thing, monotonous and fenced. Surely this was a sin, amorphous perhaps, without a definite category, but a sin nonetheless.

Marta willed her body to be shrunken, inaccessible, a vapor so that Salvador Velásquez could not find her. She ordered her body to dissolve, to become part of the darkness, a leaf dipped in pitch. She pressed her eyes together as if sewed, shut tight as the coffin of a suspected demon. Her mind was an uninterrupted vision of black satin, black birds wet with rain, glistening obsidian, black clouds, bolts of black sky and feathers.

Salvador would stumble to her, drawn by the smell of her fear the way dogs are attracted to vulnerable scents or sharks to blood. Then he was upon her, his mouth foul from alcohol and tobacco, wordlessly pulling up the back of her nightgown and pushing himself into her until she howled with an anger and pain he might have mistaken for pleasure.

It was at such moments she wished her husband was dead. Dead by a swollen river. Dead by bandits, mudslides, decapitation. When it was warm, Marta Ortega stood in the darkness of her backyard and composed lists of all the ways that men could die and she recited them out loud, alphabetically, like a kind of litany.

O arrows, o bullets, o chocking cobwebs, daggers, entropy, fire, gas, hanging, ice, jaundice, kidnapping, leukemia, murder, narcotics, overindulgence, poison, quicksand, ravagement, starvation, typhoons, ulcers, vampires, witchcraft, xenophobia, Yaquis, zombies.

As she stood in her backyard, on the grass which was not yet a garden, Marta Ortega was aware that she was no longer alone. One afternoon in late spring, two white men had moved into the intricate Spanish stucco house next to her, the house with its deliberately designed courtyards, patios and perimeter of wrought-iron fence. She assumed they were brothers. She noticed they owned a piano and crates of books. This was a fascination in itself. One dusk, as she watched them on their front-courtyard patio, she observed their fluid gestures, how the air between them turned graceful and liquid, sparkled and danced. She was startled to intuit that the men were lovers.

The lights in their house were lit as if midnight was an increment to which they were immune. She did not know whether they spoke Spanish. She did not care. Marta Ortega faced the moon and screamed, O assassination, o buildings burning bringing bridges banging on your bed, o crashing concrete cascading cruel into you and death dreams, dancing devils, evil, fungus, gorging, hideous helpless hunger, insidious ideas, jagged juxtapositions, knees kicked, lime lining your eyes, mice marching in your brain, nectars of lethal flowers, obliteration, plummeting pieces of pottery and pipe plunging and penetrating you, queasiness, repetition, sorcery, teeth in your tongue, undernourishment, vipers, wickedness, yearnings and zoos in which you are trapped, displayed, debased and humiliated.

She created lists and screamed them into the night until her head ached, her mouth was parched and her skull felt as if it were a void. Then she drifted to the grass and slept.

In the long days she observed the phenomenon of the two white lovers. She concluded that the one named Joseph was the woman. It was Joseph who began working in the garden, who stooped above his just-planted bougainvillea to inspect their crisp magenta petals as one would the flesh of a child. She watched him arrange the flowers in a vase, his movements tender and deliberate.

When the evenings were warm, Joseph and Bill ate dinner in their orange-tile side courtyard. Joseph draped the round table with a linen cloth. He placed the vase of flowers, his composition of petals, in the center of the table. Then Joseph studied the dining objects, the china or porcelain plates, the finely sculpted wineglasses and pink or white ironed napkins as if he were creating a painting or a weaving, detail by detail.

"Do you realize, Marta, between here and City Hall, only three people possess a sense of elegance in even one language, have ever read Homer or can conceive of sensibility and what it implies?" Joseph observed one spring evening.

Joseph had knocked on her door. He asked to borrow a cup of sugar. Marta was filling a glass. She dropped it, her hands trembled. She was startled. She had lived as if alone, on an island perhaps, a shipwrecked woman who had learned the intricacies and limitations of her terrain, the pattern of the tides and rains, which fish could be trapped, the edible fruits, the herbs which poisoned or cured, and suddenly someone pronounced her name. After the silence and foraging and inventing in secret, another human spoke.

"I am a primitive," Marta Ortega replied, tentatively, staring at him. "How could you tell I was different?"

"I am sensitive to the intangible," Joseph answered, this time in English. "I noticed what you read. I listen to your conversations with the moon, your alphabetical curses. I trust they are effective."

Then there is a voice, Marta Ortega realized, simultaneously terrified and reassured. This is not an auditory hallucination. At last, Joseph was speaking to her in a dialect in which she was fluent, in which she did not have to translate her thoughts through a grid where words became smooth and dull, meaningless ghostlike approximations of the truth. A mesh where nothing burned or blazed or screamed, nuances were erased.

Marta Ortega had existed in complete isolation, in an unpunctuated exile she accepted as unassailable. It did not occur to her there might be others like herself, the rare and exceptional who would recognize her by what was revealed only through implication.

Then she heard the piano. Bill was playing ragtime, dazzling the keys, making them rise from the dead and bleed, forcing them to flow as a river lit by moonlight, gaslamps, ambered, scented a faint lemon. Marta Ortega found that her body had a life of its own. It was swaying with the music. She was no longer estranged and alone. The possibilities of her new existence were disorienting. It occurred to her that she could kick off red satin slippers and dance naked in front of strangers. She could wear red orchids in her long black hair. Her lips would be painted caramel, the color of whiskey.

"Estoy loca," Marta said.

It was noon. Joseph suggested they sit in his side courtyard. The table was shaded. He was a blond man with a thick mustache of yellow hairs, silky, busy, as if his lip had been planted with a row of carnations. His eyes were green, mutable. They could be soft jade or a jungle, storm-ravished, torrential. He wore his moods on the surface, vulnerable, perpetually exposed.

Later Bill joined them. He was taller, darker of hair and complexion. "Don't I look like the black sheep?" he would often say, only partly in jest. He was complicated, Marta decided as she accepted a glass of coconut juice and rum. Bill was temperamental, emotional, the decision-maker. He was the firstborn of a wealthy family. He had scandalized the town with his flagrant love for men. Each month money was sent to him on the condition he never return to the village of his birth.

Joseph was twenty-two. Bill was four years older. They had been to the carnival in Río de Janeiro, the ruins of the Yucatán, the Louvre, the Sphinx, the islands of the Pacific and the Caribbean.

Across the street which was not yet a street, a hawk fluttered on a course vaguely western. Marta Ortega considered the life of such a creature, skimming midafternoon waters, having an alphabet of whitecaps, driftwood, kelp. She yearned for the stainless-steel eyes of a hawk navigating channels of cloud, compelled, driven, flying into shimmering wind-charged tunnels where polar and tropical meld and both burn.

"My marriage is collapsing," Marta Ortega announced out loud for the first time. She took a sip of the coconut juice that Bill spiked with rum.

She accepted a cigarette from Joseph. "What should I do?" she surprised herself by asking.

"Think about hawks," Bill suggested, and they laughed. The sound coming from her lips was a form of liquid, stunning and unexpected. She was astounded by the pleasure of it. Later, alone, as the sensation repeated itself, much like a wave caressing the lip of a shore, Marta Ortega realized that she had never laughed before, not once in her entire life.

Several days later, when Marta Ortega had completed the alphabet with *The Gin Palace* by Zola, she returned to the pueblo of her birth, to Nuestra Señora de la Soledad, the church where she had been baptized and married. As she walked, she considered the myriad of possibilities for her next reading selection.

Padre Pérez was an old man. It seemed he had always been an old man. It was possible he had been born that way. He was simultaneously implacable and irritable, a dangerous rock, a volcano which might, without warning, erupt. He received her complaints with an obvious and unconcealed indifference. She suspected he had ears of stone. It was clear he had no heart. His memory was also suspiciously tainted. When he addressed her by name, he called her María.

Actually, Padre Pérez was neither senile nor deaf. He was accustomed to the pretenses and follies of women. They flirted with insanity and drama. Birth and death were their only unassailably significant events. Then they took the center stage at last, divas in the spotlight, meaningless interchangeable sparrows who for one fluttering, one microscopic spasm, could sing. He was indescribably bored with them.

Padre Pérez was equally disgusted by their men. He was particularly repelled by the collective pretense that the city on the other side of the hill did not exist. In confession, the men recounted tawdry escapades with Chinese prostitutes in brothels on Main Street. They told him of incidents of contrived violence where they deliberately spilled the blood of the other men. They wanted penances for these actions, but in their voices he detected pride. They actually believed that their trite brutalities enhanced their masculinity. They were pathetic, perhaps even more trivial and predictable than their women.

Of course these wives confessed that they also entered the city. They pretended they were going to buy American dresses in stores near the train station. They viewed their unremarkable bodies in special mirrors where their flesh was revealed in three angles simultaneously. They studied themselves in dresses ending above their knees. They could engage in this activity for hours, centuries, a millennium. Now this pregnant girl-woman was admitting she stole books from the new library near City Hall and not merely on impulse but with the deliberation of an alphabetical plan.

Padre Pérez concluded that the details altered only slightly. The theme of them was identical. They all babbled like paganos. He was appalled by their greed for plug-in appliances, machinery, objects that hummed or glowed. They resisted magazine subscriptions and musical or theatrical productions. It was obvious he had failed them. And he felt that they had, in turn, betrayed him.

Now this pregnant child-woman was reciting a litany of the most common and innocuous domestic variety. There was not even a broken window or a black eye in her story. Padre Pérez was not deaf but preferred to think instead of the sea.

As a boy, he had one summer slept for weeks at the ocean's edge, purified by red kelp dawns, fog-wet beneath a sky blue as a flame's belly. He draped his damp shirt over driftwood logs while spent waves collapsed tame against the sea-shaped mute rock, the pivotal juncture of sea and land, sea and land at a moment of irrevocable decision. There had been pelicans then, three one morning, drilling south with rare purpose. His midmorning shadow was an arrow in cold sand tattooed where deer and coyotes had crossed, ducks and an occasional lost dog. At the shore's lip, the deeper dents of round glassy pebbles sat dislodged, tossed up as the sea dreamed, as mermaids combed their seaweed hair with empty abalone shells.

Padre Pérez pulled himself back from the warm blue embrace of the waves. "To leave a husband would be an unforgivable sin," he reminded himself and the woman.

"My life with this so-called man is a sin. What difference can one more make?" she asked, rhetorically.

There was a long silence. Padre Pérez considered the waves, the whales, and the ocean's slow broken alphabet of sweet pink dusks and irony. The punctuation of the sea was white caps, gulls flapping and pelicans stalking salmon. If one chanced upon a fortunate collection of angles and shadows, one could see the passage of whales engraving the blue surface, cubs trailing behind them like dawn-gray sails or castoff chunks of land. Surely they were the mammalian islands, the place where the ocean grew flesh and breathed. They were the original eyes. And the music of whales rising from night foam was indelible. The relentless chatter of these insignificant paganos could not mute the sound of his whales. The tongues of whales were woven red-wool tapestries, a geometry of intricate edges and numb tones. Whales were the sea's oboes, her sad gray washed-away reeds. Whale widows knew this, mermaids and men who have loved other men or insane women.

Padre Pérez remembered that he was offended. This girl-woman dared deprive him of his ocean. He was angry and confused because her questions hinted at matters of sensibility and complexity. Padre Pérez felt violated. He began to tremble with rage. Then he assigned the pregnant woman a penance of an entire rosary. He cautioned her to be patient and calm. "Muy tranquila, María, con calma," the old priest said.

He did not look at her as she left. Padre Pérez did not like to open his eyes, his cursed eyes which refused to weaken to the miseries that time brought. It was all dull and conventional, even the sordid lacked style and invention. There was a paucity of color, an absence of the bold. How could God bear the ignorance and banality of these people, these creatures who did not realize it was the extravagant gesture God craved?

Increasingly, Padre Pérez longed for droughts, swarms of locusts or bands of renegades looting, raping and burning as they passed. This would not disturb him. Such flamboyance, such an excess of red, was part of life, common as the rise and fall of waves or civilizations. What sickened him was time itself, chiseling away with rats' teeth, unspeakably sharp and insatiable.

"Muy tranquila, María, con calma," he repeated, although he knew the woman was gone. Padre Pérez thought death by time was unclean, an invasion of the flesh and the spirit, a disease. He wished to die quickly at sea or in a fire, by ambush or earthquake. There were mornings when he yearned to simply walk south along the ocean and be taken by jaguar in the mountains. Such a death would be painful but definitive. Death by time was intolerable, with its rats' teeth eating at the edges, obscuring, rubbing out the borders.

I have become obsessed with death, Padre Pérez concluded, recognizing that his fear was infinitely forbidden, a far greater sin than lying down with a woman or a man without the official approval of God. It was a greater transgression than leaving a faithless, abusive and stupid husband. It was a colossal sin compared to stealing books alphabetically from a library or telling a husband you were purchasing postage stamps while you went instead to stare at your body from a three-angled mirror in American store-made dresses which revealed your entire legs and knees. In fact, no one in the barrio could match him in sins.

No one questioned him as to the increments of his existence. He squandered the time he hated, spent entire days in bed, not reading the holy texts or visiting the sick. Instead, he merely stared at the patterns the elm beyond his bedroom window cast. He watched the elm leaves clustered thick as a fence, as flags of ships stalled in a harbor. In the meaningless horizontal wind they glinted like a catch of fish, paling identical, strung by their bellies like mackerel, some yellowing. One could observe the rise and fall of the world engraved on the elm.

His elm tree revealed patterns recurrent as birth and suffering, boredom, infidelity and death. It was the saga of the planet, condensed and specific, precise in its repetitions. There were the lean winters, the hungry nights of shifting on a cot stuck by the honed points of your own bones, in the Decembers of your life when you were leafless. Later, in spring, the elm was again splendid, leaves renewed, stretched and spread like the pushed-open skin of a fat man, a man with a belly like a fantastic cup, a chalice. And Padre Pérez thought it possible he could eat himself whole as a saint.

Now the pregnant book-stealing woman was gone. He regretted that his words had been shallow, callous and without resonance. There had been an opening, an implication of other regions, and he had refused this. And it occurred to him then, precisely as he thought of the pregnant book-stealing woman, that he was neither intelligent nor generous enough to serve God. And Padre Pérez realized he had wasted his life.

Muy tranquila, María, con calma, Marta Ortega repeated as she retraced her route back to the yellow house on the hill which was not yet Flores Street. That spring, a third house was being constructed. She half heard hammering, muted in the hallucinatory periphery. Patient and calm, she raged, spitting at purple wildflowers near her ankles. Con calma, she scorned, kicking chips of stones with her painfully bloated feet which were numb.

Marta Ortega was neither patient nor calm. She was outraged. Her surface betrayed nothing. Within, she was assimilating information, collecting, processing and revising. She read Aristophanes. At dusk, hills darkened, warm as a young lover's belly or thigh. Fields charcoaled as birds rose and sailed, proclaiming the excellence of pure process.

The context expanded. There was a clarification. The periphery was tamed and edgeless as a disc, a placated moon, silent and remote. Or a lake frozen with white lids shut. She detected a hint of roses. Shrill birds drifted across grasses, engrossed in a complicated dialogue. The nameless were named, unghosted, released to stay or go as they chose. And Marta Ortega realized that after the baby was born she might leave Salvador Velásquez. This too was possible.

"Do I expect too much?" Marta asked Joseph. It was the beginning of autumn and still warm.

"He doesn't talk to me," Marta tried. "Words have no resonance for him. They require too much thought, an activity for which he has no capacity. He cannot feel words like arrows or hear them as bells. They do not open for him like flowers, breaking the silence with fragrance."

"What should he talk about?" Joseph inquired. "Eccentric gods and the privilege of history? You knew he was ignorant."

Marta Ortega was six months pregnant. Her patio plants needed watering. Dust coated the plates and trays and glass vases they had received as wedding gifts. Everything sickened her. When Salvador Velásquez was home, he listened to the radio incessantly, as if the sheer volume of noise unleashed upon the house could somehow render her invisible.

Now, when she should be caressed, whispered to, held as if she were holy, this fraudulent and deluded man was calling her fat and lazy as he began his elaborate ritual of preparing to go out for the night, three nights, a week or a year. She found his white shoes for him and thought, I will miss you as the caged beast misses her keeper. Salvador Velásquez was viewing himself in the mirror, changing shirts, allowing the discarded garments to fall on the floor. She was a cow. Later, she would pick them up and hang them in the closet. It occurred to her then that differences could not be ignored, erased, bleached, disguised by scent or fabrics. Such disparities could not be sanded down, replastered or covered with paint.

They are our shape, she recognized, they define us.

At the end of the sixth month of her first pregnancy, she noticed that her husband had entered into a state of profound agitation. He expressed this disturbance in the form of a ferocious anger. The most trivial pretext propelled him into a fury. Since he was inarticulate, he turned his frustration to the exterior. He broke plates and chairs.

Salvador Velásquez proved to be swollen with miniature vanities. He spent hours in front of their mirror, styling his hair with an assortment of jellies and combs. He dreamed out loud, talked about purchasing a white linen suit, a Panama hat and a cane for walking. Marta Ortega thought his ambitions squalid, garish and mediocre. His limitations were becoming stifling. They were becoming bricks around her head. She was being buried alive.

The seventh month of her pregnancy seemed interminable. One night when Salvador Velásquez was in the house, a rare night indeed, Marta Ortega realized he could no longer bear to look at her. It was inconceivable to him that he had ever desired her, even as a convenience, a necessity of convention or mere breeding stock. When he touched her, he said her skin felt as if it were webbed with wire. He removed his hand from her body as if the grain of her flesh caused him actual physical pain.

Marta Ortega wondered why her husband could not pretend she was a sea creature, a dolphin perhaps. And he a sailor deluded by rum and sun, adrift in a senseless latitude. Could he not imagine her as a mermaid and find the exotic in this? But no, it was too sinuous a route for his adolescent simplicities.

She was appalled by his lack of imagination and wit. It was not the physical rejection which wounded her. She was grateful he no longer wished to violate her. It was the implications of his reasoning process that terrified her. Spontaneity eluded him. She recognized there were unsurmountable differences in their vision. Even angles and shadows were viewed with a wild and irreconcilable discrepancy. They were not of the same species.

Marta Ortega was simultaneously tentative and outraged. She felt like a woman in 1957 or 1981, perhaps, who has just gone to bed with her lover. They have known each other for weeks, months or years. They claim to share a sensibility, a vocabulary, a geography with gardens, bridges, cliffs. On this night, after several margaritas, the woman lies draped in dusk shadows, becomes the shadows and cannot speak. Word-lessly, she pulls the man's head down, a small pressure on his skull, down to the place between her legs. He freezes. The body she is gently guiding with her fingertips is suddenly composed of metal, dense and heavy as a collapsed star. The man appears stunned, angry, dazed.

"What are you trying to do?" he demands.

"Lick me," the woman whispers.

"Don't tell me what to do," the man says. He slides away, lights a cigarette. Perhaps he glances at his watch.

"But you tell me what to do," the woman says, softly, calmly. She is drunk. She permits the natural configuration within her to express itself. She is telling the absolute truth. She has often felt the fingers of the man on her hair, her head, as he steers her down to him. She has never refused this.

Now the man says nothing, rises from the bed, dresses. She has been his lover for three weeks, three months or three years. There is a shatter-ing, a revelation, undeniable. The woman did not keep her place, her pose of subservience, her falsely cemented lips. Her posture of ignorance is a requirement. She has failed to comply. She is punished.

The man leaves, perhaps slamming the door. They will see each other again, of course, but it will never be fluid between them, spontaneous, assured. The woman will weep when he finally leaves, when the door has been shut for the final time, boxes packed, keys returned. She will cry and scream, not at the loss of this particular man but at a wound, an excru-ciating burning in an inner dominion, and a sense of betrayal for which no words yet exist to define.

As she grew so swollen with child that even strangers stopped to offer their blessing on such an obviously healthy baby, Marta Ortega realized that her young husband lacked the reference points for the grotesquery she had become. They were utterly adrift. They might have eaten human flesh or transgressed some unspeakable border. It was this monumental oddity that married them. All else was superficial pretension and lies.

The church of Nuestra Señora de los Dolores had just been com-pleted. There were three houses on her hill now, four on what would be Manzanita Street, and on the next ridge two houses were partially con-structed. It occurred to Marta Ortega that the barrio and her baby were simultaneously forming. It was an easy sloping downhill path from her house at the top of what was now a paved and officially named Flores Street to the new church.

Padre Romero was a young man, tall, with fine features and an aura of nervous intensity. His elegant bearing made him a provocatively sexual presence. He was aware of the response he had upon women and often wished God had not afflicted him with such an unfortunate physical configuration, that he might accidentally injure himself and receive the blessing of a limp or a gross bodily defect, an amputation and scars.

Marta Ortega described her marriage. She longed for her husband to die. She attempted to manifest this desire by the creation of alphabetical litanies. There were moments when she wished to beat her fists into her flesh, to push her fingers directly through the skin itself and tear the breathing nest of a baby within her to pieces, returning it to its elemental condition of raw air, nothingness and dust.

Padre Romero listened to the distraught pregnant woman. A hint of summer lingered in the warm autumn afternoon. Bushes were lambent, bursting with red buds and a sense of rare conjunctions. The priest was struck by the intelligence and despondency of the woman. Padre Romero tended to be deeply moved by everything. He inhabited a realm of profound sorrow and manic optimism, the balancing of which proved irreconcilably strenuous.

He wanted to say, You have been empty but now you are filled. Waken unto this and the earth will shake with your taking. Say yes and this yes will be a flare and your hands can be candles. Behold the purple iris waving their wine-anointed hands in the wind, saying Come hither, this way, back from the glare of your sins. You must plant your lands again with prayers of yes, and forgiveness will fall upon you like rain.

Padre Romero was deeply compelled by his eloquence and concurrently utterly confused by the unresolved ambiguities of the young woman's situation. He also felt intimidated by her. "You will feel differently after the birth," Padre Romero offered at last.

He must become more objective, dispassionate, anchored, he cautioned himself. Lyricism was valuable in the seminary but useless in actual practice. He was a simple man, he reminded himself without conviction. The running of the church itself, the literal details of dealing with tradesmen and completing applications and reports, consumed the hours he had imagined spending with the deformed of soul. The hours he had intended to spend with God. And because he was displeased with himself, his physical appearance, his emotional frailties and the oppressive, tedious realities of simply keeping Nuestra Señora de los Dolores from falling back into slabs of stucco and dust, he ordered an unusually severe penance for Marta Ortega.

Her insomnia worsened. Now she constructed lists of names for babies, silently, alphabetically, it was her new litany, the way she beseeched the gods for sleep.

Often, when she was alone in the bed, and it was cold and raining, she would place the other pillow close to her monumental belly and compose lists of names entirely in English. Marta Ortega alternated her lists between Spanish and English. She never considered names for sons. By then, she knew the baby within her was a girl.

The curandera came in the early afternoon. The baby was born ten minutes before midnight. The moon was one day past full. It was a cold December and the orb of the moon was stunningly white and the pull of it was colossal. In the final hours before the birth, she screamed and bled and twice bit the curandera on the wrist. She begged the unexpectedly sturdy older woman to have the mercy to simply murder her. Then Marta Ortega prayed only that the baby have four limbs, no tail, two eyes and not one or three and that it be female. Grant me this, Dios, she vowed, and I promise on all that is sacred and inviolate in this and other worlds, I will never intrude upon you again. Grant me this and this only and I will enter again into insignificance. It will be as if I never was.

She offered her breast to her infant. Angelina turned her head toward the nipple like the petals of a flower sensing the sun. Salvador Velásquez was subduing with a bottle of tequila his conventionally acceptable disappointment that his wife had borne him a daughter rather than a son.

Actually, Salvador Velásquez was shocked as he stumbled into the house on Flores Street at dawn, exhausted from four nights in a variety of brothels, his eyes yellow, to encounter an unanticipated profusion of women, including his mother and his mother-in-law, the village midwife and an infant. His wife had become peripheral to him, she was almost nonexistent. He had managed to entirely forget she was pregnant or why this was supposed to be significant.

Marta Ortega sat on the terrace of her backyard. She was whole, as newly born as her daughter, Angelina, her infant with black hair, moss soft, elusive as ferns, filaments not yet formed. Angelina's many breaths were seeds and mist, expressions of the substance, the fundamental earth tones. Night was undivided. A warm wind blew from the south. Angelina's weight numbed her arms. Marta Ortega felt her flesh transmuted into wood, limbs of a tree. She merged with her daughter, their grain identical. Her daughter's feet brushed against her torso like wings or feathers or fins as Angelina rocked in her infant sleep, still part creature of the ocean, with memories cyclic, unmolested, liquid. And Marta Ortega thought, I am jacaranda, manzanita, palm. Lean farther into me, be me.

Marta Ortega was part of a process beyond transformation. It was a metamorphosis, an act of the elements which was, strictly speaking, older than God. And she was scraping something from her flesh and drifting, stinging, into the not yet known. She could not know whether her fragile and uniquely self-invented umbilical cord in reverse would be enough. She lay her infant on a blanket on the grass. She dug her first flower bed. She planted seeds. The air was unexpected, sharp and white as a slap from a glove. And she realized that one survived not by plan but by chance.

Then it was a late blue May afternoon, the sky a gauze, thin as a slim-skinned belly. She worked in her garden, creating a border of camellias, canna and rosebushes. Her body was light, weightless. As if by prearrangement, wild iris and red geraniums appeared on the hill that was becoming Flores Street. Marta Ortega needed no secret code for this. Obviously, she was the lady of the loom. She held spindles of red, yellow and jade-green silken threads. As she recognized this, bright-blue buds erupted on a branch and fell, a veil of petals across marigolds and asters and the crocheted blanket covering her sleeping daughter.

Marta Ortega began her experiments with orchids, with the miniature spikes of red and green and yellow which were cymbidiums. Their subtle fragrance was veiled, not unlike the blossoms of oranges and lemons. She was startled by their complexity, delicacy, how they seemed almost to breathe and speak through their tongues and their spotted magenta mouths.

Later, she would come to know these and other orchids with an intimacy and passion which would, on occasion, be termed excessive. Orchids would consume her entire backyard. She would terrace the hillside, build redwood shelves, recombine and create. As she mastered their alphabets of necessity, she would learn to think in terms of decades.

The garden work suited her. The earth required a merging, an agility and a caress. It was a kind of musical instrument. Of course the dirt could sing. Her body hardened, contoured like a sculpture. She was freed of excess. She waited for Salvador Velásquez to return to her. Surely even he recognized that she was a carved fertility statue, a goddess of the harvest, his sister, a deity of the moon and flowers, ancient, perfected by pain. She had presented to him the ultimate proof, the blood offering, the infant she had named Angelina. Angelina, bearing not the name of a saint or literal angels, but rather syllables inspired by the city in which she was born. Salvador Velásquez was not her father. Angelina was a daughter of this particular barrio and Flores Street; this intersection of textures and scents and chance had formed her. The man was incidental to the process.

Salvador Velásquez stared at her without recognition. He was changing his shirt, combing his hair, perfunctorily picking up Angelina and then, almost immediately, handing her back to Marta. The baby could not be trusted, must be avoided. Liquids spilled from her mouth. She left fingerprints composed of strained foods on his clothing. He ignored his daughter. Marta Ortega was then on P. She read Plato. She glanced at her husband and thought, Dios mío, this man is absolutely vacant.

On Wednesday, the day of his weekly visit, her brother Enrique mentioned that he had seen Salvador Velásquez near the old town square of Olvera Street. Her brother was unloading groceries. Salvador Velásquez's absences were notoriously prolonged and unpredictable. In response, her family had developed the habit of supplying her with necessities on a weekly basis. Enrique was handing her a five-pound sack of sugar. He was removing a bag of potatoes and rice. "Y qué?" she inquired softly. Within her, there was an opening, a stirring silent and forbidden.

Enrique studied the floor, in embarrassment, as he would if he had chanced upon his sister not fully clothed. He recited the story slowly, as if syllables offered in a monotone would lessen the pain. It was the familiar grid, the screen through which ordinary women and men engaged in the illusionary activity of communication. The veil which made words innocuous, conforming, still.

Salvador Velásquez had been seen at the Cinco de Mayo fiesta. There were bands, dancing, church bells ringing. The plaza had been decorated with colored streamers like a pueblo in Mexico on a special saint's day. And Enrique had seen Salvador dancing with a woman, gliding across the plaza and laughing.

Marta Ortega filled her sugar bowl. This was not another rumor about her husband with una puta, a prostitute in a brothel. This was a public event Enrique had actually witnessed. Marta Ortega washed each potato separately, almost tenderly. She placed the individual potatoes on the sink as if she were building a small brown pyramid. She produced movements which were calculated, deliberately casual. She must not appear startled or frighten Enrique. As if they were merely engaged in idle chatter, she gathered additional details. Was the other woman pretty? Yes? Was she dressed in the style of a Chicana and not a Mexicana peasant? Her brother said yes.

Marta Ortega nodded and calmly poured pinto beans into a metal container. She offered Enrique a glass of horchata. What was the other woman wearing? A yellow dress, Enrique told her. She looked almost Americana. Marta Ortega suggested that her brother sit down. She indicated a chair near the kitchen window. He must be tired after walking from el mercado del pueblo where he worked with their father. Enrique sat down. He maintained that he could not adequately evaluate the other woman's face. She wore a yellow dress and a hat with a wide brim. No, she did not appear to be a puta. And no, he could not actually see her face. They had passed quickly. The plaza was crowded. After all, the woman wore a hat and there were shadows, trumpets, ringing bells, mariachis, confetti.

That night was warm. Angelina walked among the stalks and vines of the backyard, pushing her tiny face into the bushy petals of marigolds and carnations. Marta Ortega grew these common flowers to divert Angelina from the orchids. She also enjoyed their texture, the contrast they provided against her backdrop of cymbidiums.

Then she held her two-and-a-half-year-old daughter on her lap. The moon was nearly full. Marta Ortega pointed at the glowing disc, staring at the moon with her daughter until her neck ached.

She rocked her daughter. Then Marta Ortega mentioned the fact that her father, Salvador Velásquez, might have to leave the house on Flores

Street. He might have to leave the house very soon and permanently. Angelina said nothing. They watched the moon in silence.

"What do you think of divorce?" Marta asked Joseph. It was the following afternoon. Joseph was staring at a shelf of burgundy cymbidiums. He thought people might wish to purchase them.

"Who would buy flowers?" Marta inquired, startled by the idea.

"People who crave the opulent and rare. The extravagant gesture," Joseph replied. "Mangoes out of season. A spray of magenta orchids in a cut-crystal vase. A string quartet in the parlor."

It was a hot dusk. Birds, summered and untamed, began their incautious night flights above the lush moist star-grazed grasses of the hill which was officially named Flores Street. The sky unfolded in layers of violet and scarlet scarves, in plumes and capes. The gods of the night glided above her backyard in their dusk disguises.

"As to your marriage, it is a deformity. A disgrace to the sensibility," Joseph said.

She watched Joseph cut a spray of yellow cymbidiums, their interior a rain of near-red drops, a blood storm. He would place them in a crystal vase on the courtyard table where he and Bill would eat on a round table draped this night with a coral linen cloth. The folded napkins were ironed and white. There would be candles in pewter holders. The orchids were an intrinsic component in what Joseph called ambiance. El ambiente.

"What about God?" Marta asked.

"Your marriage is an offense against God," Bill offered from the far side of his courtyard. "And God is a busy man."

"He's drinking absinthe and playing poker in Paris," Joseph said.

"Don't be absurd," Bill snapped. "Paris, you idiot. Your geography is worse than your cooking. I don't know how I tolerate you."

"Not Paris?" Joseph retreated.

"God has moved to Los Angeles," Bill announced. "He's in real estate. He buys orange groves and converts them into apartment buildings."

Marta Ortega thought of the pretty girl in the yellow dress and the wide-brimmed hat, the woman she had never seen. There were shadows, Enrique had explained, mariachis and confetti.

"Life is a density of shifting fragments," Joseph said.

"The art lies in the selection and arrangement," Marta agreed.

"It is the sole definition of the self," Bill said with authority, "the only manifestation of sensibility."

"To betray one's sensibility is to die," Joseph offered. He poured rum into their glasses.

"It is to commit the mortal sin of suicide," Bill pointed out.

"Then I am caught between sins," Marta realized. She shrugged her shoulders and lit a cigarette. "Some women are born to sin," she concluded. "It's a calling, like the cloth or politics. A certain form of perception, a kind of music."

"I am going to divorce him," Marta informed her brother when he delivered her groceries six days later.

Enrique laughed. He thought Marta was joking with him. His sister had always been an odd person, he suddenly realized. "Divorce?" he repeated. "For having another woman?"

"Yes," Marta Ortega replied without hesitation, trying to simplify the matter.

Her brother, who was not offered horchata this day, returned to el mercado del pueblo smiling. No woman in her right mind, not even a woman like his sister, who had developed a curious amnesia for church bells and possessed a private calendar in which the traditional rituals were excluded, even a woman like Marta who, as rumor went, had not entered Nuestra Señora de los Dolores since the day Angelina was baptized, even a woman like Marta should not say the word *divorcio* out loud. To utter certain words was a kind of sin. Words could conjure evil. Everyone knew this, even his sister, who, as Enrique thought about it for the first time, was becoming less accessible with each season.

There was the matter of her books and bizarre flowers, her American magazines, her refusal to participate in the ordinary activities and diversions, even fiestas. She might be losing her mind, Enrique realized. As he pondered the situation, it occurred to him that it was possible she had always been abnormal. Actually, Marta was fortunate to even have a husband, Enrique concluded.

And what reason would she offer for so precipitous an act? That her husband had taken another woman? This was the nature of men, an expression of their special needs. It was a sin, of course, but an acceptable transgression and unavoidable.

Enrique found himself laughing as he walked up a path of wildflowers. Certainly, in her irregular fashion, Marta was merely jesting with him. It would be a scandal. Father would walk over the hill from the pueblo and beat her. He would have to close el mercado for several hours and this would be a definite monetary setback. As for their mother, she would no doubt drown herself in the river.

Marta Ortega sat her two-and-a-half-year-old daughter on her lap. There were no divisions between them. She was not divorcing Salvador Velásquez because he was publicly unfaithful, erratic, utterly mediocre or even cruel, she explained. He was simply too small for her, for them.

"There are limits, Angelina. I cannot permit you to have a father with subadequate grammar in two languages," she informed her daughter. "I regret he has the sensibility of an armadillo and the vision of a maggot. And el ambiente is a concept he will not master in this or any other life."

Marta Ortega imagined her future with Salvador Velásquez. She would never laugh. She would have to translate herself indefinitely. She would exist in a condition of permanent fraudulence, pretending to be something very different from what she was already becoming.

She cupped her daughter's hand. "Angelina, do you understand?" she began. "I will never be able to say to your father, Salvador Velásquez, I am yours, yours, yours. Alabaster and flawless as the madonna, as square root or history. I will fit in your hand. You can mold me, taste me, polish me, use and own me, like a god."

Angelina stared into her eyes as if she comprehended the situation completely. Marta Ortega was startled by their connection, since she was herself only beginning to realize and articulate the dimensions of her marital catastrophe. Angelina slept on her lap. Their fingers were intertwined.

Marta Ortega worked in her garden with a vengeance, driven by rage, trembling with exhilaration and fear. Angelina watched her plant a bed of violets, then carrots and a sixth row of tomatoes. She held her daughter in her arms, walking slowly through the garden, surveying the vegetation with exaggerated care. The orchids were shooting sprays of yellow, red and green, their centers lava and wine, corals and amethysts. In the front garden, there were the simple purples of the violets, asters and iris and the bold yellow punctuation of the canna.

"It is all a matter of details," Marta Ortega told her daughter.

I will make sacred what I touch, Marta Ortega vowed. She realized, at that precise moment, that it was not history, events of men, but the process of selection, the intangible scents and gestures, that defined a life. Stalks of yellow canna rising insistent beside a yellow-painted fence. The quality of dusk light brushing the faces of marigolds. Integrity was measured solely by what could be held, could be pressed with the lips. Immortality lay in one indelible kiss, in one unrepeatable arrangement of yellow-winged cymbidiums in a glass vase at nightfall, not in all the stones of all the pyramids.

"Remember this, Angelina. Defend no borders but those of sensibility."

Angelina nodded in agreement, not speaking, as if sensing that any syllable would desecrate the moment. And it occurred to Marta Ortega that to be one woman truly, wholly, was to be all women. To tend one garden was to birth worlds.

Two weeks later, Marta Ortega and her daughter walked to City Hall. Marta filled out the forms for her divorce. She hired an attorney. As they returned to Flores Street, Marta Ortega reminded Angelina that Salvador Velásquez was not actually her father, was her father in only a technical and literal sense. Angelina was a daughter of Flores Street and the barrio which was now called Echo Park. That was the fundamental reality. All else was shallow, convention and hypocrisy. This was a region they had transcended.

As Enrique had predicted, her father crossed the hill from the pueblo of her birth to the yellow wooden house on Flores Street. He beat her for the second and last time in her life. He beat his daughter and then he held her in his arms and wept.

"I am responsible for this misfortune," Víctor Ortega recognized. Tears spilled from his eyes and ran in two streams down his cheeks, like channels of water from melting snow, cutting a crease in rock. This is how rivers are formed, she thought, valleys, the gashes that slice planets. She had never seen her father cry before. His entire body convulsed in spasms. Marta Ortega was witnessing the configuration of a heart breaking.

"The train I missed. The delay in scheduling. I should have been in

Mexico City or Havana. None of this would have happened. Not your marriage or mine. Not you or this city."

"Don't be ridiculous," Marta Ortega said, almost lightly. "It isn't your fault. Life is random, happenstance, inexplicable occurrences. The world is an intersection of incongruent elements. The streets we walk cover sudden portals and mysteries."

There was a long silence. Marta Ortega lit a cigarette. She had never smoked in front of her father. Víctor Ortega did not notice. He was weeping, silently, tears falling in two streams from his eyes, and his chest was shaking from the earthquake within his ribs.

"It could have been worse," Marta Ortega offered. She poured herself a glass of rum.

"Cómo?"

"You could have fallen in love with a dancer in Río or Caracas," Marta Ortega mused. "A woman who had other men, stole your cello, compromised you publicly."

"Es verdad," Víctor Ortega admitted. He seemed relieved.

"Or you could have returned to your family in Spain, walked into a war, been forced to make difficult and irrevocable decisions," Marta said.

Her father stood uneasily in her living room as if subliminally responding to the density of fragrance and amber. There was the matter of her books and magazines, the rumors of the white lovers next door, her refusal to attend church. There were many in the pueblo who suspected she had powers. He was afraid to look into his daughter's eyes.

Marta Ortega poured her father a glass of rum. He drank it slowly, replaced the glass near the sink and quietly thanked her. Then he walked out of the house he had built and painted yellow. Then he closed the wooden door of the house on Flores Street and it was done.

Two years later, in a cold autumn, a young man with a light complexion and dark-brown hair thick with curls rang her doorbell. Octavio Herrera had been sent to pick up an order of orchids for the flower shop where he had recently become employed. Marta Ortega assembled the orchids. Then, on impulse, she went into her bedroom, removed her clothing and scattered the sprays across her flesh. "Señor Herrera," she called, "here are your orchids."

Marta Ortega lay on the cool sheets, waiting. Perhaps she intuited that this man would have to be taken by surprise attack, ambush rather than seduction. Two months later she married him in a civil ceremony at City Hall.

Her family treated this second marriage as if it were not, in fact, occurring. It was an hallucination, a miscommunication rather than an irreconcilable act of excommunication. Under the circumstances, they elected to be absent from the ceremony. Marta Ortega accepted their decision. It was not a surprise.

Marta Ortega and the nearly five-year-old Angelina wore green velvet dresses of an identical design. They both carried bouquets of green orchids. Joseph and Bill were her witnesses. The ritual was short and anonymous. The judge added nothing of originality to the official ceremony. He recited words and seemed bored. Behind his eyes he thought, more Mexicans, hordes of hungry children, tenements, knives. It was a cold afternoon, the wind gray. They returned to Flores Street by red car. The barrio of Echo Park was not accessible by bus.

Octavio Herrera was an improvement over Salvador Velásquez, but Marta lacked the ability for pretense. She was quickly dissatisfied. Within weeks, she realized she had invented a personality for Octavio, a set of characteristics, a pattern and contour without a basis in reality. She had imposed a composition where there was none. He was a contrivance. Octavio Herrera accepted this because he was passive and still unformed.

She designed an identity for him. Octavio Herrera had no interior architecture of his own. He was a void, willing to assume whatever Marta gave him. He was grateful. He had been nameless. Now he was named. Marta Ortega imbued him with purpose and direction, complexity and substance, but she recognized that her husband possessed none of these qualities.

"He was like a chanced-upon buried fresco," Marta explained to Joseph later. "In the moment of actually seeing him, in the instant of revelation, the air simultaneously began to eat away at the paint. Upon examination, he became dust."

"Marta, mi amor, most men must have a script," Joseph sighed. "And you improvise, exaggerate, lie."

"You inhabit an area beyond the accurate," Bill said.

"You will always be too much and not enough," Joseph concluded.

When Octavio Herrera first kissed her mouth he said, "Your lips taste like flowers." In her desperation for resonance, Marta Ortega perceived this observation as an intimation of a shared sensuality. Their intimacy would engrave a design across the surface of their lives, an erotic fabric, petals and tongues. Of course this was a delusion. Octavio Herrera's remark was not an implication of illumination but an accident, a random sentence, a happenstance of syllables disconnected to a central core.

Octavio Herrera was almost six feet tall, strong and intense. Marta convinced herself that this implied a sensitivity and a capacity for passion. It did not. It was rather that Octavio wore his emotions close to the surface. What she had interpreted as flames proved to be occasional sparks, inconsequential. Actually, with the exception of his confusion, Octavio Herrera was an extremely ordinary young man, mediocre at best and perhaps less.

Marta Ortega no longer stole books from the library near City Hall. She traded books with Joseph and Bill or ordered them from catalogues and bookstores. She read the short stories of Ernest Hemingway and another young man, Christopher Isherwood. She tended her orchids and attempted to banish what was disturbing in her second marriage. The grid had been removed from her mouth and the screen erased from her eyes. She could not deny her discontent.

Octavio Herrera's personal history was tainted. Marta Ortega had known this before their marriage, but she camouflaged and justified the implications of the details. She had seen the landscape of him, the vacant and undistinguished, and pronounced it not dull but rather dormant. She would take this wasteland and make it abundant, fertile, surprising. There were only four elements, water, fire, air and earth. Liquid elevations were possible.

Marta Ortega discovered that her second husband resisted the broadening she required. Increasingly, she could not ignore the literal facts of him, his parched geography, absent pulse and lack of grace. He had been born on a farm in the San Joaquin Valley, in the northern interior of California. One morning he had awakened sick of the sounds of plows and chickens and children. He had walked south, he explained, because it seemed downhill.

When Marta Ortega asked her second husband to push into her hard, no, much harder, in their bed, Octavio Herrera stared at her with wide astounded eyes like startled light-brown moons struck from their orbit. His eyes seemed to open and drift, glazed as a blind man. He became paralyzed. He curled on his side. He felt chilled and small. His experience with women was limited and conventional. And he was profoundly disoriented by this book-reading, orchid-growing woman he found himself inexplicably married to. He thought he was dreaming. He believed in Jesus Christ. Women were mothers or whores. The city called Los Angeles terrified him. In particular, he was frightened by streetcars and signs in Chinese. Perhaps he had been kidnapped by bandits and clubbed on the head. He kept waiting to wake up.

Marta Ortega touched him constantly despite the fact that he was embarrassed by this. She wanted to make love in the afternoons when he returned for lunch from the flower store and the day stalled, and the palms were draped with languor, air amber. She was hungry for sudden pleasures. She desired him at noon, when the sky was a borderless cerulean, an inverted ocean, a lagoon in an undamaged August. Yes, she said, now, naked, our bodies an offering the gods can paint.

Octavio Herrera became nervous and uncomfortable. The density and persistence of her constant attention was an irritant. He perceived the succession of her caresses as a demand. He offered unimaginative excuses. There were flowers he must deliver, orders were waiting, he feared he would be dismissed. Octavio preferred to embrace his wife beneath the cover of darkness. But somehow, Marta Ortega managed to pierce even the cloak of night. Yes, this woman could outwit the black elements themselves, mute their power, make them whisper through violet mouths.

Marta Ortega brought him breakfast in bed on a cloth-covered tray. His first meal of the day proved to be a fruit drink thick with rum. Octavio Herrera stared at a large glass in which she had sculpted slices of melon and pineapple. There was a vase of purple orchids. The cloth was coral. The sheer color of the liquids and fabrics seared his just-opening eyes. He half expected her to serve him human blood one morning, mercury or lava.

Marta recognized with regret that Octavio Herrera was offended by the absence of the ordinary. He declined the tray she had presented to him. He cooked himself eggs, frijoles and tortillas. He left the house for work, kissing not her mouth but her cheek or forehead instead. After he left for the flower shop, Marta Ortega drank his breakfast. She noticed that her consumption of rum was increasing dramatically. She was on L then. She read *Sons and Lovers* by D. H. Lawrence. Then she read the poetry of Edna St. Vincent Millay.

Angelina followed her into the garden. They weeded and watered. They searched for signs of virus, the spottings in the leaves of the cymbidiums that were the portent of disease. There were none. Now, at noon and in the early afternoons, her doorbell rang often. White women and men arrived in cars that glistened. They walked through her terraced backyard, wandered as if dazed among the redwood slatted shelves and selected orchids. They paid her with cash and checks. She opened a bank account and did not mention this to her husband.

When Marta became pregnant she told herself she would be content with the small, the peripheral, the occasional gesture. Perhaps her desires, her surrender to heat and intoxication with the flesh, had been excessive. She began experimenting with cattleyas, a hybrid orchid she grew in a tiny greenhouse Octavio had constructed for her. At dusk, she bent above bushes of roses and camellias and cut blossoms. Angelina helped her arrange them in vases.

"Do you think Octavio will notice this?" Marta asked her daughter. They had just created a bouquet of extraordinary sprays and blooms, yellow orchids and roses. The vase was radiant with heat, like a lamp. It glowed, a hot globe, remarkably fragrant, magical.

"No," Angelina had replied.

"Then why do we do this?"

"For us, for ourselves," her daughter said.

"That is absolutely correct, precisely. For the beauty, for the process, for the rituals we invent in secret, for the intangible details that define us. Yes, Angelina, for us." Marta Ortega was pleased.

Octavio Herrera offered to repaint the house. On numerous occasions, Marta had revealed her love of green to him, her attraction to the verdant, the purity and curing power she felt it contained. She told her husband she dreamed their child would be born with green flesh. Verde, she repeated in the darkness. Then she let Octavio select the color, wondering whether it would be a lime, an avocado, a jade. Or perhaps he would devise his own combination. Octavio Herrera returned to Flores Street with gallons of an innocuous blue. After that, Octavio found other houses to paint, on Manzanita and Alta Vista Street, on Sunset and Alvarado Boulevard. It paid more than delivering flowers.

"I love him with a passion," Marta told Joseph.

Joseph laughed. "You have an enormous capacity for the opulent gestures, the exotic and lavish. Recognize the distinction."

Of course Joseph was right. She had focused the force of her emotional extravagance upon Octavio Herrera without provocation. She worked in her garden on her knees, her belly swelling with her infant, and repeated his name out loud hundreds of times, like a mantra, an incantation, chimes. She permitted herself this illusion. Marta Ortega knew that she had created him and that his contrived form lacked substance. It was, by its nature and artifice, temporary. He would pass, like a fever or a storm. Then her second daughter, Orquídea, was born.

Marta Ortega returned to her garden. When she cut red roses, it occurred to her that she could serve them to Octavio Herrera for supper.

"Push into my ribs, my heart. Kiss me until I bruise. Leave your fingerprints engraved on my flesh. Let me find them like small flowers on my thighs and breasts for weeks," she whispered above a white porcelain vase of white camellias ambered by candles. Octavio smelled of turpentine and paint. He said nothing.

"Take all of me," Marta suggested. "Pretend I am a continent and you are an explorer."

Octavio Herrera stared at her like a man who has just been startled from a profoundly deep sleep, his eyes wide and uncomprehending. "Conversas como una puta," he said with disgust. Then he blew the candle out.

Marta Ortega wanted to memorize the sensation of longing she experienced. It was like wind, holy water or the rare poison of high air. She realized that her passion and intensity drew Octavio Herrera to her. It made him feel important. She also recognized that it terrified him. Octavio Herrera was a young man and obviously in transit. Only motion could soothe him. He longed to journey everywhere, but, she intuited with absolute clarity, only once. He saw the world as a series of postcards. He dealt in surfaces, in quantity rather than quality, which was a distinction that did not interest him.

Still, Marta Ortega managed to fascinate him for a while. She called to him with an incandescent and dazzling heat. She seemed to glow from inside. When he held her in his arms, after making love, the night yel-

lowed, as if everywhere women and men leaned over balconies and terraces with torches lit. He thought she was a genuine bruja, this woman
who read poetry and novels and deciphered the science of recombining
the elements of rare flowers. This skill was indisputably valuable. Even
white women and men in expensive automobiles came to the house to buy
her orchids.

There were moments when Octavio Herrera believed he was bewitched. This woman who could redesign the color of flowers was capable
of anything. She had cast a spell upon the earth of her garden. It was
possible she had also draped her invisible net of transfigured particles over
him. She could probably foretell the future and see beneath his layers to
his past, to the shadow-laden edges of stale rooms where he shed all
pretense of mastery and wept alone for hours.

Perhaps Octavio Herrera recognized that he could define his manhood
on the dangerous banks of her love. And he thought of her in liquid terms,
as a kind of river. He wanted that clarification and sense of substance she
offered, but he did not want to stay. Octavio Herrera experienced an
intense conflict within himself. He felt as if he had mysteriously fallen
through a secret hole in the world, into an enormous and inexplicably
radiant region where he did not belong.

Octavio Herrera lacked the vocabulary and intuition for ambiguity. It
was a channel he could not navigate. Essentially, he could not convince
himself that this strange book-consuming woman he had married actually
loved him. Yet he could not resist surrendering to the wind which she
transformed for him, made lush and elegant in a manner he had not
imagined possible. She trained his eyes. Starlight did not simply fall but
pierced the night in spears and daggers, deliberate, aiming for the lean
trunks of acacia, lime and orange trees. Then he complained that she gave
him an excess of starlight and heat.

Octavio Herrera began to exhibit signs of anxiety and a deep internal
disruption. He developed a difficulty with eating and sleeping. He found
himself incapable of making love to this woman who was somehow his
wife. He wondered whether there was an element obscene and sinful in
her eagerness for his flesh. He translated her sensual yearnings into a form
of command. And within him, in silence, Octavio Herrera rebelled. Everything seemed liquid, glowing, and he was filled with shame.

You want to say your nerves are being seared, Marta Ortega thought, but you are inarticulate. You sense I am twisting the fibers of your flesh, attempting to construct an interior architecture for you, but this is a concept you do not understand. Marta Ortega was almost sympathetic.

Then Octavio Herrera was saying goodbye, was saying his mother was sick, the farm was falling into ruin. He had an obligation. Of course, in a few months he would send for her, for them. They were standing in the train station near the original pueblo at Olvera Street where Salvador Velásquez had danced with the woman who wore a yellow dress and a wide-brimmed hat and there had been shadows, trumpets, confetti. "Mi madre. El ranchito," Octavio Herrera was relentlessly repeating.

They both knew he was speaking lies. Marta Ortega wished to release him from the strain of his banal inventions. It would be better to leave in silence or with a knife, Marta thought, holding the nine-month-old Orquídea in her arms. Angelina stood at her side. A wind blew from the north.

"Stop it, please," Marta finally said. "Your leaving was an inevitability. This marriage is not finished. This marriage never was."

Octavio Herrera no longer knew how to respond to this woman. He could not decipher her private code or determine whether he was being absolved or cursed or perhaps, simultaneously, both. Then he kissed her cheek.

Marta Ortega watched the train until it was small and indistinguishable as a sparrow in a cloud-crowded sky. She wanted to feel griefstricken, abandoned, wounded. She did not. Actually, she experienced a surprising sense of relief.

"It is remarkable how locusts invade farms at precisely the right moment," Joseph noted, reading her face with an accuracy which made her tremble with gratitude. "Thank the gods for aging mothers, floods and ravaged crops."

During the eighteen-month tenancy of Octavio Herrera, Joseph and Bill had been barred from her house. This was after Octavio realized they were not cousins but lovers.

"Don't apologize," Joseph said during one of their clandestine afternoon conversations. "Just enjoy yourself. He will be gone soon enough, mi amor."

"Are you certain?"

"Absolutely. Your layers cannot sustain his interest. He will fill his pockets with what glitters, oblivious to the substance."

"Will he realize he has taken only trinkets?" Marta wondered.

"No," Joseph said. "I do not think he will recognize that, ever."

As if on cue, her brother Enrique reappeared with the weekly Wednesday delivery of groceries. He simply left the bags on her porch, as if entering the house he had constructed now contained a form of contagion which frightened him. Enrique declined her offer of juice, horchata or rum. Perhaps he also thinks I am a bruja, Marta thought, smiling. She had scandalized the family twice and was officially excommunicated. She created flowers which had never existed before. Her idiosyncracies were accumulating and assuming a magnitude perceived as ominous. She accepted her brother's distance. Then Marta Ortega returned to her garden and the raising of her orchids and her daughters.

It was said the country was suffering from an economic depression. Marta Ortega did not notice this. The women and men who craved the opulent gesture still rang her doorbell. She was besieged with orders for orchids at Valentine's Day and Easter. Two summers later, she repainted the house on Flores Street by herself. Angelina held the legs of the ladder, and the three-year-old Orquídea dipped the brush into the pail.

Marta had allowed them to select the color. As they walked to the hardware store on Alvarado Boulevard, she reiterated the virtues of green. Verde es mágico, she intimated, tranquilo y curativo. She wasn't sure they were listening. I am certain green has a positive effect on the lungs and the intelligence, she informed them, her voice loud, as they walked. The sea was green, Marta reminded them as they stood at a traffic light. Green was primal, the first color God invented. Angelina and Orquídea selected a pink she abhorred. It could serve as a kind of undercoat, she rationalized. The house could be repainted later.

Marta Ortega expected her daughters to evolve their own textures and find the combination of elements which would nurture and sustain them. Angelina and Orquídea proved to be nothing like her garden. She had categorically failed them.

M̲arta Ortega walks to her kitchen window. She can feel the heat of the fires in the hills, a persistent glare. The wind is harsh. Next door, Bill is playing a phonograph record. "Now you say you're sorry, for being so untrue. Well, you can cry me a river, cry me a river, because I cried a river over you," Dinah Washington sings.

Flames and rivers, Marta thinks, attempting to dissect her inadequacy with her daughters, her defects, the exact methods she employed in scarring and poisoning them. She has memorized their accusations, but there was an era before they possessed their vocabulary of blame.

As they worked in the garden, Marta taught Angelina and Orquídea that each day was significant, unique as a human being. There were four seasons like the four limbs of god. No, a metaphorical god, she explained. They watched rain fall and when the rain ceased she drew their attention to the oiled sky and how it shoved clouds like a runaway train. Together, they charted the sheet-gray clouds hurtling recklessly fast, obviously drunk, on a path which was vaguely southern. Just before nightfall, sun elbowed the clouds apart and shattered the sky with patches like coral reefs or newborn red islands. In these regions, palm fronds arched slow shadows delicate as hand-painted fans. In such dominions, forgiveness was automatically granted.

Six o'clock was the hour of communion. It was sunset, and sunset was a spectacle and a sacrament. They would watch it with silence and respect. No, they could not talk on the telephone then. No, the radio was out of the question. Each sunset was unrepeatable, indelible, like a love affair. Sunset was a battle fought with fire amidst a flotilla of warrior clouds. This is all the alphabet you need to know, she assured her daughters. It is this which engraved your destinies in eons of green and blue air.

Marta Ortega wonders if this was the initial seed she planted in the deformation of their personalities. She had imparted a texture of sensuality and opulence to her daughters, a sensitivity to nuance and gesture. They possessed a capacity for lyricism and intensity. But there was an imbalance within their interior corridors and secret chambers.

They were constantly in love, even as young girls, reeling as if sunstruck or drunken, coupling in cars with boys in spasms, as if in a kind of consumption. They craved sweet heat and excess, a piano played at midnight while a moon raged furious. They wanted to squeeze the keys until their fingers bled. And they wished to do this every night. They lacked a sense of the finite, the rare moment which could not be caught, lured or trapped, stuffed, owned and mounted. They were convinced they could take the fluttering of a remarkable transitory juxtaposition and turn it into a lifetime.

Angelina and Orquídea ripened and blossomed, their dimension and design were as expected but the pattern was disrupted. They left home, went to college, collected honors and came back to Flores Street. They found apartments and jobs, married, divorced and returned to Flores Street. They insisted upon the dangerous, the abnormal and the self-destructive. Their choices in men were atrocious.

Angelina left the university, her scholarship and honor seminars to live with a man who had come to repair her telephone. His eyes were startling, glacial blue and yellowing with disease. Obviously, he consumed alcohol in dangerous excess and still could not sleep.

"His eyes are glazed, unfocused, ruined," Marta had pointed out, softly.

Angelina was a psychology major. Perhaps this was merely a complicated research project, a covert collection of factual material, perhaps subconscious.

"After all those pachuco frauds who wrecked my youth, I am willing to compromise. I want this relationship to work," Angelina told her. During the three years her daughter had been a psychology major, Angelina studded her conversations with the word "relationship," as if it contained magical qualities. The incessant repetition of this was becoming intolerable to Marta.

There were grave defects in the man's personal history, Angelina had conceded, but she was capable of transcending his excessive alcohol consumption and the number of automobiles he had, by his own admission, demolished.

"He is subliterate. He is considerably dumber than the Chicano boys with the long watch chains you used to fuck in cars," Marta observed. She had no patience for the tedious. She wanted to get to the point.

His vocabulary was limited and his youth grotesque, Angelina had agreed, but she was convinced he could be altered, enlightened, refined. She refused to recognize that the facts of his previous existence formed a definitive pattern. The landscape of him was irrefutable, decimated, radiated, atomic bombs had fallen. He had been dishonorably discharged from the armed forces. He had spent sixteen months in a prison for a liquor-store robbery which was, among other details, ineptly conceived and enacted.

Angelina perceived his abnormalities but translated them. These were not the actions of a disturbed man but rather the expressions of an authentic nonconformist, imaginative and untamed. There was an unpredictability. This excited her.

Then Angelina was ringing her doorbell. She was sobbing, carrying not a suitcase but a brown paper grocery bag in which she had apparently randomly tossed articles of clothing, her toothbrush, numerous pens and bracelets, one pair of dirty panties and a jar of instant coffee.

"We were eating breakfast. I felt casual, safe, loved," Angelina begins to explain. "I said, in passing, 'Where were you last night?' And he answered, 'With a whore.' He did not remove his eyes from the newspaper while he told me this. He was reading the horseracing results. I was sliding raspberry jam across the surface of a slice of toast. I put the knife down. I put the toast down. I said, 'Pardon me?' And he repeated, 'I was with a whore.'"

Marta Ortega poured Angelina a second cup of coffee. "Entonces?" she asked.

"Then I said, 'Do you mean a prostitute?' I was actually quite calm. I was rather interested. I asked him how much it cost. He said fifteen bucks. He did not even say dollars. He said bucks."

Marta Ortega was struck by the linguistic significance these words contained for her daughter. It had taken Angelina three months before something finally grated against her nerves. Marta Ortega realized there was a profound problem with Angelina's system of logic. "Qué dijiste?" Marta inquired.

"I said I had been under the impression that it cost more. I kept repeating the words 'fifteen bucks' inside of my head, as if in the repetition I would discover clarity. Then he told me the prostitute had been black. She had wanted more money but he convinced her he had no more. Mother, are you listening? He was reading the basketball scores while he described this unspeakable event."

Marta went into the kitchen and began to brew a second pot of coffee. It was, without doubt, going to be an exceptionally long morning. "Pues?"

Angelina paused, presumably to allow this information and its nuances and complexities to infiltrate her consciousness. Then she said, "I just sat at the dining-room table, lit a cigarette, looked at the coffee in the porcelain cups I bought for my birthday. Sunlight was pouring through the white polished-cotton curtains I made for the kitchen, recuerdas? With the ruffles at the top and bottom, you helped me stitch them? Sun caressed the leaves of the huge old philodendron you gave me. I had a therapy appointment at eleven-thirty and a manicure at one. I reminded myself I was a modern woman. These things happen, of course. I simply never thought these things might happen to me."

"I see," Marta said. It was too early in the morning to pour a glass of rum, although she was strongly tempted. Later, her daughters would accuse her of having rum drinks while their worlds fell apart. They claimed she distanced herself from them, veiled herself behind alcohol and orchids and failed to supply the necessary emotional support.

"Then I asked him if he enjoyed it," Angelina continued. She was apparently going to describe her morning in exhaustingly specific detail. "And he said, 'Enjoyed what?' He was preparing his pouch of tools, his wrenches and screwdrivers and pliers and gadgets. And I said, 'The black whore you fucked last night.' And get this, Mother. He actually thought about it. He was strapping his leather belt which contained his pouch of tools around his waist. Finally, while he was buckling the thing, he said, "Yeah, it was OK."

"Y ahorita, qué?"

"I will move out, naturally. Today, immediately, while he is at work, while it is safe. That man is a potential maniac."

"Adónde irás?" Marta inquired, just to complete the ritual.

Angelina stared at her. "Well, I will move back here, of course, where else? And I will return to college immediately," she added.

They drank coffee in silence. Angelina waited for her Tío Enrique to pick her up in his automobile, drive her to the apartment she had shared with the demented telephone repairman, help fill and carry cardboard cartons and transport her to safety. Then she would simply vanish from that particular configuration.

"So this is how it is. One moment you are spreading raspberry jam across the surface of a slice of toast, and in one instant your entire universe collapses, explodes, disintegrates," Angelina noted. She said this with sadness and a hint of something which might have been delight.

They should be with me now, Marta thinks, watching the fires flow, etching their fierce calligraphy across the hills. Angelina and Orquídea were collectors of ash and flame. Embers and burns fed them.

They took ludicrous jobs as barmaids or boutique salesgirls and moved into apartments at the ocean which they could not afford. Then they returned to Flores Street without warning. They were constantly coming and going like confused birds, increasingly elaborate in their sudden and chaotic migrations which had no seasons, no elements of predictability. Then her daughters had children. They no longer arrived on Flores Street with grocery bags or one suitcase. Now they were cluttered with sofas, rugs, record albums, books, paintings and appliances. They arrived in the nest of their birth with infants and cribs and cardboard boxes filled with stuffed animals, yellow bears, pink rabbits, blue dogs. The baby strollers, of course, the bottles and cases of formula and diapers.

Angelina met her first husband two months after she disappeared from the deranged telephone repairman and returned to the university. Aaron sat next to Angelina in a psychology class at UCLA. It was a seminar on abnormal behavior for honor students, Marta remembers.

When Aaron graduated from college, his father gave him two dress stores in the San Fernando Valley. Eventually, Aaron would abandon his family and his religion for Angelina. He would be at her side when she gave birth to their son. Fourteen months later, Angelina would run away to South America with her gardener, a Mexicano named Federico who was also a part-time dance instructor on Tuesday and Thursday nights.

The doorbell rang at 11 P.M. Angelina was handing her fourteen-month-old son, Antonio, to her like a mailman delivering a parcel. Marta noticed that her daughter had already lined up the cardboard boxes of stuffed animals, the boxes of diapers, crib and playpen, bags of pajamas and carton of toys before she rang the doorbell. She reaches through space and accepts the sleeping infant. A taxicab is waiting at the curb.

"What the hell is this?" Marta had demanded.

"This is a blood matter. This is passion, risking everything," Angelina announced, breathless. Marta recognized an intersection of rare elements and the fluttering, the fluctuation of the soul. "I am leaving a husband and child to fly to Guadalajara at midnight."

Angelina was gone five months. She did not telephone. Antonio followed Marta through the garden. Then the doorbell rang.

"I lived for his cha-cha, his rhumba, the light glancing off his pointed and shined black shoes. We danced until dawn, slept at sunrise and woke at dusk every day for months. From Buenos Aires through Quito, Lima, Caracas and São Paulo. We crossed the Andes twice," Angelina said. "Then I woke up broke, in an unspeakable port, regretting nothing."

Marta now drank vodka rather than rum. It calmed and cured, simply, almost immediately. She poured a glass for herself and her elder daughter. She could not think of anything to say. At the moment she was on O. She was reading *Long Day's Journey into Night* by Eugene O'Neill.

Angelina kicked off her shoes. She did not inquire about her son. He was sleeping. Angelina sat down on the sofa. "It's your fault," Angelina informed her.

Marta Ortega watches the flames commit their slow-motion atrocities upon the hills. That was the worst part, she decides, they blamed her for everything. They even quoted her, an act Marta considered unnecessarily heavy-handed and cruel.

"You would not permit us to go to church. You scorned the ordinary rituals and conventions. You would not even let us paint Easter eggs. We could not even have a goddamn Thanksgiving turkey. Can you imagine what lepers we were at school?" Angelina lit a cigarette. "You forced us to transcend convention, to be extravagant, demanding and lavish." Angelina stared at her. This was after she woke up broke in an unspeakable port, regretting nothing.

Marta Ortega weighed her options. She would be on P next. She had decided to read the poet Ezra Pound. Her firstborn daughter was lying flat on the sofa. Perhaps she would fall asleep. "Are you taking Antonio back?" Marta asked.

"Tony," her daughter corrected. Angelina sat up and stared at her as if she were missing an eye, perhaps, or had a fresh red scar across her cheek. "Of course I'm taking Tony back."

Marta noticed she could breathe again. "OK. Let's simply forget it," she offered. Her firstborn grandson was now named Tony. And Angelina was going to resume her duties as a mother.

"I will never forget it," Angelina assured her. She reached across the sofa and seized her hand.

Marta Ortega prepared herself for the possibility that, in her torment and rage, Angelina was going to break her fingers. She would be able to turn the pages of books with a cast, she decided, but her gardening would be seriously impaired. Then, instead of crushing her hand, Angelina pressed her lips to Marta's fingers and began weeping softly.

"I experienced passion, Mama," Angelina sobbed, caressing her hand. So, Angelina was not going to break her bones and she was going to take her son back. Marta Ortega realized she needed another glass of vodka, but Angelina was still holding her hand, gently, tracing the veins with her fingertips.

"You imparted this sense of passion in me, this capacity for feeling. I would have died for Federico. You gave me a gift beyond description. Gracias, Madre." Angelina was kissing her tear-dampened hand, then her mouth.

Angelina telephoned a friend. A car honked in front of the house. Then Angelina and Antonio who was now named Tony were gone. In the morning, Marta noticed that the boxes of stuffed animals, the blue and pink and yellow dogs, bunnies and bears, the crib, the playpen and the cartons of pajamas had vanished.

Marta Ortega is assaulted by scenes without chronology. It is later. It is Orquídea, leaving the teaching position for which she had studied five years, abandoning her duties in midsemester, in disgrace. She was returning to Flores Street to write her memoirs, her autobiography. Orquídea, with three children and a moving van. Orquídea, after her first husband, the lunatic Viking, and before the second, the professor of history.

Angelina stood at the edge of the courtyard. She was supporting her sister in this moment of crisis, this channel which had opened beneath Orquídea's feet. It was noon.

"You taught us to take risks," Angelina begins.

"I never did," Marta replied firmly. "I offered you imagination and you turned it into a curse."

Her daughters consider this. They light cigarettes, pace, pour themselves drinks.

"You said we were all continents, vast, uncharted, eccentrically indigenous," Orquídea begins, tentative.

"I offered you alternative realities, and in each region you managed to construct contagion." Marta is holding an empty glass. She refills it.

"You said we were mutations, white and Indian. A new species to inherit a new world," Angelina tries.

"I said you were hybrids," Marta shouts, annoyed. What was the matter with them? They went to universities and still their knowledge of the physical world remained appallingly inaccurate.

"You made us proud and demanding," Angelina persists.

"That is your interpretation," Marta Ortega replies.

"You said defend no borders, no fronteras but those of sensibility. You made us idiosyncratic, spontaneous and authentic. You instructed us to take laughter as a given and exuberance as an inalienable right," Orquídea reminds her.

On this occasion, Angelina and Orquídea are working in unison. Marta finds them formidable. Silence. Marta leans against the back wall of the kitchen. It is dusk. Angelina and Orquídea are carrying lamps, boxes of books, a typewriter, porcelain cups wrapped in newspaper, a mink stole, stacks of record albums, a crib and toys for children.

So, this is it, Marta Ortega thinks, watching the accumulation of Orquídea's life parade itself through her house. It was not a celebration but an invasion. I am the nest, Marta realizes. I must open my tired wings, my stained feathers, and take them in, over and over. I must guard their eggs, explain the hatching process, demonstrate techniques for capturing food and feeding the young.

Now Marta Ortega stares at the flames in hills which were once brush, jackrabbits, poppies and wild barley. She lies down in her bed. She can smell red smoke. She closes her eyes. Her daughters are engraved on the inside of her lids.

Angelina and Orquídea are returning, resplendent with the details of their disasters, their self-inflicted catastrophes, the festering lesions they hold out for her to examine as if they were displaying jewels. The interminable succession of midnights where she is blamed for their predicaments, now, in the indescribably horrible past and in the no doubt equally abusive and brutal future.

"You said it was all a matter of chance," Orquídea repeats in one hot August dusk or another.

"You taught us to never take shit from men," Angelina accuses her one summer evening while her second marriage is dissolving.

Marta Ortega remembers this particular incident with clarity. It was after Angelina abandoned her first husband, the Jewish man she met at the university, Aaron. The man who owned two dress shops in the San Fernando Valley and was the father of her first grandchild, Antonio.

Aaron had provided Angelina with a house in Sherman Oaks. Sliding glass doors led to a swimming pool. Windows offered a view of hillsides draped with fruit trees. Aaron studied Spanish one night each week. He wanted them to speak her language together. He planned excursions to Mexico. They would take airplanes to the cities, trains to the sea resorts and then drive to the ruins of the Yucatán. When Angelina became pregnant, he attended a special course at the hospital so that he would be permitted to be at her side when their son ripped his way out of Angelina's womb. In short, he was too easy for the twenty-three-year-old Angelina, who craved not a reasonable life but something tempestuously treacherous and self-destructive.

It was after she had run off on the midnight flight to Guadalajara with her gardener and part-time dance instructor, the Mexicano named Federico. It was after she reclaimed her son, returned to college and received her Ph.D.

She was a psychologist. She was officially permitted to call herself doctor. Angelina had new stationery printed, plaques engraved, embossed business cards. She hired a telephone-answering service which picked up her calls with the phrase "Dr. Angelina Ortega." She insisted everyone address her as Doctor. Her hairstylist, manicurist and astrologer quickly complied. Marta and Orquídea ignored her.

Marta suggested that Angelina open an office of some sort. She was a doctor. Should she not practice her healing profession and seek the afflicted? Marta implied she had a duty to cure.

Angelina looked for an office to rent. That was how she met her second husband. She stopped referring to herself as a doctor. She spoke instead of her impending wedding. Her tone retained its abnormal intensity. Angelina seemed to have simply switched obsessions. The man was tall, dark, of Italian ancestry and strikingly handsome.

Marta Ortega read *The Penal Colony* by Franz Kafka and *Under the Volcano* by Malcolm Lowry. Then Angelina arrived on Flores Street. She was going to remain with her mother until the ceremony was satisfactorily completed.

The wedding had been expensive. Angelina insisted upon a dress from Bullock's Wilshire, a traditional white dress with a train and an even longer white lace veil studded with pearl-like beads. The veil was so intricate in its attachment to the head that diagrams were provided. Marta found herself suddenly disoriented. She sat down. The veil alone cost four hundred dollars.

"Angelina, es ridículo," Marta said in the cubicle dressing room. "Only virgins do this white-lace bit. You are already a mother."

"You, of all people, dare talk to me about convention and proprieties," Angelina screamed, attempting to adjust the excessively elaborate veil to her head. "This is my baptism, my communion, my saint's day, my painted Easter eggs, the Thanksgiving turkeys I was denied, the Christmas trees, the piñatas, the fucking Girl Scouts, the cake sales and carols." Angelina glared at Marta through the mirror.

Then there were the bridesmaids in matching pink satin gowns. And, yes, they must have the pink hats, Angelina insisted. And the dance band in the backyard, and, yes, they would have to construct a platform. Angelina asserted that the band with a platform was a detail fundamental to the composition of the event. It was essential for the ambiance.

"When he wears black he looks like a panther," Angelina revealed. "In white, he looks like a movie star."

Marta Ortega waited for her daughter to provide an outline of the man's character, disposition, the texture of his opinions. She waited for Angelina to illuminate his sensibility. She was curious. She wondered which composers and poets he preferred, what were the directions of his sympathies.

Angelina applied another coat of coral to her lips. She seemed to be wondering why they were sitting in a dense silence. Angelina glanced at her mother and blotted her lips with a tissue.

"What about his substance, Angelina? Su arquitectura interior?" Marta finally demanded.

"His interior architecture? He's a goddamn Beverly Hills dentist," Angelina exploded.

Now, after the veil that even Angelina could not assemble correctly, now this second marriage had collapsed. The man who looked like a panther in black and an Italian film star in white had found another woman. The man who drove the silver sports car and took her on cruises to Jamaica, Puerto Vallarta and Veracruz was deserting her.

The panther who gave her two sons, Brian and Richard, and a daughter, Jessica, was leaving. He was moving out of their house. And their house was going to be sold.

"His receptionist, can you believe it?" Angelina wailed. "A girl from Wichita, Kansas. A girl who cannot spell the word *neurotic.*"

"It is not surprising behavior from a man who enjoys the surface pleasures, the conventional, the images of billboards," Joseph observed. "You were too complex."

"Shut the fuck up," Angelina shouted. "I am only six years older than that goddamn Wichita telephone answerer."

Yes, her daughter is taking it hard. Angelina is taking it like a war lance in the gut. She sits at the kitchen table, doubled up with agony. She has not brushed her hair in days. Joseph pats her gently on the shoulder. Marta finds a hairbrush in her daughter's purse and slowly works the bristles through the tangles which have formed around Angelina's shoulders, the hair mirroring the confusion within her daughter's mind, fragments, soiled strands, a web broken, confetti savaged by wind. The unmistakable configuration of a party that is over.

Marta holds her daughter's hand. She rocks her against her breast. Gone the veil of green with its waterfalls and tamed lagoons. Gone the sailing excursions, vacations, the jewelry at Christmas and even the house. Angelina weeps. Marta Ortega is immune to the sound of crying. She erases it from her consciousness automatically. She is trying to remember how many children Angelina has, whether cribs are compulsory or will cots and sleeping bags suffice?

Then, miraculously, the house is empty. Marta Ortega is drinking rum-and-fruit concoctions with Joseph and Bill. Black women sing about heartbreak, pain, what it is to be exquisite, perfumed, draped in red silk and to have your man pack, find another woman, leave you in debt. And their voices are a scented smoke, magnolias and bruises, molasses and gashes which never heal. And Marta suddenly thought of Salvador Velásquez, for no particular reason, how they saw the night under stars from a mutually exclusive galaxy. It was the light itself they perceived differently, she realizes.

It is summer on Flores Street, another August of jasmine, the amber arcs of streetlamps, barking dogs, orchids, camellias and roses reflecting the pastels of the sunset.

"We became strange, Momma," Angelina is asserting. "You taught us to drift gossamer, married to the air."

"We became difficult to live with," Orquidea adds, after a pause designed to sting.

"Bullshit," Joseph says. "Marta merely refused to compromise her integrity. She told you resurrection was not a formula or a chemical in a bottle. She warned you there are no mathematics to marriage, no guarantees of love or sanity or honor."

Then they are dressed as gypsies, gitanas, with sandals and earrings that dangle. They enroll in the university again, share apartments with unsuitable men and return to Flores Street. Then there are new houses, sofas to upholster, they plant rosebushes, dye their hair, spend summers in Europe. Angelina and Orquídea practice their professions, are therapists or own businesses. They remarry, purchase houses in the Pacific Palisades and the Hollywood Hills. There are more children and assertions of stability. Then the doorbell is ringing.

It is Orquídea, an older Orquídea in this image, this particular summer night rising in her memory. An Orquídea who has already been Olga but not yet the Orquídea who will live in San Diego. This version of Orquídea has taken a vacation in the Mediterranean. Her children are on an excursion with one of their fathers or in a camp in the mountains.

"I have committed an atrocity." Thus Orquídea begins, pouring herself a glass of scotch.

Always, they come to her to confess. When they are not berating, blaming and abusing her, they depict the lurid and indecent episodes of their lives in graphic and compelling detail. When she is not their personal criminal, she is their oracle. They beg for her consejos, advice and absolution.

When Marta Ortega hears the doorbell late at night, she immediately studies the street behind them, searching for police cars, ambulances, mobs of enraged men, pools of blood. She was on O. She closes *1984* by George Orwell and assumes her quasi-priestess posture. She indicates the living-room sofa.

A trembling, scotch-drinking Orquídea sits down. She does not kneel at her mother's feet. Marta is relieved. Orquídea has not kissed her feet, at least not yet. And she does not begin with Forgive me, Mamacita, for I have sinned, at least not yet.

"Pues?" Marta has already poured herself a glass of vodka, her voice is soft, she turns off the kitchen light. The one living-room lamp is soft.

"It was Crete," this version of Orquídea begins. "He was nineteen, spoke no English, Spanish or French."

Orquídea describes a hotel swimming pool and the green-eyed boy-man who passed her almost-naked body. He carried a net designed to capture stray leaves and drowned insects. His eyes were the identical green of the water. Orquídea stared at him through sunglasses, struck by his casual indifference, how elegant and remote he was. She watched him eradicating from the perfectly uncorrupted pool an occasional stranded insect. He attempted to attract the attention of a young beauty from Texas.

"I stared at the water, his eyes, and thought, There is so little time, so little time," this Orquídea says. "Then I told him my name. I told him the girl from Texas was extremely pretty but she would not fuck him like I would."

"This was in Greek?" Marta is mildly interested.

"And a bit of Italian." Orquídea lights a cigarette. "The boy asked me how I knew this. I explained she was engaged to be married, a situation she took seriously. And I was thinking I knew this because she was twenty-one and I thirty-seven. I told him to come to my room and he did."

"Comprendo," Marta offers. "You communicated in flesh and blood."

"On the night beach, with my spine congruent with the sand, my eyes open to the stars, my mouth was flagrant. I amazed myself. And he tasted of the island, of the ruin a blistering sun makes of water, chlorine, sweat, mud, and I realized this is how men are born, from sandy loam and nightness, a sudden womb."

Marta is becoming annoyed with this extensive prologue. She senses half an hour of olive trees, dancing drunk in cafés and clothing shed in alleys, courtyards, roadsides. "Entonces?" Her voice is sharp.

"I knew it was wrong, doomed, disastrous, incautious."

"I am fully acquainted with your mode," Marta Ortega, oracle of Orquídea's evening, replies.

"I took him to London with me. One morning, in a perfectly charming hotel, sun sliding across pink floral wallpaper, I realized I was bored. I packed his clothing while he bathed. He didn't have a suitcase. I folded his clothing in my Louis Vuitton bag. I called a cab. We went to the airport."

Orquídea is agitated, pacing, lighting one cigarette after another. "I had promised to take him home with me, to California. I actually believed it at the time. Then I offered to buy him a ticket to whatever city he chose."

"It is O.K., mi amor," Marta assures her daughter.

"He said I lied to him, betrayed him. He began to cry, Mamacita. He was sobbing without control, there in Heathrow. People were staring." Tears form in Orquídea's eyes. "I told him that was what being nineteen was for, to be lied to. I packed his jeans and cotton shirts in my suitcase. I kept thinking, This is the only Louis Vuitton suitcase I have ever had, and this oblivious pool-maintenance kid was holding it as he stared at the board of flight departures. He chose Vienna, of all things. I was prepared to pay the fare to Tokyo or Katmandu if I had to. Then he took the Vuitton bag and boarded the plane. I watched it take off."

"Es todo?" Marta is prepared to offer her daughter absolution.

"I couldn't stop thinking about the stinking Vuitton suitcase. I had engaged in an act of deliberate fraudulence and I was obsessed with my luggage," Orquídea admitted. "That was the last thing I said to him. Something about taking care of the bag."

Then Orquídea reaches for her hand. They stare into each other's eyes. "Now I understand why I cried in the airport and on the plane to New York. It was what I didn't say, Mamacita."

"That you were the more wounded?" Marta intuits, her voice a whisper. "That you were simply his first woman and he your last boy."

Orquídea is saying yes as she sobs, as Marta rocks her younger daughter against her breast. There are no divisions between them. Their grain is identical. And that night they weep together.

Always the cycle begins again. Angelina and Orquídea do not need extravagant events to tear them adrift. A listless sea breeze could as easily sever their fragile roots, the tendrils that lie on the surface, limp, refusing the journey into the dirt. Their harvests are disappointing, inadequate, tarnished. They blame her when the earth is barren. Anxiety makes the air rotten.

"They don't clap correctly," Marta tells Joseph. "It sounds hollow, shallow, as if even in celebration they were saving their hands for a more important purpose."

"You taught us to flaunt our triumphs, to sentimentalize our defeats. We learned to demand both awe and pity," Orquídea says.

"We became bad winners," Angelina says softly.

"Bad losers," Orquídea adds, her voice intense, angry.

They are sitting at the kitchen table. It is dusk and her daughters are between marriages and love affairs. They need flesh like addicts, the architecture of bone and how it burns, that tightrope-walking between men.

"I am bored by your narcissism and laziness," Marta Ortega finally informs them. "Your small rituals of selfishness, the whole long sleep of you."

They enter psychotherapy and become increasingly unstable. They feel their behavior is justified, is the obvious result of her egocentric influence. They complete courses of study for occupations they do not practice, diet and exercise between periods of indulgence. They join groups for enhancing their feminine consciousness, take yoga classes and circulate petitions for the protection of whales and dolphins. They equate the accumulation of experience with wisdom. Something of their fathers resides within them, Marta Ortega concludes with sadness, an area unformed, that which perceives the landscape in terms of what is downhill.

They discuss their personality defects and the deformities of their psyches incessantly. They have learned to dissect their psychological abnormalities with the dispassion and precision of one who has traveled innumerable times to a particular foreign land and returned with charts, slides, artifacts.

Es verdad, she admits, in one midnight or another. She refused to socialize with the other mothers. Their subservience and lack of variation repelled her. She refused to attend PTA meetings, bake cookies for school festivals, allow them to paint eggs at Easter or decorate Christmas trees. Yes, she pronounced such activities as pagan and shallow. She did not permit them to attend confession or mass, alienating them from their friends, reducing their social stature and popularity. They were not given access to the telephone or television, an object Marta Ortega refused to purchase. Yes, she admits, she told them science was delusionary. Angelina and Orquídea inform her that she committed crimes to their interior regions during what they refer to as their formative years, and for this she will always be a felon.

When they are wrenched by impending divorces, intensely painful love affairs or changing careers and what they now refer to as lifestyles, a phrase Marta Ortega abhors, they accuse her of being self-indulgently egocentric. Angelina and Orquídea are reciting their standard litany. She failed to provide them with a viable nuclear family. She insisted they were the substance and their fathers the accident, the random catalyst. She scorned the ordinary amenities and pronounced the residents of the entire barrio as excruciatingly dull. She did not even baptize them, they re-member, over and over, like children picking at a scab. They imply she scarred them from birth, deliberately, perversely.

"Would you have preferred acts of fraudulence?" Marta Ortega asks.

"We would have preferred a mother who was normal," they reply, even after they are themselves mothers and, in her opinion, far from the conventional feminine ideal.

"It is becoming banal," Marta admits.

"Mi amor, I agree," Joseph says. "If I were an anthropologist recon-structing their remains, I would be surprised by how small they were. I would be mildly curious. Did they invent music, forage for berries or conceive of wine?"

"My inquiries would be desultory. They are an irrelevant culture, their remains intact but unexceptional," Marta Ortega sighs.

"They teach us little about God or poetry," Joseph notes, also sadly.

"Their language has ten thousand words for saying 'Give me,'" Marta reveals.

"They would eat themselves into obesity. If the terrain were hard they would starve," Joseph decides.

When they are not dissecting their emotional oddities, examining each deviation as if it were a singular work of art, when they are not quoting her or recounting the history of her criminality, they plead for her advice and attention. They cannot select an apartment unless she tours it with them, opens closets and drawers, peers beneath carpets, studies the view from each window and then blesses or dismisses the dwelling.

Orquídea has entered the garden, pretending she is not hysterical. This is truly frightening and Marta begins to tremble. She puts down her shears. She knows the crisis cannot be marital. Orquídea's marriage collapsed three or four years ago. Her husband had been broad-shouldered, blond and blue-eyed, an image of a Viking come alive. She had married this man during the era when she called herself Olga and claimed to be of Greek and Scandinavian descent. He was the vice-president of the company where Olga was employed as personnel director. She wore suits and silk blouses and carried a leather briefcase with her initials engraved in ornate brass letters. Olga, a woman executive, with a private secretary and a company car.

Within a week, the Viking named Bob took Olga to dinner and then to Las Vegas. He was married. He filed for a divorce on the day of their return from the illicit weekend in the city of contrived pleasures. Olga worked only the one year necessary for the processing of the Viking's divorce. She performed her tasks without conviction, sat at a large oak desk and filed and polished her fingernails. Then they were quietly and inexpensively married in a chapel, alone, near Big Sur.

"He looks like an astronaut," Orquídea/Olga revealed during the twelve-month obligatory waiting period before they could be officially joined in holy matrimony. "His family has been here so long, they fought the Indians."

Marta Ortega wondered what response Orquídea/Olga expected from this particular information. His family slaughtered Indios, and Olga perceived this as a virtue. There are nuances profoundly disturbing, a wavering, a sense of a tide powerful, chaotic.

Two or three children later, the Viking who resembled an astronaut will be dismissed from his job amidst rumors of inexplicable absences of monies and stock, gambling debts and clandestine journeys to Las Vegas. The house perched on a cliff of majestic burgundy succulents with a view of the ocean in the Pacific Palisades is being sold. The cars and the jewelry will be sold. Her husband will still be in a mental hospital when their divorce is final.

Now Orquídea has edged into the house, furtive, stilted. Her conversation is inane and formal. She is not wearing makeup. Marta Ortega is struck by this absence of the usual. Even in crisis her daughters paint their faces and pick up their clothing at the cleaners. They sit in the kitchen.

Marta glances out the window, searching for a taxicab or a moving van. She remembers there are three children, Sandra and Scott and Jeffrey.

Orquídea/Olga had just become pregnant when the Viking vice-president who resembled a rocket-ship pilot was pronounced mentally disabled. Orquídea/Olga had returned with her two children to Flores Street. They endured that pregnancy together. Marta remained with Orquídea in the labor room. She had seen the grandson named Jeffrey moments after he was born. And now what was Orquídea saying? She has located what? She seems to be saying she has located a lump on her breast.

"I did not actually find it," Orquídea admits. "Jim discovered it."

Marta Ortega does not ask who Jim is. She suggests her daughter remove her blouse. Orquídea stands paralyzed. She laughs, dismissing the suggestion. Of course there is no abnormal growth on her body. It is a mistake, a passing aberration.

"I might be hallucinating. I have not been able to trust my reference points in years," Orquídea realizes. Then, slowly, as if in a dream, Orquídea unbuttons her blouse and unsnaps her brassiere.

Marta Ortega accompanies her daughter to the doctor. When the nurse calls her name and indicates the door through which she must walk, Orquídea refuses to release her hand. Marta realizes she must enter the inner office, locked by the five surprisingly strong fingers of her younger daughter. The doctor, a specialist, presses Orquídea's breasts. This is after Marta has undressed her daughter. Orquídea has lost the power to move her limbs. The doctor must reach across Marta, must navigate around Marta Ortega's body to touch Orquídea, who is shriveled up on the examining table like a run-over dog. The specialist makes notes on a clipboard in a code Marta cannot comprehend.

No, she tells her daughter repeatedly, she cannot describe the script in which the doctor wrote. No, she repeats, she is not hiding anything. The language seemed vaguely Arabic. And Orquídea is staying in the house on Flores Street while they wait for the medical report.

Orquídea follows her mother into the garden, into the kitchen, the bedroom. Orquídea is promising to become a Catholic if she is pronounced well. She is vowing to donate money, go on retreats and dump bedpans in hospitals. Her behavior has been arrogant, immature and excessive. She will correct this. She will purge her emotional imbalances by counseling terminal cancer patients. She will wash the wounds of lepers.

"Did you inform her there are no lepers in southern California?" Joseph inquired.

"I didn't want to interrupt her lyrical flow," Marta admits. "She was actually rather compelling. She was on a roll."

"I have been irradiated with clarity," Orquídea announces at breakfast. Despite the intuition that she will die in a grotesque fashion in a matter of weeks, her appetite is unimpaired.

Irradiated, Marta repeats silently, savoring the sound of the word. It is as if Orquídea had transformed the experience of having her breast placed like a slab of meat between the cold metal vise of the X-ray machine into an other, a splendor.

Marta was with her daughter. Orquídea was instructed to remove her clothing. Since Orquídea's arms no longer functioned, Marta undressed her daughter. This occurred in an attractive white cubicle with a coatrack, a mirror and a white hinged wooden door like the dressing rooms in beauty parlors. Two nurses guided Orquídea into the X-ray chamber. Orquídea described how her breast was placed on a cold metal slab like meat in a butcher's shop. Technicians tightened the vise. The radioactive beam was invisible. Orquídea walked out unsoiled, noting that her blouse would not even have to be sent to the cleaners. Irradiated, Marta thinks. Her daughter has transmuted the X rays into bands of starlight.

"You have had a revelation?" Marta Ortega encourages.

"Once I thought I required insight and purpose, an absolute and final answer," Orquídea said. "Now I only need that fucking doctor to say I don't have cancer."

It is Marta who must telephone the doctor, receive the report and transmit it to an Orquídea who, having finished four tamales and three plates of frijoles, is sitting on the kitchen floor, rocking back and forth like a mental patient in a locked ward. She babbles about cremation, ashes scattered across the sea, the agony she will bear with dignity, setting an example for her soon-to-be orphans. Marta interrupts her to report the test results, which are negative.

Orquídea does not rise from the kitchen floor. She crawls across the tiles and kisses Marta's feet. Today, Marta Ortega is not an engineer of disabling neurosis and an architect of deliberate acts of cruelty upon innocent children. On this particular afternoon, she is a saint, an oracle, holy. Her flesh is worthy of veneration. She is a bulto, immaculate, wise.

"I could not have survived this without you," Orquídea the reprieved announces. Then she telephones Jim.

He arrives on Flores Street an hour later. He is gracious, quiet, innocuous, his smile modified by his beard, his eyes shielded behind glasses. He is cloaked by pipesmoke. He is a professor of history at USC. He is unexceptional, hardly a romantic figure, Marta thinks.

"At this point, I merely desire stability," Orquídea explains.

Orquídea will marry him six months later. It is a civil ceremony in an outdoor plaza on the campus, a tiled area surrounded by statues, monumental outbursts of abstract metal. The grass is thick and ordered, a web of carefully tended paths connecting huge buildings. It is a miniature world of lawns and edifices, a surface with a curious absence of deviation. Marta senses a disturbance then, an excess of the linear, external definitions, concrete certainties.

Orquídea will bear a daughter and a son, a Jennifer and a Robert. They will live in the Hollywood Hills. Orquídea will embrace schedules and calendars. There will be an abundance of divisions as if the future was tamed, reliable, already known. Orquídea will play tennis and bridge, have manicures, charge cards and luncheons with wives married to other professors. A world within a world, duplicating itself in each detail. Orquídea will accompany her husband to academic conferences in New York and Honolulu.

On a night calm and undifferentiated, Orquídea and Jim will decide they have nothing in common but the common. They are civilized, modern, well educated and controlled. The ivy walls have grown across their eyes and through the channels where they once had blood. They recognize that the well-tended paths, acres of perfect square lawns and dinner parties with colleagues, are not enough to sustain them.

There will be no breaking of windows or vases, no fists into flesh, bruises or the revelation of fraudulent acts or the longing for others. There are no implications of inadequacy or failure. Orquídea and Jim sip brandy as they discuss the logistics of their separation, dispassionately, as if planning what to pack for a vacation. It will be a quiet divorce, and the child-support payments will arrive precisely on schedule.

Women are spawned by the moon, Marta Ortega reminds herself. They are her replicas. They too endure a similar passage through darkness, phases where they thin and go fat, one side luminous, the other perpetually hidden and black. Angelina and Orquídea were no different. They drifted through the void, living as if posthumously, divorced or betrayed, stumbling lost and uprooted. There were eras of rage, flirtations with garrets, musicians, criminals. She observed their development, how they learned to lie with ease, contriving a glamour, reeling wildly out of control, careening down the center divider, striving for the plate-glass shell, wrists first.

"Suicide is too accurate, like geometry, with the mystery at the edges erased," Marta insisted.

"What about the swallowed scorpion? The leap from a roof in Dior? Angelina or Orquídea demanded.

"Trite and contrived," Marta replied. "Make the world kill you. Be singled out by lightning. Have the cliff where you sit disappear."

Of course her daughters had their personal orbits, years of calm, the diversions of children and the myriad expressions of renewal. Then the anchor disintegrated, the sea rebelled, the waters rose and defied their contours. Then they had to swim for it.

Marta recognizes that her daughters are like statues in plazas in regions profuse with history. They are a momentary arresting glance of bronze which men see from a train and let slip into the periphery, nameless, not pausing to read their inscriptions, their rare design. Her daughters are sped past, like the out-of-focus backgrounds in tourist photographs where any bridge or hedge or stretch of muted blue water will do.

Angelina and Orquídea were mahogany, finely crafted instruments with a scale no man would master, a tone that would never open. Men would not permit this. Her daughters possessed immense inner regions which were sealed shut as the locked rooms in a house where you have not yet lived. Men could not know them. The refinement and sophistication of their gestures were rejected, their charm, intelligence and vulnerability ignored. And Angelina and Orquídea were like peaches or rocks or strips of confetti, shattered by wind, adrift in an interminable free-fall.

Marta Ortega wanted to shake them by the shoulders and scream, Idiotas, it always rains too early or late, the crops rot and you hock your diamond wedding ring for a sack of rice, a blanket and a candle. Betrayal and cruelty are not aberrations but predictable cycles on this and all other worlds. Always you pull the quilt to your face and he is drunk and blazing behind you, wide-awake, with the strength of a bull, the moon is full and your flesh a red cape. Where is the surprise in this?

Then the telephone is ringing, the doorbell. They are grateful, extravagant with devotion and remorse. She had cared for their children in their not-infrequent periods of chaos and crisis. She has never denied them. She has the generosity of a saint, the intelligence and compassion of a prophet. Soon they will kneel and kiss her feet, a behavior pattern Marta Ortega finds excessive and disturbing.

"Wake from your damnable static and black in your private abscess of night," Marta Ortega orders. She takes them into the garden. They are amnesiacs. She must teach them the alphabet again, their names, addresses, occupations. She holds their hands, noticing that their fingers are encased in expensive rings which they had collected and managed to retain between disasters. Marta guides them between rows of orchids at dusk. They are children again.

They stand tentative as car-crash victims separating themselves from glass and twisted strands of metal. They are mute as wrenched kelp stranded on hot sand in an August of frenzied green flies. They are uncertain of the methods for reentering the domain of the living, of tangible delineations, hours, laws, hairdressers, psychiatric appointments, manicures, the children that must be, by their own definition, driven to ballet classes and football practice. They stare at the tracks their feet leave in the innocent moist earth of her garden. They are transfixed by their footprints as if they no longer knew what species they were born to. They look at her with wild eyes that ask, Did I fly or crawl, burrow or bark? Later, they begin to cry. Howls rip their throats. Marta notices, somewhere in the periphery, as she passes between the house and the garden, that their lungs are good.

The mirror is a sacrament and a theater. They drape their bodies in tight red dresses, wear high-heeled sandals, gold bracelets, rings. They paint a river of purple half moons above their eyes like bridges into an irresistible interior. They reenter a quasi-Indian phase, announce they are gitanas, paganas, more extraordinary and sensual than other women. In their purses they carry invisible tarot decks, hand-painted Spanish fans and cuchillos.

Angelina leaves a restaurant and walks, half drunk, across a parking lot, laughing, on the verge of singing. Her fingers are flutes, her lips bells. She is encased in silk and pearls, impeccable, lean, dark, elemental. Her hips are arches men long to touch as they would carved alabaster. Men open their mouths like circus spectators or hungry fish. He is whispering into her ear. He is saying that he loves someone else and will never see her again. Then he hands her cab fare.

"I'm going to San Francisco," Angelina, in one of her early incarnations, announced. "I'll dye my hair red. Let it blow like a mane of fire in the knifey North Bay wind."

"That has a lyricism," Marta noted.

"I'll fill my life with sailors," Angelina mused. "I will collect them like rare glass."

"Men of the sea can be sweet," Marta encouraged.

"I'll dance in satin sandals in saloons with a blue bay view. I will get a tattoo, a lush rose, engraved on my thigh, blue as the sea and permanent as a stone, as a kiss on a rainy night you never forget."

"I would not object to that," Marta Ortega, the oracle of Flores Street, concluded.

"Then I'd pawn my ruby ring and keep going. Catch a Greyhound to Seattle. Find a barge to Nome."

"Y tus niños?" Marta inquired, mechanically.

But Angelina wasn't listening, Marta realized. Her daughter was not serious. She was constructing a metaphor. She was designing a composition of words only. Marta sighed.

Of course, Angelina was merely threatening. Her elder daughter would never walk into a sunset without a suitcase, without her porcelain hand-painted lamps from China, her perfumes from France, her sofas and the accumulation she kept in storage or on display in one apartment or house or another. These external objects had become part of her, like flesh or indelible passages from a book, ingrained, a design within the fabric.

"I will sit at the feet of the Sphinx," Orquídea screamed into the telephone. "She knows what it is to be deserted by love. I will lose myself in an air of jasmine and locusts. I will let the moths of history feed on me, on this obsolescent flesh."

"Es una idea fascinante," Marta replied, somewhat intrigued. Orquídea was howling in Spanish. Marta noticed they tended to make their most dramatic vows and curses in Spanish.

"In some alley whiter than a dried scalp, in a night stinking with ginger and urine, I will lie in a gutter and let winos and lepers fuck me," Orquídea informed her. Ah, Orquídea and her lepers, Marta sighed.

Orquídea was weeping. "I wasn't his kind, of course. Not blond enough, with too much belly. I loved too hard, desperate and clawed, with the intensity of a wounded bird, with the wisdom of a thing that has died over and over and risen with the precision of a sun."

"Pues?" Perhaps she should have encouraged Orquídea with her acting lessons, her voice training.

"He said it bored him," and Orquídea is slowly calming. After her communion with the Sphinx, she will journey to the Nile, a river she imagines as yellow as a hill invaded by wild mustard.

"I will, of course, be tending your children during this extensive expedition?" Marta asks, trying to remember how many Orquídea has. Four or five or six? She is certain none of them still requires diapers and cribs.

Orquídea does not hear her. She is engrossed in her image of the river, the Nile on this particular occasion. "I will get blessed on the shore of the river at dusk, when it is bloated with drowned men and typhus. Then I will slide in eyes first and begging for blindness."

"Did you point out that there are closer rivers?" Joseph inquired. "The Río Grande, of course. The Missouri, the Mississippi, and although it lacks mythological grandeur, the dependable Sacramento delta?"

"No," Marta replied. "I was interested in her rendering of the Nile. I was reading Lorca at the time and it had a flow I appreciated."

"Of course," Joseph understood immediately.

Marta Ortega considered the lure of rivers. She remembered when she had filed for her first divorce, had freed herself from the abomination that was Salvador Velásquez and left the church. Her father had beat her then. Enrique, the brother only one year younger than herself, the brother who would inherit el mercado del pueblo when Salvador Valásquez finally drifted north, had informed her then, "Mother will drown herself in the river."

Yes, the irresistible mystique of those liquid channels. There was still a river, then, in the pueblo of her birth. Of course her mother did nothing of the kind. She died as she danced, died dancing at a wedding reception for a cousin's son, died beneath streams of confetti with mariachis blaring on a platform in a brick-tiled courtyard resplendent with bougainvillea and jacaranda in blossom in May, when she was seventy-two.

Angelina telephones on Christmas Eve. "I did everything," she is saying, her voice drifting, cloudlike, her words a kind of fog. "I bound my feet, metaphorically, of course."

"Some things do go without saying," Marta Ortega cannot help but reply.

"I bound my feet and limped. I assumed the posture of deformity and subservience. I bided my time, made no demands, not even peripheral financial ones. And for what? To be bereft, alone, deserted again in a feasting season?"

"Angelina, if he can live without you," Marta paused, deliberately and then said, "he will."

"Y entonces?"

"Any woman waiting for a man is a whore. I know this and the secret pulse of men who kill in winter. The hare is not enough. Or acres of fox, jaguar, mountains of eagles and puma."

"What letter are you on? What does this mean?" Angelina demanded. She seemed interested.

"My current reading is irrelevant. I am saying herds of buffalo are not enough. It is the more fragile hide they prize. He will skin you in the end. They pack the sweaters their mothers knitted, their photographs and sketchbooks. They take their guitars. They go home."

"Yes," Angelina agreed, her words dreamy, drifting like petals in a warm sea breeze. Marta assumed that her daughter was taking the yellow pills which were supposed to still her agitated brain. "Y qué más?" Angelina asked.

"You smell suitcase leather for weeks," Marta said. "You breathe it in like ether."

"Y después?"

"After you conclude this ritual celebration with grace and dignity? After you decorate your tree and amuse your children?" Marta said pointedly.

"Yes, after this particular night?"

"Lo mismo," Marta concluded, "More of the same."

Marta Ortega imagines her daughter deserted on Christmas Eve. Angelina's hands are frozen on tinsel. Wind savages the rooms of her private regions, eating at the disarray, the bright yellow and red ribbons and bows on the boxes of gifts for her children. In her bedroom, empty tequila bottles sit on night tables, evening gowns are twisted on the floor beside ashtrays spilled across mistletoe. Later, after the children have been put into their beds or cribs or escaped into the night for more exotic festivities with their peers, Angelina will take a handful of yellow pills and fall asleep on the floor, perhaps near the tree she has decorated, beneath the flickering neon bulbs. And on the floor, the yellow and red ribbons lie like confetti.

And Enrique said he could not adequately evaluate the other woman's face. There were swarms of people passing, a chaos of arms and legs, bells and laughter. The plaza at Olvera Street was decorated like a pueblo in Mexico. There had been trumpets, shadows, confetti.

It was Christmas Eve. Marta found herself weeping for her daughters, her body convulsed with spasms like waves. And Marta Ortega realized it was not their frailities but their strengths men most despised.

Joseph and Bill expanded her greenhouse. This enabled Marta Ortega to evolve a system of working in her garden on a twelve-month basis. It is the only conceivable method for avoiding her daughters. The noon heat discourages conversation. The dusk breeze makes them shiver. They never seem to have sweaters, as if they inhabited a permanent tropical July. They always wear high heels, it is a necessity, they are elevated, leaner. Their movements are restricted. They stumble in the grass. They will not risk the terraced hillside.

They retreat to the house and shout complaints and miseries from the bedroom window, the courtyard. Marta kneels in the damp soil, digs, prunes and replants, just to keep her body in motion.

"What should I do?" Marta Ortega hears from the porch, the terrace, the kitchen window. They seem to be following her by scent. The constant demand for attention, advice, solace and analysis shatters the air like bullets.

"It is your imagination which created you, syllable and breath," Marta offers, directing her voice toward the window of assault.

"What letter you on now?" Angelina or Orquídea would demand. "A for All Knowledge? M for a Monopoly on Thought? What the hell are you talking about?"

"Be done with your traps and acid baths. Cease pretending and burn your masks. Be naked as a tree in high desert wind, stripped to fingers and tongue," Marta advised. "Seek what lies beyond transformation and metaphor."

When this did not soothe them, she returned to the surface details she had memorized. "Fondle your rosaries, refill your prescriptions, find new diets and palm readers," she would answer. "Take another college degree. Take a dozen. Dye your hair, have another horoscope charted. Investigate the mediocre. Trivialize your lives. You are incapable of more."

Now Angelina and Orquídea had daughters and sons who drove automobiles, went to universities, took lovers and apartments, bred and divorced. Still, her daughters were returning to Flores Street. "What shall I do?" they were shouting from windows, from the patio, the terrace or the telephones in their homes. "Qué hago yo?"

In one broken midnight or another, Marta Ortega filled their glasses with rum, vodka or mineral water and said, "All that you fear will come and pass. Abandonment, betrayal, disgrace, failure, loss. It is natural, inevitable as the slow arc of bored stars in their concentric paths, glaring down with blistered eyes, answers hooded and remote."

"Es todo?" Angelina or Orquídea asked, in one tortured dusk or another.

"That and the fact that with time, the defects startle less, the frailties, the falls from temporary grace."

"Comprendo," Orquídea or Angelina replied, in one chilly wind-driven autumn afternoon or another.

Marta Ortega was certain that they missed the point entirely. There was only death, resurrection and the arbitrary chaos in between. And, studded like embers or antiquities, an implication of the architecture of the dazzling camouflaged interior, the rare revelations of seamless green. Moments when the air was wide and wild with wind and the scent of green rum. Evenings when sudden moths rose, their dialogue verdant. And gulls picked the vivid lime dusk and streaked above green flames of grass, delirious with summer, trusting the cadence in heat swells, the suggestion of music. Of course substance is continuous, is the process refining and perpetuating itself.

Angelina returns. Orquídea returns. They curse her, her of the strange climate and aversion to the ordinary. Yes, she who did not braid their hair or baptize them.

"I baptized you, Angelina," Marta remembers. "It was Orquídea who was denied God's infinite blessing."

In between, they beg for her counsel and forgiveness. They have transgressed, been self-indulgent, egocentric, obscene in ways she does not even suspect. Marta Ortega is amused by this concept. There is nothing about them she does not know.

"Qué hago yo? Mamacita, are you listening? What should I do?" She is brutalized. Their syllables are a swarm of wasps.

Marta Ortega pretends she is losing her hearing. She thinks of the old padre in the church in the village of her birth, Padre Pérez, with his ears of stone. Of course, it was a pretense. The tedium and the repetition must have sickened him. On her most recent alphabetical book journey, she reread Keats and Shelley. She considers Keats, coughing blood in his hotel room. Did he clutch his chest, his throat? Did he doubt his destiny? And what of Shelley, drowning only one year later, also in Italy? Shelley, lost to the elegance of uninhabited water, surrendering his illusionary man limbs into the hurtling green other, and, somewhere, a kingdom of seahorses, salt and elaborate metaphors. An entire fluid and hidden architecture, arches of blues and greens, plazas of aqua and liquid resolutions.

Angelina and Orquídea do not discourage easily. They shout louder. "Qué hago yo, Mamacita?" Jesus, this is impossible, Marta realizes as she begins another bed of begonias, a strip of violets, a sixth pot of orchids.

Her daughters brave the night air. They are following her around the garden, tripping in their high heels, catching their skirts on the thorns of rosebushes. They are disturbed. They have given their sons the names of American astronauts like Brian and Scott and Jeffrey and Robert and Richard. Even Antonio was long ago transformed into Anthony. Despite the frequent, abrupt and sometimes savage dislocations of their lives, they have diligently provided guitar lessons, Little League, handmade Halloween costumes, museum excursions, summer camps, sailing weekends, Christmas-tree decorations, turkeys at Thanksgiving, theater productions, even tutors when necessary. They have supervised homework assignments and attended counseling sessions with teachers. They have supplied the correct paraphernalia and accouterments of ritual and culture, all the conventions they were denied. Still, these sons remain immune to any stimulus but the most obvious and barbaric.

"What do you think I am growing here?" Marta finally demands. "These are cymbidiums, not crystal balls."

Angelina and Orquídea telephone with increasing frequency. Now there are problems with their daughters, la sangre de su sangre, her granddaughters. Marta can no longer remember their names. They continually change them, just like their mothers. Orquídea who called herself Olivia in college, then, briefly, Opal, and finally, during the marriage to the lunatic Viking, Olga. That was when she claimed her ancestry was Scandinavian and Greek. That was when she dyed her hair a repellent yellow she called platinum blond. Marta Ortega expected her to arrive on Flores Street with ice skates draped over her shoulders and those silvery blond strands braided and pinned like a crown to her head.

Then it was Angelina becoming Angela, Anna, and at one point, between her second and third marriages, Angie. Olga and Angie. They were impossible. They could not even settle on first names. Now their daughters were replicating the process. Angelina and Orquídea were frantic. They suspected that their daughters, her granddaughters, were smoking marijuana and having sex.

"I've had a terrible experience," Orquídea began.

"You will, no doubt, give me each garish detail," Marta said. They were speaking on the telephone. It was late at night.

"It was Sandra. Now she calls herself Sunshine. She's fourteen, you realize," Orquídea said. "Anyway, she got caught in bed with a neighbor's kid. The father, an aesthetic and intellectual abomination, a real-estate agent, came home early and found them. He marched them over to my house. Thank God, Roger wasn't home."

Yes, Marta remembered, Roger was Orquídea's current husband. That was another problem, keeping track of the names of their husbands.

"The kids admit they have been having sex for months. The boy announces that he wants to marry Sunshine. Meanwhile, his father is becoming so agitated he is chain-smoking and his hands are shaking. He says to his son, 'Do you think she's knocked up?' And the kid replies, get this, Mamacita, this is a direct quote, the kid says, 'No way, José. She's on the pill.'"

"This is a surprise for you?" Marta asked.

"Of course not. It was the tawdry quality of the entire situation. Then this fat chain-smoking real-estate agent says to his son, 'Do you want the car, boy? The red Triumph we talked about?' And the kid says 'Yes.' Do you understand, Mamacita? They are engaging in this conversation right in front of me and Sandra, Sunshine, as if we weren't even there."

"There is more, I presume," Marta said, resigned.

"Fucking A. Then he says to his son, this nice kid who wanted to marry Sunshine, the father says, 'Do you want to meet women? Divorcees who have kicked around and know how to give great head?' And the boy says, 'Huh?' He actually gulped. And the father is sounding like the announcer on one of those ghastly television game programs, offering the kid a choice of curtain one, two or three. 'Do you want to go to college, son?' this horrible obese man is saying. 'Meet women, take them to Hawaii for vacations?'"

"Tacky," Marta agrees.

"Then he looks at the kid and says, 'Well, son, you can't do that if you are married, right? So let's just say goodbye to these nice people. A short and simple goodbye. And you promise me that you will never touch that Sandra Sunshine girl again.'"

"And he did?"

"Yes," Orquídea sighed. "I can't take it anymore."

"En particular, qué?" Marta inquired, almost interested.

"The pollution. TV. The epidemic of cancer and cruelty. The senseless violence. The religious maniacs. The mediocrity everyone accepts. The war in Vietnam. I can't watch the news anymore. I tremble. Every time I hear sirens, I want to rip off my clothing and scream, Fuck me, fuck me while it blows up. Fuck me at the moment of impact, in the red flash, in the center of the radiation and falling glass."

"Get another college degree," Marta suggested. "Talk to your priest, your therapist, your hairdresser."

The telephone rang incessantly. It was Angelina. The situation was deteriorating. Her grandchildren, su sangre de su sangre, were becoming hippies, incomprehensible, bizarre and without focus.

"As a pose, it is bereft of inspiration," Angelina informed her. "If it is genuine, it is grotesque and terrifying."

Her grandchildren were sent to Flores Street for evaluation. They sat on her living-room floor and spoke about the lotus, a flower she had never grown but one which contained symbolic importance for them. They emulated this particular blossom and arranged their legs to mirror its unique configuration. They played guitars and composed songs about women with hair like black rain. They embroidered their clothing with stitches which formed flowers and stars. Marta Ortega thought they were charming in a banal manner and absolutely harmless.

In retrospect, Marta Ortega realizes she enjoyed the hippy era. She regrets it was merely another passing fashion. Her grandchildren had been with her constantly then. They respected the garden, hammered fence stakes, patched the roof, dug new terraces for her cymbidiums and built more redwood shelves. They seemed to take pleasure in the earth. They worked without complaint.

At dusk, she brought them plates of watermelon, peaches and oranges. She let them plant their marijuana between her tomatoes and maize. They smoked the herb and ate leisurely, enraptured by the variations of sunset, the lights of the city appearing as if by miracle, dense with sculptures of neon streaks and globes which glowed. They said the city below Flores Street resembled an open box of writhing jewel-encrusted snakes. They watched sunset together.

Her grandchildren spent their nights in sleeping bags in the back garden. Marta sent them back to their mothers in autumn. Angelina and Orquídea did not say they were cured but rather that the disease had entered a period of remission. Marta Ortega could detect relief in their voices.

Then the hippy era passed. At least now, for close to a decade, her daughters seemed settled with new mates, nested, cluttered with objects, their chaos controlled. Marta returned to her garden. She had more orders for orchids than she could fill.

As she worked in her garden, it occurred to her that women should live within walls where time was rendered obsolete, where there was only the shifting of mats as the sun circled and new shade appeared in a patch, cool as the words uttered by a swiftly passing god. Yes, it was good to live within walls where days were divided by water spilled from a clay jug, green flies, the cries of infants and one raven someone said they saw too distant to be an omen. Within such walls, noon became indistinct, a boundary without resonance or edges. It meant nothing. Time became like a granite mountain range or a river. It was all a fluttering, hot and brief and not meant to be more. And Marta Ortega realized that she had spent fifty summers surrounded by the skins of melons and opening petals. She had learned the subtleties of sun and shadow enacting their ritual battles across her courtyard bricks. Within such walls, all things were possible. One could predict the precise trajectory of rain clouds before they even dreamed of opening. One could accumulate more information about heat and dust than science. In time, it would be possible to alter matter at will.

"Do you mean this metaphorically?" Joseph had asked one dusk.

"No." Marta Ortega replied. And somewhere, there was absolute resolution and a silence.

There was an invasion outside, beyond her courtyard walls. Marta Ortega could not ignore it. The fires in the hills. The ash cascading from the sky like the last snowfall on a dying world. The night wind was ruthless. Then the elm on Juan Martínez's front lawn snapped off from its roots. After more than a century, this particular virulent spring had finally broken its heart and severed its sacred connection with the earth.

The elm lay on Juan Martínez's front lawn like a beached sea mammal, colossal and unexpected. It looked as if a passing god had jabbed the ground with a huge white spear. Marta Ortega could not dismiss the sheer three-dimensional actuality of it. The tree had sprung up of its own accord. It was not a metaphor. The suicidal elm was an indication of an opening, an abrupt denuding of the ordinary, an expression demanding recognition.

Marta Ortega had not traveled far, not if distance is measured in terms of miles or flying hours. Her journey had been one of increments, tangible, a bed of seeds, a row of melons and tomatoes, one daughter, one orchid in one pot, at a time.

Now something was shattering her private unmolested stillness. It was lying wounded on its side, appearing almost alive, staring at her. The elm on the lawn of the house where Juan Martínez lived. And fires encircled the city. Ash fell like the shredded gray eggs of a winged dying creature. A female bird, perhaps, who dropped her offspring through space, sensing there were no places to nest, that the species had reached the end of its line. The female bird decided it was preferable her unborn crash to the ground rather than witness what was impending. And it was possible the dead elm lying like a slaughtered carcass on the lawn at the bottom of the hill of Flores Street was merely a beginning. At night, the tree that had chosen to die gleamed white as a certain type of pewter. The bark felt hard beneath her fingers, like bone.

"Es la mano de Dios," Consuelo López pronounced.

Consuelo López lived at the bottom of the hill, directly across the asphalt gash of street from the house of Juan Martínez and the stricken elm. She claimed she had seen it fall. Not fall, precisely, she corrected. It was more like a thing rising.

Marta Ortega glanced at Consuelo López, who was standing near the tree, holding her rosary between trembling fingers. Consuelo López was twenty-four years old. She had painted her wooden frame house an obscene and graceless shade of pink and she was, in Marta Ortega's opinion, a classic hysteric.

"First the heat, then the fires. Now my tree. Something is coming and it is getting closer," Juan Martínez said. The fallen elm was a moment of tremendous significance for him. He was elevated by the occasion and assuming the stance of a sage. He was behaving as if he had just been elected barrio president. This is ludicrous, Marta Ortega thought, turning her back from them.

These people are insufferable, she concluded as she climbed the low hill that was Flores Street to her yellow wooden house. She had felt them as an oppressive presence for years. She had smelled their raw animal terror when the American baseball stadium was built, when the pueblo of her birth had been eradicated. And Flores Street had shuddered then, hallucinating La Migra behind every bush. The baseball stadium had been erected more than twenty-five years before, but she was only now placing the incident in proper perspective. Age had made her subject to extraordinary lapses of consciousness, to a suspension of the obvious and appropriate linking of specifics into patterns which were blatant and irrefutable.

"Why don't you move?" Angelina shouted at her over the telephone.

"It is because you feel superior there. A woman who has read the alphabet of world literature eighty times surrounded by ignorancia, paganos, subliterates. It nourishes you. You can be La Reina de la Calle Flores."

"You must be in therapy again," Marta had replied. "It always makes you abusive." Angelina had slammed the telephone down.

Still, the insistent speculation about omens and retribution was disrupting her silence, was seeping into her inviolate courtyard walls. The rosaries being taken from drawers. The pilgrimages to Nuestra Señora de los Dolores. The framed photographs of saints being polished and placed on bedside tables. The babbling about los signos mágicos, las manos de Dios. Her neighbors with their mouths forming incantaciones y penitencias.

Marta Ortega was attempting to save her garden. The heat was ferocious. She wrapped her head in a wet bandana, dug up beds of fuchsias and replanted them in terra-cotta pots. She placed them in an avenue of shade below her bedroom windowsills. Then she strung sheets across her front patio, constructing pools of cool and shade. She worked as the fires ravaged the hills. She dug and potted as ash fell, as the great female birds jettisoned, their eggs shattering to premature deaths. She moved her hands through dirt and fibers until her fingers trembled.

"The natives are restless tonight," Joseph observed from his side of their bamboo backyard fence. He said this lightly. But his eyes seemed weary, uncertain, stained like the ozone layer, the sheets which were being torn and rendered unusable from human abuse. Ash was falling into the petals of flowers and into the fragile orbs of eyes.

"If I go to church on Sunday, then cabaret all day Monday, ain't nobody's business but my own," sang Billie Holiday, the woman Joseph called the voice of the twentieth century, the quintessential distillation of this particular cycle of time. And it was a silk torment, the pain of tiny metal needles, an intoxication with passion and ruin. It was a fragrance, pungent, irresistibly exquisite and without exception lethal. It was a juxtaposition of blossoms, wild inventions and lime pits where entire tribes were murdered by the millions. It was genocide and spearing the moon and offering your flesh to the night, knowing it would be tattooed by malevolence and indifference and the bruises embossing the skin like purple flowers strung.

"Sometimes I feel the door has already closed, slammed shut. Not just on you and me but on all of history," Marta Ortega whispered. They looked at one another, exchanging information wordlessly, aware of nuances in the air between them.

"Still, there are crossroads and choices, even in the Apocalypse," Joseph said, his voice soft. They sat in her courtyard in a night more red than black. The air was abnormal, charged, chaotic, gashed.

"Always, some will behave better than others. Some will stand in line and not stampede for rations," Bill mused. His hand trembled.

"And some will say the substance mattered, even at the end. Some will say it was more important than oil and food," Marta added, her voice soft, hushed. She felt as if she were taking a vow. Then they looked into one another's eyes for reassurance and found none.

Marta slept and woke early, the fear erased from her mind. She was saving her garden. She ignored the relentless speculation about fires, ash and the fallen elm in the yard of Juan Martínez. Her courtyard walls were intact. She would permit no more debris, babble or hysteria to invade her private terrain.

Then Gloria Hernández went mad. Marta was working with a fierce determination, her fingers enticing petals into shade, and, abruptly, she intuited a disturbance. Instinctively, she traced the source. Gloria Hernández was standing in her courtyard. She poured two glasses of horchata. Marta sensed a severing of the ordinary, but she did not pursue this. She had long ago dismissed Gloria Hernández from her consciousness.

The moon was full that night, bright as a bulb, taunting, almost demanding. This was significant. Across the street, Gloria Hernández entered the house of the white clerk, Barbara Branden. Perhaps there had been a confrontation, a struggle. And Gloria Hernández plunged a kitchen knife through the white woman's chest.

The geometry that was Flores Street became treacherous. It assumed a dimension beyond decimation which is a state of utter ruin and therefore measurable and known. Gloria Hernández was a charcoal sketch which had peeled itself off a wall. The gradations of gray erased themselves and where there had been vacant lots and strips of sand, bridges of vermilion appeared, monuments of magenta and blood. The field which was barren issued forth abundant, spectacular. The dismissed and insignificant pack-animal had dared to form a mouth. From her camouflaged void there was an eruption, a hissing, spit stones, steam and lasers.

The landscape that had been Flores Street was simultaneously inspired and mutilated. Arches manifested themselves, sculpted deceptively from severed flesh. Marta Ortega did not recognize this terrain which was neither destruction nor birth. The design was crafted in another region, alien, resistant to definition.

Then the men in blue uniforms, the sirens and ambulances. The linear assumptions shattered. In the altered sky, female birds dropped their eggs to the pavement. And the street was stained, scorched, dense with a sense of contagion.

After the murder of the white clerk, terror encased Flores Street. Marta Ortega's courtyard walls could not withstand the inflamed pressure. The air spoke now, undivided, clear, and it said Cataclismo, sangre, catástrofe. The border was damaged, unsolid, and Flores Street was a series of locked doors in which candles blazed, lips formed incantations, fingers followed the instruction of ritual. The intimation of disaster was no longer amorphous.

"What about portents, signos mágicos? Metaphorically, of course," Marta asked Bill. It was the evening after the murder. He watered a peach tree with exaggerated intensity. He avoided her face.

"A terrible madness is lying upon the land," he replied. He studied his peach tree. They were silent.

"Madness?" Marta repeated, surprised. "Isn't that a bit lyrical? A bit like walking through the moors in mist. You are not serious."

"It has always been a chaos," Joseph said. "A stumbling through vines and branches in regions of green streams, green gullies and clouds, perhaps. An area of green density where compasses and maps and prayers are irrelevant."

Marta Ortega considered this. They sat in silence. Flames ate the hills slowly, delicately, like a form of brutal calligraphy, a deliberately dull blade in flesh. Later, as Marta Ortega stood in her garden alone, it occurred to her that the Apocalypse had already come and gone. Like all other American fashions, it had proved less startling and durable than predicted. Perhaps Flores Street was merely living on in altered form, ash after the conflagration, ash waiting for a sea breeze to take the dust they had become into the air, into oblivion, nothingness.

●   ●   ●

Now the stupid white clerk, the insipid and pretentious Barbara Branden, was dead. Now Gloria Hernández was incarcerated, locked in an institution, a subject for interrogation, a statistic or a curiosity, perhaps. And her garden sat ravaged by sun. Even the canna and bird of paradise, plants born to endure the wrath of the sun, had turned brittle on their stalks, browned and bent back into themselves, unsalvageable.

Perhaps she had committed a terrible error in perception, in her entire system of logic, by not considering the circumstances of her personal history and the events which placed her in this yellow wooden house on this particular hill. Those were her thoughts, precisely, when Joseph knocked on her front door.

It was early morning. They did not knock upon one another's doors. Such formality implied a distance, a set of proprieties they had abolished and transcended. She wondered why Joseph did not simply enter her house and sit in the kitchen as was their custom. Bill and Joseph stood in her courtyard. Finally, bowing her head slightly, Marta Ortega said, "Entre."

"Mi amor," Joseph began, his voice sad, "we are going home."

She felt disoriented, as if she had been struck. She dropped the coffee pot she had been holding and stood paralyzed as the hot brown liquid slid across the kitchen tiles. Then Bill was pressing her tightly against his body. Joseph was kissing her forehead and eyes.

"It is conventional, the nostalgia to die in familiar dirt," Bill said. He was speaking about the village of Joseph's birth in the southern state Louisiana. His voice strained for the casual. He was almost cheerful. The sound of it was intolerable.

"To cruise the French Quarter once more." Joseph seemed excited.

"We are ludicrous," Bill noted, "two ancient queens who have lost everything but our banal romanticism."

Marta Ortega recalled their anecdotes of the French Quarter in New Orleans. It bordered a port in a land of brothels, bars and pianos, perfumes and alleys of cobblestones smoothened by passion and the caress of sin. Black women sang and saxophones poured from hallways and doors, hot and amber. It was a sound and texture you could not resist, a music that intoxicated, insisting upon the shedding of clothing and sudden embraces. It was a perpetual midnight, gulf-warm, fragrant. An elegant port in which to die.

There the bones would not merely be buried but would gleam, freed of the excess of flesh. One drifted from the earth like sails or petals into the green warmed wind. The skeleton could become liquid, transmuted into ambers, saxophones, silvers and pewters, horizons of fluid benedictions.

Marta accepted the necessity and wisdom of their decision without hesitation. She forgot her garden, realizing with a start, a jolt which was physical, that her garden was no longer important. She recognized this but did not pause to examine its implications.

She entered the elaborate house which she had watched being constructed. They opened drawers and closets, rummaged, folded, discussed and discarded. Bill played the phonograph at full volume, the scratched ragtime and sultry bruised blues that created their own warmth, that were a flame within the blistering day. They jitterbugged and waltzed between the cardboard boxes, kissing one another on the mouth in all combinations, the three of them drunk on heat and pain and piña coladas, singing and dancing and stumbling amongst the debris. They packed the phonograph last.

Later, it would not seem possible lives could be so easily disassembled. Joseph and Bill had been collectors. Mementos served as their children, their legacy. The pebbles from a beach in Greece where they made love on warm sand near olive trees, waves a fine indelible caress across their flesh, fragile as flowers, the hands of infants, whispers and vows. They embraced at dusk, in an hour of small blue portals and, somewhere, an echoing bell. The air was aqua and taut as a canvas starved for the brush. Night was vivid as oils for painting.

They packed black beads with white dots like a swarm of insects, intricate and delicate, bartered from a vagrant trader in a village in the interior of Nigeria. Then the vases from Europe, the flame-blue tiles from the Middle East, the dyed scarves from a region then called Siam. They wrapped wooden sculptures from India between bolts of batik, filled a carton with woven baskets, ceremonial knives, hand-painted face masks, goblets and flasks.

Bill carried a cardboard box of phonograph records into the car. They filled the trunk and the backseat. The house was silent. Whatever did not fit into their car they left, their furniture, piano, books, tools, rugs, silverware, pots and pans. They were vestiges which no longer contained significance, like her garden. Bill surveyed what remained and advised her to give these objects to her grandchildren.

"We'll write you," Joseph said.

"When we get an address," Bill added.

After hours of embracing and weeping, Joseph and Bill sat down in their car, turned the corner and were gone. Marta Ortega experienced a sadness so sharp and pervasive, she considered the possibility that she was physically ill. She stood on her front porch all evening, certain they would change their minds, reach the desert or mountains or some symbolic border, a frontier of literal geography or of the sensibility, and return.

Marta Ortega is assailed by the specific events of their lives. Joseph, excited and indecisive before each summer vacation. She considered the permutations of what to wear on the boat, train, bus, plane. She shared the confusion of their packing, the logistics of their journeys, analyzed and advised. Later, she studied their photographs, intrigued by the periphery and the edges. She memorized the names of trees, bridges, cathedrals, harbors. She sailed with them through the Caribbean, the young green sea, the blessed infant child of an undeformed God. The inland passage to Alaska where everything was tinted blue. The mosques and temples of Asia where she heard brass gongs, chants and the songs of jungle birds. In Java and Hong Kong she slept on straw mats and walked beneath a sun sullen, opiated, exhausted from experience.

Suddenly, she remembers a year Bill had taken a young Chinese lover. The sadness in Joseph's eyes, his desperation to appear undamaged, peripheral, invisible. Of course it was a temporary fancy, that almond-eyed boy who visited nightly and wore a carnation in his jacket, whatever the season. A cycle like any other, she assured Joseph, it would pass. And, in silence, Joseph endured.

Then the Chinese boy with the carnation was gone. Now Joseph and Bill were gone. And gone was their unique terrain, their alphabets of implication, the gestures of opulence, the recognition of the intangible and rare, the music, the illusions of incorruptibility they had invented.

In the morning, on rare impulse, Marta telephoned Angelina in San Francisco. "Joseph and Bill have moved back to Louisiana," she began. Of course she would not mention the fires, the ash, the elm which had committed suicide or the fact that the inarticulate, dull and dismissed Gloria Hernández, the housewife without imagination or skill, had mur-

dered the white clerk, Barbara Branden. Fourteen times the metal penetrated the breast. That is what the police report said. I dug in my garden,
Marta Ortega thinks, in my exclusive domain, in my delusion of untarnished permanence, and permitted Gloria Hernández to go insane.

"Lo siento," Angelina said, obviously shaken, "es como una muerte.
Anything I would say seems inadequate. How do you feel?"

"Quite well," Marta Ortega decided. From Angelina and Orquídea,
she had learned to lie with ease. Gone the sacraments, the antique magic,
the mass in Latin, the fabric of Flores Street, her orchids and courtyard
walls where time had been rendered obsolete. Gone Gloria Hernández
whom she might have saved, gone Joseph and Bill and the nights of the
sudden doorbells and moving vans and infants. And gone even the rage of
her daughters. Then, suddenly, "Angelina, I regret I discouraged your
acting classes."

Angelina laughed. "That was Orquídea. I wanted to be a singer, once."

"I regret my failure to support your aspirations, your voice training,"
Marta amended.

"Don't be absurd," this final incarnation of Angelina assures her. "I
was absolutely mediocre."

"You have always been exceptional," Marta recognizes. "I have always
loved you."

"I have always loved you," Angelina replies without hesitation.

Marta hung up the telephone. If she said, Do you believe blood
creates a channel through time and recognizes its own in other configurations, her daughter would become frightened, would intuit a disruption.
Marta Ortega was the anchor, the port, the inviolate shore. She would be
their buoy until the flood and, if need be, beyond.

Suddenly Marta remembers a summer Angelina had spent with her.
Angelina was in the midst of another identity crisis, her possessions scattered in storage in at least two cities, changing colleges, attempting to
make herself useful.

Marta appreciated that her daughter was, with unusual grace, trying
to take up as little physical and emotional space as possible. Still, her
presence was an intrusion. Marta Ortega had a lover that summer. She had
to make a decision. It was simple, requiring only one telephone call. Marta
sent her lover away.

It occurred to her then that she had been either too indulgent a mother or not even adequate. She realized she would never have the answer. She thought the paradoxes and subtleties of the situation would amuse Joseph and Bill.

Angelina was pacing the front courtyard patio, obviously agitated, even for her, a young woman who constantly took yellow pills prescribed for her by the university hospital doctor for a condition termed anxiety. Or was it Orquídea who took the yellow pills, who swallowed them like candies or perfect round moons?

"They actually make love with each other," Angelina announced, lighting a cigarette and staring at her.

"Not extremely passionately, at this point," Marta had answered. She laughed as she walked into her kitchen.

"But they embrace, they engage in acts of sex," Angelina realized out loud, following her in a kind of trance. "I never quite understood before."

"Claro," Marta replied, thinking their conversation was edging into the tedious, even in Spanish.

"I saw them dancing together," Angelina revealed, as if discovering a vital clue of the universe, a new equation which rendered her breathless. She was a woman who chanced to glance at the sky and observed a planet no one had ever noticed before.

"Pues?"

"I knew intellectually," this early version of Angelina said, "but to see them dancing. They dance extremely badly." Angelina had concluded, unwilling to explore her thoughts.

"They dance as a gesture. It is symbolic rather than aesthetic," Marta Ortega explained. Then Marta entered her garden, reached for her gloves and shears and dismissed the matter.

Of course it was all a fluctuation, a subtle current, the earth itself was fragile, a hide not a shell. Always, the cortege arrives at the appointed hour, the body is lowered into the waiting ground and it is too late to scream, Why carnations, you fools? Idiotas, it was violets and orchids she loved. Then the dirt falls. Night falls. You think you will go mad, will not recover from this severing, will be crippled forever. Then you find you are washing dishes, astounded by the chorus of birds above your courtyard and the music from a radio in a neighbor's room. That is all.

• • •

Now the ebb and flow has come to Flores Street. Flores Street has three empty houses like teeth knocked out of a mouth. Black gaps, windows without lights, lawns of seared grass, doors chained and padlocked. The scent of blood and abandonment lies across pavements, courtyards and lawns, a decimation irrefutable as a pueblo where bombs have fallen.

Marta Ortega reads Neruda, listens to Billie Holiday and waits. Transformation comes as it will, as it must, intricate and inexplicable. Flores Street is an intersection, an opening into an other. There are no voids.

The fires sated themselves and winds removed the ash. Gradually the heat lessened, abated and turned natural. Gloria Hernández's husband, Miguel, endured the police reports, the filling out of forms and the visits of real-estate agents. The house was sold. It was rumored that Gloria, who had crossed into the terrain no tribe would tolerate, who had murdered the white clerk and was removed from her cottage in handcuffs, refused to see him. Not her husband, it was said, nor her sons, a padre or anyone.

After a period which seemed inordinately short, Miguel Hernández and his two sons returned to the pueblo of his birth in Jalisco. He left with a quiet which implied guilt and complicity, vanishing in the night, saying farewell to no one. The method of his departure was not unnoticed by the residents of Flores Street. And it would not be forgotten.

Miguel Hernández had waited for the moon to enter remission, Marta observed, and then removed himself beneath the cover of darkness. The blistering sun of Jalisco in summer would not cure him, or the seasons of torrential rains wash him clean.

The stucco cottage next door to his, the house where Barbara Branden had been murdered, was empty. And the two-story Spanish structure Marta Ortega had watched being built, the house designed by an architect where Joseph and Bill had played their scratched phonograph records of women singing of abrupt loss, betrayal and the breaking of a heart while they ate by candlelight, while they danced until the sunset, was also vacant, waiting to be sold.

On Sunday afternoons, real-estate agents brought young American and Chicano couples to tour the empty houses. These women and men shaded their eyes as they stood on the dead lawns, the patios and porches and courtyards bearing the stains of what they perceived as merely rain and natural aging. Such abuse could be cured with plaster and a brush. They studied the wood and the stucco from a variety of angles. They seemed dazed, staring from roof to courtyard to the lawns of brittle grass, to the blades which were brown and dead. They mistook this butchery for carelessness. A gardener could be employed. They noted the bougainvillea tearing the courtyard wall and the rows of malformed rosebushes. The implications were obvious, but these young women and men chose to rationalize what they intuited, to banish from their consciousness the revelation of a street disintegrating.

Marta Ortega observed them from her front-courtyard patio. When they noticed her, they crossed the street and walked to her front door with extravagant gestures of goodwill, with casual poses which were transparently fraudulent and offensive. After what they considered an appropriately gracious greeting, their words innocuous, they inquired whether she knew anything of these houses.

The real-estate agents sat in air-conditioned cars, smoking cigarettes, anxious. They knew that Marta Ortega was una bruja, la Reina de Calle Flores. They turned on their car radios and avoided even a peripheral glance in her direction. Later, they would not deny anything she said to their clients. One did not argue with the judgment of la bruja del barrio.

Marta Ortega answered the young women and men in accordance with her mood, intuiting precisely what they did not wish to hear. "There are nests of hornets and rats in the attics," she told the American couple, softly, conspiratorially. "I have lived here for twenty years," Marta revealed, realizing that the truth would not seem credible, "and the mudslides are notorious. These hills are impossible. If only I had the strength to move." Marta sighed. And she did not see them again.

"The flood damage was extensive," she informed the Chicano student with the pregnant wife. She could not imagine them inhabiting the house where Joseph and Bill had lived, placing a crib where the piano had been, crucifixes on the walls, stuffed bears and dogs where Joseph and Bill had danced. She poured horchata for them. "One more storm and the entire roof will collapse. You know, the city building inspectors are considering condemning the structure," she said, as if admitting a painful secret. They too disappeared.

The real-estate agents stopped bringing potential buyers to Flores Street. They did not analyze the complexities of the situation. They realized la bruja del barrio did not wish these houses sold. They accepted this.

Marta Ortega decided she wished to be alone. She would send her grandson, the quiet one, back to his mother in San Diego. That would be Orquídea, her younger daughter, currently married to a man named Ian, an engineer of prominence who consulted with other men, who dealt with the problems of aircraft designs. Orquídea, who had married this man and become a Catholic and remained one for more than a decade now.

"Which one are you?" she asked her grandson.

He had just entered the house. It was dusk. He seemed startled by the sound of her voice. She rarely spoke to him. She noticed he carried rugs across his shoulders like a multitude of bloated boa constrictors.

She knew he was Orquídea's, but there had been so many fathers and changes of first and last names. It had become an ordeal for her to remember.

"Yo soy Roberto, Abuela," he replied softly. He was patient, grateful they were speaking. "I was Robert before that. Then I was Bobby, remember? I came here with my brothers and sister and cousins. We had the van with blue flowers painted on the sides. We lived here for three summers in the back garden, Abuela. We painted the house yellow."

"Of course, Roberto," she replied. She did not remember him or the van embossed with blue flowers. But she recalled vividly the painting of her house. This had occurred during the era when the offspring of her daughters were Los Niños de las Flores. They had done this as a surprise for her, an offering of gratitude. They had heard that the house was once yellow and they assumed this had been her preference.

She had returned from an orchid symposium held in a downtown hotel. She had entered several varieties in this competition. She had been awarded prizes. It was late afternoon and she intuited an irregularity immediately, even before Bill turned the car up the hill of Flores Street. Then she saw the wood glaring yellow at her. That particular moment had been disturbing, startling. She walked into her house breathless, feeling the wood glistening arrogantly.

Now she was studying the coiled carpets her youngest grandson was wearing around his neck and shoulders. "What do you do with those rugs?" Marta Ortega inquired.

"I install them in the apartments Tío Enrique buys and rents."

Enrique, her brother, who had attempted to raft the tributary leading to el río de Los Angeles, to sail back to Mexico, had become a slum landlord. He purchased dilapidated buildings and then further subdivided them, renting to terrified immigrants, to refugees from the wars in Central America who spoke no English at all. That was why she had dismissed Enrique from her consciousness.

"You may put the carpets down, Roberto," Marta Ortega informed her grandson. She watched him release himself from the rolled burden of fibers and cloth. They formed a surprisingly large pile across her living-room floor. It was not the intimation of a monument but a stain.

Marta Ortega sat down on her sofa. She motioned to her grandson to join her. "Do you enjoy your work?" she inquired.

"It is hard and depressing," Roberto admitted. He seemed relieved to be sitting near her. He also appeared to be straining to express himself in Spanish.

"Why don't we speak in English?" Marta Ortega suggested.

"Abuela, remember what you told us? When we lived in the backyard? When we asked if we should call you Grandmother or Abuela and if we should speak to you in Spanish or English?"

"What did I say?"

"That we should address you as Abuela. You said we should speak in Spanish about matters of the heart, and what was literal, inconsequential and tedious in English."

"That is interesting," Marta noted, wondering what her reasoning had been at the time.

"You said English was a description of the surface and Spanish more lyrical, more like the flowing of the substance," Roberto clarified.

"I remove that stricture," Marta Ortega informed him. "Do you drink?"

"Yes."

"Make us two vodkas, please."

They sat on the living-room sofa. Roberto seemed content with their proximity and silence. "What else did I tell you?" Marta Ortega asked.

"Everything, Abuela. You explained the cycles of the planets and stars, and how the garden was arranged by texture and scent as well as color and obvious form."

"Yes?"

"You said we were the debris of surface fashion, lacking an interior architecture, incomplete. You suggested we create unique paths, built from inspiration and intuition. You said we were all continents, eccentrically indigenous. And if we failed to explore this, we would betray our sensibility and integrity."

"Was I harsh?" Marta Ortega asked.

"Of course not," Roberto assured her. "You spoke as a Zen master."

"Continue."

"You taught us to compose lists. When we had bad acid trips, sabes, problemas con drogas, you convinced us we could calm ourselves by creating lists and reciting them silently, alphabetically, like a litany."

"Of what elements did your lists consist?" She is interested in this.

"Places to go to. Alaska, Brazil, Caracas, Denmark, Fiji, Greenland, Hawaii, Iceland, Java, Klamath Falls, Lima, Morocco, Nairobi, Orange County, Philadelphia, Quito, Rumania, Santo Domingo, Trinidad, Uruguay, Valley Forge, Washington, Xochimilco and Zaire."

"I see," Marta replied, not quite as interested.

Roberto sensed this. "There were numerous other lists, Abuela. I was satisfied by inventing lists of foods. Avocados, burritos, cake, donuts, French fries."

"I get the drift," Marta Ortega said, silencing him with her hand. "Did it bring you solace?"

"Always, Abuela. It was superior to Thorazine."

"I have appreciated your company," Marta says, realizing this is true. "You have been gracious and undemanding to the point of invisibility, which I demand and admire. However, you will now return to your home."

"Mom says someone has to be here with you at all times," Roberto informed her.

This surprised her. Marta Ortega assumed her grandchildren came to Flores Street of their own volition. "Why is that?" she asked.

"No estoy cierto," Roberto said with an absence of conviction. He stared at the floor, at the mound where he had shed the carpets from his shoulders.

"Sangre de mi sangre," Marta Ortega lashed, "did I not clarify my feelings about lies?"

"Claro."

"Did I not tell you I have an aversion for insolent insects? You dare engage in deliberate fraudulence with me?" Marta demanded. Then, softer, "Roberto, I require a precise summary of all that you know."

"They say you must be guarded, protected. Mom and Tía Angelina. They say you are an artifact which must be kept safe between glass."

"Roberto, I recognize your intelligence and elegance. Did I not attend your graduation from college?" She dug through the shelves of information in the storehouse of her brain. "Comparative literature, no?"

"Sí, Abuela, exactamente," Roberto replied. "I was inspired by you."

"Of course. Now spare us unnecessary subterfuge. Give me the bottom line."

Roberto lit a cigarette. She had never seen him smoke before. He was respectfully peripheral, he did not even violate her air with the fumes of his cigarettes. "They are afraid you will go off in Indian style," Roberto revealed, inhaling smoke.

"What does that mean?"

"That when your time comes, you will take a blanket into the hills, lie beneath stars and let coyotes eat your flesh." Roberto looked up from the rolled carpets on the floor. Their eyes met and connected, the sensation was physical. She removed her eyes from her youngest grandson. He seemed deeply relieved.

"Gracias," she said softly. "I expect you to be discreet in your report to your mother. You will from your consciousness erase certain events you have recently witnessed. They never happened. You know your mother suffers from a hysterical disorder and must take yellow pills."

"That is Tía Angelina. And she's on the ten-gram ones now, the blue ones," Roberto corrected. "Also Seconal and amphetamines. But I will not betray you in any way."

"Gracias, Roberto. Now pack up." Marta Ortega walked into her back garden. The orchids were ruined. She did not even glance at them. She simply watered the roses and the camellias, cut an assortment of the least-tainted blooms and placed them in a vase near her bed.

Roberto was packed. Sons were certainly less cluttered. One jacket, a few shirts, two pair of blue jeans, a guitar and it was done. Boys did not even require suitcases. They went to war. They went to the moon. They married women of the wrong color in inferior areas of the world and had their names removed from the family Bible. Roberto was sitting on the edge of the sofa, obviously disturbed.

"Was your father an executive who gambled?" she asked on impulse.

"No, Abuela. That was the father before mine. My father and the

father of my sister Jennifer who is now called Jasmine teaches history at
USC."

"Did he recover?"

"Who?"

"The father before yours. The one who was in the mental hospital."

"Oh, sure," Roberto said. "We see him in the summers. He has a
sailboat."

"Está bien," Marta replied, her tone an unmistakable dismissal. She
wondered why he did not rise from the sofa and leave.

"What letter are you on?" Roberto asked.

"R. I am rereading Rimbaud."

"Will you do it?"

"Do what?" Marta was becoming annoyed.

"Go with a blanket into the hills and let the coyotes eat you?"

Marta Ortega sighed. What was the matter with these people? The
death pilgrimage was strictly a phenomenon of certain North American
Indian tribes. Certainly, with the multitude of college degrees in the family, they must know that simple ethnological fact.

"What do you think?" Marta Ortega asked, mildly curious.

"I believe you are a genuine bruja," Roberto replied. "I would expect
nothing less."

Marta did not say anything. Roberto was looking directly into her
eyes. She felt a fluctuation of the impulse, an opening into a sudden
glistening green channel.

"What about the rugs?" Roberto asked. He stood up.

"I will take care of them," she assured her youngest grandson.

Marta Ortega walked with Roberto to the curb where he had parked
his truck. He tossed his clothing and guitar into the backseat. He wished
to linger. Then he kissed her cheek. Inside his mouth lived fog, volcanoes,
clouds, opals, waves. His lips were not flesh, were hard, transmuted, as if
he were deliberately attempting to imprint her skin. Then he drove slowly
up the hill. At the crest, he rolled down the window of his truck, reached
his entire arm out and waved to her before turning his vehicle around the
corner. The arc his arm inscribed in the night air remained.

Marta began to carry the carpets from her living-room floor out to
the gutter. She considered Enrique and the mania and greed he had developed. It was after the pueblo of their birth was taken by the city to form a

home for the new baseball team. The store their father had built and literally died in, had a heart attack in one warm afternoon while lifting a carton containing cans of tomato sauce, had become worthless, bulldozed back into its original elements, into the dust and ash of its fundamental structure.

Enrique did not perceive the eradication of the barrio of their birth as an omen of destruction. It was a beacon of opportunity. He was illuminated, radiant with knowledge. If the city would eat a thing as insignificant and meaningless as their home, then it would consume anything.

With the erasure of their village, Enrique was struck with a vision. The landscape was transformed. He saw the wooden and stucco houses perched on the hillsides of the periphery of the city as a deformity. The scalped hilltops were punctuated by television antennas. The new gods spoke from electronic boxes. Everyone could own one. There were no more penances. And the colors streaming from the square screens were more compelling than paintings of caped saints, bluer than the robe of La Virgen de Guadelupe, whiter than the banks of clouds on which angels sat. These colors glistened, glazed as the underbelly of abalone shells. Obviously, the saints were obsolete. And the people who inhabited the low hills bordering the central city were less than cattle.

Enrique began buying stucco houses and brick apartment buildings in the path of the mouth of the spreading city. He provided the fat woman, this city, with her next meal. He accumulated what she pronounced unfit and subdivided the already derelict structures into apartments which he rented to men who had crossed borders illegally, who had left families and who trembled in his three-piece-suited presence. The refugees who could not afford these apartments, but somehow did.

"It's the modern world, Marta," he told her one afternoon, optimistically, luminescent with cynicism. Now Flores Street appeared shabby to him. He could find her something cleaner, closer to the ocean, Santa Monica perhaps.

"El mundo moderno?" Marta had repeated. "There is nothing modern about fraud and avarice."

"Then I am absolved in both the current and historical context," Enrique laughed. He was no longer a Catholic. The wife of his youth had grown fat and dull, displeasing to his eye. He had shed her even before the tractors and the bulldozers turned the store their father had built into dust. Now he was married to an American woman. They had their own children.

"We have a choice in the archetypes we select," Marta had parried.

"I thought you transcended conventional morality eons ago." He seemed genuinely surprised.

"Morality does not alter," Marta replied. "Only the conventions of fashion which surround it are subject to change."

They rarely saw each other. Enrique would ring her doorbell when he was, as he euphemistically described it, in the neighborhood. What he meant was when he was in the barrio, searching for buildings he might buy. They did not discuss the nature of his activities. She remembered this as she dragged her brother's carpet out to the curb, one arduous foot at a time.

Enrique purchased a house with a view of the ocean near Malibu. The geography was a metaphor for the distance which had grown between them. They were separated by what could not be measured in miles. It was dimensional, a manifestation of the sensibility, a gulf which could not be driven across. This is what Marta Ortega was thinking as she half dragged, half kicked the last of the carpets into the gutter. She was breathless, her hands trembled.

Marta Ortega expected passing vandals to cut the carpets with knives, the night breeze and the heat of midday to shatter their threads, and innumerable dogs to piss into the cloth. Then the entity stalking Flores Street could make these fibers its feasting ground. Let nests of insects form in the threads. Let them lay their eggs in the coils. And their eggs would hatch daggers and flames and beasts with the agility and venom of cobras. Beneath the amber arcs of lamplights and the fronds of palms, the new configuration would be born. After the nests and eggs and cobras, let a hot wind blow from the south, an ancient wind studded with seeds of brilliant yellow vines that glowed. And their offspring would be amber jaguars, thrusting their heads silently, telephathically, always hungry and almost invisible in the coral orchid underbrush.

PART FOUR

Now Roberto, her youngest grandson, has gone. The house assumes a dimension of quiet, dense, unexpected. She is startled by the intangible scent and rhythm of rooms which are not shared. The change in the texture of the air is chemical, as if she is descending a stairway into a basement, walls damp, transparent.

Marta Ortega recognizes that she has rarely been alone. She remembers her bedroom in her father's house, with the wide arched windows and the greens of the back garden rolling across her body like waves. A warm ocean, the still-young green Caribbean perhaps, wrapping her in an embrace and rocking her tenderly as it would any creature of the sea, as it would a shell or a drifting piece of a broken ship.

The house on Flores Street has never belonged to her, she realizes, shocked and enraged. She has not even managed to have the house painted green, despite the fact it was green she worshipped.

Marta Ortega is surprised by her anger. She has been oppressively subjected to the presence of others, the jolt of unexpected footsteps, the abrupt scent which annihilated a moment, a season, a decade. Salvador Valésquez and Angelina, then Joseph and Bill with their piano and their black women singing the tortured blues which she came to love. Then Octavio Herrera, her second husband, the man who had walked south because it seemed downhill, and Orquídea, the Wednesday ritual of Enrique with her groceries, her grandchildren, occasional lovers and the unremitting gossip which was the dialect of Flores Street itself.

Marta Ortega realizes she has been continually invaded by the clutter of accumulation, not merely the debris of objects of fashion resurrected with intensity and then thoughtlessly abandoned, but the weightier rubble of ideas and words which have fallen like rain, fog, storms upon her. The squalid dreaming out loud of her first husband and the invisible white Panama suits, hats and walking canes he left behind.

It occurs to her that the residue of all the broken midnights and dusks remains, somehow, within the walls of her house. The vows and curses of her daughters settled across the floors and carpets like a curious form of dust. It could not be swept away. There was the lingering of the constant profusion of new gods who proved inadequate and flawed, husbands and revolutionary leaders, diets and occupations. And, of course, the furniture, the mink stoles and cardboard boxes of books sliding through the rooms of her house, leaving indentations, scars which were permanent. The pregnancies, children, dislocations, and the lesions adorning the flesh of her daughters and their daughters, every one extravagant with a portable cache of bruises.

Suddenly, standing on her front-courtyard patio, in the hot near-midnight, she is aware of the portent in this interminable spring and summer. She should have recognized the clues immediately. Yes, she detected the disruption, but she refused to acknowledge its significance. Within her mind, she locked what she intuited into a cell and convinced herself she did not remember where she had put the key, there was no reason to find it, to unlock the door which was not a door but an opening into worlds. She had been overwhelmed by a sense of enormities, inexplicable and raw. And in arrogance born of fear, she had deliberately denied what was irrefutably obvious. It was a foolish act of self-subterfuge.

Of course she knew that her cymbidiums had blossomed much too early. Spring had been a flare, as if the sun were punctured and bleeding hot streams through the womb which men called space. The sun was in torment, perhaps betrayed, and she scattered her rage across the surface of the earth. Roses and canna pushed themselves up prematurely into the ferocious sun. The city had collapsed, catatonic beneath the weight of the heat and the intensity of the light. Streets were drained and bleached by early February. By mid-March, the city was a blanched plain where even the puma, mistress of the night, would starve. Then the elm had committed suicide.

Nuestra Señora la Reina de los Angeles was pulling up her illusionary pastel skirts and flaunting her wounded womb, the mutilated contours which were the residue of birthing countless mutations. Everything she grew this spring and summer was diseased, like the infants born to aged women, children with enormous heads who remain three years old forever.

It is after midnight when the telephone rings. It is cloudless, the moon gibbous, struggling to be whole. It burns behind bruised clouds.

"You sent Bobby home," Orquídea begins.

"I thought his name was Roberto."

"He calls himself Roberto with you, Madre, from respect and the magnitude of his identity crisis for which you are a focal point. At home, he is known as Bobby," Orquídea explains. She pauses. It is a pregnant pause. Marta Ortega counts an elephant being born, a redwood tree and two small islands. Somewhere, sunset through half-drawn drapes, sending a coral flush across stained beige courtyard walls. The earth shivers as if with fever. Then Orquídea says, "I do not want you to be alone."

"I wish to inhabit my own house for a few months, if you don't mind," Marta Ortega replies. She thinks she sounds reasonable.

"Bobby said the street is laden with bad vibes," Orquídea announces.

"Roberto said that?" Marta is surprised.

Orquídea considers her response. "As a matter of fact, no. It is my interpretation that Flores Street is inundated with bad vibes. Bobby actually said there was a mala onda."

"This is untrue," Marta says, calmly and firmly. She notices the hand holding the telephone is trembling.

"Madre, Roberto was discreet. I put my husband on him, his father, then his brothers. I had to crucify the kid. But I have assembled certain disturbing information. Gloria Hernández stabbing the Branden girl. The state of your orchids. Juan's elm breaking from its roots without reason." Orquídea lights a cigarette. "I cannot permit this. I am sending you Jasmine."

"Why would you send me jasmine?" Marta finds herself asking. "You are fully aware of the loathing I have for common plants."

"Jennifer. She still calls herself Jasmine, although this divorce may give her the maturity to return to the name of her birth. You will like her." Orquídea says cheerfully.

"Give me one month alone." Marta digs her feet into the linoleum of the kitchen floor as she speaks. Her voice plays back to her like a recording. She sounds as if she is pleading and whining. This admission of her confusion intensifies her panic and disgust.

"No," Orquídea decides. "Jasmine will arrive by noon on Friday. She is already preparing. She needs the cure, Mamacita."

Marta sighs. Another sick bird to enter her nest. Another amnesiac, a nameless sphere to be reassembled molecule by molecule. She is expected to invent a habitable region for this lost thing, show her the way day dissolves into the verdant and it is possible to be justified by green. She will have to explain the blossoming, how surprising it is, nothing like what one may have imagined, not the red silk dresses of a frantic calypso in a May stained burgundy. The process is subtle, an attitude built from the inside out, the delicate recombining of a cellular structure. A quality not purchasable, not from Bullock's Wilshire, not from a bottle in a botánica or from an American doctor.

"Lo siento, mi hija," Marta says finally. "The voice training, how I discouraged you."

"I don't remember singing lessons." Orquídea seems mildly surprised.

"I belittled your singing career. I called you a dilettante, a nihilist, an exhibitionist. I made you have neurosis," Marta Ortega remembers.

"That's absurd. I'm not a neurotic. There is no more neurosis." Orquídea laughs. "I have a personality disorder."

"A personality disorder?" Marta Ortega repeats, stunned.

Marta finds it deeply offensive to her aesthetics that neurosis is no longer in fashion. Neurosis has been pleasing to the ear. She has imagined it as a kind of flower, a night-blooming cactus perhaps, purple with luminescence and fragrance, growing abundantly along the shore of a miniature and deserted wharf, a port which had disintegrated, reclaimed by the jungle.

A personality disorder grates against the ear. It seems the description of a faulty appliance, a broken crankshaft in an automobile. It makes Orquídea seem inhuman, an interchangeable object, deprived of unique significance. It lacks lyricism and drama. It is an abomination.

"Forget it, Mother," Orquídea says, gently. "It was long ago, in a distant land, and besides, that particular wench is many times dead."

"Orquídea, I regret the baptism, the communion dresses, the saints' days, the PTA meetings. I was arrogant and inadequate. I always loved you."

"And I always loved you," Orquídea replies immediately. "What letter are you on?"

Marta Ortega is startled. She was rereading Neruda. Then Rimbaud. She has skipped letters. She is out of order. The illusionary increments she created are tearing themselves loose. Her garden was the basic structure of the existence she had idiosyncratically devised. And she had refused to perceive the details of this particular spring and summer because they were brutally obvious.

She had thought her garden permanent, Marta Ortega silently admits. She was convinced that it could serve as an anchor and that the ocean would not claim her. She thought the ebb and flow would be confused by the density and purity of her design. It would be awed and pronounce her inviolate. She would outwit it. She, who had dared dismiss the behavior and rituals of other women as acts of fraudulence, is fully exposed, a creature of absolute delusion.

"Mamacita?" Orquídea, her youngest daughter who lives now in San Diego, repeats.

"F," Marta says arbitrarily. F as in false, failure, flawed and fool.

"Ah, the possibilities," Orquídea muses. "Faulkner again. Carlos Fuentes. Freud."

Marta Ortega is expected to respond in kind. Her head is empty. In the long silence between them, an entire mountain range rises from the floor of the ocean. A continent shifts. Five million women recite rosaries on their knees in their separate but oddly identical darknesses. Five million candles burn on bedside tables between vases of dying flowers, hand lotions and silent telephones. Five million rooms torn by barking dogs, neon and loss. It is the ambered stasis of a broken-in-half heart.

"What are you wearing?" Marta Ortega suddenly asks.

"What am I wearing?" Orquídea repeats, genuinely annoyed. "Ian is sleeping. He has to be in the office at eight. Bobby is babbling in Spanish about mala onde. I have to meet Jasmine at the attorney's at nine-thirty. You can't remember what you are reading and you ask what I am wearing?"

"Tell me," Marta implores, her voice soft with longing.

"My bathrobe, Momma."

"The yellow one? Your favorite?" Marta asks.

"Yes."

"The yellow flannel with satin on each cuff? A paler band of satin on the cuffs and a sash that matches?" Marta whispers. Her eyes are closed.

"Yes, precisely. How can you remember that?"

"There is nothing about you I do not know. There are no divisions between us. Our grain is identical. I am intimate with your dreams, Orquídea, your contrivances and what is most delicate and hidden. I am familiar with what you do not yourself yet know," Marta tells her younger daughter.

"Es verdad," Orquídea sighs. "Madre, Jasmine will arrive by noon Friday." Then Orquídea hangs up the telephone.

It is Tuesday night. The granddaughter who has retained the name of a deeply scented but ordinary night-blooming flower will arrive on Friday. Three days, Marta realizes, that is all the reprieve she will be granted. Marta Ortega lies down in her bed, in the house on Flores Street which is at last, briefly, empty. The accumulation of curses, vows and sobbing, strategies and analysis is deafening. The air in her rooms is irrevocably damaged.

Her bedroom windows are open. Pink camellias and yellow roses in a crystal vase near her face startle with fragrance. She falls asleep, widening her nostrils, her lungs, embossing the inside of her being with the odor of her garden. As she closes her eyes she wonders what has become of Antonio, her firstborn grandson, who was now Anthony or, perhaps, a man named Tony.

"You always ask about Tony," Angelina says, annoyed. "I tell you repeatedly he lives near me, in Mill Valley. He is a professor of Chicano studies at Berkeley. He has three sons. You know this and then forget. Is this deliberate?"

So, Antonio has become Tony. And what of Scott and Bernardo, who is perhaps Brian again. And the one named Jeffrey whom she saw moments after his birth. And the one named Sandra who was once Sunshine, is presently married, a mother and Sandra again. And now this Jennifer, who persists in calling herself Jasmine and will arrive in the house on Flores Street in three days. And three days is an insufficient time in which to rebuild a life, Marta Ortega recognizes.

She decides to have her morning coffee with Joseph and simultaneously remembers he is gone. Gone the sacraments, the quest for excellence, courage, the jaguar and the fabulous night-blooming cactus called neurosis. Gone the mahogany forests of the Yucatán, the plumed caped lords of Tenochtitlán, the pottery, plazas and temples, the stars of divinity and augury. Gone the pueblo of her birth, her youngest grandson, and now Joseph and Bill.

And what did they put in the vaults, Joseph? Only nerve gas and the

Bill of Rights? And what about her face, Enrique? It was impossible to see her eyes, her mouth? Only the yellow dress and the hat with the wide brim. There were young women on a platform dancing in layered skirts. Mariachis were playing. There were shadows, the sky was webbed with streamers of colored paper. The air was confetti.

Marta Ortega walks through her backyard aimlessly, like a boat adrift, surveying the damage. Then, abruptly, she stops.

At any instant, Angelina and Orquídea would speak together. Angelina who lived now in a suburb of San Francisco, in a house an architect had designed, in an edifice of glass and redwood, with massive windows viewing the bay from a prized angle which included both bridges. Angelina, with a husband who spoke to London and Caracas and the islands of the Bahamas from the telephone in his car, instructing a select few where to buy oil wells, when to sell gold or move their surreptitiously gathered money to or from Panama.

Now Angelina served hors d'oeuvres on a vast expanse of redwood terrace, captivating her guests, telling them how she had once left a husband and an infant to run off to Buenos Aires with a part-time dance instructor named Federico. Angelina would be standing, her movements subtly integrated with the words of her story. It was a matter of phrasing and timing, nuance and pause. The wind would be rustling her burgundy or coral silk skirts as she acted out the scene for her guests. And the sails of the boats in the bay at her back passed swiftly, as if for punctuation and emphasis.

Then Angelina would continue, "I lived for his cha-cha, his rhumba, the light glancing off his pointed and shined black shoes." As Angelina revealed this, her body would sway in a deliberately slow cha-cha, then an exaggerated but graceful rhumba, her skirt swirling in the wind as if the wind were an intrinsic part of her monologue. Of course with the wind it was more dramatic. It was transformed into a dialogue.

Suddenly, as Angelina was reenacting this anecdote, it became the carnival in Río. The bay wind was transfigured into a dense green breeze of ginger and rum. There was a suggestion of jungle vines. And even the uniformed maids carrying the silver trays of elaborately arranged sea creatures and cheeses surrounded by coils of meat in pastry shells would pause, recognizing that this moment was a kind of sacrament.

"We boogied all night for months. From Santiago to Lima, we crossed the Andes twice," Angelina would recite as she poured white wine into the cut-crystal glasses adorning the linen-draped antique dining table. And the wind seemed abnormally warm and her eyes would be red as the sun setting across her shoulders. Her eyes would be radiant and aflame, mirroring, precisely, the sky. Of course Angelina had learned that clouds, sunsets and sails could be choreographed and used as a backdrop.

"Well, I woke up broke, in an *unspeakable* port." Angelina paused, allowing her guests to envision this monstrous landscape, how it must stink of urine and typhus and night-blooming cactus with poisonous spikes, how it was rotten with women in rags followed by packs of hungry dogs. And the barefoot boys in torn t-shirts, dreaming of cars and knives and of becoming boxers or singing stars. The boys in packs, scratching like dogs at the edges of ripped sidewalks and the dust of alleys that led nowhere. "And I regretted nothing," Angelina would conclude.

And then the sun erased itself behind her back. Her timing was impeccable, flawless. Yes, the sun itself came down like a curtain across a stage, falling in folds as if she had ordered it.

Then her guests would laugh, delighted and relieved. The uniformed maids would again move with their trays among them. Angelina, the wild one, the sought-after, with more dinner and reception invitations than she could possibly accept. Angelina, with that spontaneous wit and that hint of danger and the unexpected. Oh, her unique Latin flair, that hot spice. Yes, Angelina the rare one, with her brood of mismatched children, her university degrees unframed in a drawer and her mother in Los Angeles who was a bruja, a woman who grew orchids, read an entire city library alphabetically and, in isolation, invented feminism. Angelina was remarkable, her guests agreed. She always seemed to be caressing an invisible long-stemmed red rose in her mouth. Of course an ambassador or a mayor would wish to sit at her side. She was an adornment, a jewel. Angelina, that wickedly strange one, with that intelligence and style.

Angelina no longer rang the doorbell of the house on Flores Street to hurl insults at her or sit at the kitchen table at midnight, weeping about the men who came and went, leaving only artifacts like small premature burials. Or perhaps men were like dogs, marking the path back. Angelina did not rage bitter, screaming that her life was a perpetual Christmas where men left pieces of themselves on her shelves, in cartons, as if she were a hotel or a warehouse.

"It's your fault. Es tú culpa," Angelina no longer screamed. "You, with your damned ambiance, your stained oracle lips, your deranged geography. You made me into this thing, this creature that I am. You invented me, with my special darkness and heat that both attract and terrify. Oh, I'm rare, Mamacita. I'm unique and spectacular. Everyone loves me for minutes."

Soon this final incarnation of Angelina would receive a telephone call from Orquídea. Orquídea, who now lived in San Diego with a back garden facing the mouth of Mexico. She was soothed by the burning southern wind, her tennis afternoons, confessions and mass. From the front windows of her house, she watched the sails of the boats in the bay aiming themselves south. And the sails were wide and absolutely white, white as the baptism and communion dresses and Easter lilies she had been denied and the sails were not canvas but alabaster as the faces of saints, white as the lace of the gown of a virgin bride married by a bishop in a cathedral. And the sails were white as the eggs she had been forbidden to paint, white as the flesh of Mary and Joseph and their infant who was a god.

Every day was a communion for her. Orquídea could see God's hands gliding across the waters like a man playing a piano. God's hands were gently guiding the lazy south-sliding vessels with their perfect acres of sails, the sails opening like mouths of supplicants to the winds which were the breath of the Lord. And the winds offered them blessing without asking, divinity and absolution. From her front-room windows, Orquídea could study the bay of white sails, the calligraphy of God which was pure, calm, fluid and southern beyond confusion or doubt.

It was inevitable that Marta Ortega's daughters speak together. They would plot across the miles of wires, the vineyards and reddening walnut trees and the soft-sculpted coves nestling against the shore of the ocean like an infant at a breast. Across the road embroidering the lip of the sea with its cliffs of succulents, wild strawberries and rocks flushed with the fever of sunset, they would assemble data. Through the layers of clouds, lingering bruises and uncountable sails in their bays, their words would connect and float above lime-green lawns, alleys of bougainvillea and canna and then over the low hills of wild barley and scrub oak. They would gather the details.

Perhaps Orquídea would begin with the elm which had sprung from its roots on the front lawn of the house where that paranoid, Juan Martínez, had lived for half of their lives. Orquídea would gracefully prepare her sister for the brutally inexplicable events which would follow. She would make certain Angelina understood that the elm was without disease.

"Are you asserting that the tree defied gravity?" an irritated Angelina would demand. She was hosting a dinner party that night for forty people, including two congressmen and an Italian tenor. This was definitely not the moment for Orquídea to launch into another of her periodic conversion trips. Angelina glanced at her watch. She could allocate her sister three minutes, she decided. The caterers, the bartenders and the florists were standing in the hallway.

"I am convinced it committed a mortal sin, yes," Orquídea would pronounce calmly. "It committed suicide."

Then Orquídea would describe the unprecedented heat, fires and ash. She would mention the pervasive fear encompassing Flores Street. Then she would tell Angelina of the murder of Barbara Branden, how Gloria Hernández had stabbed the white clerk though the breast with a kitchen knife.

"You are joking," Angelina would reply, although she recognized instantaneously that her sister was not engaging in a grotesque jest with her. She was, for the first time, alert. Angelina would turn her back on the bay. This was not the appropriate moment to devise methods for choreographing dinner-party conversations and sails.

"Dear one, it is true," Orquídea would admit, her voice dull, her tongue tasting oddly of sand, swollen, hard, alien in her mouth. They would speak in Spanish.

"Gloria Hernández stabbed her? She murdered her? She is dead? This is not possible," Angelina would say, feeling herself sway, feeling herself reel. And the hand-woven Persian rug on which she stood would seem unsolid, as if it were fluttering, as if it contained liquid currents within the threads. Rooms were temporary, she remembered, places which existed by delusion, artifice and sheer will.

Angelina and Orquídea would collect the specific details like women arranging flowers for the centerpiece of a feast for a lord. The exceptionally brutal spring, the ash that fell from the skies, gray and ugly as the last snowfall on a dying world. Then they would discuss the departure of Joseph and Bill.

"They drove away with only the clothing on their backs. Angelina, they were running for it," Orquídea might say.

There would be a silence then, a pause which was a physical sensation, running through the miles of cables and wires, through the curvatures of the roads and wave-eaten beaches, through the curvatures of their ambivalence and personality disorders. They would sense the severing of the ordinary, the sudden opening which was a gulf, a vortex. And it had appeared like a rare red bird on the sloping hill that was Flores Street. And white sails would drift at their backs. Angelina would be wearing a burgundy gown a designer had created for her. She would stop thinking about the composition of sunset and wind and silk she had been devising for that evening. She would cease wondering which melons to serve, which wine and which cheese.

"The garden is ruined," Orquídea would say, finally.

"This is extremely serious," Angelina would recognize. And the floor where she stood would still be swaying.

"She is not reading alphabetically," Orquídea would tell her sister. This detail, perhaps more than any other, would outline the dimensions of the situation.

Then perhaps Angelina would take a handful of blue pills and pour herself a martini. Later, Orquídea would walk to her church. It was nearly three miles, but Orquídea preferred it, the sense of her feet on cement, the feeling she was gradually approaching a final destination. The walk elongated and intensified the ritual for her. Before hanging up the telephone, Orquídea would have informed her sister that she had already dispatched her daughter Jasmine. It would serve as a temporary stopgap until they figured out precisely what to do. The mala onde, the bad vibes, the murder, the ash, the lifetime of scorched orchids.

Yes, they would send her another granddaughter, Marta Ortega thought sullenly. A Jasmine who would have been instructed to occupy less space than a vase of sun-seared camellias or a just-dusted brass lamp, but a granddaughter who would manage to consume her remaining moments, the yellow-tinted granules of sand, of opal and quartz. The fundamental dust, drifting down in a spiral, torrential and accelerating. It would be unavoidable, this eating of her final silence. Always the daughters of her daughters arrived with psychological gashes. Of course, they concealed their wounds artfully, knowing that Abuela was a bruja. Abuela would find their scabs and cure them. Abuela, La Reina de la Calle Flores. Their private Lourdes.

Marta Ortega walks through her terraced hillside of separately potted cymbidiums, her patches of side and back garden. Her roses are malformed, strangled on the bush, twisted by noise and dust, ash and heat and the murder of the meaningless white clerk who called herself a social worker, that random juxtaposition named Barbara Branden. Her garden has been rotted by the subliminal lash of the insanity of Gloria Hernández with her magnificently concealed capacity for malevolence. Her garden has been ruined by what the radio termed inverted layers of air and torn clouds of ozone, ripped like stained sheets, linens violated by the debris of fraudulent couplings and destructive severings. And her garden has been poisoned by what the clergy terms an accumulation of sin, what her pagan neighbors pronounced as omens, what Roberto recognized as a mala onda and what his mother translated into bad vibes.

Marta Ortega studies the wooden structure her father constructed for her, the house she has never contrived to paint green. Green moist as moss at the softening edges of rivers beneath leaf and shadow, intertwined like nets, perpetually modified by branches and fronds. The green of the always dusk of the jungle, tranquil and hushed. Green air and its variances, its music. Green across the palms and broad-leafed philodendrons after rain, glistening, cleansed. The green of wind in banyan, a subtle drumming. And the green rain that falls after birth. The way the sky greens when it prepares to open its womb and push forth an infant star. Or how the sea greens when she prepares to open herself and produce an island, a continent.

Marta Ortega is assaulted by images, vivid, distinct, their clarity an astonishment, undamaged by the passing seasons. Once, she held her daughter Angelina to her breast, recognizing that this was the primal theme of which all else was insignificant variation. It had been raining that December. The air was damp as a river and she knew mother and daughter were the fundamental cord of the world. She nursed her infant. In time, Angelina would offer her breast to one daughter, two daughters or ten. And between them they would keep the planet on axis. They would feed the process. They were the sea and all that dwelled in it. They were the oracle, the current and mystery, the one authentic inspiration in a cacophony of accident.

But her father painted the house yellow. Marta Ortega cannot dismiss the portent in this recurrency, repeated in her terraces of scorched yellow orchids. And the hot jaundiced sun hanging suspended in the sky since January. The yellow of the bathrobe her daughter Orquídea might be, at this precise moment, wearing. The glaring of the yellow taxicabs which brought and then carried away her daughters in their tempestuous and irregular seasons. The house her grandchildren painted yellow again, as it had been at the beginning. And the yellow dress the nameless girl wore, dancing with Marta Ortega's husband at a Cinco de Mayo fiesta half a century before. The girl in the yellow dress, setting in motion a fluttering, a quake in Marta Ortega's hidden regions, the undergrown forests near the invisible lakes of her being.

Marta Ortega notices that her hands are caked with dried dirt. The fundamental brown threads of the earth, the brown of bodies and graves, the bark of trees, the skin of violins and cellos. The brown of simple aged clay vessels which have served their temporary purpose.

She had glimpsed something when Angelina and Orquídea were born, an implication of the fundamental expression manifesting itself in the greens of ferns, orchids and the shape of birth, how the air remained damp and green after her daughters pushed themselves from her womb. The revelation of the impulse had anchored her miniature world, providing her the design. In this way she charted her continent.

But she had betrayed the substance, had thought she could possess and sculpt it. Marta Ortega is horrified by the perversity of her motives and how relentlessly she pursued the elusive. Her regrets are monumental. She sits alone in her ruined garden until nightfall, enduring.

And, somewhere, an aged priest who also realized he had wasted his life called out, "Muy tranquila, María, con calma." And as Marta Ortega remembered Padre Peréz she said, "Gracias," and felt the syllables float from her lips and drift into the night like breeze-driven petals, carving a channel through what was not empty space and what was not dark.

• • •

There would be a second telephone call. "It cannot be true," Angelina would begin. "Gloria Hernández? I did not think her capable of such passion, of so bold and irrevocable an act."

"We all underestimated her," Orquídea would realize. "Her disguise was brilliant."

"Was Miquel having an affair with the Branden girl, that dumb cunt?"

"I doubt it," Orquídea would intuit.

Orquídea would correctly decipher the situation. She would not know that one warm night, when the wind was a gentle and irresistible caress, Roberto had knocked on the door of the house where Barbara Branden lived. He had showered, washed his hair and put on his clean white ironed shirt. He offered her a bouquet of orchids he had selected for their flamboyance, their sheer dazzle.

Barbara Branden would pour him a glass of wine and then another. Finally, Roberto would say, "I want to make love to you." Barbara Branden would laugh then. "I have not been with a woman in more than a year," Roberto would admit. "I could give you pleasure."

Barbara Branden would place the orchids in a vase. She would not tell Roberto that they were remarkable. She would not say thank you. Then she would send Roberto from her house, unkissed. When he reached for her, she threatened to call the police. "I may not have made it in Hollywood," Barbara Branden would tell him, "but I am not ready to make it with Mexicans."

Roberto would remember how she said the word Mexicans, how her lips twisted with scorn and disgust. And her eyes said I would no more touch your flesh than I would a dog.

"Then why?" Angelina would persist. She had canceled her dinner party.

"Because she was not a dead volcano, merely unusual and dormant," Orquídea might reply.

"Perhaps it was a form of ritual," Angelina might intuit.

"We were deceived by our scorn," Orquídea would say.

"We betrayed her," Angelina recognized, surprised.

"And ourselves," Orquídea would add.

"And Madre is not reading alphabetically? The orchids are decimated?" Angelina would repeat. She was making notes for her husband's secretary. She would not accompany Barry to Barbados the following week. Their Friday dinner party and reception for the mayor would be canceled. Future invitations would not be accepted. Angelina was going to return to Flores Street.

"The street is dismantling itself," one or the other of her daughters would realize.

A silence would fall between them. The bays would be stilled, chill. Angelina would momentarily lose her balance and her control of red. Orquídea would experience a wavering in the white serenity of her waters. In the silence they would be sensitive to the shifting of the climate, to a rawness in the texture, an exposure of the interior. In silence, they would share their terror. They considered the possibility that they are drowning. I could be as a shell in the waters, Angelina and Orquídea think. All beaches are the same. I could be refined by the incessant beating of waves. A shell which is found, is lost. I could be a daughter of the salt-webbed waters, blue into blue where there is liquid and rhythm only, a camouflaged and more final reality.

It is early evening and Marta Ortega does not wish to listen to their conversation. She must concentrate on glimpses of the definitive moments. Angelina or Orquídea is reaching an arm through the warm air for her hand. They are walking through the garden, their feet caked with mud. They are staring at the moon, watching the sunset, clouds, rain. It is a spring dawn of yellow roses, and listen, my daughters, observe how elegant and hushed they are, now, at dusk. Notice the ferns awakening, uninhabited and vulnerable, preparing for the sea breeze which will embrace them with passion. It is an Angelina who does not yet take yellow and blue pills to control the liquid enormities flowing in her head. It is an Orquídea who has not yet been divorced three times and embraced God as an infant wraps her not-quite-formed arms around the neck of her mother.

Chronology is irrelevant. You are never quite finished with girl children, Marta decides. They can return at any moment, in taxicabs, cars, airplanes, with children or even grandchildren. She would take them into her garden, her shrine, her delusion of permanence. Of course the bird of paradise lies, she would remind them. Always red roses and blood canna grow in still corner groves tortured by the inadequate shade of palms. Do you think you are different? Do not reply. You are not. Now come watch my morning ritual, she would call across the dawns and dusks and winters and summers of their lives. See how I wind the worn-out fan and push the desert back with my thumbs?

"Is this some sort of koan?" they would demand.

They claimed to be shipwreck survivors, but their vocabularies were intact. She ignored their sarcasm, recognizing that it, too, was merely passing fashion. Listen to the cool breath of dusk rising with night wings from the secret gutted well. Find a riverbed, she would instruct, take reeds from the water's edge. Pit the reeds with small holes. You must create the instruments of your survival. Now enter the wormy forum, yes, here, where you sit, where you stand. See the pavement fill with fine white sand? Yes? Then go. Invent your own salvation. Put the flutes of your design to your mouths and blow, my daughters, charm the snakes that come.

She rebuilt her daughters. She was La Reina de la Calle Flores, a constructor of planets. Can you hear the rustling of the exploding trees? his is the dawn of the dog bark and spring. I tell you the sun is freshly spun. There is gold in the hills. Widows are itching in their black robes, in their travesty of woolen servitude which follows them, even after the burial. Angelina, Orquídea, it is behind you. Come, here we go again, wandering down the same paths, following our old footprints, drunk on the nectars of antique promises fat red and yellow on the vines.

"Tell them always the great palace gates are besieged by refugees," Joseph had suggested. "Children with glaring physical defects, lame old men erased of wisdom. Barbarians and savages. This is natural."

"They resist the obvious," Marta had sighed. "Las ocurrencias accidentales, las circumstancias inexplicables."

"Do they think they alone notice the winds stink of decay, the corrupt are enshrined, the sacred chambers violated and justice arbitrary?" Joseph had wondered.

Now, drinking coffee alone at her kitchen table, Marta Ortega considers the possibility that she failed her daughters by her scarcity of sympathy. Women inhabited the region of unceasing transition, in the liquid gulfs and eddies. It was women who walked on water. Should she have applauded them for what was inescapable and ordinary?

"Gloria Hernández?" Angelina is somewhere repeating. "She of the dull eyes, the inarticulate mouth, the pervasive lack of grace, wit and imagination?"

"The epidemic arrives on two legs," Orquídea replies, sighing. "What did you expect?"

Marta Ortega is remembering an earlier version of Angelina. Angelina who became Angela and Angie. It is Orquídea becoming Olga, dyeing her hair a deranged yellow she called platinum blond, as if she were bathed in magic chemicals or draped in starlight. Olga, who claimed she was actually of Scandinavian and Greek ancestry and refused to speak Spanish for more than two years. Later, Olga would sell her imaginary ice skates and fjords and become Orquídea again and a Catholic. Later, she would find solace in the confessional, the mass, the particular metallic clang of church bells punctuating her days and nights, caressing her with their expression of the collective metaphor. Angelina, with her South American adventures and the professions she would abandon, would become Angie and then Angelina again, the one prized for her Latin flair, her insistent implication of red and her refusal to be tamed.

Then they were surprised when their children changed their names, gave themselves extravagant spellings and invented relatives blatant with prosperity and incredible ancestry. These grandchildren did not have a family tree but a jungle vine, replete with Indian princesses and brujas in continual bloom, mahogany corridors, hurricanes and exiled musicians.

Her daughters are now gliding or draped in apathy and barely moving across the surface, the fluid regions without borders. In between the love affairs and the divorces, there are flirtations, stolen afternoons and weekends in Aspen and Ensenada, the moments they squeeze out from the rubble, the mopping up, the sandbagging, the rebuilding of their miniature cities, their diminutive civilizations, reconstructed brick by brick. In between their bitter assaults on her inadequacy, her eccentricities and how dissatisfied they were with the shape and texture of the youth she embroidered for them, they were exuberant with gratitude.

"I could not have survived this without you," Orquídea is saying, after Marta has pronounced her free of cancer. Orquídea who will now wash the wounds of lepers is preparing for her new vocation by kissing Marta's mud-caked feet, literally.

"I would not be sitting next to ambassadors if it were not for you," Angelina reveals during one late-night telephone call. "Yes, you instilled this passion and sensitivity for the opulent in me. You permitted me to sprout eccentric. You demanded it, forced me to become rare. Gracias."

These were simply the fluctuations of the soul made visible, Marta Ortega realizes, las fluctuaciones del alma, refinements of necessity. Somewhere, Angelina and Orquídea reenter an Indian phase. They assert that a uniquely red heat has invaded their blood, their limbs are molten, volcanoes erupt in their breasts and their lips are blistered, inflamed. She was not empathetic. They were reading texts about Mayan rituals, architecture and art.

Always the Maya, Marta had thought with disgust as she potted orchids in her garden. They study the Maya, despite the fact that she has repeatedly informed them that her mother was born on the Pacific coast, in a region of another tribe entirely, a group lacking even linguistic similarities with the books they are memorizing. And in between, they wanted to be singers, actresses. They craved careers and professions and then abandoned their work to be with their new husbands and children.

Professions were a mere salve for the ego, they inform her, gratuitous, perhaps even unwholesome. Instead they will dedicate themselves fully to their family, implying that this was something she failed to do. She who had been married not to a man or a god but to her books and garden.

Within months, they were sitting at her kitchen table, admitting to a restlessness, an agitation. The routine of domesticity was an atrocity, they concluded again. Marta Ortega was working in her greenhouse. She was not supportive. She lacked patience. She had forgotten the conventional posture for accepting tedium.

Angelina and Orquídea arrive for lunch and accuse her of having been harsh and unrealistically critical with them. By dessert, they inform her she was criminally permissive and lacked even the concept of discipline. They recite their standard litany. Marta pours herself a vodka on the rocks while they repeat their complaints. She had not provided them with even the semblance of normal fathers or healthy male role models. She denied them the ordinary rituals, on all levels, religious, sociological, even national. They insist she cared only for her garden. It had been her profession, they shout, and she pursued it with the devotion and compulsion of a man greedy for success and money. It was not a sanctuary but a private avarice, a green contagion, a hillside of terraced poisons.

"But you are my garden," she tells them, resigned. "You are the plants that resist my fingers. I cannot invent the right soil or find the conducive climate. No combination of sunlight or shadow proves nourishing or sustaining."

It is midnight. Marta Ortega lies down on her bed. The garden is gone. Suddenly she remembers that it had taken only one day to dismantle the exterior of Joseph and Bill's lives, of what they had collected, what had served as their fabric and design. When you are running for what remains of your life, physical objects render themselves invisible, meaningless. They have no context. They disappear. Gone the rocks saved from a beach in Greece where they slept naked, their feet washed by waves as they embraced in a night hot, ancient with comprehension. The stones meant nothing, were less than the indentation their bodies had briefly engraved in the innocent and indifferent sand. No objects, no mementos, no charade of permanence. Gone the two-story Spanish house on the lip of the hill of Flores Street, the Grecian rocks, the scarves dyed in Siam, the flasks painted in Borneo. Gone the centaurs and saints, Minotaurs and mermaids, the trilobite and mastodon, Java and Peking man with their gods, alters, ceremonies, songs and flowers. All of it, gone.

Marta Ortega closes her eyes. Angelina and Orquídea appear. They demand recognition. Always you could see them across a room. Their eyes were bruised as if saying, Use me, get a stick, go in deep and sharp. I have nothing left to give but the truth. Are you man enough for that? Mi madre es La Reina de la Calle Flores, una bruja. She has taught me the intricacies of recombining elements. I can cast spells and transform. I can give you back your youth, softer and greener than it actually was. Or I can turn your skin the color of debased linoleum. Do you want to play for real stakes? Say, life and death, just for a start?

They think they have found him in a spring when love speaks in tongues. A blue-eyed man, and they dance to a jazz band, in transit between worlds, planning their marriage in Arizona or beneath redwoods or in rumored ruins purposeful and mythic. They sleep like berthed ships, rocking gently, her hand on his thigh which is a kind of anchor. Months flow as if miraculous, inflamed, unflawed, as close to perfect as a woman and a man get in this world. Then something goes wrong.

It was Orquídea. And the blue-eyed man proved to be married. The man with eyes blue as the flames on stoves in cold rooms when you are alone would not divorce his wife. His eyes were the blue of betrayal and desertion. Orquídea rang the doorbell, weeping. It was a cold night and raining. Thunder and spasms of lightning an electric blue. Orquídea must have been wandering in the rain. Her hair and clothing are soaking wet. Marta helps her remove them, finds her a bathrobe, a woolen shawl.

"I won't beg my married lover to stay, to unpack, to commit his inviolate unformed self to this raw persona, this female intelligence that terrifies," Orquídea said.

"Pues?" And since it was night and raining, Marta must have poured rum into their glasses. In the silence between them, rocks fall, slabs of round onyx, glittering shreds of the garish moon, the blue thunder, blue lightning, blue petals and glass. And the rain was an elegance of black.

"Just say my mouth tastes like Hawaiian flowers and yes, come and go, no demands. Just pass through, baby, I'm a fucking hotel," her daughter sobbed.

Orquídea looked out the window at Flores Street. It seemed skeletal at midnight, the lawns empty, roses and wild iris plucked and stuck back into a trunk. "I am forty years old," Orquídea seemed stunned to realize.

"And you have broken your heart often and with precision," Marta added, softly, carefully. "Is it not enough to have silence at two A.M., Baudelaire and no one you love rehearsing suicide, lying in agony or dying?"

Her daughter considered an appropriate response. The wind was wailing, a wind from the north, of Pacific tundra and a harsh rocky coast. And Orquídea was thinking, I am nameless, limbless. It is ice I grow in daggers and sheets and I am a web of gashes and salt is offered me. Orquídea heard dogs barking and thought, This is a city of dogs, of half-buried bones and anger, of a mean wind aggressive as a lover drunk and thwarted, stumbling where alleys collapse. And I will die without love in this haunted obscure hour of lamplit leaves fallen in deserted culs-de-sac where loss is deafening. She wondered how she could be so empty, how she could have forgotten so much. She felt thin, derelict, as if she were wearing her bones on the outside, allowing her ribs and spine to show, hard and solid as an answer. But there is no resolution.

"When you have lost everything, the world softens," Marta told her younger daughter. "You learn by trial and fire. It is finite. The music, the roses, love and your tumultuous follies. All transitory and arbitrary. Then the world quiets, undemanding. It dissolves like the smoke from a worn-out spell."

"Is this it?" Orquídea had asked.

Marta Ortega refilled her glass. She pantomimed a toast to the catatonic wall. "This?" Marta smiled. "This is as good as it gets."

Angelina and Orquídea believed in love. They moved slow, as if recognizing they were a vanishing species, like the buffalo. They hid their pervasive mourning unsuccessfully beneath too much perfume. Their voices were tropical, moist palms, metallic green insects, a sense of something hot, unpaid for, pagan.

They were refugees from the wars one never hears about. They were minor ballerinas who lost their legs. Or women who married the wrong men, ceased to embrace the music, forgot that it was dancing they loved. Their devastation was internal. There was no body count. The dead kept walking. It was not blood they spilled but some nameless fluid, equally the stuff of life, the invisible joy within atoms motivating their celebration and spinning, their bonding and mating. Marta Ortega observed her daughters and wondered what would happen if the molecules too forgot their lines and purpose.

Angelina and Orquídea are accenting their dark skin, letting their hair blacken naturally. It cascades across their shoulders like a waterfall on a moonless night. They wear shawls and mantillas. It is earth and sun, amulets, the lakes and volcanoes of the southern valleys which birthed them, they assert. They abandon their diets.

Marta is watching them overeat. Idiotas, she thinks as they consume a third plate of frijoles. You were born in Los Angeles. I was born in the shadow of City Hall. My mother was born just outside Mazatlán, even then a tourist trap. She never wore the skin of jaguars or embossed her face with clay or paints or feathers. Her father owned a hotel which catered exclusively to European vacationers, my angels, my utterly flawless fools.

Her daughters shed weight and enter, again, their American phase. They are Olga and Angie, hair dyed auburn, platinum, strawberry blond. They refuse frijoles, queso, tortillas. The avocado, that caloric hand grenade, becomes their personal enemy. For an entire summer they subsist solely on melons, water and appetite-suppressing pills which make them

314 · Palm Latitudes

chain-smoke and talk incessantly. Sleep is an impossibility. They are hiding on Flores Street with their chattering mouths, trembling hands and red eyes until they thin to a configuration designed to allure. They take apartments in Westwood and Santa Monica, and still the one with the tourniquet and laughter, the mangoes out of season and the Swiss bank account does not come.

Angelina and Orquídea do the swing, the jitterbug, the pachuco hop, the tango and twist. They go to New York and Vienna, Madrid and Veracruz and Rome. Somehow, they are always disappointed. Cities and harbors prove to be precisely as depicted by the advertisements, only smaller, dirtier, more cluttered, with the colors not as sharp as the photographs. The Champs-Élysées and La Gran Vía and El Paseo de la Reforma are boulevards like any other. Stonehenge and the pyramids of the Yucatán, even the Pyramid of the Sun and the Pyramid of the Moon, are merely stones, after all.

Angelina and Orquídea know only two climates, summer or winter. There are no gradations. They are luminous with heat or glacial and remote with self-pity and loss. In their summer phase, it is always afternoon in a lethargic July in a country or century unmolested by time. They paint their fingernails and toenails with the deliberation of artisans. Their bodies are a craft. They push the hot air with imaginary imported silk fans. A river sullen with sun flows beside back porches laden with fireflies. But, goddamn it, something goes wrong.

After the university degrees and the women's magazines, the immaculate apartments and impeccably tailored skirts, after the priests and hair stylists, starvation diets and tranquilizers, the night classes in French and anthropology, the sitting in museum lobbies and cafés, still he does not come. The one with the bouquet of long-stemmed red roses. The one with the sack of mangoes. The man who is going to love them as if they were the last princess in the final tower at the end of the map. Or he appears and proves to be dented, scratched, maniacal, subliterate, unemployed, alcoholic, devious or physically ill. He lacks the sheen promised by the brochures, the durability and dimension. This was not what they ordered. They send it back.

They enter their impenetrable winter. They are shells, empty husks left by winds. Their grief is disproportionate. They cannot believe that the shrunken sun has abandoned them, night presses and the dead return, partial and indifferent as scarecrows. They smell of fear.

"Perhaps only the lean cycles will remain," Marta suggests. "Consider the elgance of seeds that have stood without complaint or vision, becoming guardians of hills and models for saplings."

"Somewhere elephants drag tusks through brush, burial grounds lost," Joseph says softly.

"You have known the life spans of small things. Kingdoms of inch-worms, frogs, moths. Generations of what flies and crawls," Marta offered.

"Indeed," Joseph agreed. "An enormity, resplendent, incandescent."

"Mierda," her daughters screamed.

"The day closes a black shade. Darkness locks. And even suns tumble blind," Marta Ortega concluded.

In their winter realms, they are extravagant with lace and sadness. They sit on her living-room sofa, playing her Billie Holiday records incessantly. "She knew the pain of tiny needles. She too longed for flowers, a gesture. It was love that killed her," they recognize.

They purchase black silk negligees to weep in. They wait at cold windows in high-heeled satin sandals, fixed like moths in reverse, drunk on the draft. Their feet turn blue. Young men refuse them, say they hate women that cling. Marta Ortega watches as her daughters let their arms fall off, as they become exquisite with contrived silence, undemanding as gardenias in January, perishing quiet as transplanted flesh.

Rage keeps them alive. She hears them pacing in the living room at 3 A.M. Their anger eats the air in the house. Their anxiety accumulates. It becomes difficult to breathe. It is these residues that litter her rooms, even now, when she is finally alone. It is Angelina or Orquídea, pacing, smoking, sobbing. They are recalling their mistakes, astonished that these errors of the soul and perception are, in fact, imprinted within their skin. The garish heartbreaks of their lives are beyond mere dinner-party anecdotes, they recognize, startled. Their personal horrors are actual tattoos across their nerves. Sleep is impossible.

"Make lists," she calls out to them. "Hagan listas. Count all the ways I have been inadquate, alphabetically. Identify each separate seed of neurosis I implanted."

They count instead their lovers, chronologically, by age, profession, city. In between, they ponder their mortality unceasingly. They search for unusual bodily markings or secretions. They fear the darkness, the angry redundant dogs barking in what they perceive as a chorus. Of course the barking dogs have a design, a purpose that is evil. Surely something will enter the house on Flores Street, rape and maul. A thing drawn by their bruised scent which rises like a tarnished moon above the orchids and the camellias. Terror makes them lethargic. Insomnia eats their energy. They are charting their numerous abandonments, in specific, as if cherishing the nuances of the loss, as if wanting to keep it vivid and alive, still burning.

They are reappearing, shouting from her bedroom window, the courtyard and the terrace, begging for the consejos. Within the grain of her flesh a voice is wailing, "What should I do?" The voice has a recurrent rhythm. "Qué hago yo?" sails at her like an arrow from windows, courtyard, terrace and patio.

Marta Ortega wonders whether they think she is a botánica, with potions and tin medallions. "Make lists," she repeats from her greenhouse. "Hagan listas," she calls out from her terraced hill. She knows that composing lists and reciting them, alphabetically, like a litany, is superior to the pills they take, their yoga classes, their psychiatrists or entire rosaries intoned on their knees.

"I will bang my head against the wall and drink the blood," Angelina threatens. "I will slide off a cliff. I will slice my wrists."

"There are uncountable styles of ruin and death. They open with clarity, a sudden vista, dazzling with possibility," Marta notes in passing. "Your version is bereft of flair."

"I will drive along the lip of the ocean, where the blue mouth yawns resplendent with promise. Where the wind and waves shriek, This way, this way," Orquídea improvises.

"That has a flow," Joseph admits.

"Can you continue with something unexpected and compelling?" Marta inquired. It was late afternoon. She was carrying a watering can.

"Driving along the ocean, where the wind is saying, Come to me. The rock will complete you. This is the secret spray your lungs crave, the formula you have longed for." Orquídea lit a cigarette. "The wind is saying, These harbor swells will enter the place between your legs with greater grace than any lover's tongue. It will be more precise and certain, a kind of absolution, like the moment you were born."

"I remember the moment you were born," Marta says softly.

Orquídea is not considering birth. She is planning her death and carefully avoiding the word *suicidio.* "And the wind will say, You cannot deny this return, this small shudder, the brief thunder of earth into earth. This is the answer you seek."

"Is there more?" Joseph is pouring vodka into their glasses. He seems interested.

"Fucking A, there's more. I can imagine it, yes," Orquídea says. "To be stunned by the simplicity. One into one. The concept of zero. The universe deciphered mathematically. A stack of red ones, blue twos, yellow threes, clear as a child's toy blocks at the moment of impact."

When Orquídea is not watching, Marta removes her daughter's car keys from her purse. She gives them to Joseph for safekeeping. Then she watches Orquídea until she falls asleep, tossing and moaning at daybreak.

"**I** am taking the vow this time," Angelina informs her. She has dropped her children off at a movie theater. Marta senses immediately that her climate has altered, that she has entered her private winter.

"Indeed," Marta says, "Something new?"

"No, the original black veil that never changes style. The one you nail to your skin."

"Have you told this to your therapist?" Marta asks. "Your astrologer?"

"I hate it when you are glib," Angelina said.

"Then make lists," Marta instructed her elder daughter.

She has been telling her daughters to compose lists since they were children, since they had measles and chicken pox and could not sleep.

Marta Ortega is surprised she can remember the lists of their lives as clearly as she does their apartments or their hubands. It is winter. Angelina or Orquídea is composing a list of authors, alphabetically, reciting it out loud like a penance, the names of writers she plans to read but probably will not.

"Aleixandre, Burroughs, Hart Crane, and not just selections but the whole damn thing," Marta hears and smiles. "Dante, T. S. Eliot, Faulkner, Goethe, even if I don't understand a word I can tell people I conquered it, like a fucking mountain..."

Marta Ortega is standing just beyond the closed door of her daughter's bedroom. She is listening, smiling, wishing Joseph were near. It is Angelina or Orquídea, trying to put herself to sleep, now that the pills don't work, not even with vodka or brandy.

Angelina and Orquídea return in their dark winter phases, if only for an afternoon or an evening. They come to Flores Street when their night is damned as if by hidden gas lamps. It is some era before electricity. Their bones are chill as the rained-into basement rooms where forbidden seances are held and the occasional dead enter edgy as insomniacs, nerves bitten raw by worms, flesh diaphanous as incense. Marta Ortega knows the secret of her daughters. They say they are tough as glass. If you sang to them they would shatter.

"Do you still compose lists?" Marta Ortega asks Angelina on the telephone. Angelina glances at the bay, the whitecaps, the sails of the boats. The bay with its cold currents, its torment of wind, its implication of scars and lips. Angelina is thinking that the bay sings a black woman's blues.

"Lists?" Angelina repeats. "Not very often."

"Have they changed your medication?" Marta inquires. "You can sleep now?"

"It's Barry. He's a maniac for me, sexually. It does strain one's credibility, at my age, after everything. But I turn him on. He calls me from his office, a restaurant, to say he has a hard on thinking about me."

"Sex makes you sleep," Marta notes. "No hay más listas?"

"Imaginary dinner parties, sometimes. Artaud and Bogart, Coppola and Plácido Domingo. Elvis, Betty Ford and Judy Garland. Hemingway, Ionesco and Elton John. Should I continue?"

"No," Marta sighs. On Flores Street, she is squeezing oranges into a glass. Then she will pour vodka into the glass and watch the sunset.

In San Francisco, Angelina is staring at the bay, at the white sails of the boats and the whitecaps opening across the waters like a series of teeth. The bay is hungry, sensing the impending sunset, the release into darkness and the elegance of uninhibited currents, depth, sculptures of dolphins and sharks and sudden awakening islands. She is stretching. Soon she will part her dark-blue lips and sing. "But the children make lists," Angelina offers.

"You taught them this?" Marta is surprised.

"You taught them, Madre. When they lived in your backyard. When they ate those goddamn Mexican mushrooms and had bummers, problemas con las drogas. When they tossed haunted, seeing monsters in their sleeping bags under the stars. Las estrellas mágicas de la Calle Flores. When you let them grow that stinking marijuana in the garden," Angelina remembers.

"What lists do the girls invent?" Marta is interested.

In San Francisco, the sun is beginning to set. Angelina is composing a menu for the dinner she will serve in the dining room with the windows overlooking the bay. They will eat inside, this night. It is chilly, the wind is already slicing. This will not be a spectacular sunset. It is too overcast. The rack of lamb is fine, she reassures herself. The wild rice with the mushrooms. But something is definitely missing. Angelina is aware of this void and it is gnawing at her. She pours herself another martini.

"Pues?" Marta persists.

"The girls create lists of men they wish to fuck," Angelina reveals. The mint dressing for the lamb, that dash of green. That is not the problem. The rice with the mushrooms and almonds is adequate. The crab hors d'oeuvres. Still, she senses a lacking.

"Angelina, las listas," Marta repeats.

"The lists? Woody Allen, Jeff Bridges, Fidel Castro, Bob Dylan and Albert Finney." Angelina notices that the night is draped with clouds, shrouded, the cold biting. She will not have the clouds speared by sunset to help her tonight, no backdrop of magentas and reds, no inverted coral reefs dangling from the sky. She must compensate for this. She has already had the table set with a fuchsia-colored linen cloth. The napkins are a shade darker, closer to burgundy. She surveys the tableau, dissatisfied.

"G," Marta Ortega prods.

"Jackie Gleason, whom they recently discovered. And Che Guevara, of course. Dennis Hopper. Julio Iglesias, naturally. Or maybe Billy Idol. Don Johnson. And the entire Kennedy family. John Lennon and Paul McCartney." Angelina stares at the table. The pink roses seem a bit lost. Is it possible the inadequacy lies with her floral arrangement?

"The Beatles," Marta Ortega says. "I remember."

The endive salad, is it too placid, perhaps? The composition is pink and green, subtle but coherent. The integrity is subliminal. No, the problem is not the salad or the roses. Yet there is an imperfection, a flaw. And she will not have the sky tearing into streamers of red and purple confetti tonight, or the wind rustling the silk of her skirt. There are factors for which she must prepare herself. It is a challenge, an improvisation. She could change her dress, of course. She could wear a gown, black, floor length perhaps. The statement would be formal and severe, elegant, naturally, and unexpected. If she wore black velvet, she could bring the bay, contoured, into the room. "Where am I?" Angelina asks.

"N," Marta reminds her.

"Oh, Paul Newman, Daniel Ortega. Al Pacino. I don't know what they do for Q. Then Smokey Robinson and Martin Sheen and all his sons."

Perhaps the problem does, in fact, lie with the pink roses. She could have Barry stop for something more surprising, dramatic and flamboyant. She wonders what would be more compelling. If the composition is one of pinks and greens, the vase might require additional greenery, ferns or even cymbidiums.

"Is there more?" Marta finds herself fascinated. The sun is setting on Flores Street. Soon she will say goodbye to her daughter. It has been an overcast day. Now the sky is speckled as a flock of black-and-white ducks glued to a gray and agitated sea.

"I don't know what they do for T or U. As for V, it might be the entire Viking football team or the male population of Venezuela. Where am I?" Angelina is still undecided about dessert. Perhaps that is the problem. The mousse. Is it not exotic enough? It could seem predictable.

"W," Marta reminds her daughter.

"Orson Welles, I suppose. Or every black running back named Washington. I have no idea what they do for X or Y. As for Z, perhaps herds of zebra grazing between their legs."

"I see." Marta finds herself sighing, audibly.

"What do you think about mousse for dessert?"

"It lacks majesty and impact," Marta replies without hesitation. Then she hangs up the telephone.

In San Francisco, Angelina orders cartons of strawberries. The details define us, Marta Ortega remembers, watching the sunset, the rituals we invent in secret where it is always dark and remote. The selection and composition sculpt the great nothing into temporary shape. And Angelina and Orquídea have been her elements, the seasons and orchids her expression of the impulse made momentarily tangible.

Angelina and Orquídea are an insistent red pulse, inseparable from the landscape which they pollute. Red sunsets, red-painted fingernails, mouths and the silk scarves draped around their necks. Red is their rage, their delirious tropical summers. Always, they sit at the kitchen table, stare at Flores Street and imagine harbors with cliffs lost beneath the liquid fire of flamboya above ports where boats with red-patterned sails dock. The red of their thoughts as, somewhere, Angelina or Orquídea lights a cigarette and suddenly envisions Joan of Arc, vividly, as if she knew her intimately. Angelina or Orquídea, shrugging her shoulders, concluding that Joan of Arc also had visions and burned her lungs. Her daughters, with a logic to their images of fire, how they bled their flames into their perceptions, their dreams. Always red, with its nuances of danger and pain. Red without increments, a promise of intoxication and disaster. And the red which resonates belongs to the painted mouths of her daughters, lips lacquered in crimson, wine, vermilion and, if fashion dictated, the blood of bats.

The red mouth is opening. It is Angelina, deserted by a man who looked like a film star or a panther. The red lips are parting and vowing, "Know this, Mother. I am his greatest mistake. I will hate him as the planet turns, in each increment of her shifting orbit, in each nuance of her seasons. I will hate him in August heat and in sudden autumn storms. I will become a certain way the neon will scratch one window after another, relentless and haunting. He will come to know it, taste and dream it. Me, lit from the inside, whispering his secret corrupt beast name, mixing my burned lips with the Santa Ana winds, becoming part of him and the landscape. In the smog and mist, in the moonlight and jasmine, I will dig in under his skin in a way he will never forget."

"You are creating a magical arrow," Marta observed.

"This is a tracer bullet. It is an army of rats marching through his veins, nesting in the chambers where he once had blood. He will feel them scratching with their many claws and infinity of teeth as he drives into the pastel distance that will always open for him, beckoning like desperately lonely arms. That insatiable scratching from within, as he drives from one woman to another, one blue velvet sofa and slice of city view to another, he will feel this following him, this corrosive eating from within," Angelina promised.

The air in the rooms of the house on Flores Street reddens. It is the accumulation of curses and vows, the glittering shards, embers, tiny volcanoes and crystalized blood, compacted, hard and incandescent as stars.

And the air on Flores Street bleeds as Angelina or Orquídea spears a car up the hill. Angelina or Orquídea in dangling garish earrings shouting from the window of a speeding vehicle, "Life's a ten-cent postcard," the red mouth laughs, brazen, cynical, "it's gone in a flash." The laughter lingers, red, an implication of an intelligence deliberately debasing itself. The red of irony, a certain recognition of mortality perhaps. "Run where your blood runs," the lacquered lips shout, "all the rest is lies."

Then, without warning, their summer passes. They enter their interminable winter which is amber. Amber the candles and lamps switched on at dusk in winter. This amber is specific. It is the amber of perfumes in tinted-glass vials on nightstands, the liquids of ambergris beside rosaries and bottles of tequila. It is the bedroom of Angelina or Orquídea. Their eyes are the amber of love-haunted women in a stalled December, on nights when the Santa Ana winds blow sand into their bones. And the sands too are amber. In the night, amber is a kind of clarification and purity. Amber the seeds, the bones and petals, the cold air craving an embrace, the lamplit arcs and random definitions.

The telephone is ringing. Marta Ortega turns from her greenhouse of sleeping orchids. She enters her house which is not yet painted yellow again.

"I have sinned," Orquídea begins. It is an Orquídea who has already been Olga but does not yet live in San Diego. She prepares herself to receive another confession. She wonders what orchids dream in their winter sleep.

On Flores Street, the lamplights are amber. The Santa Ana winds are amber. The vodka in her glass is amber beneath the kitchen light. Marta Ortega intuits that her orchids dream only of themselves, their slow birth and perfection. And Marta Ortega absolves her daughter.

M arta Ortega awakens with the inexplicable sensation that she is falling. She remembers that her house is painted yellow again, as it was at the beginning. Cycles, she thinks, completion and return. And even in a long life, one knows so little, less than cattle or scrub brush which are limited but at least substantial. In her kitchen, there is no silence. The red mouths of her daughters are erupting like wounded stars, enraged orchids ripped from slumber, and their lips are birthing atrocities and benedictions. Marta Ortega can sense this debris, this stain of rage. It is dense, fused with the vases of her flowers, the uncountable arrangements of bouquets which have been the increments of her days. It is these fragrances and bruises which linger in the house on Flores Street, in the house which will never be empty.

She realizes someone else will live in her house. Perhaps a grandchild with the name of a jewel or a flower will inhabit her rooms with their intangible shards of tempestuous conversations which would remain as an undercurrent.

"I was too large to mount, too rare to eat, too exotic to be acceptable," Angelina weeps in a warm dusk in a distant summer. "I was too oblique for a mirror, too jagged for a rug. What did he want me for?"

"It was an experiment," Marta intuits.

Angelina spills her anger into the house on Flores Street. She has arrived with suitcases. This is going to be an extensive procedure, Marta Ortega realizes, a real surgery. It was August. Angelina's children were in camps in the mountains. An old fever had returned to her daughter. There is no cure, merely random dormancy. Then the sky turned smoke white and fat with imminent cataclysm. The typical sky of August in Los Angeles. "It is earthquake season," Angelina observed, simultaneously agitated and pleased.

Then it is Orquídea, also in summer. Summer was a bad season. Their children were in camps or with their fathers. Now her daughters were free to indulge their grief without interruption. In summer they polished the secret jewels of their terror.

"We ceased speaking," Orquídea is informing her. Orquídea has also arrived with a suitcase. There will be another surgery. The walls and floors of her house will be anointed with yet another coat of the incandescent syllables, the glistening invisible dust spilling from their plum- or mauve-tinted lips and lying as abscesses beneath the foundation of the house, forming pools and wells, gulfs and eddies.

"Is that significant?" Marta inquired.

"I became useless, nonlucid, luminous only in private. He willed me to fade and I did and I have except for the residue, the new scar I can trace with my fingertips. The ridge of ripped skin, Madre. The fine metallic line of how he said I hate you."

Marta Ortega is seized by the recognition that virtually no time remains to her, for her. Tomorrow, the daughter of her daughter will arrive. Marta Ortega stands in her garden. She feels as if seas are washing over her, at least seven of them, each utterly distinct, like geological epochs, husbands or children. She is amazed by their singularity and magnitude. The context expands and she realizes that the core is fluid. Of course all women knew this as they sewed shirts and buttons and drapes, as they designed the direction of the waters. Women created the seams and margins, their fingers forcing the nameless implications into definable hills, jungles, coves. Women wove storms and droughts, children and rivers. Men built boats. Men sat in metal and canvas shells. It was women who embroidered the sails, contoured harbors. It was women who took what was empty and birthed geography.

Of course solidity was an illusion. The motion was constant, changing as winds dictated, tides, fences of kelp, driftwood, gulls. Marta Ortega is aware of the significance of her discovery. This was the swaying which women often felt. It was the lapping of waves, the rising and dying and mating of winds within. This was the source of the pain she had experienced, the sensation of stabbing in the heart which is not the heart but a masterfully hidden region. It was a refinement in the composition, like the distant fluttering of a forest or a star or a daughter being born in the subliminal shadows of a not-quite-erased antiquity.

Suddenly, Marta Ortega considers the implications of the mixture of white and Indian blood which comprises her, the two distinct rivers which should not have intersected but did. Marta Ortega's mother had been Indian, yes, but by pigment and the accident of geography only. Marta had dismissed the blood facts of her mother because she had been seduced by the European culture with which her mother cloaked her dark-as-mahogany flesh. Her mother had been educated in Mexico City, spoke French, attended operas and ballets. She wore shoes and leather gloves crafted in Spain and Italy. Her mother's father owned a hotel renowned for its costly European ambiance and its view of a placid harbor where time stalled and the waves were green as the fields of one's imagined youth. Her mother had gone to confession and mass, but the god of her father was the dollar, progress, the imported and not the indigenous.

She thinks of her father, Víctor Ortega, born in Madrid. He had been a prodigy, a cellist who toured the capitals of the New World, Buenos Aires, Rio de Janeiro, Caracas, Havana, Mexico City. It was by chance, by a variety of delays in travel arrangements, that he found himself in a seaside resort just north of Mazatlán.

The mahoganies of the hotel corridors and saloon, the staircases of marble and the white arched windows opening like sails onto the jade-green harbor pleased him. He was satisfied with the seafood and the wines, the arrangement of candles set in silver between vases of tropical flowers, orchids, opening mouths and tongues, deliriously red and purple, as if certain petals had been bathed in wine. These blossoms were subtle with fragrance and radiant with heat. They were born not from seeds but from some secret process of the sun itself.

Víctor Ortega had also been struck by the hotel owner's nineteen-year-old daughter, delicate, her flesh brown as the skin of cellos or earth caressed by eons of a gentle and more forgiving sun. They sailed the harbor and embraced as waves spilled tame at their feet, stars hung above their shoulders dense and intricate as the constructions of spiders.

The Indian woman was a virgin and would remain intact until he married her. Perhaps Víctor Ortega was simply exhausted and the tropics opened raw and intoxicating, disorienting him. In his weariness and trance, he saw the slow-rising coastal hills of infinite green gradations and equated these vines and branches and fronds with a form of absolution or revelation. He was sensitive to the sounds of the verdant, the moss and night-blooming vines, and thought he had discovered balance and grace. The unexpected music, the scales which were green, liquid and scented, made him rash, made him veer from the predictable and the tour he did not rejoin. His luggage and musical scores were delivered to Mexico City and Havana, where he did not go. In Spain, his family crossed his name from the front leaf of the family Bible. From the day of his marriage, Víctor Ortega was considered a son who had died.

They were married in Mazatlán by the bishop. Then Víctor Ortega took his dark-skinned bride by boat to America, to a port called San Pedro, to a city named Los Angeles. The land proved oblivious to his unique skills, the region arrogantly indifferent to the craft he had mastered.

Víctor Ortega was unprepared for this inexplicable and undeniable reality. His wife's dowry kept them from starving as he asked himself how it was possible that in a country so vast, there were so few positions for cellists. He found himself living on the outskirts of a squalid and pathetic village called Nuestra Señora la Reina de los Angeles, in an ignorant pueblo where culture had not yet been invented.

His wife gave French lessons to white women while she waited for her husband to awaken from his stupor. When she became pregnant, Víctor Ortega began to build el mercado del pueblo, blistering and callusing his musician's hands on cardboard boxes, wooden crates that splintered, and burlap stapled bundles of beans, corn and rice.

In the warm nights, Víctor Ortega spilled his pure European seed into the clay vessel that was her mother. Sons and daughters issued forth and they were not American or Mexican but simultaneously both and neither. They were not mutations, she repeatedly told Angelina and Orquídea. Mutations were erratic. Rather, they were hybrids, more colorful and sturdy than the original. Yet even after Angelina and Orquídea completed the university and collected additional degrees like women compelled to possess rare coins or stamps, they seemed incapable of comprehending this essential distinciton.

There were connections, instants of revelation and absolute definition. Las conexiones complicadas, resonantes, irrefutables. Once, when her grandchildren were Los Niños de las Flores and lived in her back garden, they had convinced her to journey with them to San Francisco, a city which contained symbolic significance for them. She had been driven north on Highway 101. It was a clean gray slate, a solid gash with San Francisco in front and La Paz beating hot and persistent at her back, watching her like an eye.

It was the pale-purple June of jacaranda on the roadsides. The ocean of amethysts and not yet fully formed or named metals lapped gently below scrub and thistle ridges. Beaches bore the names of Spanish warlords noted for their savagery, the water glistened blue with wind-jettisoned jacaranda, like tiny purple orchids, floating across the waves.

Santa Barbara became Avila, Santa Maria, San Luis Obispo and Paso Robles. The day elongated into gauzes of sheared purples. And within, the interior was called San Joaquin, Salinas and Modesto. The coast had become dense with palm trees and succulents cascading across rock, transforming cliffs into acres of magenta and burgundy. The composition was blatantly and irrefutably tropical. It was a culmination of the uniquely Mexican and Spanish which manifested itself in subtle shifting greens and delicately curved coves and farming towns named Gonzales and Aromas.

And, always, the jacaranda was drifting and the car was rocking her tenderly, like a cradle.

It had been a Sunday. They stopped for lunch in a village with a centuries-old mission in the town of San Juan Bautista. The pueblo rested anchored to the valley floor, still gripped by the Spanish impulse, those first lords in black who painted murals on adobe walls. Although Marta Ortega had long been excommunicated, she toured the church and lingered in the corridors and chambers. There was a certain residue in the blanched walls, in the air of the church which was cool and dusty. And she was assailed by an intimation of the familiar.

Later in a garish tourist shop with shelves of electric madonnas that could be plugged into walls where their blue eyes could be made to glow, Marta Ortega purchased a book about saints. As she walked through the town of San Juan Bautista, beyond the mission, past the bougainvillea-draped walls of white courtyards shadowed by fruit trees, she was again seized by a sense of the intimate.

She responded to the repetition of the pattern, a specific setting of white courtyards with fruit trees in their centers, church bells and brick patios. She felt as if she had always lived there, in the pueblo of San Juan Bautista, not merely for decades but for generations. It was a terrain, a grain, a weaving she knew absolutely. Even the canyons of soft scrub oak rolling in slow rows to the foothills and the deepening green of the village of Santa Cruz seemed to exist within the fibers of her flesh.

An old man, a farmer wearing a sombrero, called out to her, Marina, Marina. When she turned, the old man apologized. He had mistaken her for the wife of his primo. They paused in the shadow of a fig tree. He explained that badgers were the problem that year, bobcats and wild pigs. And Marta Ortega thought, Here they mend what breaks, they tend what grows. And this village is no different from my garden on Flores Street, or the pueblo of my birth, she realized. Then a sudden rain rooted into the low foothills, and the wail of Sunday church bells sealed a black veil across the valley, blessing them that dwelt within the walls.

It had been a definitive moment. She had refused to journey farther. Her grandchildren accepted this without argument. As they turned their car around and began driving south again, Marta Ortega said, "I have already seen San Francisco."

Her hybrids left her in silence. Marta Ortega considered the possibility that she too dwelt within the walls. It was simply that her walls had no conventional edges. Rather, it was all a fluttering where there are no borders, pretenses, vows or phrases to recite like fences, the penances that were dull atrocities, trying to contain the infinite possibilities of the night.

We pretend our hearts sleep in the night, Marta Ortega realizes as she lies down in her bed, sleep and do not dream of monsoons and mutiny, of regions of uninterrupted jacaranda and papaya and abandoning us to our rows of dull plants in identical terra-cotta pots, to our interchangeable patios, gardens and children, our predictably graying sheets and assorted linens strung to dry above postage-stamp yards.

There is a fundamental substance, she recognizes. It is not a trick done by slide rules, formulas or sleight-of-hand. Not with the prayers of one passing god or another. Not with the unceasing transitory rituals and accessories of arbitrary fashion. It is perhaps connected to the subtle shifting patterns of a migrating sun striking glass panes strung with hand-stitched curtains of polished cotton, but it is not this, precisely, either. It is not the passing seasons or even time as a concept frozen and visible. Beside the intricacy and the resonance of the substance, all the names invented by women and men are banal.

Marta Ortega wakes with an unusual sense of clarity and purpose. Sunlight bathes her rooms, luminescent, gentle liquid yellow channels outlining each dusted surface and polished lamp, ceramic vase and clay-colored flower pot. She notices the grain in the wood of her tables, the swirls and waves and solid grooves which differentiate mahogany from redwood and oak with the precision of fingerprints. She can see beneath the patterns in the wood grain to the trees which were felled to form the object, and further, to the patch of forest that existed before the seed itself was accidentally planted. The separate details of the world are accessible and unambiguous as artifacts in museums, labeled, protected by a form of invisible glass.

Marta Ortega is overwhelmed by a profound desire to visit the river of her youth. She will walk down Flores Street and follow the curves of Sunset Boulevard east into the city and traverse the treacherous web of characterless towers and office buildings, find paths between the vertical ruins where men sit in a stupor of delusionary purpose, there in the monumental abscesses of concrete. Yes, she will journey to the dried gully that had been el río de Los Angeles, the gash that lay butchered in the shadow of the sunsores of steel.

Once, her brothers attempted to raft el tributario del río de Los Angeles, had sought to navigate a fluid blue thread. They sensed a rare opening, an irresistible impulse into an other. It was the moment when they had most clearly understood the nature of the world.

Of course the river was gone now, erased. It could rain incessantly, but there would always be drought within its chained asphalt mouth, its bricked lips. The mouth longed to open and curse the architects of its premature burial, who had dared sever it forever from the sea, making it an orphan, denying it grace.

The river lived only in memory. It occurs to Marta Ortega that much of the world exists in precisely this manner, as fragments, juxtapositions, dreams and private revelation which can be expressed in no tongue, in no coherent image. The ebb and flow is moving recklessly, careening and splintering into gullies, ridges, paths which are, from the instant of their conception, already shattering into otherness and more.

It is early morning. Today, the daughter of her daughter will arrive. "Abuela," Marta Ortega will hear, startled. And this granddaughter will consume her remaining instants of celebration and regret. This granddaughter would bide her time. Then, in a vulnerable configuration of shadow and quiet, she would say, "Sometimes I am crazy. It is cellular, a disturbance of the nerves. The edges disappear. I consider suicide. Don't tell my mother."

"Of course not," Marta Ortega would have to respond.

"Pills help, herb tea, a hot bath and sometimes it passes," this granddaughter who was filing for her first divorce would reveal.

"You will heal," Marta Ortega would find herself compelled to answer, when she longed to think only of the river which was dead and her orchids as they had once been. And the house on Flores Street which was never painted green, and how that particular green might have affected the composition, the individual events and their destinies.

"Abuela," this granddaughter would whisper, "sometimes I get angry and ashamed. My hands shake, longing for contact with glass or knives. It is a physical sensation, almost sexual, the desire for absolution by blood or poison."

Marta Ortega is expected to absorb the debris of the second cycle of her birthings. This crop of girl children born to her Angelina and Orquídea who now insist upon her counsel, her consejos. They are like their mothers, of course, restless, eccentric and demanding. The shallow and mechanical will not satisfy them. They have an intuition, a craving for the inspired insight.

"Abuela," she hears, startled. "Forgive me, I was in the vicinity."

Marta Ortega must open her door for them. Now her granddaughters sit at the kitchen table where their mothers once sat. Now she pours coffee or brandy for the daughters of her daughters, implicitly responsible.

"I went to a clinic on Vermont," a Jade or a Jasmine or a Sunshine reveals, voice soft, conspiratorial.

Marta must wait. They will supply her with the details. They have a flair for the graphic and compelling. It is intrinsic to them, landscapes which are spectacular, windless moons, worlds breathless, static, as if at a final edge. Perhaps she should have encouraged Angelina and Orquídea with their voice lessons and acting classes.

Then one of her granddaughters will light a cigarette. She will open a purse, extract a match, each gesture intricate and refined. It is Sunshine in this image, the young woman who has returned to the name of Sandra, slowly lighting the cigarette, pausing to study the match flame as if it contained mysterious equations. "Fat women were sitting on bridge chairs, women with bellies like rotten moons and legs of blue ridges like rivers on a map," her granddaughter Sandra is informing her. Or was she still Sunshine, then? And next door, Joseph was playing "Cry Me a River."

"Such women do not mate," Marta commented, "they spawn."

And in the two-story once-white mansion, a black woman was singing, "You told me love was too plebian, told me you were through with me. Now you say you love me, well, just to prove you do, you can cry me a river, cry me a river, because I'm tired of crying over you."

"Precisely. And there were tattooed men coughing. Their words an amphetamine guttural rush of Vietnam ambushes and being jobless with a box full of medals."

"Is this an anecdote or a novel?" Marta inquired. The cymbidiums needed watering. It was late afternoon and Sandra was still Sunshine then, Marta Ortega is certain.

"I waited six hours for the doctor. The fan was broken. I could smell the lush underbrush of the Mekong Delta, frozen dinners, abortions, the dirty shirts hurriedly plucked from an unwashed floor." Sunshine paused. "It was a unique sort of stench," her granddaughter recognized. "A certain ambiance, like a permanent stain."

"Nothing is permanent," Marta remarked. Not the chinampas of Xochimilco, not Tenochtitlán or the pyramids, the magic, science or flowers. No, she thinks now, not the gardens or rivers, not the rituals or music.

"And the traffic rushed beyond the smeared windows. The air was greasy and tormented. At last, the doctor appeared," her granddaughter Sunshine is telling her. "He wore a sports shirt and strands of thick gold chains around his neck. He was tanned. I let him rub my breast and run his stethoscope along my thigh."

"Indeed," Marta replied, thinking about her orchids, her miniature civilization which she had somehow convinced herself was impervious to time and rot.

"Then I told him I never tried to die, coughed blood or had problems of a mental kind. I bit my lip and smiled. Then I handed him my last twenty-dollar bill for one bottle of Seconal," her granddaughter who was still named Sunshine concluded.

"Es muy interesante," Marta Ortega lied. "Now get a watering can."

Her granddaughters arrive on Flores Street begging for consejos. Just give us a shrug, a moan, any indication that you are listening, they implore, they demand. Marta Ortega thrusts the appropriate items into their hands, shovels, shears, gloves. They bend in the earth near her. They are explaining their longing for the opulent gesture, the gift with the sheen of black pearls, embraces by candlelight when the flesh is ambered and the molecular structure transformed. They yearn for sailing ships which will transport them to islands that are better than the postcards.

"Qué hago yo?" her granddaughters ask.

"Compose lists of all you desire, alphabetically, of course, until you are empty," she tells them.

"That could take years," they realize.

"If you were exceptionally fortunate, it could consume and gut an entire lifetime," Marta Ortega, La Reina de la Calle Flores, says. "And don't stop watering."

Granddaughters arrive with and without warning. Marta Ortega cannot separate the occasions of their coming and going. They have returned to their original names. It is later. She is no longer diapering an infant. The cribs and the cartons of stuffed bears and dogs are gone. The yellow bunnies and fat pandas are gone. She does not have to teach them how to count their five fingers, their five toes, the miracle of ten digits. No, this particular series of repetitions is behind her. Now they are married.

"Abuela," she hears, and the morning dissolves. They reveal that their husbands do not make love to them often enough, lack imagination, resist the impulsive and raw invention, even simple experimentation. They claim they find themselves moving in a trance, almost indolent.

Her granddaughters are listless, exhausted, shorn of conviction. The constant masquerade and the unceasing task of concealing their rage and disappointment are debilitating. They offer their mouths in apathy. They no longer expect bouquets of lilacs, martinis and Bach at sunset. They find the absence of this specific configuration tragic.

"Ashrams and feminism," Marta, who has never been compelled by convention, snaps, annoyed. "Freud and combat boots, numerology and sex until you are numb and diseased and nothing works."

"Abuela, this is not an age of anxiety," they insist, "this is an age of terror."

"It is always an age of terror, unless you are dull or an opium addict," she dismisses their complaints. "Get a clippers and shovel."

She erases their faces. They actually believe their century is unique in its abundance of atrocities, as if women did not always fear plagues, droughts, wars, the disappearance of their men and their children, the arrival of new gods with rituals demanding the heart or eyes of the first-born son, the skin of the virgin daughter, the rains which come too early or late, the limbs of the elements disfunctioning. This is fundamental to their dance, to the impulse, that unpredictability in the winds and currents which is the substance insisting upon innovation.

"Abuela, did I startle you? Lo siento," and a granddaughter is bending over her in the garden. It is Jessica or Jade. Marta refuses to remove her eyes from the pot of orchids she is pruning.

"He was wild, a dark cloud. He was nervous, sentimental, spoiled. He drank too much, liked the soiled night too much and all it implies," this granddaughter is revealing.

Marta Ortega glances at the feet of this Jessica or Jade. They differ from their mothers in their garments. That, at least, is an improvement.

This granddaughter is wearing not high heels but sandals. "Pues?" Marta offers in the direction of the sandaled feet. "And hand me my shears."

"He thought there was a thrill in ruin," her granddaughter says, lighting a cigarette with elaborate deliberation, pausing to stare at the flame. This granddaughter, who herself is intoxicated by disaster, is disparaging the man for a quality she also possesses in excess.

"His life was a collection of four A.M.s in punk dives, not sleeping for days and waking in stucco bungalows with marginal redheads." This granddaughter holds the gardening tools for her, gracefully placing them before her, as if they were sacred objects. Then she continues, "He had boxes of silk shirts, Neiman-Marcus ties, jet-set criminal pals. He left his Mercedes in towaway zones. He could lie in three languages, scratching an itch with a blowtorch. He had style."

Now Marta Ortega allows herself to stare at her granddaughter's face. The woman wears sunglasses. Her hands tremble. Soon Marta Ortega will put down her gardening tools and rock the daughter against her breast. She will permit this Jessica or Jade to weep. Marta Ortega is immune to the sound of a heart tearing itself into fragments. She absorbs the anguish.

"I loved the private planes, his imported high-tech watch. I bought white gloves, renewed my passport, planted six rosebushes. I just didn't have the strength to grow him up, grow him through his greed for inexhaustible Saturday nights. I couldn't cut through or cut it and found it empty, fraudulent, the beast to be not yet formed." And Marta Ortega hears the voice wavering, the lips which will soon shatter into a howl.

"Still, I miss his kisses, his relentless indifferent precision. Tanqueray gin on his breath," and now the voice is breaking. Marta Ortega is placing her shears on the redwood slatted table on her terraced hillside. "And how much losing him hurt," her granddaughter moans, reaching through the air for her.

And somewhere, an aged padre in a pathetic church who had also lost his faith counseled, "Muy tranquila, María, con calma." And now Marta Ortega takes the injured thing into her arms and whispers, "It is O.K. Be calm, mi amor." And the sun slides down behind them, their embrace profound, their grain identical.

• • •

But today, Marta Ortega will not be Abuela. She looks at Flores Street, noticing that the heat has lessened, like a cancer entering a period of remission. It will be a good day to walk, she decides. Marta Ortega stands at her front door, aware she is forgetting something. It asserts itself, insistent.

Yes, the blanket she has been subliminally instructed to take with her. You are a bruja, her youngest grandson said. I would expect nothing less. Marta Ortega smiles as she chooses a woven fabric with bands of primary colors and fringed edges. An ordinary serape a grandchild brought her from Mexico. Cycles, Marta Ortega remembers, completion and return.

She is carrying a vestige from one of their Mexican adventures. Her granddaughters telephone her from raw wet Mexican nights, the black of drying blood and elements which are exposed, ancient and hot. The sun poisons in a too-blue sky above agave tattooing the sides of roads. On highways, signs point to villages which do not exist. Death licks the land and stands just behind the shoulder, like a friend. The New World thins. Freshly painted arrows indicate towns aborted, coughed dry before birth.

"Even ships were ruined, stuck like spears in the sand between rocks. Torn in half like arteries with the waves washing the dead center," one of her grandchildren is telling her. They are wordless. White rock and rough brush speak for them.

"I watched fishermen cutting bonita, tossing the red heads to gulls. I realized nothing is wasted here. The sea birds are fatter than longed-for children. They shrieked above the harbor where abandoned boats sat like bloated fish, engorged on their own rust. And the wind was raw, a salt-and-rock wind mixed with bits of fish and bloodied flesh."

"The wind that laughs and spits down towns," Marta Ortega understands. "The wind of amulets."

"Sí, exactamente, Abuela," one of her grandchildren replies. "I sat on a cliff, feeling naked and unprepared. I could be plucked now and sucked clean. A thing left for the wind and the wrinkled Indian women. They could arrange my bones like their stacks of painted belts, their pyramids of watermelons and cantaloupes. A body used and returned."

On Flores Street, it is after dusk. Marta Ortega wraps a shawl across her shoulders. Next door, Joseph listens to Billie Holiday.

"What should I do? Where should I go?" this granddaughter asks.

"Drift," Marta Ortega offers. "You are freed from the cold geometry of absolute direction, which is an illusion. Let this be a time where time fills itself in, in dogs barking, in drugged insects between hot flowers and the songs of worms and the sweet gossip of stars in a pure black night."

"Drift?" she repeats.

"And find less conspicuous clothing," Marta Ortega adds. Then she hangs up.

Suddenly, her granddaughters are twenty-five years old. They sit at her kitchen table, between men, with infants on their laps. "Once I thought my confusions rare and unrepeatable," they admit. "And the borders a trick of mirrors and bastard stars. I was seduced by the intrigue of a moody sky beckoning, jammed awake like a lunatic that seemed accessible."

"It happens," Marta Ortega says, her voice soft.

"I lived like a maniac," one of the daughters of her daughters recognizes.

"You were lucky," Joseph observes.

"There is mercy, however arbitrary," Marta concludes.

Today, the granddaughter who has retained the name of a flower, Jasmine, will arrive at noon. And she will not be Abuela. As Marta Ortega begins walking, she is struck by a sense of impending autumn. Of course the planet will continue its relentless spinning, weaving its personal tapestry across space, birthing seasons and stars and men, trees and oceans in their turn. This exceptional spring and summer of ash and flame and blood would become an autumn of muted charcoals and occasional chestnuts and lindens. The air would gray with the smoke of burned leaves, the smoke which lingers, categorically refusing banishment, as if the leaves themselves were aware they existed. They had pushed their version of a quarter into a slot, and the game had been brutally indifferent and far too short.

As Marta Ortega walks down the sloping hill that is Flores Street, she feels the ground beneath her feet rock and sway. The sidewalk is a kind of ship, a strip of tinted paper or cloth floating across waters, less solid than confetti. And Enrique could not adequately evaluate the woman's face. She wore a hat with a wide brim. There had been the blare of trumpets, the shadows, the women on the platform dancing, the siege of bells.

At the bottom of the hill, Marta Ortega notices that the elm tree in the front yard of the house where Juan Martínez has lived for twenty-five years is gone. She heard the metal mouths of the saws chewing the bark, the hide. The sound had been unbearable. She experienced a twinge then, a stab in the place which might be the heart but is not, is a subtle and less identifiable region. A refinement in the composition, Marta Ortega realizes, a thread pulled through the tapestry, that is all.

It had taken three men half a day to hack the carcass of the ancient elm into pieces, uniform, smaller than the span of a man's spread arms. They stacked the bark flesh and carted it away in a truck, to a specifically designated area where it would be burned. Marta Ortega was offended and disturbed by this casual desecration. The elm had been a catalyst. It had invented its own logic and defied gravity. It had performed a remarkable feat. It deserved, at the least, an actual burial.

Then she walking, the cement beneath her feet swaying, liquid. The air tastes of sand, rock, bits of fish flesh and blood rising into a sea breeze of intoxicated ginger and wine-scented vines. It is these inexplicable conjunctions which cause the inexorable rot and burnout which is actually turning the planet, Marta realizes. It is this that generates electricity and hurricanes and all the ideas of women and men, the chaos, the genius and the mundane. It is a shifting of paradoxes, a random assortment of unresolvable artifacts and emotions, all of them brief, transitory and resisting contours.

Consuelo López, in the obscenely pink wooden house at the bottom of the sloping hill that had become Flores Street, who dwelled within an atrocity she herself had painted, offers a partial smile in her direction. The house is not the color of lipstick, Marta realizes, but the pink of genitals. It is not alluring or decadent but merely strange and pathetic.

The young woman is pale, drawn, thinner than Marta Ortega remembered, and oddly vacant. It is after nine in the morning and Consuelo López is still wearing a bathrobe, her hair uncombed. Her feet are bare and soiled. It is a posture instantaneously decipherable, indisputable, this precise arrangement of details unchanged from antiquity. This is the rendering of a dominion bereft, simultaneously turbulent and listless, stricken and dazed.

Pobrecita, Marta Ortega thinks, deciding she will not exchange platitudes with Consuelo López but rather continue her journey, the planting of her feet into the strips of cement bobbing like buoys on the surface of waters. I have nothing to give you, Marta recognizes. Ask consejos of a pebble, a mute or a lunatic. I will not even tell you to compose lists or to be tranquil and calm.

She is aware of the eyes of Consuelo López hot at her back as once she had felt the sun of La Paz watching her. She was being driven north by her grandchildren to a mission in a pueblo where she discovered that she had always lived.

And the eyes of Consuelo López are twin suns behind her. Consuelo López had waited two years for her lover to come to her from Mexico. There were obstacles, reversals, gulfs and acres of ambiguous communications. Consuelo had inhabited an abscess of private grief, her nights bloated with forbidden botánica candelas while the lights of her front windows blazed like lasers.

Now her lover was finally with her. Marta Ortega intuits that Consuelo López has experienced her version of Rome and Paris, Mexico City and the islands of the Caribbean. Always, Angelina and Orquídea were disappointed. After the airport, the cab driving aimlessly through miles of orange-terraced projects, clothing drying everywhere, forming a web between balconies. And the plants pushing out of old oilcans on cell-like cubicles, the disabled cars abandoned on patches of irregular lawn. The air steaming greasy as a vague breeze pushed the fronds of the palms growing alongside wooden shacks, growing beside fruit stands, gas stations, pizza parlors.

Consuelo López realizes that her lover lacks the sheen, the durability and the promise of the photographs. But Consuelo López is different from Marta Ortega's daughters. She does not send this flawed object back, does not have her billing adjusted, take her credit and disappear into another dimension.

The man for whom Consuelo López prayed on her knees in the church of Nuestra Señora de los Dolores and made illicit visits to botánicas spends days merely sitting on the front porch of the pink wooden house. It is rumored he refuses to work, to find a tío or primo who knows of a restaurant where he can ask white women and men whether they desire more water or coffee, refuses to cut vegetables in a kitchen or unload trucks in night depots where no questions are asked.

On Flores Street, it is noted that on blistering hot days he wears long-sleeved shirts. His arms must bear a self-inflicted deformity, like the tattoos engraved in flesh by tiny metal needles. It is said, in whispers, that he sticks a brown substance into his arms with syringes. He forages in the night like a dog, seeking not bones or edible creatures, which would be natural, but rather latches which can be broken and houses which will offer him watches, bracelets, televisions, silver.

Of course, marriages are like the sea, Marta thinks, with cycles soft as green porcelain, as seamless lagoons. And there are seasons of merciless storms when the currents rage savage, confused and abusive. All couplings are a sculpting by battering and caress. This is the way shores and beaches, cliffs and babies are formed. And the colors are never as compelling or vivid, the outlines not as well defined, as the postcards. Always, there is a clutter, a scattering of unexpected debris, a waiting in line for the museum, the palaces and plazas which prove to be merely buildings after all, an assemblage of stones, magic gone. There is merely water, bridges, ports, the infestation of souvenir stands, the air stained.

One day Consuelo López would awaken bruised, pack a bag, plan a divorce. She would walk to the corner of Alvarado and Sunset Boulevard and either go or stop. No one could predict such a matter. The decision would be based upon the unique qualities of the moment, the angle and density of the sun or clouds, the scent in a hallway, a radio on a balcony, the way the wind does or does not move. What appeared to be choice was accident, a response to a subliminal current, nothing more.

Perhaps Consuelo López would perceive that the edifices were edged with rust and the nests of long-extinct birds. A bus would appear bearing the number 6. Consuelo López might have no idea what it meant, not the inscription and not the purpose of the huge metal machine. She might run from such a monster. Her head would contain no vocabulary to describe the object she would enter or let pass. It was possible Consuelo López would decide the earth was not as she remembered, with its odd slant and foreign alphabet. And Consuelo López would recognize the vehicle as her means of escape, of entering an entirely different configuration, or she would not. The doors would slide apart, yes, and Consuelo López would climb the steps and venture into the unknown or she would not. Later, after the bus passed, perhaps Consuelo López would toss a coin and, depending upon how the metal disc fell, decide to kill herself or else spend the morning shopping.

Decisions are a manifestation of the ebb and flow, a symptom of how

we drift, Marta Ortega recognizes as she turns the corner to Sunset Boulevard. And Consuelo López and her dog husband are insignificant in all
that is now forever behind her.

And compasses and charts of the latitudes and stars cannot save you.
Penances and offerings, mathematics and intuition, astrologers, chests of
gold, books, feathers, parchments and discs of music cannot save you. Not
the songs of women floating through inflamed lips, their misery a hotter
gash of fire in the darkness. Or decoding the language of stars, the history
of individual trees and their sagas which rise across gashes of pavement
and alleys, that merge with clouds and are taken across continents webbed
with the sheets women have strung between terraces and courtyards, no,
this cannot save you.

Marta Ortega pauses in front of the courtyard of Neustra Señora de
los Dolores. She remembers when it was built. There were three houses
on what had just become a paved Flores Street and she was still married
to Salvador Velásquez. The church had loomed before her then, elegant
and remarkable, her own personal outpost from God.

As she stands in front of the church, she feels no implications from
Dios, no intimation of an other. The church is small and shabby, the paint
browning. It occurs to Marta Ortega that everything is weathering badly.
It is a phenomenon born not from smog, smoke, flames, ash, sin or spray
cans polluting the air but rather from absurd promises and self-inflicted
obligations, the distorted expectations and inhibitions worn on the inside,
like a cage within the skin.

The church is debased beige. Nuestra Señora de los Dolores has assumed the color and texture of its flock, of its decades of conventional
confessions from tiny hearts which tremble at the unusual, fear expressions of mystery and long to placate the fluctuations of the soul, the
ambiguities and paradoxes. The church has been draped in insignificance,
like the women and men who imagine only identifiable transgressions and
wafer-sized absolutions. Even the aged avocado and orange trees in the
courtyard, with their roots tearing at the wall, forcing eruptions in the
bricks, seem shorn of vibrancy. Here, there are only seams and borders.
The designs are deliberately derivative, repetitive without resonance, bold
strokes, ambition or risk.

Marta Ortega realizes that such confessions are a monotony which render the padres numb. After a certain succession of bells and masses and predictable admissions, the priests become bitter, arbitrary with their penances, in a world where everyone is named Juan and María and there is no delirium, vehemence or dazzling deviation, merely a dense mediocrity like a stalled and aggressively stagnant sea. This is the geography of sunken mountain ranges and abandoned ports. And the men commit acts of banal infidelity, motivated not by a desire for flesh or pleasure but for accumulation, quantity and number. And their women commit sins of idolatry. This design is a contrivance, a region where one discovers nothing which is not already known and the world is one of careful restatement, cells within cells.

"Muy tranquila, María, con calma," the aged Padre Pérez in the church of her baptism and marriage, in the pueblo of her birth, had said. Now she appreciates his gesture. It was an effort for him to speak, to offer indifferent, shallow phrases rather than to say what sat heavy and irrefutable as a stone in the center of the place where he once had a heart. He longed to open his lips, to hear spill from his mouth, I know nothing, I am tortured by my own transgressions. I have failed absolutely. You would do better to ask consejos of a torn leaf, a beggar, a blind man, a drunk.

And Gloria Hernández had attended confession and mass shortly before she murdered the white clerk, Marta remembers. Surely the words of Gloria Hernández blazed with rage, contempt, images of a continent of insinuating reds, radiant and edged. Her terrain was alien and she was unequipped, her mouth damned, a well of delirium, insistent and fluid. Perhaps she let only syllables which were innocuous, dulled uniform by the grid, drift from her lips. Gloria Hernández sought solace and relief. Her fever intensified. Grace was denied.

Consuelo López often went to Nuestra Señora de los Dolores. She attended church between her journeys of sin to botánicas, between her potions and candelas shaped like men. She recited her rosary, fell to her knees and longed for her chaotic impulses to be still and meaningless as dust. And suddenly Marta Ortega remembers that Orquídea became a Catholic again and has remained one for a decade.

"It is a metaphor," Orquídea explained, softly. "A grotesque simplification, but it soothes me."

"You believe in Dios as they define him?" Marta had been curious.

"Don't be insulting," Orquídea replied. "You taught me to transcend definitions."

Marta Ortega stared at her.

Orquídea had laughed. "The grandeur of the ritual calms me. My bones are sanded. I can feel the edges again and they glisten. The connection to a collective impulse and shared belief that some things are not finite is intoxicating," Orquídea said.

Was it winter? Was Orquídea ringing the doorbell on Flores Street, clothing wet from rain? Were they drinking brandy while a wind brutalized the hill? And Orquídea was saying, "Yes, I know it is all finite. Tenochtitlán, empires and dynasties. They are chicken scrawls in dust."

"Then why?" Marta had persisted.

"I am not uncomfortable with paradox. I rub myself raw by repetition. It is purifying, like washing dishes. Surrendering to the confined and insignificant, which is also unassailable."

Was it a cold winter? Had Orquídea journeyed to Flores Street to curse her, to weep or beg forgiveness? Somewhere Orquídea said, "It is a bit like the lists we used to compose, refined and with an aesthetic element. The stained glass, the spires tall enough to trap clouds, the chants, the eruptions of magenta and amber squeezing through the chapel windows as if God had prisms for eyes and blood which could grow flowers. The linear assumptions dissolve."

Marta was silent. She was thinking about nothing and how in nothing there is a shifting of light, afternoons are sliced in two, diagonally, like a cantaloupe. Marta was thinking that after the illnesses of transformation and the exhumings, there was solace in the unspoken and the simple acceptance of night wind.

"It is practical," Orquídea had laughed. "No expeditions across continents or oceans. No hotel reservations or airport terminals. There is a shrine on every corner."

Marta Ortega had smiled. Orquídea slept now without pills or hysterical telephone calls. Her rosary rested like a rare coiled snake on her bedside table. The daughter she had refused to baptize had become a child of God of her own accord. Orquídea had done as Marta Ortega designed. Her daughter had invented herself, her own solutions and embroidery. And Marta Ortega did not argue with Orquídea. She was, in fact, satisfied.

Now she finds herself entering the church. She has not been inside a

church since she toured the mission at San Juan Bautista with her grandchildren, on their abortive northern adventure, when she understood that
she too dwelt within the walls. Yes, in the northern pueblo when she had
responded to a certain pattern, recognizing it as intrinsic to the fibers of
her skin. And Nuestra Señora de los Dolores is unexpectedly cool. She sits
in the chapel, which is deserted, watching candles burning like a field of
planted amber-flamed arrows. Amber the vigils, the longings and terror.
Amber the fever and communion.

"Señora Ortega?" She studies the padre who has entered the chapel
and silently sat down at her side. She does not know him.

"Sí?" softly.

"We have not met. I know you by reputation, of course, La Reina de
la Calle Flores," the middle-aged priest says. "La bruja del barrio."

"I have already been excommunicated," she reminds him/herself, the
candles flickering in their perpetual graves of amber, the cool dust of the
chamber, the specific details of this composition.

"A technicality, a matter for linguists and Vatican councils. We are
beyond that, no?" The padre is silent. "Would you care to engage in an
ordinary ritual such as confession?"

"Is it permitted?" Marta is curious.

"Officially, no. Neither are the botánicas, the infidelities, the betrayals,
the myriad ways we trivialize our days." The padre shrugs. His hair is still
black. "I was thinking of an informal sort of confession," he offered. "And
who knows? The mass in Spanish now, the constant invention of new
definitions, the incessant reinterpretations."

"Morality is unalterable," Marta Ortega remembers. "Only the conventions of fashion which surround it are subject to change."

"Es verdad," the priest agrees. There is a familiarity between them, an
intimacy. They share this recognition. Explanations are unnecessary. This
priest knows that many and varied are the dominions. He knows that
inspiration and purity and prayer cannot save you.

"What became of the other padre, the young one, Romero?" she
inquires.

"Romeo, he was called in the seminary," the priest remembers.

"He succumbed to the flesh?" Marta Ortega is not surprised.

"After prolonged suffering, yes."

They are silent. The candles flicker. Oceans are born, carve shorelines, lagoons, coves. Arrows and musical instruments are invented. Cities are devised and flourish. Then the trade routes shift. Hurricanes and erasures. A vanishing. The priest knows this.

"Orquídea comes here from time to time," the padre informs her, his voice soft. "Joseph and Bill before their departure. And your grandchildren in moments of crisis."

"You have an intuition," Marta Ortega recognizes.

"Why are you here?"

"I am going to die today." Marta Ortega is shocked.

"Pues?" the priest inquires.

"I have committed sins of arrogance and misperception," Marta Ortega begins.

"That is a definition of a human being, is it not?"

"I contrived to make myself immortal," Marta Ortega says. "My garden. My elaborate exclusive dialect. My perversity."

"A fantasy of the intellect? A corruption of the imagination?" The padre weighs the concurrencies and possibilities. "But was there not an integrity within this?"

Marta Ortega does not reply. The priest touches her shoulder. "You birthed and tended. You did what was required. Are you afraid?"

"No," Marta Ortega realizes.

"Do you have the power?"

"Yes," Marta Ortega replies without hesitation. This too is a revelation.

"Such a gift and a burden," the priest recognizes. "You have been restrained, Señora Ortega."

"What about Gloria Hernández?" Marta suddenly asks. "We betrayed her."

"Betrayed?" the padre shakes his head. "Always, there are realms which are disguised and inaccessible. Gloria es como tú, Dama de las Orquídeas. She is like you, an inhabitant of another area entirely. Within that other, I believe you will both be absolutely absolved." The padre's voice is firm, assured.

"This is a clarification," Marta Ortega admits. "Gracias, Padre." Then she rises and walks slowly out of the church.

Marta Ortega is following Sunset Boulevard east, the Mexican blanket folded under her arm. The street is apathetic and sullen, beaten into submission by heat, confusion, traffic and agitation, the disruption of the elements, some of which are artificial and others the residue of the human soul in transition. The air is white.

The Mexicano carnicerías and lecherías rise between the El Maya and El Azteca taco and burrito stands with their banners of "Horchatas y Aguas Frescas" brightly painted in bands of yellow and red which are familiar, reassuring. The dentistas and clínicas, the Centro Jurídico de Familia are shielded by iron gates. Advertisements offer Cubano goods, Salvadoran foods, Guatemaltecos. Their texture is slightly different, as the fragrance of a white rose is from that of one which is yellow or pink.

The density of restaurants and stores offering productos Latinos is overwhelming. In this world, one consumes obsessively, trying to fill the sense of the void with the tangible of enchiladas, carne asada and chile verde. And there are women in the carnicerías and pastelerías, young and already fattening, the women eat at intersections, overripe, trapped.

Marta Ortega notes the profusion of botánicas with their Artículos Religiosos, their Consejos Espirituales, their plastic replicas of saints and cards to predict el futuro. And the women, obese with inarticulate rage, cluster at the counters, purchasing potions to induce love, inflame the blood, entrance and bind.

As she walks, Marta is aware of numerous storefront churches. Iglesia de Dios, Iglesia Evangélica Latina and Iglesia de Dios Pentecostal. These new churches squat below old brick buildings, their crosses embossed on windows covered by plywood. Everywhere, murals are painted, on cement strips alongside schools, beside freeway entrances, bridges, steps. Brown faces in the acts of battle and prayer, their bodies draped in primary colors, in this world of red and blue and yellow.

Nightclubs with música tropical y disco wear red and yellow awnings over their carved wooden doors. Iron grates web small stores with their signs of "Cambio de Cheques." Wedged between restaurants named Casa de Tacos and Casa Carnitas, Casa Michoacán and Casa Veracruz, tiny stall-like shacks flaunt their "Fotos Para Pasaporte." This is a world where everyone is eating and journeying. And, always, the inducement of "Cerveza" and the implication that the unformed gaps can be filled with liquids, meats in hot sauces and an airplane ticket.

Between Raúl's Beauty Salon and Margarita's Coiffeurs, Rubén and Alberto's Barber Shop, haircutting parlors define themselves in an Oriental

script. And between the tacos and burritos stands, restaurants offer Viet-
namese and Chinese dinners, markets promise Thai and Korean goods,
Filipino and Japanese spices and newspapers. And the wooden and stucco
churches with their small white crosses announce services in the languages
of Asia.

This is the confluence of Los Angeles now, Marta Ortega recognizes.
The conjunction of the Spanish and the Pacific, etching an unforeseen
configuration. The arrival of more gods, with their unique shrines and
postures of supplication. Yes, an invasion of rare spices and combinations,
some from farther south and others from across the ocean.

Marta Ortega is sensitive to this assertion of the Pacific in the visible
structures and in the intangible, the sense of old women with yellowish
skin planting seeds smuggled from a vastly different climate and architecture. They have brought calendars which have years assigned not to saints
but to dragons and tigers, roosters, dogs and oxen. This is a future she will
not see. Marta Ortega dismisses it.

The sky is a drained blue, birdless, seamless, it could be composed
of a sheet of thin metal or tin, a construction cognizant of only the surface
of necessity, a fabric which is a contrivance of durability without variation
or tenderness. And on each hillside and street, bungalows of wood or
stucco squat like scorched camellias on slats of browned lawns. This is La
Reina de los Angeles as she has known it. Still, Marta Ortega is unprepared for the density of this specific composition, its incessant duplication,
its miles of nearly identical rooms facing their mirror images, uniformly
graying, ignorant, mute.

Marta Ortega is crossing alleys of bougainvillea. Insistent yellow and
orange canna stud paths between walled courts. Palm-slatted shade falls
angular across rooms where walls are a debased beige, lashed by barking
dogs, sirens, salsas and laments. There is the smell of frijoles and children
and crucifixes. Women bulge out of themselves as if to numb an insatiable
emptiness, a well of anger that gnaws, physical, eating them alive from
within. Marta Ortega is intimate with this design and its constant repetition.

There is a seepage, a loss of color and distinct outline in this cluster-
ing. It is obvious on the stained surface and a symptom of a similar ruin

beneath. There are no longer any sacraments, not in the pueblos of the jungle or in the capitals, not in this Los Angeles or any other city. Blood and marriage, rites and magic are ineffective. There are no idols, no incantations, no combination of the elements which can provide solace.

Here, women and men sleep as they walk, as they wait, perpetually, for birth or buses which transport them to jobs of no significance. The posture of apathy and stasis in a world where only televisions, radios and dogs speak. Women and men drift catatonic in cycles of long silence punctuated by sudden flurries of violence. And the church bells, the rosaries, the random acts of sex with strangers and the sporadic spilling of blood bring no revelation. And she was wearing a wide-brimmed hat, Enrique said. He could not actually see her face. There were trumpets, shadows, confetti.

Suddenly Marta Ortega is jolted by the realization that Enrique had deliberately averted his eyes from the face of the woman in the wide-brimmed hat who was dancing in the arms of her husband. Her brother had been stunned by this flagrant public violation. He had shut the eyes within his heart, turned his head away, automatically, as one does from the scene of an accident. She underestimated his discretion. She should have forgiven him decades ago, she recognizes, with a sadness, a wavering, a pain which passes immediately. There are no more rearrangements.

Marta Ortega stands transfixed at the corner of Sunset and Alvarado Boulevard. Traffic lights go green, amber and red. They are similar to stars, she realizes, stars being born, aging and dying. They are green as infants, then amber in an adulthood of subtleties and sculpted flesh, amber with cravings for the ineffable and finally red as they grew bloated with wisdom, rage and transgressions, their bodies in flame. Red as they prepared to explode, to become nova, nada, to return to the belly of the void where they would rest as silent green particles and green veils in space. The womb would receive an impulse, an inspiration, and gather them individually, with delicate precision. They would be reborn, fresh spheres with a capacity for seas and swamps, jungles and pyramids, sharks and moths and cobras. Young worlds with distinctive seasons of innovation and necessity.

She studies the traffic lights executing their diminuative lives, their limited but remarkable cycle of green and amber and red, green and amber and red, hypnotic as the rhythm of oceans and the syllables of wind. It is a juncture, the opening of a door, a mouth.

How simple it is, Marta thinks. We turn a corner, answer a letter and the course of a life or a generation is changed. It happens at noon under an erratic radiant white sun. It occurs at intersections of bougainvillea and iron-grated liquor stores, stucco sides embossed with spray paint in the graceful script of local hoodlums. The fundamental and yet utterly inexplicable, why we chose that tourist hotel or flower shop, why that dawn, that jade-green polished summer lagoon, that port, that apartment building, that particular man and not some interchangeable other.

No, she will not return to the river of her youth, she decides, or let it be decided for her. She is the vessel, a leaf or a shell or a sail. The substance moves through her as a current, steering her away from Sunset Boulevard and toward Alvarado. Of course the river would be erased of meaning. It would speak as ash speaks, that which is limbless. Sun had baked it clean of memories or yearning, of the aspiration for revelation or vengeance. It was rageless. And the river too was behind her.

She will walk to the park with the lake instead. Years before, her grandchildren had insisted upon a picnic. They had prepared a basket of fruit and sandwiches. She sat on the grass, surrounded by the children of her daughters, the second cycle of birthings dressed to mirror their misconception of pueblo Indios, guerrilleros and putas. Her hybrids, glittering in beads, in hand-stitched garments which formed moons and flowers. They were a ring around her. She was the centerpiece, the jewel.

There had been a certain connection that day, beyond the obvious circle of generations etching itself on the deep-green face of the grass. Her guerrilleros and gitanas were playing guitars, singing their own compositions about women with hair black as the feathers of rain-wet birds and planning journeys to ashrams in India, temples in Japan, shrines in regions with customs and climates too alien and inaccessible for her to seriously consider.

It must have been a Sunday. Beyond the circle of her grandchildren, on a nearby bridge, a bride and groom stood while a photographer took one picture after another. The bride wore a traditional white dress with a train and a longer avenue of white veil. Bridesmaids were walking wild iris in gowns of purple taffeta. Wind rustled their amethyst skirts. There were water lilies in profusion beneath the wooden bridge. Young boys maneuvered boats between outcroppings of weeds and rock. Children were pushed in swings embedded in a patch of sand near the lakeshore.

Marta Ortega had been struck by the languages rising and drifting from the surface of the lake. That day, the lake had a mouth, yes. From the parted lips she heard English and Spanish in numerous varieties, the accents slightly different as are the songs of birds. An English at times exceptionally angular and severe, sharp as northern architecture. A Spanish strangely fragrant, curved like islands or peninsulas dense with spice. She heard what might be Chinese, and then a kind of Slavic, and, in the wind, dialects she could not identify. Her grandchildren did not seem aware of these disparate alphabets, these gulfs and eddies, magnificent with possibilities. They were talking of Tibet and Java, the Himalayas and the Andes.

Her hybrids were discussing the strategy of their pilgrimages. They would procure passports, pack bags which could be worn on the back, wear white clothing the sun would accept and caress as they sought revelation across the Pacific or Atlantic Ocean. Her grandchildren were chattering, and suddenly Marta Ortega was disturbed. It seemed incredible that they did not realize they were, at that precise instant, sitting in a city park planted at the exact vortex of the world, at a rare and unrepeatable opening where the ordinary dissolved in a chaos of infinite articulation. No, her grandchildren did not recognize the significance of that particular afternoon, the mixtures of blood and gods and alphabets, the confusion of channels and climates which comprised the city of their birth, which was irrefutably Los Angeles defining herself.

By tilting her head, she could imagine the city park where she sat to be any miniature palm-draped lake in any tropical city. A plaza in Caracas or Mexico City, San Juan, San Salvador or Havana. Marta Ortega had been startled, realizing then, by implication, that the city of her birth was neither Mexican nor American but rather the capital of another sort of region, an area defined not by maps or borders but by scent, rhythm and texture. It was a demarcation of the sensibility and perception. There were verdant latitudes cutting across nations and continents, centuries, fashions, armies, time and debris. Here, where the indigenous could not be erased.

Wind rustled the palm fronds and the gypsy dresses of her granddaughters and the purple taffeta skirts of the bridesmaids posing for the photographer on the arched wooden bridge rising across the mouth of the world. A hot wind pulled at the long white veil of the bride, standing at a juncture of worlds in a city which was the capital of a region called the palm latitudes.

Marta Ortega regretted that her grandchildren failed to sense the exotic juxtapositions surrounding them, the familiarity of the design, the deviations and mutations. Resolution opened like a fan, a door or a portal where they sat. It was in the air above them, definitive as calligraphy. It drifted across the waters of the lake. Yet they remained oblivious, ignoring this startling composition, resisting the intimation of revelation and babbling about Nepal and Maui.

Then one of her guerrillero grandsons chanced to glance at the lake, the bridge, the tender breeze tossing the folds of the gown of the bride. He observed the just-married couple and laughed. "Six months from now, he'll be kicking the shit out of her," this red-bandana-headed hybrid announced. "He'll have a mistress burning candelas for him, and a whore on Saturday nights."

"Apologize for cursing them," Marta Ortega had demanded.

The boy with the red bandana and the guitar, with strings of tin beads and eyes dense with Java or the pyramids of the Yucatán looked startled. "No one heard," he said softly.

"I heard. The air and palm trees heard. The ducks and water lilies," Marta Ortega assured him. "God and history heard," she added, for emphasis.

The boy with a red bandana across his forehead, the son of a father who had run away with his receptionist from Kansas, a woman who could not spell the word *neurotic*—or was he sired by a Viking who proved to be a lunatic, by a dress-store owner or by a professor of history?—had said, "Lo siento, Abuela. I meant no offense. I apologize."

"No, not to me, idiota," Marta Ortega had replied, calmer. To the confluence of worlds you are obliviously sitting on. To the channels and eddies etching stunning equations at your feet. To the door which would open if you let it, the chamber into a region you could enter that has no name. Las latitudes de las palmas, tu tierra natal, she thought, the kingdom which you were born to. The realm of the multifarious accidents which constitute you. The palm latitudes, where no passport is required.

Her grandson separated himself from their circle. Marta Ortega watched him walk with measured steps through the park, alone, stooping to dip his hands into the warm waters of the lake, rising to touch the fronds of palms. He rubbed the grass and the water weeds. He studied the clouds, then the shadows, straining for clarity, as if sensing an intangible other. When he rejoined his relatives, he sat on the periphery, subdued, frightened and perplexed by his experience with exile and the persistent intuition that there was something fundamentally significant he had somehow failed to perceive.

As Marta Ortega turns down Alvarado Boulevard, as she changes purpose and direction, she realizes lives are a record of such variations, of incidents camouflaged as innocuous and inconsequential. Viewing the phenomenon with her expanding context, she recognizes that these deviations are the expression of the substance itself, the individual moments accumulating and forcing the great nothing into temporary shape, continuous, unceasing.

The horizon is virescent, the impulse concurrent in water and air. Space is laden with messages, letters strewn in leaves, sentences strung between branches, epics unfolding like pages of a book, entire texts embossed across the underbelly of clouds stalled above a lawn.

Perhaps these were the hieroglyphics which consumed Gloria Hernández as she stood mesmerized at her front-room windows. It was not stupidity but an intuition of the substance, the process, the relentless music, now temperate and measured, now nonsymmetrical and turbulent.

She could have told Gloria Hernández that to hear voices is not enough. They must be orchestrated, taught technique, made to lie at your feet like the tamed beasts they are. She might have explained to Gloria Hernández that her season of bloodless beheadings would pass. Her chairs and tables would again master gravity. The snakes coiled along the living room would leave on their own accord. And the snake charmer with his wicker basket.

Growth is slow and misleading. One morning, you call yourself dog, then worm, boy, bouelvard, stone. There are long arcs when we are immune to failure. Eventually the outlines harden. Shadings, beige and orange, appear between the edges. You discover that the ambiguities of your personal history are ordinary, an abundance and a shearing no different from a tree. It rains. Your roots drink and you sense an acceleration. Afternoons are erased of terror. The sky slopes at a bearable angle, cleansed of cataclysm and the monsters of invention. One day, as if without effort, you recognize a purification. You will survive.

She could have told Gloria Hernández that all awakenings stun. Walls reveal their contempt for fraudulent mystery. One encounters the density of reality head on. But one can lose only one's third eye. One can be lucky. Then she could have shown Gloria Hernández the secret of the litany of the lists.

"Listas de qué?" the pretense of dead rock would have asked, her eyes the color of stagnant wells and mud, of vacant lots where winds collapse and the lungs are a sculpture of dust.

"Lists of all you value and love," Marta Ortega could have suggested. "You begin with A, of course, which can be amethyst, amazement or absolution. B which is brilliance or..."

Gloria Hernández, with her moonlike disguise, her contrivances of barren fields and dried seas, would have said, "No me gusta nada."

"Then create lists of all you hate. The poisons and evil. The stalled sea breezes which have savaged you and rendered your mouth useless. A is America, mi amor, a region you never craved. B might be Barbara Branden, that accident, that happenstance who moved into the house next to yours. C as in cooking and cleaning and caring, for the chains and cells of your motherhood, your wife years. D is the desires you cannot express because the magnitude of the subliminal incantation has flooded your lips and you are awed by plentitude. E is for English, that language of points and angles, of compasses lodged in the tongue. F is for what?"

"Fear," Gloria Hernández might have replied, her first word like a faint shudder of thunder before a storm, a rumbling which is indistinct, hallucinatory.

"And G?" Marta would have prodded, gently, letting her tone and eyes say, This afternoon is like all others, long and without edges or borders. We are women stitching the shoreline of a continent. There is no reason to hurry.

"G is for Gloria. I loathe her lies, her private drowning. And H is for her, all of the hers, pasteled and laughing in lobbies. I is for the invoices across my thin gray metal desk, invoices which are slabs of sheared skin, as if, on the floor above our windowless room, unwanted children were being separated from their flesh, infants perhaps, without anesthetic. J is for Jesus, whom I hate and curse. Then kissing, Los Angeles, men, night, outside. You are surprised that I can recite the alphabet? P is for promises which are lies and Q is for queers like your Joseph and Bill who have invented a terrain of sin, of the defective and twisted and whom you accept."

I should have filled a glass with orange juice or horchata, Marta Ortega realizes. I should have said, "That was excellent, Gloria. What about R?"

"Rape," Gloria Hernández could have replied. And in the continuing, in the forming of her words which were a network, a structure, she might have again connected to her orbit and axis. "And rage and roses and Rome, where the priests live. S is for the suffering. T is for traffic. Then U is for under the house where the waters I alone see rush and churn, their sound an obscenity, like a fat man eating. U is for the universe God did not intend to create and still regrets, this universe which stained his hands. Then V for the medals of valor my husband has discarded."

"That was wonderful, Gloria. You will have another glass of horchata? It was made only this morning. What about W?"

"White women on billboards with their white teeth and skin which is like a cream that shines, a form of alluring armor. White anything, particularly white which is soiled and used like my shoes and the ruined courtyard walls of Nuestra Señora de los Dolores which now repel me. W is for walls, notably walls without windows. And W is for women who wear skirts transparent as insect wings and flaunt their knees and laugh in elevators. They smoke cigarettes and wear high-heeled shoes. Their feet are gardens, lilac and peach. You expect them to turn the ground where they walk into perfume. W is for winter, the wind, the way the street froze the afternoon Barbara Branden arrived with her moving truck, unchaining the last of the air."

"X and Y and Z are difficult, Gloria," I might have explained, Marta Ortega thinks. "Would you prefer to begin again with A?"

"Still you think me dull," Gloria Hernández might have said and laughed. "X is for Xanadu, a kingdom which does not exist, like heaven and hell, grace or the sanctity of marriage. Y is for youth and yearning and yellow hair, like the blond curls Barbara Branden brazenly lets the winds caress, the yellow strands I detest, individually, one by one. Z is for zero, of course, which I am, empty, nothing, gutted. I cast no shadow."

"That was exceptional," I could have encouraged, poured horchata, inquired whether she would please begin again. It is one slow syllable at a time that turns worlds. I should have known this, Marta Ortega recognizes.

Perhaps Gloria Hernández would have agreed, leaned back in her chair and let their eyes meet. "A is for your Angelina and her posture of arrogance, her acres of carelessness, how she says without words she could never control her eyes, with their compulsion to open like sails in the wind, to widen and drink it in. Your flesh sculpture, Angelina, who is a biologist of disaster. Her middle name is ruin. She is the epicenter. She considers herself an astonishment. Beneath her silk, she is hollow. And A is for angels who are corrupt, the constructions of white men, a contagion in the clouds. B is for boys, my sons and all others. Then crazy and crippled and catatonic, which I am."

"C is also for cure and cleansing which I will demonstrate for you," I should have vowed, Marta Ortega admits. Her regret is an agony.

Yes, Marta Ortega thinks, yo, La Reina de la Calle Flores. Yo, La Dama de las Orquídeas, recombining the skins and faces of flowers. I was the woman with the scalpel, the monumental spindles of thread. My fingers were cactus and needles, more articulate than her madness.

"You are on D," I should have said, including her in my composition.

"D is the devil, watching me in the night, his breath of scales and dead fish salt against my flesh. E is the eagles my husband and sons discuss, the significance of which no one has bothered to explain to me. F is for the force of his flesh, swollen, cruel and ugly, and the penetration which is a wifely obligation I long to be freed from. Then grace, grandeur and gratitude, qualities I will be denied in this life but not necessarily in others. H is the heat. I is the ice of the village of Barbara Branden's birth, the ice she loves and the white sheets I would bury her bones beneath. J is for Jesus whom I hate twice. Then K is for the kites my sons desire and which I will never purchase. My sons, with their private alphabet of eagles and tigers and raiders and steelers and rams. My sons with their kingdom of animals and renegades, their secret fascinations and how they have erased me. If they procured their own kites, I would tear and burn them. You realize they think me ignorant?"

"We are more sensitive, you and I. Inhabitants of another realm entirely. We know the configurations the substance forms," I should have offered, Marta Ortega acknowledges. I should have made my voice an anchor, my embrace a port. Be moored at my breast. Yo, la bruja del barrio. "You are on L."

"L is for living and the suffering of it, how I wish to simply shed my flesh, allow vultures to scatter my bones and be done with it. M is for Miguel, my husband who I also wish would die, painfully, in the tradition of the Yaqui, by having the soles of his feet removed, there in the high grounds of wind and rock, beneath a hierarchy of clouds in an area God abandoned. N is for the nothing that I am. And O is for your Orquídea and your rows of orchids and all things that proclaim their beauty dramatically. Yes, your Orquídea, with her passport fingers, her nights warm as wood burning and the moon above her in permanent estrus. She thinks herself a phenomenon, spectacular as an artifact. She is pathetic. And you seem pale, Marta Ortega. P is for your paleness and priests whom I particularly detest with their pretenses and penances and propaganda. Q is the quicksand where I dwell in solitude, invisible. R is for the remembering and rearranging of the world into coherent form, an activity which requires the hours of my days. S is for studying, my sons sitting at the dining-room table above their American books, staring at the English inscriptions which they think will bring them answers, security and resolution. T is for the tunnels I have torn beneath the earth, under the house where Barbara Branden lives, and one day these corridors will collapse and swallow her. And T is for the skin of tigers which white women on billboards are draped in. Their images consume hills. Tight their dresses, taut their paper skin. And T is for their teeth which are white, invulnerable as marble or granite which time itself cannot violate. Then unhappiness, unworthiness, and waiting and walking up the hill of Flores Street, walking from my bus to a house where I no longer live. A house infested by herds of animals where my husband and sons are bewitched by a white woman."

It was possible Gloria Hernández could have been cured of her mania and venom, Marta Ortega concludes. I could have absorbed and transformed it, Marta thinks. But I dismissed Gloria Hernández as inarticulate, thick with weight and bereft of imaginative gestures, the capacity for invention or song.

Marta Ortega realizes she has become accustomed to the flamboyant expression, to the pitch that is Angelina and Orquídea and their children. Her internal vision has been corrupted by exaggeration, deformed by an excess of the lush. Her range has grown limited. There are entire tones she does not hear. Wails, screams, lamentations and curses have rendered her numb. The tempestuous has become the mundane. She sees only the flagrantly singular. I am an instrument profoundly out of tune, she admits. I no longer hear the whisper, the soft moan, the estranged stray syllable beseeching with grace, undemanding, patient and enduring. I know only that which insists with red, threatens and seeks the ruthless, the danger-ous, the embers and the edge.

Marta Ortega recognizes that, like Angelina and Orquídea, she ex-pected revelation to arrive with bullets and drums, a colossal radiance and a chorus of dancing girls. She had assumed that definition would rise like a sudden rumbling earthquake, irrefutable. Now it occurs to Marta Ortega that the remarkable is ordinary, is merely an expression of the ebb and flow, coming with and without trumpets and confetti, often in stillness, camouflaged, amorphous.

Of course nothing is abstract, Marta Ortega recognizes. The passing seasons inescapably etch our flesh with the same precision and dispassion accorded to the trunks of trees. The circular planets have a purpose to their dance. That is why we wear the rings of their passage. They birth and bury us as we drift on a world of water and weeds, purely incidental to the journey of stars, less than a photograph or a postcard, not even an afterthought, a footnote or echo.

Marta Ortega is aware of her exceptional clarity and sense of irresist-ible momentum. She feels the wind. It is the distillation of all the winds of her life, the first breaths of her daughters, those soft filaments rustling from their barely formed lips. It is a gulf-warm green wind which prom-ises and disappoints, turns greasy, stagnant. A wind which has lost convic-tion and become an oppression. The winds are scented with sagebrush and sand, salt-charged as the breeze which blows with vehemence from churning whitecapped bays. And she is being carried into the air like a leaf, uprooted, no longer of the earth.

Marta Ortega is quickening her pace like an exhausted beast, a horse or a mule sensing water and shade at the end of a terrible mountain trail. The lake is beckoning, its voice the tone of a flute played at dusk in rooms which are tiled, ambered, cool. Night grazes blue and hushed. Sandals brush stones smoothed by acres of smuggled silk. And the lake has the voice of one lone exiled cello and the resonance of Sunday church bells across a damp valley floor in winter at nightfall. The sound is simultaneously primitive and refined.

Of course the day at the lake with her grandchildren had been an opening into a geography measured by fragrance and implication. It had also been a confluence of time. Once, when the lake in the city park was recently formed and substantially less damaged, her first husband had taken her to ride in a freshly painted red boat across the liquid surface she had perceived as a phenomenon of blue, insurmountable as an ocean.

She had been young, not yet pregnant, a girl. Salvador Velásquez rowed the glistening red boat. The world was fluid. They were liquid and air, steam, fire and clouds. The day had been hot. The palms were draped with languor, the air amber. The red boat slid across the miniature light-blue lake, and Marta Ortega realized she had been born for the sudden pleasures. She did not intuit then the price of such pleasures, or, more sadly, their rarity.

Marta Ortega abruptly stops in front of La Flor de Oaxaca, a stylish Mexican restaurant she has never seen before. The windows are leaded glass and arched, gracefully designed, striking. The ceiling is wooden beams, studded with ferns in hanging pots, an inverted forest. The ambiance is primordial, shadowed, a door into a beginning. She is at the verge of a fantastic discovery. It has something to do with variations and recurrencies. Yes, it is always precisely the same cast of characters exchanging roles at random in an interminable drama, its theme both brilliantly improvised and unbearably predictable.

She understands the scenario in all of its nuances, permutations, shadings. The desperation and contrived excitement, the pretense of ignorance and then the inexorable spin into acceleration. She knows how it begins. One day you are watering an azalea. You are twenty-four. You turn your back, reach for a match and you are thirty-one, sitting in a bar, asking a strange man to press against you. And you're saying, I get drunk and reckless, drive my car too fast. Don't give me promises. Just show up with cash.

One dusk, in a season hot and airless, sky a dark insomniac blue, you bend above a bed of begonias, moist earth a caress at your feet. You are thirty-six. You answer the telephone or a letter and you are forty-nine or sixty. The numbers are unimportant, metaphors, an implication of the day the wind calls you by name. It is intimate with your intangible transgressions, the self-inflicted betrayals of your sensibility. It is the serpentine Rio Grande of your subconscious, forcing its way out of the suffocating dark we cling to and defend as life.

"You are La Reina de la Calle Flores," Angelina taunts her on the telephone. Angelina wants her to move to San Francisco, to live in the redwood-and-glass house on the hill overlooking the bay from an angle displaying both bridges. Marta refuses.

"I know why you won't move," Angelina screams, furious. "You are the only woman in the entire barrio who has read Freud or Lorca, attended a ballet or spent a day, voluntarily, in a museum. You surround yourself with ignorance like a fat woman with boxes of chocolates. It was cute, almost chic, in your typically eccentric style," Angelina informs her. "Now it is deliberately perverse."

"What do you expect to create here?" Orquídea demands one afternoon. She is pointing at a shelf of near-burgundy cymbidiums. Orquídea is trying not to stumble in her four-inch-high heels. "You spend your life on your knees here." Orquídea is outlining the perimeters of the back garden with a hand terminating in fingernails painted purple, lacquered and long as a kind of fan. "Are you growing emeralds? A crop of diamonds, perhaps?"

"Is it only jewelry that compels you?" Marta Ortega had asked her younger daughter.

They stared at each other. The air was a strange unraveling azure. Night fell in pastels on anchored hills solid and green as the childhood of her daughters, which she had destroyed. It was a silence of enormities and absolutes.

"What do you suggest?" Marta was interested.

Orquídea had shrugged her shoulders. "Life is a ten-cent postcard. It's gone in a flash."

Then Orquídea was driving away from the house on Flores Street, the radio in her car abusively loud, the music concurrently amplified and muted, utterly distorted. The air shattered, an exploded shell, and shards fell from the car window, the wake of noise Orquídea left behind, the splinters of sound filtering into the house, becoming part of the intangible residue.

Then it was Angelina, driving precipitously fast, turning onto the Hollywood Freeway, weaving between lanes at eighty-five miles an hour, car windows open, the radio a tortured screaming mouth. Always, her daughters courted danger. They were brazen, flagrant, in sordid phases when they lived like exiles without papers, perpetually at the edge. They designed catastrophes as if to propitiate the gods. They created their own cataclysms, committed acts of obvious self-sabotage, planted mine fields one slow seed at a time. Then they rang her doorbell, proclaiming themselves victims, mutilated, desperate for solace.

It is a montage, images floating and bobbing and swaying like tree limbs in the sea after a storm. They are blaming her, quoting her, telephoning taxicabs, gliding across the front-courtyard patio with infants and bassinets. The constant changing of apartments and names. The shuttered windows of their lives. The fluttering polished-cotton-print curtains of their lives. The iron-gated balconies above miniature suggestions of gardens of their lives. The round rattan tables and chairs behind stucco walls draped in the shadows of orange and lemon trees of their lives. The sound of wind and dogs mating and rising from the alleys of bougainvillea and flickering neon of their lives. These have been their increments.

They wanted to be singers, actresses, to wear elaborate mantillas and long-stemmed red roses in their hair, their mouths. They slept on floors, spare sofas, a vacant dusty chair and lived for months without telephones. They claimed to be that which served fate. Their allegiance was to the tides and the moon, to the random lust born above jasmine and neon. They called themselves mutations, creatures born to the green felt and dice.

"Madre, some women open their eyes on the ride," they informed her, gliding through days like glass, their feet growing invisible blades in the area where they lived, in a darkness icy past blue, past grace, glazed, almost innocent. In between, they consorted with musicians and actors who defrauded them.

Marta Ortega leans against the side of La Flor de Oaxaca Mexican restaurant. She is simply an aged half-breed woman, darkening with the years, carrying an ordinary blanket of primary colors in wide bands under her arm, a common Mexican serape. An old woman catching her breath.

The street accepts her as it would church bells, the petals of magenta crepe bougainvillea the sea breeze blows, canna, dogs, a lamppost or a palm. And I am not merely part of this landscape, Marta Ortega suddenly recognizes. I am more.

It is noon. She is without illusions. It was no better in the original pueblo, in the first village which chanced to appear from the earth, a neutral blossom, eons before the invention of nomenclature, saints, sins or plunder.

Marta Ortega does not long for clay on her face, stacks of obsidian and chipped flints, nets or sails to repair while the afternoon is stagnant, suspended. Always, senile men recite the history of the world in a monotone, a drone, worse than a priest who has lost his faith. And each slow syllable grates against the ear like a tossed stone. Boredom is fundamental, Marta Ortega realizes. And even then, they dreamed of sharper daggers and a harvest of rare feathers, hunting and skinning jaguars, barter, accumulation and more. In the exceptionally long cycles, when it took one million years to invent the wheel, women and men were stoned, burned or dismembered on the basis of transitory fashion which justified itself as knowledge, sanity, order, one hallucination of permanence or another. And Marta Ortega is aware that, at this precise instant, somewhere in the Yucatán or the mountains of Guatemala or Bolivia, a shaman's firstborn son is moving to the capital. He will drive a truck, buy a refrigerator, an electric clock, a television and a phonograph. He will consider himself intelligent and fortunate.

"Muy tranquila, María, con calma," the padre in the church in the village of her birth had said.

Marta Ortega, an old woman, indistinguishable from a legion of similarly shaped and pigmented women, glances into La Flor de Oaxaca restaurant. Within the dimly lit eating room, it is worse.

A young woman and a man sit at a round table in a corner, beneath the hanging plants, the inverted forest dense and verdant above them. The table is covered with a cloth of red linen. A white carnation floats in a thin vase beside their wineglasses. They are discussing the assets and liabilities of marriage, softly, in Spanish. The young man is talking about their relationship as if it were a country, with a surplus of raw materials, regions with borders, a fully charted typography and a projected gross national product.

The woman sitting at his side is supposed to smile. She has purchased a lipstick specifically for this occasion. She has practiced applying this shade of lilac to her lips and studied the effect from various angles. Her name might be María, Angelina or Orquídea, Olga or Angie. On this day, at this particular conjunction, this vortex and portal, it is not.

The young woman is expected to say Yes, please, come gut me. Gouge me for oil and shale. Carve and cut and own me. She is prepared to intone these phrases but finds she cannot. And this noon, for no reason she can explain, her mouth is a collapsed grid. Her lips are a river damned with asphalt. She experiences a sudden vertigo. She is stunned by the force of an inexplicable rage she cannot begin to express because she is dizzy and there are gigantic ridges of concrete in the place where she once had lilac-lacquered lips.

There is a wavering, a sense of a liquid magnitude. The young woman thinks only of rivers. She is disoriented, cold and hot. It is a malaria of the soul. It is generated by Marta Ortega, leaning against the wall of the restaurant, glancing through the window and impaling them with her eyes. And this noon, the young woman drinks four margaritas and vomits.

Later, in an hour of desperation, in a stalled dusk which seems to be the accumulation of all the suspended and broken nightfalls of her life, after she has claimed a bout of food poisoning and successfully drawn the man back to her, they will embrace. There will be a sense of trespass and enormity such as vandals must feel while desecrating a shrine. Between the woman and the man there will be a catalogue of inadequacies and a gauze of tenderness which will vanish almost immediately.

Prayers and bank accounts, cut-crystal bottles of imported musks, university degrees, clinics and preparation cannot save you. The young woman who is not named Angelina, Orquídea or María will recognize this, later, after Marta has passed.

Still, the subterranean will be exposed, will flutter, rock and sway. Perhaps the man will take a shower. The young woman will pull the window shade shut, noticing for the first time that the paint on the wall is graying, stained. A chill slices the room. She is startled. She has always detested harsh climates.

She decides to leave. She cannot remember where she put her purse, her car keys. It occurs to her that she has nowhere to go, escape is an impossibility. After all, this is where she lives, here in this stucco house or brick apartment with her pastel-print curtains, her wrought-iron balcony above a tiny slice of courtyard, an implication of a garden. This is her home. And there is flute music floating eerie and cool, a fluid blue, from a nearby terrace. The young woman is perplexed. She has never heard this instrument before, not in the three years she has inhabited this structure.

Perhaps she will recognize that her bedroom is a portal, a transformed intersection of extraordinary textures and shapes. Rivers of raw wind pitted with sharp sand and hot breezes fragrant with spice. The rivers mate, their scent is sagebrush and salt, mangoes and ginger. Perhaps the young woman will notice that her floors have turned green as moss-embossed rocks, smooth as an equation. She intuits that this is the specific configuration which often precedes rapids.

The young woman recognizes that innovation and routine, tenderness and vows, fraudulence and augury, the stripping of lies and all that is contrived cannot save you. She experiences a lucidity which feels ancient.

The young man will telephone her again, repeatedly. She will find excuses to delay their rendezvous. She will change her telephone number, cut her hair. Time will elongate. The young man becomes peripheral, partial. She forgets his name. For no reason she can explain, she will never see him again.

Of course all afternoons are confluences of happenstance, unexpected intersections, vortices of ambivalence, a mysterious geometry that is not an abnormality but organic. The impulse insists upon manifestation, demands gestures, choreography, proofs and pyramids. It rises in vines and mists across cliffs of young palms and banyan. It assumes the form of tin shacks which rains erase or stucco bungalows ringing absurd configurations which pronounce themselves cities. It is the substance expressing itself. And it is urgent, incautious and mad.

Meanwhile, on Flores Street, in the house which was never painted green, the daughter whom Orquídea has dispatched sits in the living room waiting for her abuela. Jasmine's movements are dreamlike, deliberate, as if she knows, intrinsically, there is no reason to hurry. There was a crisis, she senses, but it has passed. Jasmine removes her blue jeans, takes a hot bath and shampoos her long hair. She feels the necessity to drape her body in ritual garments. This intuition is absolutely compelling. She decides to wear a floor-length light pink cotton dress, newly purchased, never worn before. She knows her feet must be bare. She stands in front of a mirror and thinks, suddenly, of rivers.

Later, the mailman will deliver two postcards addressed to her grandmother. They are from her Tío Bill. Jasmine reads them without hesitation. The first is a photograph, dazzling with streams of what appears to be pure liquid neon leaking into a sultry purple night sky. A bruised sky, Jasmine thinks, exquisite with paradox. She reads a short inscription about the French Quarter in New Orleans, Louisiana.

"Mi amor," the message says. "We did the French Quarter. Two nights, in fact. Am en route to a pueblo where Joseph instructed me to bury him. Love. B."

The second postcard seems muted and stained. An undistinguished cannon squats on a slice of thin lawn. The handwriting is smaller this time. Jasmine must strain to decipher the letters. "Squalid beyond description here. Was not surprised to find a son & grandchildren at funeral. Always suspected J of youthful indiscretions. Am ensconced as best friend, etc. B."

Jasmine notes that the second postcard bears an address and a telephone number across the bottom border, beneath the initial of her uncle. Then she realizes her Tío Joseph has died. She puts the postcard down. She feels as if her fingers have been burned. She wonders what to do. She knows she is not to telephone her mother. She trusts this sudden intuition. Instead, she plays a Billie Holiday record. She pours herself a second glass of horchata. She leans back against the sofa cushion. Time will fill itself in, she knows.

Later, the telephone will ring. Jasmine will answer it immediately. What has been amorphous will be resolved. Jasmine anticipates the release she will experience after the definition.

"Orquídea?" a man's voice demands.

"I am her daughter, Jennifer." She pauses. "Tío Bill?"

"Where is Marta?"

"I don't know," Jennifer admits. Then, with a surge of panic, "I've been waiting for her all morning."

Jennifer feels the depth of silence between them. It is like a door opening into a chamber cold and vast, a frozen ocean perhaps. She is going to express the pain she is experiencing at the death of her uncle, her Tío

Joseph. No phrase comes to her mind which does not seem trite, empty, a form of impropriety.

"That's a good girl," her Tío Bill finally tells her. The telephone goes dead in her hands, which begin trembling. The only coherent image which rises in her mind is the desire to cut flowers and pin them in her hair.

Jennifer stands in her grandmother's garden. The sky is pale blue, unfamiliar. It seems to be a kind of river. She is placing pink camellias behind her ears. In the silence, she senses an implication of music, drumming, a flute and a haunting plaintive sound of a reed, perhaps, or the deep strings of a cello.

Her Tío Bill is telephoning her mother in San Diego. He informs Orquídea that Joseph has died. He allows Orquídea to cry. Then Orquídea becomes aware of a density in the silence which has settled between them. In this wordlessness, entire regions are born, molecule by molecule. Storms and tides are invented, hillsides terraced and erased.

The years of their lives are lying in this silence, in increments of black women singing blues, in the garden of orchids, in the channel of birth and death which has bound them. The midnights when Bill played the piano. She jitterbugged with Joseph. She practiced new dialogue with them, postures and strategies. She borrowed their car, books, souvenirs. There was a scarlet scarf from Siam. She never returned it.

Then Bill says, "Orquídea, I believe your mother has gone off to ease her body into the flesh of the earth. Will you indulge yourself in an excess of grief?"

"No," Orquídea realizes. "It would disappoint and offend her."

"It was you she loved. The garden was a metaphor. She loved you without borders or division. She loved you in this life as she will in all others. Substance is continuous."

"Yo sé," Orquídea finds herself replying, stunned by her sudden tranquility.

"To exaggerate this event would degrade and trivialize it," Bill reminds her. "She was not una santa or any permutation of its opposite."

Orquídea glances out her front window where boats are sailing drugged and lazy, like white petals drifting in a current south. "Was she a bruja?" Orquídea hears herself ask.

"What do you think?" Bill lets the question dangle.

Orquídea is confused. She does not reply. Images of death and fragrant green islands, the relics of an inspired god, orchids and infants, flood her. Her skin is imperfect. The air is water.

"Marta possessed a certain intuition and discretion," Bill said, after what seemed like an exceptionally long time, an entire eon, perhaps. "In any event, cease your hysterical searching. You will never replace her."

Bill immediately telephones Angelina in San Francisco. Their conversation is almost identical, in the phrasing of words and in the intervals of silence. "Are you going to make melodrama of the mundane?" Bill inquires, his voice sharp.

"It would be an offense to her sensibility," Angelina responds. She is surprised by her voice, calm, measured, somehow assured. "I believe she was a bruja."

"Marta said we are all continents, vast, uncharted, eccentrically indigenous. Labels and definitions will not save you." Then Bill hung up the telephone.

Now, on Flores Street, there is the momentum of accelerated activity. The granddaughter, who was Jasmine and has been transformed without warning into Jennifer, speaks to her mother, her tía. They are making airplane reservations, calling taxicabs, packing suitcases, quickly, easily. There is an order to their pace and movements. Marta Ortega is aware of this static in the periphery, but it is behind her, in a cul-de-sac where she is already dead.

Marta Ortega is passing a five-story red-brick apartment building which has assumed the texture and scent that is an accumulation of a particular form of misery and the passing seasons which are raw and blistering. Here, women and men are vulnerable, stunned, chaotic. A combination of disappointments, sun and wind and silence has nested in the brick itself. The building is now a tenement. The bricks have been bleached of their original red connections to the earth. The building is a shell, and the women and men who dwell within it are severed from the world as it is ordinarily known. The windowpanes are broken. There is a pervasive sense of a tearing and a weeping, of rituals which are private and useless. Marta Ortega perceives this structure as the unmistakable manifestation of exile.

She is drawn by the sound of radio music erupting from a fourth-floor window behind a partially tiled balcony. There are no curtains. Julio Iglesias is singing about the curvatures of love. Marta Ortega observes a woman in a beige nylon slip standing in silhouette. Near her, a man smokes a cigarette, crosses in front of the window, shirtless, and walks into the shadows consuming the recesses of the room, in this region where darkness is pronged and dangerous.

The woman is staring at the man, yearning for him to recognize that her eyes are lined not with common chalk but with a more exotic substance called kohl. She imagines that a former lover smuggled this gray chalk for her from a country of mountains and veiled women across the ocean. She wishes the man to notice she is anointed with gifts. Of course she is the one he has always longed for, the woman waiting perfect and alone in a Mexico City or Los Angeles nightclub. The woman with clean flower-print sheets and a slice of city view, a window which looks out upon a wall of wine-colored flowers and two ancient palms. The woman with the red-painted mouth which could open and change his life.

The man is barely aware of the woman's physical presence. Her layerings, her interior architecture and psychological dimensions do not interest him. Perhaps he is thinking about his wife in a northern province of Mexico, how he broke his hand when he attempted to punch her and she glided from his fist and he hit the wall instead. He is curious whether the baby she was carrying was a son and whether she is going to divorce him, officially. The man is considering boxing results and a bet he may have lost. He is wondering whether it would be possible to simply pretend this wager did not occur, to vanish from certain cantinas and street corners. He is trying to remember, precisely, how much money he has in his pocket. It occurs to him that this woman might take it. He has made love to her on several occasions, but their connection is one of random necessity. The man is not certain he knows her name. That is why he addresses her as corazón or querida.

Something is disturbing him. The man concludes that this annoyance is somehow connected to the radio. He turns it off.

Later the woman will wear a chenille bathrobe, a pale pink, bleached by years of machine washing, soft as muslin. She will brush her brittle dyed reddish hair. She knows that the potion she is opening is ridiculous. The appearance of youth cannot be purchased in a bottle for three dollars. Such a combination would be far more expensive. Still, the act of rubbing the bótanica-herb–scented lotion into her flesh is soothing. It is an insignificant ritual of purity for which she expects and receives nothing.

Her name might be Angelina or Orquídea or María. On this particular midday, it isn't. She is thirty-six years old and thinks this man, who does not actually know her name, might be her last, her final chance for a connection. Not marriage, of course, but a continuity. She has imbued this man with qualities which are, without exception, the product of her conventional imagination.

The woman drinks too much, has twice been dismissed from jobs, even sewing in the fabric factories. She crashed a car she had borrowed and finds she cries abruptly, without provocation. She recently sent her son to live with her cuñada in Sacramento. For the time being, until she finds another apartment, new employment. She does not mention the school which telephoned her. They had discovered the bruises on the stomach and thighs of the boy and threatened to report this to la policía, La Migra. The woman cannot sleep, smokes one cigarette after another, watches television constantly and trembles.

This man will finish the last beer, angry there are no more. He suspects that this nameless woman drank one. The thought of this enrages him. Then he will take the woman from behind, simply, as one mounts an animal. Quick and relatively clean and it will be done.

Then the woman will cross the room, switch off the kitchen light and suddenly sway. She will be seized by a violent vertigo and nearly fall from the fourth-floor balcony as the air dampens, as the walls become shapeless as sails at the edge of a horizon.

It will occur to her that rooms and walls are transitory, symbolic, meaningless without the consent of shared context. She can no longer consent. Then she begins screaming.

Later, after the clinics or the bloodletting, the potions of ground moth wings and cow intestines, the reciting of entire rosaries, the electric shock to the brain or the dancing all night around a campfire with rattles, after the yellow and blue pills or whatever happens to be the local custom and current fashion, the woman will find herself intangibly altered. One noon, in a suspended summer of excessively burgundy flowers in a plaza flaunting a plaque for a saint with a record of redundant and marginal acts, the woman will say, "I lost control, that is all."

That is not all. After the various treatments and the transformation, she will recognize that she stumbled through an unexpected gulf. It is possible she will intuit that it was merely a stitch in the fundamental fabric, a wavering caused by an aged mestizo carrying a common Mexican serape who quietly passed on the street below her, on an avenue chosen by happenstance and accident. Perhaps the woman in the plaza of burgundy flowers longs to say, "It was a refinement in the composition, that is all."

Marta Ortega stands on a fantastic mesa. The recognizable borders between object and event have dissolved. She is walking on weeds, floating leaves, bits of grass, slabs of concrete bobbing like streamers of colored paper across an infinity of agitated waters.

Then the brick tenement is behind her. She is walking, glancing at the familiar pattern of rows of beige-and-brown bungalows perched tentative on small squares of lawn behind courts with hedges and gates. This config-uration is deliberate. It is designed to reinforce what is alien, insular, that which can be measured only in increments of human blood.

In hallways, unshaded bulbs are dying in spasms similar to the rise and fall of waves. Strangers embrace in corridors between the scents of metal, knives and flowers. There is a sudden severing of the ordinary, green below, magenta above. And in between, the constant chattering about love. It rises from the stucco courtyards where women hang sheets to dry on lines beneath the sun. It drifts into the air of tin and blossoms, floats above alleys and terraces of geraniums in terra-cotta pots and old oilcans. From Buenos Aires to Lima, through San Salvador and Guadalajara, the islands of the Caribbean, Havana and Miami, San Diego and Los Angeles, the chorus of women exchanging strategies, offering elaborate stagings, the recipes of temporary resurrection.

Marta Ortega sighs. The weekends of silk quilts, stained sheets and the amber of tequila bottles and eyes which do not close in the dark. The insistent need to be used up as if empty implied cleansed.

She feels a tiny quaking within, a fluctuation of the soul, neither divine nor cruel. It is merely a wavering, less meaningful than the amber of autumn lamps at sunset or a shadow spilled by an ordinary yellow daisy in June. Of course the texture is complicated, more deeply rooted than all the cities built by men since the start of time, since the first drum, the first renegade son of night conceived of foraging for silver. It is layered in shadow, memory, dream. It is written in braille, camouflaged, the chemis-try of a city dying, surrendering to weeds and wildflowers, which is not a corruption but a form of music.

The borders are defined by the elements. It is not by their benediction but by their indifference that we exist. And Marta Ortega is now aware that somewhere in the enormity of all that is forever behind her, Joseph has died.

Marta Ortega approaches the city park, aware of a radiance and heat. It is a bed of magnificently tended geraniums, perhaps, but no, it is a woman, blouse and skirt a conflagration of scarlets. She sits at a bus bench near the edge of grass where the city park begins.

This lake is her water hole. The acre of city park is the silk predator's backdrop. She is the red of inflamed neon and content in her waiting. This woman recognizes that waiting is a form of art like ballet or origami. Women wait on cassia-covered patios, on terraces of fuchsia and ferns. In the waiting, there are nuances, images appearing incessantly and dissolving as sun shifts, as a window shade is pulled open or shut, a door or a mouth. In this waiting, civilizations rise and fall, alphabets, gods, science, songs and magic.

The lake is an empty slate reflecting the palms standing in a tormented circle around the shallow dirty water. Cars honk and slow near the red-silk-dressed young woman. Cars circle, return, responding to the sphere of heat she projects. She is sliding in and out of cars.

For a moment, Marta Ortega thinks the prostitute is Angelina or Orquídea in one of their gitana phases when they were seduced by flame, carrying bottles of tequila in cars. Her daughters, speeding between lovers, mestizos in zoot suits, men who made them dance and laugh and carried cuchillos. Men with long watch chains who made the syncopation of their fingers snapping into a phenomenon.

Yes, I can remember them, Marta Ortega sighs. Angelina and Orquídea in their tight red skirts, flaunting their slim architecture, flesh draped elaborately in coral and fire. Angelina or Orquídea, leaving the house on Flores Street, layered in jewelry that glittered, brazen, deliberately offensive. They bathed in oils pungent enough to make the night itself notice them. They were speeding up the hill of Flores Street in specifically mutilated automobiles, music from car radios shattering the air in their wake, in their loves with boys who called themselves pachucos.

Then Angelina and Orquídea revealed that these men bored them.

Her daughters were sophisticated, could smell the future of these boys with their long watch chains and exaggerated jackets and hats. Later these Chicanos would smell of jails, bus stations and tequila, of waiting and schemes which collapsed over and over, recurrent as waves in an ocean. Angelina and Orquídea waited for autumn. Then they left Flores Street and returned to the university.

Marta Ortega stares at the prostitute, wondering why she seems familiar. Of course this is not Angelina. Now Angelina lives in San Francisco with a financial analyst. She serves intricate hors d'oeuvres on a redwood terrace where the sails of boats drift at her feet and then, when she permits it, they slide across the two-bridged bay.

The bay is Angelina's backdrop. It is better than mere curtains and lighting cues, superior to any script. And she has found a wind which suits her, with its bite, its cold that pierces, its edge of danger. It is a challenge to transmute that wind of wire, that bruised howl into a stalled sea breeze, dense and green and drunk with sheer heat. Angelina has learned to charm that wicked dark bay, to force the cold driven waters into a vista of drowsy red sails and laughter. Wind cuts at the silk folds of her skirts. The constant barrage of salt keeps her wounds alive, burning. And Angelina has at last found her climate, her alphabet of the elements, her canvas and personal geography.

This arrogant anomaly of red silk cannot be Orquídea, no. Orquídea now lives in San Diego. From her back porch she can look across the border into the mouth of Mexico. When the wind blows from the south, it smells of a substance Orquídea describes as corruption, betrayal, decadence, starvation and regions of rock and agave which are only partially alive. She fills her lungs with this scent of dusk and ruined plazas where dogs and barefoot children roam aimlessly beneath a meaningless sky where all gods, innovations, auguries and acts of idolatry have failed. This purifies her. These astringent and severe winds have become her form of meditation and absolution.

Orquídea says the winds from the south smell of a lush rot, of what is arid, harsh and unformed, of promises overripe, broken and ruthlessly abandoned. Sin is a specific composition of details Orquídea has memorized. She embraces this wind which feels thin and derelict, which contains a sense of locked doors and the wearing of bones on the outside. As she walks along the ocean, beneath the slatted shadows of the palms, she is aware of the possibilities which exist, the ancient kingdoms invisible beneath chameleon air.

Orquídea knows that one day she will be walking to her church, along the quiet sidewalks with their embroidery of palms, and she will turn a corner she has never noticed before. A hill will erupt with orange poppies, and the air will become greener. Then she will see the church perched above a calm summer harbor. In a miniature village, women with bellies blooming with babies conceived in passion sit in a shaded plaza beneath jacaranda and banyan. They are repairing the fishing nets and stitching the sails with solar designs. "Orquídea," they will call to her. "Where have you been?"

Then Orquídea will sit on her mat. She will reach for her thread. Church bells will tell the time. This is her image of death. Now she attends confession and mass with her husband. Often, her children are with her. The wind from the south is an entity she can decipher, an unceasing process of clarification. And Orquídea has finally found her texture and terrain.

It occurs to Marta Ortega that this spectacular puta is familiar because she is a granddaughter. Perhaps this is one of Angelina or Orquídea's daughters who now claim that their blood pulses insistent and mysteriously hot. They cannot ignore it. They drape their bodies to assert a sense of raw red ambiance. Now the daughters of her daughters seek her consejos. "Abuela," she hears, and turns, startled, as the day shatters.

Her granddaughters announce that they cannot talk to their own mothers. Not this final incarnation of Angelina who is settled between her redwood deck, her yellow pills and the intricate permutations of sunsets and dinner parties. Not this Angelina who stands at her enormous expanse of window for hours, studying a bay she perceives not as a muted or cruel blue but rather as a palette of greens. She is consumed by choreographing the sails in the warm jade waters with the seating of bank presidents and the subtleties of shades of linen, floral arrangements, wines.

And they cannot talk to this final version of Orquídea, devout between her daily confession and mass. This Orquídea who has also shed her restlessness and found a capacity for enormous silences, who now stands motionless, staring south, facing the Baja of Mexico where the smell of sadness and time measured in increments of coins and terror soothes her.

"Orquídea actually hears stories in the wind?" Marta inquired one day. She paused in her garden work, glanced up at a granddaughter who no longer wore army clothing. She shaded her eyes, studying this daughter of her daughter, curious. She wonders whether Orquídea has learned how to transform the elements of her unique design.

"Oh, it's an entire novella," her granddaughter laughed. "There are characters, recurring themes, a story line. It begins in a terrible mountain village. A man deserts his wife and child. He is a drunk and even a curandera cannot erase his presence. The woman and her daughter move to a border town. Mom is certain it is Tijuana. Sometimes she walks the outskirts of TJ, looking for these people. She says when they left the mountain village they journeyed by bus. But the bus they entered was a vehicle of dream. A curandera whispered, 'Maria Magdalena was no less a saint than La Virgen de Guadalupe.' And then the mother disappeared."

Vanished into the air, into the wind Orquídea can decipher, Marta thinks. She is sitting near the edge of the lake. The water is muted beneath the sun, beaten, like a thin gray metal. There are indentations on the surface like the fingerprints left by craftsmen on certain artifacts. The gray of pewter and antiquity.

Then Marta Ortega is aware of the frail shadows of the palms forming a circle around the lake. They are the too-tall variety, all trunk without body. She is startled by their small heads. Their heads are empty, gutted, consumed. The trunks of the trees tell their story, are a weaving, hiero-glyphics in bark which winds have turned thin as straw. The palms wear thatched skirts. Their legs have been etched with precision and symmetry. They could be concubines to a powerful and eccentric lord who made a fetish of their legs.

Marta Ortega glances at the prostitute who is not a granddaughter. Now the daughters of her daughters no longer live as if posthumously, when they were what came and went in the night streets where lamplight and neon provided definition. When they claimed to be an expression of the city itself, living as the city would, could she sprout skin and legs draped in the reds of geraniums, the purples of wild iris and the blaze of canna? The daughters of Angelina and Orquídea, managing to assert a form of aesthetics in their selection of reds, in their posture, in their eyes which assured an onlooker that they had seen certain gestures of opulence and rarity.

But no, even her granddaughters are now with children. Marta cannot know this deliriously dressed whore, unhurried, absolutely alert like any animal freshly risen, hungry, tasting the first implications of dusk. There will be prey. The night will be as all others, treacherous, studded with disguised traps and graves.

The prostitute enters a battered car, an indistinct gray or blue. The man is Latino, young, slackening, his dark flesh implies a lack of purpose. He is dressed simply. He might be a student. The prostitute will tell him where to drive and park, wondering whether he is drugged or drunk. He is unconnected, adrift. His name might be Miguel or Roberto. On this particular afternoon, it is not.

Now sun and shadow carve channels into the waters of the lake. These are the eddies, Marta Ortega thinks, the creeks and gullies where we are born and drown. And it occurs to her that the veins of the earth and the veins of her limbs are identical forms of expression, the substance moving from air to liquid to rock to flame with grace and fluidity.

The miniature lake is an encapsulated world. Boys in brightly painted boats pass between ducks and water weeds. The shore is soft. Old men sit fishing and young men with the blood of warriors and the minds of caged beasts often fight and die. The lake mirrors the sky, its motion determined by the wind. It can stall greasy or startle into a fierce blue. And the lake is encircled by palms rising like many arms beckoning the sky. The palms are abnormally vertical, as if they desired to make themselves more attractive to the wind.

Marta Ortega remembers that the continent is actually held together by nets of sheets strung on lines between shacks and terraces, back alleys and tenements. It is women webbing the earth with beige cotton sheets washed weekly and bitten dry by noon wind, noon sun. The insane hands of women inching silent, hidden, collectively willing the earth to continue spinning. Women tethering the planet with cords on which clothing dries, sheets and shirts, the fragile anchor of the world.

It is women who stumble and drift, aware as their fingers move through acres of cloth that it is random and arbitrary. Why that harbor and flower shop, that dawn, that wharf, that man and not some interchangeable other? And space is also bound by the hands of women and their fabrics, the women hanging linens to dry on planets of magenta and lilac. This is the architecture of the void.

Suddenly, Marta Ortega understands why history has never intrigued her. Intuitively she recognized that even the most sacred objects have impermanent edges. They eradicated Tenochtitlán, capital of a civilization, if only symbolically. Metropolises are lost on a routine basis. Gone their inventions, formulas, sagas and genius, the instruments for producing music and curing madness. Gone the soft channels of celebration. The elements fold back on themselves, returning to their fundamental condition, raw, stripped, freed of human artifice.

Afternoon is an intersection of neon and irradiated water lilies draped in the deepening green caress of the fronds of palms. Accidents. Erratic gestures. A man walks south because it seems downhill. A woman answers a doorbell. There is a fiesta. A girl wears a hat which hides her face. There is a confusion in travel arrangements.

Marta Ortega is aware that the street prostitute has returned, she is pacing the edge of the city park. Marta is seized with the desire to touch this stranger, to call her Angelina, Orquídea, Gloria. To hold the young woman in red silk in her arms and soothe her, now, as tentative shadows claim the sleeping lake.

Listen to my lullaby, Marta instructs the prostitute she does not know. Angelina and Orquídea found London and Barbados and Honolulu less than they expected. It was precisely as depicted by the postcards, but the actual colors were muted, the outlines less intense, and in the air, clutter and debris.

Once my daughters were young, yes. They thought each day could be a calypso, February in Río and they perpetually delirious and masked, bathing in rum beneath a green ginger-scented sun. With each man they thought there would be no more atrocities to the sensibility or dingy hallways in backwater ports with squalid culs-de-sac and dysentery where they watched their ship come in and depart.

Be as a shell in the waves, Marta Ortega longs to tell this stranger, all beaches are the same. Be found, be lost. Daughter of the salt-studded waters, blue into blue, where there is liquid and rhythm only, a different and more final reality. It is merely an illusion of damp grass which separates us.

"What should I do, Mamacita, qué hago yo?" ricochets from a balcony, a bedroom window, a courtyard in the house which never belonged to her. They are following her by scent, shouting complaints and pleading for advice.

"Compose a list of all the ways I have failed you, alphabetically, like a litany of misery," Marta suggests.

"That is glib and I am desperate," Angelina or Orquídea admits.

"Then recognize that the accident of your encounter is that and that only. Cease calling happenstance a miracle in your pathetic desire to create ritual from the isolate rubble," Marta answers. She walks farther into her back garden, down the path to the terraced hillside of orchids they will not risk in their high-heeled shoes.

Now a slow sea breeze is stirring the terrible overwrought air, with its accumulation of brokenness, its wounds, its abscesses of sorrow and loss. The prostitute who is not a granddaughter must be cold, with her legs and arms bare. Night must sting her flesh which is the dark of a finely crafted wooden instrument, the textures and fibers which are similar to her own.

Marta Ortega is also chilled. She reaches for the Mexican blanket she has been instructed to take with her. She is grateful for this particular detail. As she wraps the serape around her shoulders, she is drawn again to the inflammation of red that is the street prostitute.

Come to me, Marta Ortega calls without words across the shadowed gulf separating them. The village of your youth is not lost. I will clothe, cleanse and cure you. Lose yourself among my orchids, come and go as my Angelina and Orquídea and their children. As Gloria Hernández might have come and gone, had I permitted it. Listen. We have the skin of cellos, the deep-toned strings of the world. We speak as the sea, fluid, cyclic. Release yourself from your incautious flight into the regions of red and red only. Shed your self-induced frenzy, the vocabulary of flame and ruin which adorns you. There is a beyond, an alphabet you have not yet decoded.

Marta Ortega is suddenly aware of the gaps that glisten, the punctures adorning the ground like small wells or tide-pools, these junctures into the complexities of the roots, the worlds below. These are the corridors and chambers the palms have for centuries engraved, in silence and boredom and rage, with vehemence and terror into an other, a splendor.

Approach me, scarred thing, Marta Ortega orders. Behold these verdant assertions, this stunning acre of green, luminescent and fresh, this grass, after the boulevards stinking of rot, the exhaust of cars, the exhaust of women and men, the exile and loss, heat and poisons, the fumes of savage betrayals and lies. The myriad toxins saturating a day, many not even intentional or named. The postures of abandonment, severed bricks, the nerves of women exposed like the roots of a suicidal tree. Green, these unique repetitions, Marta Ortega thinks. La región de las latitudes de las palmas.

Understand, it has always been this way. You sit on a hotel terrace, sip tall glasses of sculpted fruit and rum. The streets are pewter, brass, silver and ivory carved flasks. Women pass with veils or paper parasols, mantillas or masks. They talk as all women do, noting how bad it has been, how arbitrary the gods. And your season is like any other, Marta recognizes. It will pass. One day you will awaken wide-eyed in your own limitless hills, shedding your excess of conflagrations. You will find yourself blessing the process, your rare endurance, how you stirred and ripened private, quiet, resolving the neutral ground. This I have witnessed with my daughters.

When Marta Ortega glances to the corner where the red-silk-skirted prostitute is standing, she sees the woman staring at her, rapt. Tonight, for no reason she can explain, the puta is thinking about orchids and angels, her mothers and sisters. She is seized with a desire to embrace them. In the morning she will pack suitcases, take a taxicab to the airport and return to the country of her birth.

Marta Ortega knows this, yes. The images of orchids and angels. And it suddenly occurs to her that Angelina and Orquídea are more than fifty years old. She is stunned by the enormity of these numbers and what they imply. Fifty years of arguments and vows, curses and caresses, the pleading for forgiveness shooting from their mouths like bullets or flowers falling, joining, like streamers floating from fifty years of children's birthday parties. The confetti wrapped around their flesh was transmuted into moss, vines, a green film, molten, alive. Now it returns to its original pure liquids, the cycle complete.

We washed across one another, Marta Ortega realizes, flowed through one another like the clay vessels we are, porous, bound by an impulse beyond love or necessity. We are interwoven, refinements in my personal composition, on a molecular level, nerves entwined, memories forming the design, the filigree, the contours of our world.

Marta Ortega can see Flores Street if she chooses. Mailmen deliver telegrams. The telephone is ringing. Angelina and Orquídea are airborne, landing in terminals, hailing taxicabs. Enrique, the brother separated from her by only one year, the brother who tried to raft el tributario del río de Los Angeles, to sail south to the seamless green gulfs of jaguar and speaking birds, is driving his black Cadillac Seville from his seaside house near Malibu.

Enrique notices his rugs lying like slain cobras in the gutter in front of the house on Flores Street. He recognizes the significance of this gesture. And he feels the wavering then, the fluctuation of the soul for the first time in his life.

Marta Ortega smiles at this ironic juxtaposition. It will be her brother Enrique that Angelina and Orquídea will encounter when they walk into her house. Their Tío Enrique, banging his head against the kitchen wall, hitting his head into the wall over and over, sobbing, "Dios mío, I loved her."

No, this life was not as she intended, none of it. She did not expect such abundance, the profusion of infants in cribs or the siege of hybrids in their sleeping bags. Every day was an astonishment of lime and vermilion, each dawn agonizingly opulent with promise. Skies opened in a passion, simultaneously exuberant and wounded. And always, Angelina and Orquídea, their bodies slates to paint, etch, erase while candles ceaselessly flickered across the seductively shifting channel of what they demanded she pronounce an ordered world.

"Would you have preferred acts of fraudulence?" she would ask.

"We would have preferred a mother who was normal," they would reply, without conviction, she now recognizes.

"Muy tranquila, María, con calma," the padre in the church in the pueblo of her birth called out, even after she left the confessional, the courtyard.

"What should I do? Qué hago yo?" Angelina shouted.

"Take one of your yellow pills. Take a handful," she replied. "Plan your dinner menu. Practice your dialogue. Time your punch lines with the sunset."

But she could not lie to them, could not hallucinate fences where there were none, illuminations and constructions where there were none. It was ceaselessly flowing, fluid, blue the air, blue the wind, liquid the hills and the skies. We drift in undiscovered latitudes where compasses are irrelevant. We are the shanghaied crew of a derelict asylum ship. We slay dragons until we are empty, our dreams vacant, the seas still. We sway and reel, drunken and hysterical, feeling only the lamp of our hearts fluttering on and off of their own accord.

"Mamacita. Tell me. What can I do?" Orquídea follows her into the garden.

"Go to confession. Crawl to your shrine on your knees," she told her younger daughter. "Rub yourself clean on your beads. Start a new diet."

"What shall I do?" Angelina and Orquídea are pleading.

Silence like an ocean, incalculable, dimensional. Somewhere, she looks at them. "You know," Marta Ortega says.

T he lake lies near the core of her personal composition. Early evening is a confluence of time, chance, rare birds that speak and were thought extinct, dead rivers, curses, painted mouths, abstinence and fraudulence, elegance and greed. And there is no equation which can resolve the simultaneity of our antipathies, Marta Ortega decides, or the ambiguities of our inventions. Our avenues of warehouses with their unintelligible fruits, the vanishing ports, the wavering, the fluctuations of the soul.

"You taught us to demand the lyrical, to take risks, to know exuberance as an inalienable right and not an aberration," Orquídea or Angelina screams in one hot August evening or in the heavy fog just before a torrential downpour in one November or another.

"Take off your ridiculous shoes and help in the garden," Marta shouts. "Or make lists."

Make lists, my darlings, while the substance flows as it will, as it must. And I am the Spanish of gypsies and eight hundred years of Moors from Africa and the Indian of young women raped with regularity by bands of bored Europeans. I am a hybrid, she remembers, my blood pure barbarian. I am the product of random events, a missed train, a hotel cancellation. A man with a cello, a placid cove, a young woman with the skin of a delicate wooden instrument whispering between green vines in French.

Marta Ortega sits near the lake, the expanse of hand-crafted pewter, the fist of liquid antiquities. She is a seventy-four-year-old mestizo woman sitting in a city park on the fringe of the central city. She is ordinary, intrinsic to the scenery, the fading evening, the red and yellow and blue boats which boys glide beneath bridges and patches of waterweeds and rock. Brown-skinned children and Oriental toddlers are pushed in swings by their mothers or grandmothers.

Today there was a birthday party. Red and yellow streamers have been strung between the trunks of the palms clustered above a wooden picnic table. The streamers wrapped like sashes around the trunks, the waists of the too-tall tattooed palms that circle the lake. And she wore a wide-brimmed hat, Enrique said. He could not evaluate her face. There were mariachis, shadows, the plaza a web of confetti.

The lake is a contained body of water, erased of danger. Palms provide a sense of familiarity, an immediate recognition of texture and design, an insistence of the indigenous, resisting contrivances, oblivious to artifice. The lake is filling with shadows and graying. Once, she too had been young. Then she answered a telephone, a doorbell, a letter, held cardboard boxes of stuffed animals for children, planted a garden and she was seventy-four.

Now Enrique is banging his head against the pale-yellow walls of her kitchen, crying as he has never before cried in his life, not even when his father and then his mother were laid into the earth. Enrique is howling like a man possessed, "Dios mío, I loved her, I loved her."

Angelina and Orquídea are sitting in the living room of the house on Flores Street, in the house which was never green and will never be freed of its residue, its perfumed curses and vows, its dreaming out loud. And her daughters are not reaching for sedatives or rosaries. They are evaluating the state of her garden, discussing what can be saved. Their dialogue is expert, concise and imaginative.

Angelina and Orquídea have slipped off their shoes and walk with ease, barefoot, as they did when they were children following her between the beds of begonias and the orchids in their redwood shelves. Some cymbidiums are not irreparably damaged, they conclude, the moist earth between the rosebushes and the tomatoes in staked rows coating their feet. It feels like a caress.

Her daughters hold hands in the slow-falling dusk, loving with their secret mouths, at a juncture too sacred to name. They carry pots of orchids and speak to each other through their moon teeth. They embrace, their arms are bark, limbs of a tree, spokes rising from the ground like the hidden spine of all things. In between, they telephone sons and daughters, summoning them to Flores Street. They are arriving in airplanes and cars, with infants and children, with the third cycle of birthings.

As Angelina and Orquídea walk through the garden, their entire lives wash over them, like an ocean. There are revelations, an abundance of color, indelible. Awakenings, a deciphering and transformation. The lingering of extravagance, communion and unbearable loss.

Marta Ortega is aware of this vibration, this lamentation, this agony of regret, and she ignores it. This is their personal composition. They will create their own singular and idiosyncratic solutions, their own justifications and designs. From the labyrinths of concurrent gulfs and eddies, they will fashion their enduring histories. This is now behind her.

It is night, air neon, barking dogs, the scent of grass, the constant lake water licking the shore, the ducks, the weeds, the unidentifiable combinations rising into the thin clouds. Marta Ortega senses the palms awakening around her. They are stalks with heads pitiful, defective. Then they are calling her by name. Marta Ortega is surprised. In this unremarkable city park, the palms are beginning to open their lips to the night which will be radiant with expectation, brilliant and devious, more an equation than a lullaby.

Marta Ortega walks from the shadow-dented lake, spreads her serape beneath the farthest tree and lies down. The puta, draped like a Venezuelan orchid, a spontaneous jungle growth, is sliding across the seat of a car. Across the illusionary darkness, their eyes are meeting, connecting, inventing a gulf which is glowing. And the moon is rising, her struggle complete. She is absolutely full, whole again, the perfect mouth of the night and this night only.

Cycles, Marta Ortega thinks, completion and return. The moon was full the night Angelina was born. She held her daughter to her breast, recognizing that this infant would in turn offer her breast to one daughter, two daughters or ten. And they would keep the planet on axis. They would feed the process. They were the sea and all that lived in it, the oracle and the current, the one authentic inspiration in what was accident.

Orquídea was born in August. The heat was ferocious. Marta Ortega felt that Orquídea was a nest within her, an orb of vines perhaps. She sat on her courtyard patio in the late afternoons, in the company of ferns with their placid green presence, their ability to simply wait, like a kind of rock that breathed. And in the searing late-summer air, she wondered whether this unborn child dreamed of molecules, whether the atoms were an alphabet which this yet-unborn infant could recite. How ancient and cool they must be, edgeless and indifferent, certain of their purpose, their intrinsic sorcery.

Joseph had told her that there was music, some pattern of drumming, thought to be fifty thousand years old. In the night, she asked the unborn nest of moss and embers whether she could hear this music in the beating of her heart, perhaps, and in the silence of the intervals. She wondered whether her almost-born child could sense the ocean rustling her random shells, or the wind embossed by the wings of birds as they parted the merciless summer sun, aiming their shadows which were cobalt darts across the yard of tiles and the pale-green backs of her moistened plants.

Marta Ortega felt the warm bud, the jewel of her burning not-yet-born Orquídea, how like a tiny suspended sun she was, glowing within her personal space which was filled now in a cycle of abundance, in a rapture of summer. She had longed to touch her unborn infant. She stood naked in her garden in a Santa Ana wind, letting the bands of salt-laced desert air bore directly into what was about to become her daughter. And Marta Ortega drank the stars into her belly, there, in the twilight harbor they driftingly inhabited where nothing required translation.

It occurs to Marta Ortega that because she is female, her compositions have been laden with birthings and moons, orbits and implications of the round. The circle of her hybrid grandchildren, the perfect arc they inscribed on this precise grass in another configuration and dimension, in an afternoon when surfaces dissolved and she recognized that the lake was not squalid but magnificent, a portal, a conjunction of worlds.

Moons, births, mouths. Always the round, her affinity for the circling of planets, the phases of the moon and the nuances of seasons. Her life has been a sensitivity to the cyclic, orbs and rings, the necklaces and scarves around the throats of her daughters. Angelina and Orquídea coming and going, leaving and returning, the circular paths of their ceaseless migrations. She has been burdened by the density of wombs and wounds. The round bruises on the soul and flesh, the round of buds entering into blossom, the seeds and openings, mouths like oceans and wells, spilling their promises and vows. Round the lesions of Angelina and Orquídea in their succession of betrayals. Round the punctures in their hidden regions.

Round the spheres she rebuilt, absolved, blessed new houses, children and marriages. Round were her arms, curled in a perpetual embrace.

And the palm tree above her is ancient and unexpectedly generous and articulate. She is suggesting that Marta Ortega has remembered enough. She must cover herself and rest. Marta resists. She will telephone Angelina and Orquídea. And the palm-tree woman laughs. Do not be ridiculous. Your daughters are sitting in your kitchen now, at this particular unique vortex of an instant. They have been working in your garden, carrying plants, feet bare and muddy. And your brother, Enrique, is banging his head against the yellow enamel walls of your kitchen, sobbing, "Dios mío. I loved her, I loved her."

Now he has chanced to glance out your kitchen window. He is studying his carpets coiled in the gutter. "Don't you see the flames?" he is saying to your granddaughter Jennifer. He is pointing at the rugs, agitated. "No? Are you mad?" he is screaming. He is running across the lawn to the sidewalk, staring at the curb. "The threads are glowing," he is yelling now. "Things are growing inside, Jesus, monstrosities."

Marta Ortega can see her house on Flores Street, if she chooses. Her granddaughter Jennifer wears a long pink robe, a gown for a temple initiate. She gives Enrique a yellow pill. Still he is trembling. He is stunned, awed, vapors are appearing. He remembers his youth, suddenly, vividly, a stream he tried to raft. He feels as if liquids are washing across him. He has never experienced the wavering in the illusionary fabric before, the ebb and flow of the fluid gulfs. He thinks he is having a heart attack.

Angelina and Orquídea ignore him. They see nothing. They carry pots of green and yellow orchids. Their feet are bare, caressed by moist earth. Their movements are precise, as if they intuited the necessary procedures by subliminal instruction. Marta Ortega is satisfied.

Angelina and Orquídea are aware of the impending full moon. They walk through the garden and no lesions adorn them. They are purposeful, ripened, whole. They recognize the significance of the moon on this particular night, completing her journey into the round and temporary. They call Orquídea's daughter into the garden.

"You will note the fluctuations of the moon," Orquídea begins.

"It is the fluctuation of the soul made visible," Angelina assures her niece.

"It is not mathematics or equations but the orbit and pull of the moon which make you bleed," Orquídea explains.

"Space is not a void but fertile," Angelina adds.

"Each month, you feel eggs and stars and unborn moons die and squeeze through your womb," Orquídea remembers.

"This is all the alphabet you need to know," Angelina says.

Marta Ortega covers her body with the serape. The house on Flores Street, fantastic in her last glimpse, vanishes. This is behind you and of no consequence, she is reminded. There are no more rearrangements. You are warm now. I will protect you. Our grain is identical, there are no divisions. And you cannot rise, Marta Ortega, you can no more cross this acre of city park than you could the Andes. Lie down, hija de la tierra, you with the skin of cellos and carved mahogany. Absolution and revelation await you. Listen. You who are not frightened, you who refused to dream only that which was reasonable, bloodless and conventional. You who never craved a night rendered harmless and controllable. Listen.

Marta Ortega obeys, places her face flush against the ground. Then she begins to hear it. Of course the earth is alive. It has a heart, a pulse, beating rhythmically as waves in an ocean, verdant, hot. She can almost decipher the words the earth is speaking through her secret mouth. Yes, this is a standard-issue planet, one cop and whore, one palm and plaza, on every corner, but there is more, ceaseless, inexhaustible, rising from the lush center, from the flawless undiscovered green interior, an undamaged continuity, perpetual, ineluctable.

The white heat of the moon appearing now and dropping anchor directly above her is startling. Of course space is not empty, is simply the belly waiting to be filled in cycles of barrenness and abundance. The palms are also women. They know this. Their legs have been scratched to satisfy the transitory fancies of men. Still, they have stood, bearing witness for centuries, providing the earth with its camouflaged roots, its networks and chambers, the fundamental interior structure.

Marta Ortega lies wrapped in a common Mexican blanket beneath a palm that is one of dozens ringing an insignificant circular lake in the center of a city park which is a vortex, an opening into a realm of texture and fragrance where no passport is required. And she feels the sea breeze aggressively asserting itself as palm fronds bend and sway, responding from habit and some intrinsic necessity of their own.

It occurs to Marta Ortega that she has spent her life standing at windows and terraces, slices of courtyard and lawn, observing uncountable branches and fronds bend and sway. Perhaps that is all, she concludes, green paradigms and the fluctuations of the soul, how the music relentlessly shifts, now a calypso, now a dirge.

She relaxes her flesh into the skin of the earth which accepts her without hesitation. Marta Ortega could fall without effort into the liquid green core. For a brief fluttering, for one fluctuation of the soul, she longs for cinnabar, the blood pigment, so that any passing god might recognize and claim her. Then even that is not important.

It is behind her, the creek they tried to raft back to the southern lands of jaguar and wild strawberries. It is behind her, the hotel in Mexico with windows arched and wide and white opening onto a lagoon embellished by boats, the dark-skinned woman whispering, the special scent of bells swaying and calling to one another from the masts of vessels in the slow sea dark. Behind her, too, the first red rose of the season. She cut it and placed it in a vase near her bed, calmed by its purity and purpose, how it observed her without bitterness, choosing instead to pump each petal full of red. That is all. Red.

Marta Ortega is a clay vessel prepared to disassemble her temporary form. She closes her eyes. Gone the unmolested acres of mahogany that were the Yucatán, el río de Los Angeles, the virgin moon, the night-blooming purple cactus, the strangely luminescent neurosis. Gone Tenochtitlán, with its aqueducts and pyramids, the murals and plumed capes of the lords, the books of sacred knowledge with pages of animal skin and bark, images rendered in a plaster of lime. Gone the terraced hillsides of orchids and the flesh of infants. Gone the chinampas of Xochimilco and the garden of Marta Ortega. Gone the fierce bruises of Angelina and Orquídea, gone the women singing with their lips on flame. Gone the one lone exiled cello, Joseph, the ozone layers, the legions of women hanging their sheets to dry on lines webbing this planet and others. Gone the threads of one personal composition unraveling, strand by strand.

Suddenly, Marta Ortega realizes that all songs and arrangements of images, stones, flowers or phrases, all the rituals and gestures of women and men, are simply the transitory notations, the raw exposure of terror and pathetic flutterings of what we saw and how we endured.

Her face is flush against the earth which has a heart, yes, and lips.

Marta Ortega hears it beating, speaking, a final and fundamental configuration of syllables, indisputable, insistent and resonant as all the waves of all oceans and seas living now or forgotten. There are four elements, earth, water, fire and air, and their infinity of sculptures. The fragile antiquities are continuous, shorn of increments and ambiguity, absolutely intelligible. And the earth's heart is beating as it has always, will always, repeating the only word it knows, *daughter, daughter, daughter.*

For my daughter Gabrielle
Los Angeles, 1984